THE FORCE IS UNDER FIRE
AT FORT APACHE, THE BRONX

Captain Dennis Connolly—the tough new captain is determined to make a clean sweep . . . inside the stationhouse and out.

Officer Corelli—dressing for success as he tries to beat the odds for survival on the streets of Fort Apache.

Officer Murphy—safe neither on the streets nor off them because he saw too much the night of the riot.

Morgan and Finley—cops who believe the strong right arm of the law is always right as long as it's their arm and their law . . .

Fort Apache, The Bronx

HEYWOOD GOULD

WARNER BOOKS

A Warner Communications Company

WARNER BOOKS EDITION

Warner Books, Inc., 75 Rockefeller Plaza, New York, N.Y. 10019

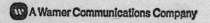 A Warner Communications Company

Printed in the United States of America

First Printing: February, 1981

10   9   8   7   6   5   4   3   2

Fort Apache,
The Bronx

1

JUNE, 1974

Patrolman John J. Murphy was passed out in the bathroom of Sammy's Rendezvous the night three stickup men killed his partner. He was lying face down near the urinal, luxuriating in the coolness of the tile against his cheek, waiting for the room to stop spinning so he could go back out and knock that wise guy Houlihan right on his ass. Only a minute or two more, just until the sirens stopped moaning in his brain. Then, he'd take a long, ecstatic piss, and he'd be fine. But first he sank into a blissful, gurgling snooze.

Houlihan, Murphy's partner, was still on his feet, a V.O. and ginger ale buried in his ursine fist, betting that nobody in the bar or in the whole fucking Bronx, including that faggot in the bathroom, knew the only man in the history of baseball to win the M.V.P. award two years in a row. Houlihan was a massive Irishman with forearms as thick as a nun's ankles. The memory of the school yard was still in him after thirteen years on the job, and he had fooled many a skinny purse snatcher with his agility. Liquor went into him like into a bottomless pit, making him garrulous, generous, and, as every bartender in the Bronx acknowledged with a sigh of relief, good-natured. Houlihan had never lost his temper, it was too terrible to imagine what would happen if he did.

They came in quietly, and stood by the cigarette machine as if trying to make up their minds. Two skinny Puerto Rican dudes with field jackets and berets, and a pasty-faced

7

white kid with tattoos crawling up and down his arms. Nobody noticed them, and there was no reason why they should. Sammy's was two blocks away from the 40th precinct on 138th Street. It was known throughout the Bronx as a cop hangout. In the thirty years it had been open, there had never been a stickup. Every heist guy knew there was no money in cop hangouts. Besides, why hit Sammy's when there were at least three fat bars in the same area? You had the Cabana Club, where all the big smack dealers hung out; Little Anthony's, which everyone knew was a numbers drop for most of the neighborhood. And there were the after-hours on Third Avenue which charged six bucks at the door and three bucks for drinks, not counting the loose joints and grams of coke that were sold by the score every night. Why hit a bust-out saloon where there was no real bread, and where every customer at the bar might turn and cut you down in a fusillade of off-duty fire? It just didn't make any sense.

That was why, when the Spanish cats opened their jackets and leveled sawed-offs at the bartender, announcing a holdup, everyone in the place immediately got very quiet and very frightened. This was irrational and unprofessional, which meant it was dangerous. There were two other cops in Sammy's, aside from Houlihan. One of them had left his off-duty pistol locked in the trunk of his car because he always got a little suicidal when he'd been drinking. The other had his in the pocket of his coat, which was on a hook only a couple of feet away. He spent the next few minutes waiting for the right moment to jump for it. That moment never came.

It took the white boy a little while to get a 9-mm automatic out of his belt. "Careful you don't shoot your dick off," one of the Spanish cats said to him.

"Don't worry about me, motherfucker," he screamed. The guy was flying. Downs, or maybe angel dust. Every cop in there knew his story. The white kid, the punk, trying to make points with his Spanish brothers. Mouths got dry and pants got wetter as he kicked everyone off their stools, and made them lean over the bar while he went through their pockets. A kid with tattoos like that—if he had any kind of rap sheet at all, and you knew he did, he could be pinned in a minute. That was bad. If he was crazy enough to finger himself, he was crazy enough to do something worse.

One of the Spanish cats stood by the door while the other

went behind the counter and emptied the cash register. The white boy went down the bar picking up the change and the wallets. The three were about to leave when he turned on Houlihan.

"Hey, this motherfucker's a cop," he screeched. "I know this motherfucker. He was there in the Forty-first precinct the night they broke my arm . . ."

Oh, Jesus. Now the guy was locating himself at the Four-One with a broken arm. Hospital records, mug shots—the kid was incriminating himself. Which only meant that he might have a brainstorm, and decide to wipe out all the witnesses.

"You a cop?" he said.

"See if he's got a piece," the cat by the door said.

The white kid started to pat Houlihan down. "You're a cop, man. I can smell you."

Houlihan shook his head. "I drive a truck," he said.

"Don't bullshit me," the white kid yelled. He jumped back and slammed Houlihan on the side of the head with the barrel of the gun. Houlihan hardly winced, but stood looking calmly into the kid's eyes. Later, everyone agreed that if he had gone down holding his head, begging for mercy, swearing that he wasn't a cop, he might have come through it. But Houlihan had never been knocked off his feet by anybody. And he wasn't about to go on his knees for some whacked-out mutt with a gun. No way!

"Drop your pants, motherfucker," the white kid said, slamming Houlihan with the gun again.

Houlihan let his pants drop to the floor. "See," the white kid yelled triumphantly, swooping down and ripping Houlihan's off-duty pistol out of his ankle holster. "I told you." His voice rose hysterically. "A fuckin' cop!"

He jumped around in front of Houlihan, and shot him in the face with the 9-mm. The right side of Houlihan's head flew off: the white kid was splattered with his blood. Houlihan stared into his face, still gripping the bar. The kid screamed and shot him again, but Houlihan held on stubbornly. He was still holding on minutes later when Murphy staggered out of the bathroom, rubbing his eyes and shouting gleefully, "Ernie Banks, you dumb bastard, the Chicago Cubs, '52 and '53." Then, as if he'd been waiting for his partner, Houlihan crumpled to the floor, his huge corpse settling in a puddle of blood.

9

2

They made it tough for Murphy. The Homicide detectives kept him for hours repeating the same two sentences: "I was drunk. I didn't see anything." They kept him sitting in that saloon staring at his partner's blood, and then, even worse, at the chalk outline of his body the forensic guys traced on the floor.

They weren't looking for leads, because there would be no problem getting the perps on this case. The three were known "cowboys," small-time heist guys who stick up four or five places a night. They'd been on a rampage, hitting a gas station and a *bodega* before they came into Sammy's. Their last stop had been a White Castle on Fordham Road where the white kid had shot the security man. Total take for a night of four robberies and two homicides: eleven hundred and thirty-eight dollars. The detectives had dozens of good descriptions, plus a stoolie who had already made the three guys, supplying names, addresses. The search would become even simpler by morning when the white kid turned up in a vacant lot on Eagle Avenue with thirty stab wounds, his partners having decided the take was too small, and the risk too great to have him around. No, the cops wanted to build up a case against Murphy and the other two guys who'd been there. They wanted to prove negligence, cowardice—anything that would fix culpability. There would be an investigation by the Internal Affairs Division, the unit charged with policing with the policemen. They wanted Murphy, and he knew it.

They made him stay while they dusted and photographed, the forensic guys searching diligently for pieces of Houlihan's skull, which they wrapped in cellophane bags. Finally, at four in the morning, when they got tired of asking him the same questions, they let him go. He drove all the way out to Mineola in a daze. The liquor had long since ebbed away, but

10

he was still in a stupor. Houlihan's dead, he kept telling himself. He was supposed to feel grief and pain. He felt nothing.

It was only when he pulled up in front of his house, saw the light burning in the bedroom window, and knew his wife was waiting to berate him for coming home drunk and to threaten to pack the children up and go if this continued, then later to beg him to please call his brother Vincent, the priest, before this problem got out of control, that he began to tremble so violently he couldn't even light a cigarette, and threw himself down on the floor and cried for his dead partner.

They called Murphy down to Borough Headquarters next day to see the Internal Affairs officer. He was a squat, barrel-chested lieutenant named Connolly, with a hard, unwavering look. He sifted through Murphy's folder as he questioned him.

"I find it hard to believe a man could get so drunk he wouldn't even be awakened by the sound of gunfire."

"I had my head next to the toilet, Lieutenant," Murphy said. "The running water must have drowned out the sound."

Connolly looked at him with disgust. "You know there is another explanation," he said. "You could have come to while the holdup was in progress, and decided it would be safer to wait it out in the bathroom."

So that's what those sonsabitches were going to try to put over—cowardice. "Lieutenant, if I'd have been awake in that bathroom I would have come right out smoking," Murphy said. "Maybe more guys would be dead today, me included, but that's what I would have done. And if I'd have been sitting at the bar when those mutts came in I would have gone to war with them right away. Maybe everyone in the joint would be dead, but that's what I would have done. I know that, so I don't have to convince you or I.A.D. or the Department or anyone else. As a matter of fact, it's lucky for me I got drunk. I think I'll get drunk more often . . ."

Connolly went through Murphy's folder.

"I'm told you come from a real illustrious police family," Connolly said. "Both your brothers are lieutenants . . ."

"Don't hold that against me," Murphy said.

Connolly's expression didn't change. He wasn't going to be charmed or bullshitted—oh no, not him, not this righteous bastard. "Your father's a retired sergeant. Thirty-five years on the job. Think you'll put in that much time?"

"If I keep hiding in bathrooms I've got it made," Murphy said, getting up.

"Sure, sure, go ahead and give me the finger," Connolly said with quiet anger. "You think I'm full of shit, that I.A.D.'s full of shit, too. I could crucify you, put you on the rubber-gun squad until we find out if you're an alcoholic, or even if your drinking habit could possibly interfere with execution of your duty. I've got a lot of power in this job, and I got it because there are people who believe that a police officer has to be better than everybody else."

"Why?" Murphy said. "Because he makes more money? Because he has such a wonderful job so rewarding and fulfilling that he leaves the precinct bursting with love for humanity? You tell me what's so great about being a cop that makes it necessary for a cop to be so great. And while you're thinkin' it over I'm going over to a wake for a real great guy, my partner for seven years. Why don't you come with me? You can tell his wife and four kids how great it is to be a cop."

Murphy walked out of the office without being excused and went right downstairs to McChesney's Tavern, where he proceeded to get plastered in full view of most of the Borough brass. He'd been drinking vodka for the last few years—screwdrivers, vodka-tonics. He liked the way it sneaked up on you. You didn't get drunk with vodka. You got mugged. One minute you were eloquent and charming; the world had never looked so rosy. And then suddenly it was three hours later and you were picking yourself up off the floor. And your partner was dead.

Murphy gripped his glass tightly. His vision blurred. He didn't dare check himself out in the mirror because he knew he was crying. He vowed then and there that he'd never drink anything stronger than beer for the rest of his life.

3

They gave Houlihan an Inspector's funeral. Murphy was one of the pallbearers. It was a beautiful June day ("The sun always shines when they bury a cop," the priest said), and the sight of all those men in blue standing at rigid attention was a stirring one, even to Murphy. The pomp and ceremony really worked, you could see it on Mrs. Houlihan's face, on the awed expression in his children's eyes. It made this sudden, violent death a little easier to bear. Never mind that among those serried ranks there were men licking their parched lips, suffering for a drink and a cigarette, while others worried about that peddler who had sworn he'd report them if they shook him down one more time. Others were hoping their girlfriends and wives wouldn't somehow meet, and most of them were scheming to make this month's bills, while the guys who had managed to connive a little extra were scared they wouldn't get away with it. Still, they looked good in formation. Uniforms did cover a multitude of sins. The Mayor and the Commissioner were on hand to decry the conditions that caused such tragedies, to call for jobs, urban renewal, and gun control, as if these had anything to do with one hopped-up heist guy who hated cops.

Murphy's brother Paul showed up with the Headquarters contingent. He was a lieutenant in the Planning Division, which developed programs for the boroughs. He had done it the right way on the job, getting off the street as quickly as possible, studying computer programming and business administration, getting his degrees, keeping his nose clean, making friends in all the Borough offices. He hadn't been out from behind his desk in years, and looked it. In spite of his success he was a worrier. A little mustache of sweat had formed over his upper lip in adolescence when he was caught cheating on his Latin finals, and had stayed there ever since.

"For Chrissake, what did you say to Connolly over at Borough?" he asked Murphy after the funeral. "He wants to put you on a medical suspension."

"Good, maybe I can get out on half pay."

"What, are you crazy? You wanna kill the old man? Ten years on this job, and you still don't know the score. I oughta beat the shit outta you for this."

The old familiar threat. Murphy was the youngest in a family of five boys. The "runt of the litter," the old man called him. He had stayed thin while the other boys had ballooned like their father. As a kid he'd been the butt of all their cruel jokes, the punching bag for all of them. But that was long since over.

"C'mon Paulie, the last time you raised your hand was to go to the bathroom in school," he said.

"Look, asshole, I'm tryin' to help you. I told the old man I'd get you off the street. Ten years pounding a beat is a disgrace in this family. It makes us all look bad. Now, I almost got you in plainclothes. The Bank squad, for Chrissake . . ." Paul looked around nervously. "You'll make more money than I do. You know what those guys are whackin' up every month?" His voice dropped to a whisper. "They got twelve guys covering gambling in the Bronx. It's a joke, Johnny. The Commissioner wants us to reorganize the system, but that won't happen for at least a coupla years. Meanwhile, these guys are getting three or four thousand a month from the numbers people alone. And that's not countin' the occasional bookmaker you run across . . ."

The Bank squad was the plum assignment of the Police Department. "Guiltless graft," the men called it. It wasn't like Narcotics, where you shook down guys who were selling poison to teen-agers. It was bookies and policy guys who were willing to pay plenty to keep their rackets afloat. Everybody gambled. Nobody thought of bookies as criminals. Guiltless graft, and safe too. Every once in a while somebody had to take pinch just to keep the quota up. So they nailed a runner with some slips, or even broke up a bank if the higher-ups wanted headlines. It was all arranged in advance. The raid might make a big splash in the papers, but the bookies would probably get a suspended sentence, and everybody would be happy.

"How'd you swing that for me?" Murphy asked.

14

"I spent fourteen years on this job makin' connections. It's gonna cost ten grand . . ."

"I don't have . . ."

"The old man's gonna front it for you. You'll have to pay him back, of course, with interest, but it'll be worth ten times as much to you."

Murphy shook his head. "I don't fit in with those hustlers, Paulie. It won't work."

"They want you, Johnny," Paul said anxiously. "You got a good street record. They like tough cops. They want you. But you gotta clear this thing with Connolly . . ."

"How do I do that?"

"You're gonna have to go on a retreat with Monsignor Ryan," Paul said.

"The ones he has for the drunks and the psychos?" Murphy said. "Forget it."

"One weekend, Johnny," Paul pleaded. "You go up there and make a confession. He has this therapy group . . ."

"Forget it, Paulie."

"The Monsignor's got a lotta weight, Johnny. He drops a word and you're in. Not even Connolly'll go up against him."

"I ain't kissin' no priest's ass," Murphy said. "I ain't beggin' for absolution, 'cause I didn't do nothin' wrong. So I got a little pissed. Cops will do that, you know. The old man's no stranger to the sauce, and neither are you. So the joint was stuck up. You drink in the South Bronx, you gotta expect that. So Houlihan bought it. You gotta expect that, too, sometimes. If it was me in that box, and him standin' here, he'd say the same thing."

"Alright, you stubborn sonofabitch," Paul said. "I tried to help you. Now Connolly's gonna throw the book at you . . ."

"What's he gonna do, put me out at half pay? I'd go on a retreat for that. I been lookin' for a way to get off this chickenshit job anyway. Or maybe he's gonna transfer me, huh? Well, anywhere I go would be a vacation compared to the Four-One, Paulie. I got the lowest job in the world. I'm lower than a pregnant ant. And I'm workin' in the worst precinct in the city. What could be more of a punishment than that?"

4

They called it "Fort Apache." No one knew who had given it the name, or when. It had to have been christened some time in the early sixties, though. It was then, while the country marched forth to conquer Kennedy's "New Frontier," that the South Bronx was forgotten and left to die.

Only forty years before the Bronx had been a frontier as well. In the nineteen-twenties, the tenement districts of Manhattan, Harlem, and the Lower East Side were bursting with hard-working immigrants, savers, and strivers anxious to escape their claustrophobic ghettos. Only a few miles north of these teeming slums rested the Bronx, a pastoral borough of dairy farms and summer estates, kept pristine by narrow country roads, rolling hills, and a determinedly rural population. The construction of the subways changed all that. Trains flowed underground through Manhattan, rising into elevated lines that traversed the length of the Bronx. This virgin territory was suddenly accessible, not only to homesteaders but to speculators as well. The movement was relentlessly northward. The farms were purchased and plowed under. Soon apartment buildings were the only cash crop in the borough. The wealthy families—the Morrises, the Freemans and Van Cortlandts—abandoned their estates and holdings to the land-hungry developers, becoming absentee proprietors, leaving only their Yankee names on the streets and boulevards that were hewn out of the rolling hills. Freeman, Simpson, Fox, Tiffany, Hunts Point, Jerome Avenue, Welton and Morris—these patrician names, these sons and daughters of the Revolution, became linked with the Jewish sweatshop workers who first settled the South Bronx, then later with the Puerto Ricans who arrived in the late forties, and finally with the crime and devastation that became the symbol of America's failing cities.

16

It was on those streets that the first apartments were built, rows and rows of five story walk-ups on Hoe Avenue, along Hunts Point and Southern Boulevard. The further north they moved, the more modern the buildings became. In the thirties the upwardly mobile moved to the cream and yellow Art Deco buildings with elevators and glass doors that had risen along the spacious, tree-lined Grand Concourse. The sound of their voices had hardly faded from the abandoned walk-ups before another family was installed, another father with the scarred fingers, bent back, and perpetual squint of a garment worker was taking the train to Manhattan at Southern Boulevard every morning.

The neighborhood was never genteel. The racketeers who serviced the illicit needs of the burgeoning population located themselves on Fox Street, Intervale Avenue, and along Southern Boulevard. Old timers spoke of "goulash" parlors, tiny casinos that operated out of storefronts and apartments; of Jewish prostitutes ensconced in basement brothels under the El on Westchester Avenue; of bootleggers running booze out of garages on Jerome Avenue; of cabarets on Fox Street where flashy Italian gangsters from East Harlem came to smoke opium. Every other candy store had a guy in the back who took numbers. In every pool room there was a guy who could get you anything you wanted, cheap. You could walk the streets safely at night, as long as you knew which streets to walk. The South Bronx became a way station. The idea was to make enough money so you could move north to the Concourse and beyond. Always relentlessly northward.

In less than a decade a metropolis arose out of what had been a country town. With no time to level the rolling hills and carve an urban grid, the builders had to conform to the dreamlike topography of the Bronx. Long, unbroken boulevards suddenly culminated in *cul de sacs*. Hills climbed steeply away from main arteries, ending in bluffs that commanded fortresslike views of the entire area. One block off a teeming thoroughfare you'd find a quiet backwater of narrow streets, quaint little squares with anonymous statuary, traffic circles, little patches of greenery. You couldn't pick your way through the Bronx. You had to know where you were going. Tiny side streets converged on busy avenues. Rows of apartment buildings were inexplicably broken up by sections of neat, two-story houses with gardens and backyards. The Bronx was dotted with landmarks, monuments, historical mansions, all unheralded and obscure, tended by dedicated souls, ignored by the rest of the population.

The Bronx became a borough of contradictions. There were no homogenous neighborhoods. Walk five blocks in any direction, and you'd stumble on a different ethnic enclave, which meandered away into a park or a shopping area as quickly as it had appeared. The Irish were supposed to be in Mott Haven, but they surfaced in little colonies in Jewish Hunts Point, where saloons with shamrocks in the window, and little boys "rushing the growler," or taking home a bucket of beer for their fathers lay cheek by jowl with kosher butchers and appetizing stores where housewives haggled over the price of herring. The smells of stale beer and garlic mingled in the fine dusty mist that descended from the elevated tracks where the train roared by every fifteen minutes, forcing an intermission in the most heated conversations, rattling crockery and window panes for blocks around. One block off hectic Fordham Road, a shopping area that was jammed day and night, the atmosphere suddenly calmed as you walked down provincial Arthur Avenue past the shingled two-family houses with the high stoops, the old women who sat on bridge chairs scowling at strangers, to a street lined with markets and restaurants, salumerias, pizzerias, sidewalk peddlers, organ grinders squeezing doleful Sicilian melodies out of their mysterious boxes. There were stout, impassive men with jewelry glinting off their wrists and fingers who stood on the corners watching, and giggly girls who huddled in groups, hardly daring to look at the boys across the street; it was a dream that ended as abruptly as it had begun when the street suddenly curved around a park, and came out on an ancient, cobbled street on which stood yellowing buildings of the former municipality.

The Bronx was a crazy quilt, a city planner's nightmare. Everything was put up quickly to accommodate the hordes of eager immigrants. Schools, churches, hospitals, precincts, office buildings—there was always excavation and construction going on somewhere. Not a day went by when a Tammany official wasn't dedicating a new site, or welcoming a dignitary to a recently completed one. It was boom town, and it stayed that way right through the depression and the war. The construction kept right on going until the destruction began.

5

No one could have foretold it. There was no precedent for decay in America. Unlimited growth had been the rule since the early nineteenth century. There had always been room and opportunity for the new waves of immigrants that hit the city. There was always a future.

And then gradually, imperceptibly at first, the growth stopped. The cities had reached the zenith of their potential. For a time, like rockets at the top of their parabolas, they traveled in the weightless euphoria of postwar prosperity. And then they began to plummet, the devastation accelerating with each passing year until they reached the bottom—burnt-out hulks, rusting and moldering away.

It was almost as if the death of the cities had been decreed, as if every ameliorative measure, no matter how benign and democratic, would not only fail but would drive another nail into the coffin.

First, there was rent control. During the war millions had streamed into the cities. To protect them from profiteering landlords, laws had been enacted limiting the amount of rent that could be charged for each unit. They were good laws, necessary ones to insure the growth of the cities, maintain a labor pool for domestic and defense industries, protect the families of GIs who were living on limited incomes. After the war there was a slump, which was only to be expected. Releasing hundreds of thousands into the peacetime labor market was sure to cause a strain. This was no time to lift controls. Especially since those *landlords* (the very word was to become anathema in the cities) were waiting to pounce, and make up for all the money they had lost during the war. Controls were good, a little socialist corrective to the entrepreneurial insanity of the wartime economy. They stayed.

Next came the immigrants. First the movement was in-

19

terior, involving a massive shift of population within the country. Southern blacks had come North during the war to work in defense plants. Millions were freed from the feudal Jim Crow economies of the South, which had flourished right up until the outbreak of the war. Afterwards, they stayed on, settling in areas that had been vacated by fleeing whites, Harlem in New York, the South Side of Chicago, the Central Ward in Newark, Watts in Los Angeles, and the inner areas of Detroit, Cleveland, Buffalo—nearly every metropolis in the country. It seemed like a good thing at the time. The thriving cities would provide opportunities that had been long denied these people, and they, in turn, would add to the prosperity of the cities. They stayed.

Next came the Hispanic migration. Because Puerto Rico was a possession of the United States, its citizens were automatically naturalized Americans, and could settle in any part of the mainland. They left their overcrowded, underemployed island and came to cities, as had so many millions before them. They were mostly *jibaros,* rural people, who could no longer make a living off the land. They had no skills, and didn't know the language, but that was nothing new. Hadn't most of the European immigrants been rural, almost hillbillies in their countries of origin? The Sicilians and Calabrese, the Irish farmers, the Jews from the backwater villages of Russia and Poland all had arrived similarly bereft. This was just another phase in the classic American process—the immigrant who makes good. These people would provide a cheap, willing labor market just as their predecessors had. They would work hard and better themselves. The tradition would continue as soon as they found jobs.

Only there were no jobs. Industries had peaked or automated. The price of real estate, the taxes, the demands of the unions were all driving factories from the cities, and no new ones were being built to replace them. You couldn't just walk into a shop, a restaurant, or a garage and get a job. You couldn't just latch onto a carpenter, a mason, or a tinsmith and learn the trade. You had to be in the union first, and the unions were tightening up, passing those precious cards down from father to son. Even the most menial jobs had been organized. Sweatshops had been virtually eliminated, and people bribed and connived to get into the few that existed. The city was no longer a cornucopia of jobs and opportunities. It wasn't like the Depression, when the whole country had ground to a temporary halt. Here, things were going along fine. Fortunes were being made. With a few bumps at the beginning, the country had slid into a booming peacetime economy. Except for these new arrivals. Nobody seemed to need them. They couldn't work cheap. They couldn't even give it away.

They settled in the rent-controlled walk-ups of the South Bronx and the whites fled from them as if they were carrying the plague. Northward through the Bronx the whites ran, jamming into enclaves in Pelham and the Grand Concourse, while the ones with money moved into the high rises of Riverdale, and the even more prosperous left the city for the suburban sanctuaries of Westchester and Rockland County. You didn't even need money to get out. Across the East River in Queens, red brick middle-income "Lefrak Cities" were going up, providing instant refuge. The swampy farmland of northern Queens was being hastily developed, much as the Bronx had been twenty years before. And for the same people. Only now it wasn't ambition that was motivating them. It was fear.

For their new neighbors weren't like previous immigrants. They were America's scapegoats, the victims of its indigenous racism. The systematic libel against blacks to justify their slavery, and, later, their oppression, had pervaded. The idea propounded as early as the Monroe Doctrine that the Spanish South was subordinate to the English North, and reinforced with countless colonial forays into South America over the next hundred odd years, had created the impression that Hispanics were somehow childlike and irresponsible with the sudden, homicidal tempers of children. These native Americans were pariah people, who would never fit into the society created by European immigrants. They were dangerously different. No sooner did they show up in a neighborhood than the buildings began falling apart. There was garbage in the streets. Women and old folks weren't safe after dark. They were rapists, drug addicts. Hysteria was fueled by conditions. The neighborhoods *were* beginning to deteriorate. There *was* more street crime, just as there had been with the arrival of every immigrant group. Everyone who could picked up and left the Bronx to the newcomers.

Now rent control became a necessity. The only people

21

who might have been able to sustain decontrol were gone. Real estate taxes and maintenance costs crawled up, but rents stayed the same. A huge welfare bureaucracy was created to help keep the new arrivals at subsistence level. Landlords, despairing of ever seeing a profit, began to neglect the buildings, preferring to let them deteriorate rather than spend money on maintenance and repairs. They refused to pay the taxes, thus forfeiting the property to the city. The more desperate among them had the buildings burnt down to collect the insurance. Arson became a cottage industry in the South Bronx, with buildings and retail businesses going up in flames every day.

The welfare system, certainly a benign, liberal response to poverty, proved to be a mixed blessing. In certain situations the monthly benefits, especially for large families, were almost as much as the wages for a menial job, so many preferred not to work. The system had been created to protect families, but its peculiar regulations tended to fragment them. No benefits went to a family with a father on the premises, so husbands and wives lived apart, arranging clandestine visits, hiding from case workers, who were known to stage "midnight raids" on apartments to catch the husbands. Benefits were cancelled as soon as the recipient found a job, thus making it pointless to work for a few more dollars than you could get for doing nothing. The Welfare Department often placed families in substandard buildings. The only way they could be relocated was if the buildings simply ceased to exist, so many desperate people, seeking to get their children out of heatless, rat-infested, crime-ridden buildings, put the torch to them. And the area was further desolated. The system encouraged cheating. The bureacracy became so cumbersome that there were many ways to loot it. This created an adversary relationship between recipient and caseworker, each trying to outwit the other. Welfare laws discouraged birth control, providing larger benefits to larger families. Unwittingly, inadvertently, and with all the best intentions, welfare became the nemesis of the people it had been created to help.

And then there was heroin, the wrecking ball that finally leveled the neighborhood. Heroin was an infection that had been controlled by social conditions and availability. In the forty years since its development as a cure for morphine addiction, it had been confined to tight, secretive circles—former patients who'd been weaned off morphine with it, medical people who took it as a recreational sedative, musicians who used it to wind down. It never became as popular as cocaine or marijuana; the dire consequences of its physical addiction frightened off the decadent bohemians who had flirted with the other drugs. The great forbidden drug of the twenties was alcohol; prohibition made it a *cause célèbre*. The culture of speakeasys and wild parties that booze spawned was the perfect complement to the energy and gaiety of the time. Heroin had no culture. It was used in dark rooms by desperate people who knew they risked illness, even death, every time they injected it. It was abhorred by fastidious racketeers, who were making quite enough at their other rackets. Trafficking in heroin became a death sentence in the underworld. The gangsters knew that its use would destroy their other rackets. Junkies don't drink or gamble or go to brothels. They don't do anything but dream.

But after the war the infection began to spread. Thousands of GIs who had been palliated with morphine by harried Army doctors came back looking for more. Racketeers, having lost their lucrative black market trade with the end of the war relaxed their scruples a bit when they realized the potential of heroin. Wartime connections had been made with opium smugglers in the Near East, and processors in Europe. Relatively negligible amounts of the stuff—fifty to a hundred kilos—were worth millions. Their consciences could be clear as well. The heroin wouldn't infect the white kids in the good neighborhoods. It was going right to the market of its greatest demand, the black and Spanish slums of the cities.

Heroin is the drug of idleness. A pain killer, a time killer, it's perfect for those without work, ambition, or self-esteem. The heroin addict is a lone wolf, forced by his craving to think only of himself. He becomes a predator when necessary. He can't think beyond his next fix. Within ten years, by the late fifties, the area was infested with addicts, stealing and killing to support their habits. Violence became a commonplace. The police were seen as either too incompetent or corrupt to stop it. And the coffin slowly closed shut on the South Bronx.

6

Somebody must have known something. In the calm, bucolic days of the nineteen-twenties when the Forty-first precinct was built on Simpson Street, somebody must have had an inkling of what the future held.

In a neighborhood with hardly any crime, and hardly any population to commit it, they built a four-story fortress of gray stone. The Four-One looked more like a prison than a precinct. It was unique in its design. No green lanterns twinkled hospitably amidst the red brickwork as in the other station houses. Here, huge slabs of stone had been cemented into the dismal edifice where an occasional tiny window overlooked the narrow street like a dinosaur's beady eye. It had a huge, square desk area, two stories in height, and a muster room that could accommodate four times the policemen who were stationed in the precinct when it opened. Up a broad, winding staircase in back of the desk were two floors of offices, locker rooms, detention areas, bathrooms, and dormitories. It was as if someone had known that one day the tranquil Four-One would be a bedlam; that on weekends there would be five hundred policemen turning out for the night tours, among them three hundred members of the Tactical Patrol Force, the elite group of the New York City Police Department sent to help keep order on a Saturday night; that there would be a squad of thirty detectives struggling to keep up with the incredible volume of major crime in the area, a hundred and forty-six murders in one year; that on any given day there would be scores of social workers, psychologists, lawyers, reporters, community leaders, and politicians in attendance. There were legions of professional head-scratchers puzzling over the social problems of the South Bronx; on the slowest day the precinct was crowded with prisoners, detention areas were overflowing, prisoners were lounging on the

24

steps, sitting companionably on benches, standing in line near the one pay phone to call lawyers or friends—or bookies— while their families clamored for their release, screaming broken English at the desk sergeants who were trying to cope with mountains of paperwork. For years the desk area had been a lonely place. Janitors wandered about sweeping the dust from unused corners, wondering at its cavernous size. But, beginning in the early sixties, every inch of available space was used. The precinct became the center of the community. People came with their problems, whether or not they were police-related. The ill and the injured wandered in for help. Those with no heat or hot water came for warmth. Old folks, afraid to walk the streets with their social security checks, came to ask for escorts. Others just checked in from time to time to see what was happening.

Now the maintenance men had plenty to do. On Monday mornings they scrubbed the blood off the walls and floors of the desk area, from a typical weekend in which victims, perpetrators, and police officers had been shot, stabbed, bludgeoned, or all three, and had bled on the precinct floor while waiting for ambulances. They cleaned the cigarette butts, candy wrappers, and coffee containers off the stairs leading to the second-floor squad room where scores of prisoners had stood handcuffed, waiting to be fingerprinted by detectives. They swept the broken glass of wine bottles that had been dropped or thrown by prisoners, sponged the desperate graffiti off the walls of the bathrooms and the detention pen, emptied the ashtrays in the squad room where detectives had spent long nights typing up reports on the cases they had investigated that weekend.

True to its prophetic construction, the Forty-first precinct became a fort. Luckily, it was built in the middle of a narrow block, its walls thick and its windows small. Because on several occasions it had been besieged by residents protesting an arrest or an instance of alleged police brutality. Had it been a smaller, flimsier building, it would have been overrun by determined rock-throwing mobs. It had even been under fire from snipers on roofs and in apartments across the street. Had it been on a corner, a favored location for many precincts, it would have provided a larger target area, and would have been harder to defend.

Even within its solid walls, policemen weren't always safe.

A patrolman had been killed with his own gun while wrestling with a psycho. A detective was killed when his gun was snatched by a prisoner he was fingerprinting. The other detectives had left the bullet holes, unrepaired, on the walls of the squad room as a reminder to everyone. You couldn't be too careful in the Four-One.

It was around that time that some anonymous cop with a taste for old movies decided that the Four-One wasn't a precinct at all, but a fort in hostile territory. The cops were as besieged and beleaguered as John Wayne and his cavalrymen in *Fort Apache*. This was Fort Apache, the Bronx.

7

Murphy went on sick call after Houlihan's funeral. He didn't want to have to tell the story a hundred times, answer a thousand questions, get a thousand expressions of sympathy. Most of all there was one sentence he never wanted to utter again. "I was drunk."

He stayed in the house, sleeping late, avoiding his family. Every morning he would hear the alarm go off in his daughters' rooms. His wife, Mary, was already downstairs on her second cup of coffee. Their daughters, Katherine and Anne Marie, seven and nine, would come to the bedroom door in their school uniforms—middy blouses and green plaid skirts. They would stare at him for a while, not knowing whether to come in or not. To make their decision easier he moaned and burrowed into the pillows, making a great show of being fast asleep. But Timothy, the little one, aged eighteen months, was not as easily discouraged. Murphy would hear the bar drop from his crib, hear the flap of his little hands as he crawled doggedly across the hall, his little puffs of labored breath as he pulled himself up on the bed, and shoved his father, sticking his finger into Murphy's nose and trying to lift his head off the pillow. "Dada, dada . . ." Murphy would

26

finally yield, taking this squirming, giggling little boy under the covers with him. He was a big baby; his large head was a harbinger of great physical stature, the doctor had said. So he'd be a big guy like his uncles: like his grandpa. He already had the old man's thick bulldog chin. There was even something cold and watchful in the eyes. Like a cop checking out a driver's license, or listening to a phony alibi. Was it in the genes? He closed his eyes, and that blood-spattered barroom in the Bronx popped into his mind like a slide in a projector. He had to open his eyes because his son's soft, infant flesh was beginning to feel like Houlihan's body before they took him away.

On Sundays, when the weather was warm, his brother Vincent, the priest, would have the whole family out to the church for a barbecue. Vincent's parish was on the North Shore, a mossy gothic church with a gym, a ball field, and manicured grounds. The rectory was a split-level house built for him by his rich and grateful parishioners. Vincent had the most prosperous parish on Long Island. It was only a matter of time before he became a monsignor. He had a Sunday morning show on a local cable station, and was writing a booklet on marriage counseling for the diocese. Vincent did alright. "Of all my sons," the old man would constantly say, "Vincent is the sharpest operator."

Murphy had managed to avoid these outings in the past, pleading work or fatigue. He was uncomfortable around his family, and always sat alone while the wives chatted in one corner, the kids played, and his brothers tried to make points with the old man. But now he had no excuse. Since he had suffered a tragedy, his presence was required; the family had decided that he needed them now, although they were the last people he wanted to see.

They put a beach umbrella over the picnic table because the old man didn't like the sun. There was a bottle of Ballantine's scotch, the old man's favorite—Murphy remembered the cases he would bring home every Christmas, "presents" from the merchants on his beat. Murphy's mother had died six months before, and the old man was taking turns visiting his sons before he went back to live in the old three-story house in Throgs Neck, where he'd lived for almost forty years. Now Murphy's turn was coming up. He dreaded the prospect.

"Johnny, Johnny . . ." His brother Eddie was calling him

over to the table. Eddie was the desk officer at the nineteenth precinct in the silk stocking district of the Upper East Side. Another good politician, another soft job. He met Murphy halfway. "Go over and talk to the old man, will ya," he snarled. "He's startin' to get pissed off."

The old man was dropping a few watery cubes into his drink as Murphy approached. "Wanna drink, John?"

"No thanks, Dad."

"Leavin' the hooch alone for a while, huh? That's a good idea."

After sixty years in this country the old man still spoke with the hint of a brogue. He was an older, thicker version of his two elder sons, a little redder in the face, toothless from a brawl thirty years before in a Brooklyn bar. As a boy Murphy remembered him dropping his upper plate in a glass of water as he settled down in front of the TV. The big, square hands trembled a bit as he poured the drink, the knuckles raw from the thousands of beatings he'd given anyone who didn't obey —criminals, other cops, his boys. He'd been a strong bastard in his day, arm-wrestling two guys at once at a July Fourth picnic. Murphy remembered that. He remembered getting cuffed around by those big hands, too, going ass-over tin cup every time the old man hit him, even if it was only a casual smack. "Wait'll your father gets home." That had been his mother's most potent threat. Because when the old man came home still wearing his uniform, booze watering his eyes and stinking up his breath, he was in no mood for tales of mischief or disobedience. . . .

"Sorry to hear about Houlihan," the old man said. "How long were you with him, anyway?"

"Seven years," Murphy said. He was watching his brother Vincent dance around the grill, flipping hamburgers, forking frankfurters into buns, his face flushed from the heat. "Why does he have to keep that goddamn collar on even when he's cookin' hot dogs?" he said.

"That collar is makin' him more money than your shield ever will," the old man said. "You know, you should forget this old grudge you have against Vincent. He really made this little party because he wanted to talk to you . . ."

"Is he gonna give me a little spiritual guidance?"

"Well, he's concerned."

"He wasn't so concerned when he held a pillow over my

28

face when we were both kids until I thought I was gonna die. Or when he tied me up with the clothes line, and locked me in the closet . . ."

"Listen, Johnny," the old man said sharply. He was impatient with other people's memories. "You know how we've been tryin' to get you out of the Four-One, tryin' to get you on the right track in this job. Well, now we're right back where we started from. Paulie can't do anything for you, not with this thing hangin' over your head. Now, we're gonna have to wait a while longer, and hope you can keep your nose clean until we can get you a transfer."

"I'll be okay," Murphy said.

"It comes from workin' in that goddamn precinct," the old man grumbled. "There's no money to be made, no important people, all misfits and drunks. I'm tellin' ya, Johnny, I'm ashamed to have a son of mine workin' up there."

"It's not so bad," Murphy said. "To tell you the truth, I kinda like it up there."

The old man just shook his head.

8

After a week, Murphy got a call from Heffernan, the desk officer at the precinct. "You still out? Should I take you off the chart?"

"Nah, I'll come in," Murphy said. He couldn't take it at home anymore. He'd begun bickering with his wife about little things, the big, unspoken problem always looming in the background. In the seven days he'd been home, he'd hardly even touched her. Before, working the night shifts, getting up early to go to court on a case, coming home so legitimately tired he could barely make it up the stairs after supper, his disinterest had been easy to camouflage. But now he had no excuse. The tension between them grew steadily. At night she'd wait in bed, her arms stiffly at her sides, her frosted blonde hair glowing in the dark. It wasn't that she wanted it so much. She'd never exactly been a good piece of ass, not even in the first romantic days of their marriage when she'd pushed him away more than she let him in. You couldn't compare her to the women Murphy had met on the job—the hookers whose casual attitude and complete lack of shame was such a turn-on to him, even though he knew they were only doing it because he was a cop; the topless dancers in the many sleazy joints he frequented, who'd clutch at you in the car, moaning endearments, shrieking when you touched them; the teachers and social workers who took Murphy to smoke pot in their cramped apartments in the Village, put the red light and the rock records on, told him their life stories, and reached for him as if he were a life jacket. Sex had never meant that much to her. It was only a gesture of propriety, proof that the marriage was solid. She just wanted him to make the move, and each day that he didn't, things got worse. So he took the easy way out, and went back to work.

Driving to the South Bronx was like going down in a diving bell. You slowly accustomed yourself to the depths. Murphy started out in quiet, suburban Mineola. He took the Long Island Expressway, passing garden apartments and industrial parks, to the Throgs Neck Bridge, where he crossed over to the Cross Bronx Expressway, and the little brick houses and lawns of the North Bronx. Traffic thickened as he moved closer to the city, and the landscape subtly changed. Rising out on either side of the highway you could see the shells of burnt-out, gutted buildings. Disabled vehicles appeared along the roadside. The Cross Bronx was a sunken drive that traversed the Bronx, and it seemed to sink deeper, the brick walls on either side getting higher as you hit the South Bronx. Murphy drove up the long ramp at the Webster Avenue exit, emerging on a street of stripped cars. Junkies scurried in and out of a few abandoned buildings on the corner. Three men sat in a shiny Cadillac having a heated discussion. Obviously, numbers guys waiting for the drop. Murphy knew if he parked around the corner, he could wait until the runner came, and collar them all with probably fifteen or twenty grand, the day's take from maybe three or four banks. He could move right in now on the dude in the leather jacket sliding in and out of the phone booth on the corner of Southern Boulevard, and probably collar him with cash, five nickel bags of dope, which he stashed in the phone, and at least one junkie who'd testify against him. A whole neighborhood full of beautiful felony collars just begging to be made. A cop could get rich or famous up here. A little shake, and you come up with a coupla hundred or more for looking the other way; or if you want to make points you drag everybody in and a chest full of commendations, which you can wear to funerals.

Murphy drove down Simpson Street looking for a parking space in front of the precinct. Cars were triple-parked, some backed up onto the sidewalk, right to the stoops of the buildings on either side of the precinct. Everyone liked to get as close as possible to the house so their cars wouldn't be stolen or stripped. The only time to get a space was when a shift broke, and the men came running out for their cars. Murphy double-parked next to the Captain. That was one car he knew wouldn't be going out all day. Captain Dugan was new on the job, but he hadn't shown too much curiosity about his new precinct, preferring to stay on the phone in his office trying to arrange a transfer.

It was a Monday morning, and the precinct was recovering from the weekend. Clendennon, the huge black desk sergeant on the midnight-to-eight, was standing at the desk, his sleeves rolled tightly over massive forearms, wading through the mass of paperwork that had accumulated during the night. Pantuzzi, the eight-to-four sergeant, stood waiting to take over. He was short and slight with sharp, dark features, and a nervous twitch in his right shoulder. After sixteen years on the job, Pantuzzi had learned how to get through the day without ever looking at anybody. He had the snapshots of his kids, which he propped up on the desk in front of him, the *Daily News,* which he read intermittently between calls, the racing form, which he studied during lunch, and a stack of contest entries clipped out of magazines, newspapers, and special contest magazines. Pantuzzi entered every contest, played the numbers religiously, put down small bets on long shots at the track, invested in cheap stocks, looked for anything that could make a quick killing. He wanted to retire, and knew that pure luck would be his only ticket out of the job. Meanwhile, he had worked out a way to endure. From the moment he hit that desk until the tour was over he was writing. Booking reports, sign-ins and outs,

31

keeping the charts up to date, his own personal paperwork: Pantuzzi never looked up from his work. The men had tried to get him to lift his head. They had exploded a cherry bomb in a garbage can by the desk, hired a hooker to come in and strip right in front of him, even played the cruelly elaborate trick of getting someone to call and say that he had hit the million-dollar lottery. Nothing worked. Pantuzzi's regard remained steadfastly downcast; his tone was calm and even with just a hint of scorn. Nobody could get him to look up.

Even at seven-thirty in the morning there was a handful of prisoners in front of the desk waiting to be booked. Handcuffed and patient, they knew the route, and talked quietly with the arresting officers. It was a mistake to make a commotion in the Four-One, to demand your rights, chew gum, or talk tough. The cops were just too tired and frazzled to take any crap, the repeaters knew that. If you acted like a model prisoner you might get out of the precinct and over to Central Booking without catching a beating.

"They got a new partner for you, Murphy," Pantuzzi said, spreading his papers out on the desk, and sitting down.

"Who's that?" Murphy asked.

Pantuzzi just pointed into the muster room. He never liked to talk when a gesture would do. There were about a dozen cops milling around the coffee machine.

"Can you give me a hint?" Murphy asked.

"He's wearing a blue uniform," Pantuzzi said, settling in behind the desk. Clendennon looked over and grinned at Murphy.

"You can relax, Murphy, he ain't colored," he said.

"Just as long as he ain't a guinea," Murphy said, walking into the muster room. "I don't wanna have to fumigate the car every week."

"Name?" Pantuzzi demanded of one of the prisoners.

A dark-haired kid was standing apart from the others looking uncomfortable and out of place. Murphy knew this was his new partner. He ignored the kid, and joined the men around the coffee machine. There were a few mumbled condolences and expressions of concern.

"You okay, Murf?"

"Sorry about Houlihan."

Murphy nodded quickly without responding. The men could see he didn't want to talk. Instead he nudged Gerry Donahue, who was lying on the bench with his hands over his eyes. "What's the matter with you?"

"What the fuck does it look like?" Donahue said. "I hit the double at Yonkers yesterday, spent the whole fuckin' night celebratin'. It's cheaper when I lose."

"Why don't you go say hello to your new partner?" Eddie Finley said.

"Think he's old enough to talk?" Murphy said, loud enough for the kid to hear.

"Look at the hair," Charley Morgan said with equal volume.

"He looks like a fag to me," Murphy said.

"You could do worse," Finley said.

"Think of all the money you'll save on pipe jobs," Morgan said. "You won't have to be tossin' those hookers at Hunts Point every night."

"Murphy don't like the hookers," Donahue said. "He goes and hangs around the Catholic school. Gets those twelve-year-olds with big tits."

"All in the interest of science," Murphy said. "I wanna find out what they eat to make their tits grow so I can feed it to my wife."

"They eat the Irish inch," Morgan said. "Accelerates their development."

Murphy tuned out, and stared across the room at his new partner. When Morgan got started he made Hitler sound like a liberal. With a little gleeful prompting from his partner Finley he'd run through his whole repertoire on the "boots" and the "pineapples," the current precinct names for blacks and Puerto Ricans. Morgan's routine was pretty funny the first thirty times you heard it, but the jokes stayed the same, and when you saw him beat up on a collar in the back of a radio car, you knew there was something sick behind his humor.

Morgan was big and strong. Murphy, that great bestower of nicknames, had christened him "Godzilla," and he loved it. His face was red and blotchy like a slab of raw meat, his thick knuckleless hands hung limply until he balled them into huge, lethal fists. He liked to hit, and didn't care where or when he got the chance. You couldn't call him a coward; Murphy had seen him wade through a riotous crowd, his blackjack cracking against skulls and collarbones. Murphy had once kicked in the door of a shooting gallery in an abandoned building to get at a psycho who was taking pot shots at people with an M-16, and had found Morgan right behind him, pistol drawn, breathing angrily through his nose, ready for anything. He'd also seen Morgan throw a handcuffed prisoner over the hood of a radio car and break both his knees with a billy club. Morgan had the reputation of being a good man to have behind you in a beef, but maybe he was too good. Maybe he wanted to hit so badly that he'd get himself killed one day doing it. Murphy had always avoided him. Several times Morgan had let it be known that he might consider becoming Murphy's partner. Most of the men would have called that the best matchup in the precinct, but Murphy had stayed with the big, affable Houlihan. In seven years, Houlihan had never pulled his gun. All he ever had to do was slap a guy in the face, and all the fight would go out of him. Houlihan got a kick out of talking guys into the radio car, of getting them to turn around with their hands out to be cuffed. Only he had this stupid pride. He had never been knocked off his feet, never really been intimidated, and he was willing to die to keep that record clean. That stupid sonofabitch . . . Murphy would have forced him to go down on his knees and cry and beg for his life if that was the only way out. Or he would have gone for broke if he sensed that kid was going to shoot Houlihan. He would have known, too. Murphy had the best instincts in the house, everybody knew that. He would have known which way to go. . .

"Hey, Murphy!"

Lieutenant Heffernan shuffled into the muster room, shaking his head. He was a florid, gray-haired little guy, his upper row of teeth protruding just enough to merit the secret nickname "Bucky Beaver," which he knew about, and hated. His nose had more crisscrossing red lines on it than a road map. He had twenty years on the job, and hated it. Every single task he had to perform, from signing out to going to the john, was painful to him. Every cop who made him do thirty seconds more work than he absolutely had to was on the shit list forever. As soon as he entered the room, he knew what was going on.

"You puttin' this kid in the barrel already?" he said.

"Hey, Loot," Murphy said, "do I get a bib when I go to work with this guy? Just in case I have to burp him."

"C'mon, you ain't such a bargain to work with. Corelli," he called.

The kid took his time about coming over. He had a resigned look as if he knew he was in for a lot of grief.

"Say hello to Johnny Murphy, Corelli," Heffernan said. "You'll be riding with him until the smell gets to you."

"How are ya." The kid had a thick Bronx Italian accent. He sounded more like a racketeer than a cop. He looked Murphy right in the eye, and gave him the soft handshake, not the wet fish of a mutt, or the bone-crusher of a guy who had something to prove. He was a pretty boy, and he wanted to be prettier. His dark hair was long and carefully combed, rising to a glossy pompadour, and falling over his collar. His uniform pants were pressed, and his shoes were shined. He was clean, too, as though he hadn't dragged himself out of some grungy gin mill fifteen minutes earlier to come to work. And he was strong: Murphy had sized up enough guys in his life to know the strong ones when he saw them. He had the confidence of a guy who could take care of himself, you could tell by the way he looked at everybody. He wasn't intimidated.

"I guess you oughta meet the other guys," Heffernan said reluctantly. Making introductions came under the heading of unnecessary labor. Corelli waived the introductions, earning himself a warm spot in Heffernan's heart.

"It's okay," he said. "I'll get to know everybody in due time."

Yeah, Murphy thought. This kid could definitely take care of himself.

When they went out on patrol, Murphy asked the kid to drive. "That is, if you're old enough to have a license."

The kid took it real good. Like he was used to it. He was probably the youngest in a large family, just like Murphy, and had learned to take the beatings and the insults from his older brothers.

"How old are you, anyway?" Murphy asked.

"Twenty-three."

"Just outta the Army?"

"Marine Corps."

"Oh, tough guy, huh?"

The kid looked casually over at him. "Yeah, that's right."

"We'll see," Murphy said. "Where were you before you came up here?"

"The One-Four."

"Down on Fifty-fourth in Manhattan? Jesus Christ, it's a piece of cake. What did you do to get up here?"

"I came in with my numbers on backwards, so they sent me up to the Four-One."

The kid was smart. The first thing cons learn in prison is never to tell anyone about what they did, or why they were there, but always to protest their innocence. Smart cops never publicized their infractions, either.

"Well, you got a lot to learn up here that they didn't cover in the Academy, tough guy," Murphy said. "You gonna listen or what?"

"You tell me something worth hearin', and I'll listen," the kid said.

So Murphy told him. He tried to cram as much of it as he could into the first day, so the kid would make it to the second. "The first thing you gotta learn up here is respect," he said. He pointed out of the window at a bunch of Puerto Ricans standing around an old Caddy, peering under its hood. "Don't ever go to sleep on these guys. They got a lotta frustration in their lives, and the slightest thing'll set 'em off. And they got heart, too. A hundred-and-twenty-five pound P.R. will fight you to the death. He'll make you kill him. So treat everybody with respect, and if you make a move—" Murphy slammed his fist into his palm with a resounding smack that startled Corelli. "—make it count."

The next thing to learn was caution. "I meet a guy who takes a lot of chances, always wantin' to fight, and gettin' in jackpots all the time, I don't see a brave guy, I see a suicide," Murphy said. "And I stay away from him. You see I like guys who are scared, who take a lotta precautions. That, means they wanna live. I like guys who wanna live."

"So what are you tryin' to say?" Corelli asked impatiently.

"When you get outta the car, what's the first thing you do?" Murphy asked. "You look up to check the roofs just to make sure nobody's gonna throw a brick on you. When you walk down the street, especially when you're responding to a call, you walk as close to the buildings as possible, so they can't bomb you. You don't go rushin' into dark hallways, you take your time. You don't get too close to people, you don't try to intimidate them with your size, or your mouth. Up here the shield ain't worth shit unless you got something to back it up. And these people know if you got heart; they can smell it on you."

Murphy interrupted his lecture to respond to a call.

"Four-One, Ed," the dispatcher said in a bored voice.

Murphy picked up the radio mike. "Ed K."

"Respond 4330 Hoe Avenue. Report of shots fired."

It was one of those half-occupied, half-devastated buildings where working-class families struggled to maintain apartments next to burnt-out shooting galleries, crash pads, and numbers drops. Murphy knew the building. There'd been a few drug busts in it the week before. When they pulled up, the street was deserted. Murphy shook his head. "There's usually a guy pickin' up numbers on that stoop," he said, pointing across the street. "Plus a couple of his boys standing around. Fuckin' numbers guy'll stay here in a hurricane. If he's gone, you know there's trouble."

Murphy noticed that Corelli looked up at the roofs as they approached the building. Someone had pulled all the lights out of the hallway. They found a man sitting against the wall in a pool of blood. Murphy shined the flashlight into his face. The man mumbled something, and a torrent of blood-flecked spittle poured out of his mouth. Murphy turned away to stifle the nausea. Corelli was staring at the man, his eyes wide with horror.

"You can wait outside if you want," Murphy said.

"It's okay," Corelli said. "I've seen this before."

"Better call for an ambulance," Murphy said, "and tell the dispatcher to get the Eighth Homicide over here, too."

The streets were still empty when they came out. Murphy wandered around trying to find the super. There'd be no witnesses on this case; there rarely were. While they were waiting for the ambulance, Murphy continued his lecture.

"You gotta make friends on this job. Supers, for example. They run the neighborhood. The good super is like a cop. He keeps his building clean, chasing the junkies and the thieves. He knows everybody on the block. The landlords usually give the supers up here a cut of the rent they collect, so the super wants a good building and a quiet block . . ."

The ambulance arrived, followed by Sergeant Applebaum, the patrol sergeant, who wandered over to them with his clipboard. Corelli was more amazed by him than he'd been by that bloody derelict in the hallway. Applebaum was built like a huge pear. He walked and talked with irritating slowness. His neckless head looked as if it might roll off his body with the slightest exertion; Applebaum saw to it that that exertion was never made.

"Why'd you shoot this guy, Murphy?" Applebaum said.

"Didn't like his deodorant," Murphy said with a straight face.

People were filtering out of the neighboring buildings, drawn by the arrival of the ambulance. Applebaum looked around bleakly. "Did any public-spirited citizens come forward to identify the perpetrator?" he asked.

"Not so far," Murphy said.

Applebaum shook his head. "It's gonna be a hot one today. That hallway'll stink for the next ten years." He took off his hat. A little yarmulka was pinned to the back fringe of hair around his bald head. Corelli gaped at it in disbelief.

"Just what I love, a DOA before breakfast," Applebaum said.

"Go in and take a look," Murphy said. "Maybe it'll kill your appetite."

"The only thing that kills my appetite is food," Applebaum said. Wiping the sweat off his scalp, he waddled across the street.

"What the fuck is that?" Corelli said.

"Sergeant Applebaum. He's an orthodox Jew," Murphy explained, "which makes him about as popular as crotch rot. Plus he refuses to take the beanie off, even though it's not Police Department issue. So they stuck him up here with the rest of the misfits."

Corelli looked around at the ruined street, the vacant lots and crumbling buildings, the stripped cars, the rubble. He looked at Applebaum standing outside the buildings talking to the ambulance attendants, the corpse on a stretcher on the steps next to them, covered casually with a blood-stained sheet. He looked at the people, impassively watching. Old women with bulging bellies, winos clutching their bottles to their chests, young hoods, hard-eyed, casing the crowd, innocent kids, nicely dressed, holding school books, people stopping off on their way to work for a look at the dead man. A few blocks away a cloud of acrid black smoke billowed up from a burning building. Fire apparatus roared by. The street was filled with the stench of burning rubber. Everybody looked in the direction of the fire. A few people started off to check it out. The radio in the car squawked more signals in ten minutes than Corelli had heard in three months at the fourteenth precinct, but nobody seemed at all concerned. Murphy lit a cigarette. The sheet slid off the corpse as the attendants took him to the ambulance.

"Where the fuck am I?" Corelli said.

"You're in the Bronx, my man," Murphy said. "And you ain't seen nothin' yet."

9

JANUARY, 1980

Hunts Point was so cold the hookers had gone inside. There wasn't a soul on the streets. Even the winos, who warmed themselves around garbage-can fires on Westchester Avenue, were gone. The wind roamed like a hungry dog through the desert of Charlotte Street, howling in the desolation. On a morning like this it was nice to be sitting in a warm radio car with a cup of coffee, an apricot danish, and the *Daily News*.

Loomis opened the window for a second to flip out his cigarette, and got a blast of cold air. "Whew, the hawk is out today."

"The hawk," Shoup happily echoed. He was a white kid from Queens, fresh out of the Academy, and he loved his black partner's colorful expressions. Loomis had been in the same graduating class, but a few years in the army and the cynicism of a street kid made him seem older. Loomis and Shoup had been part of the first class graduated from the Academy in four years, since the bankrupt city had put a freeze on hiring new police officers. They had been sent to the Four-One because, as Loomis put it, "We must have

39

scored real low on the psychological test. Which means we're too crazy to arrest white people."

Shoup laughed uproariously. That Loomis was a pisser. He was glad he'd been paired with him. Some of those older guys looked at him like he was a piece of dogshit on the street. A lot of them were lushes. You could smell the stale beer and booze on them during the turnout. The muster room stank like a Bowery saloon. Shoup didn't drink or smoke. He ran five miles a day, and worked out on the *Nautilus* three times a week. He was one of the "new breed of police officers" the Mayor had referred to at graduation. He liked working in the Four-One. He'd have more police experience up here in a few months than guys got in thirty years in other precincts. Even on a freezing night, working the midnight-to-eight, he and Loomis had responded to a family dispute in which the wife had pulled a knife on the husband and had collared a burglary suspect coming out of a building on Jennings Street. And that was because of Loomis's street smarts. "What's that cat doin' out on a night like this?" he said when they drove by and saw the guy walking out of the building carrying a shopping bag. Shoup had to admit he wouldn't even have noticed the guy himself. And yet when they called him he started running, and fell on his ass on the ice. He had a radio, a cheap watch, and a toaster in the shopping bag, a couple of rings and sixty-two dollars cash in his pockets. You couldn't call it a major arrest, but the people who he had ripped off would be happy to get their stuff back, and that's what being a cop was really all about.

"Check this out," Loomis said.

A black chick had come out from behind a gutted tenement. She was in gold from head to toe. A golden wig cascaded over her brown shoulders, a gold lamé halter top stopped just above her midriff; gold lamé hot pants looked like they'd been painted on her. Her light brown legs were bare, and she tottered through the rubble on golden spiked heels.

"It's a mirage," Shoup said.

"Think she's got a john in that building?" Loomis said. "I don't see any cars around."

"Shit, I'd take the subway just to get a little piece of that," Shoup said. He hoped Loomis wouldn't be offended by this sexual reference to a black girl. Shoup had never slept

40

with one; he hadn't exactly cut a swath through the white population, either, but guys always told him how good these black chicks were, and he thought it was about time he found out for himself.

"Dig it, bro," Loomis said. "That chick's got some germs they ain't even discovered yet."

The girl began to saunter across the street toward them, swinging a little gold handbag, smiling enticingly.

"I do believe she's makin' a move on us," Loomis said.

"Ain't she cold?" Shoup said, trying to cover his excitement.

"Cold? That chick's so stoned she thinks she's in the Bahamas."

Loomis rolled down the window as the girl approached. "Been partyin', baby?"

She stopped about three feet from the car, put her hand on her hip, and stared at them. It looked like she was having trouble focusing. She was oblivious to the cold, she wasn't even shivering, just staring into the car, swaying a bit, stoned out of her gourd.

"I party all the time, lover." She drew her tongue slowly across her teeth, producing velvet tingles in Shoup's groin. "I'm a pahtay girl . . ."

"Well, party on home, mama, and get yourself some rest," Loomis said.

"Rest?" the girl said, jumping back as if she wanted to fight. "Shit, I don't need no rest. I'm on the case, baby." She came over and leaned into the car, her breasts almost falling out.

"Wow," Shoup said involuntarily. Loomis turned slightly, and gave him a wink.

"Y'all wanna come pahtay with me?" the girl said in a slinky whisper.

"Not right now," Loomis said.

The girl smiled at Shoup. "Pretty little white boy. You wanna go out? I got somethin' fine for New York finest."

Shoup's voice cracked. "We're on the job."

"Well, I'm on a job just like y'all. Important job, too. Y'all just take a look." She bent over far enough to give Shoup a peek at her nipples, and reached into her handbag. All the while Shoup was thinking that if Loomis agreed they could put her in the back, and ride her around Charlotte

Street to one of those areas where there was nothing but rubble for blocks around, and . . .

Something glittered in the girl's hand. It looked like a cigarette lighter. Loomis fell back against the seat clutching his face as it jumped in her hand. He was screaming. The girl's teeth were bared, and she was saying something. It was like a dream. Shoup reached forward to stop her, but couldn't move. It felt as if someone had hit him in the forehead with a pool cue, and then in the cheekbone. Hit him so hard that it didn't even hurt.

Jose and Angel and two kids from the neighborhood, who Angel swore could move a lot of dope, had ducked into an abandoned building on Jennings Street when they saw the cop car. It was freezing. Jose had the down ski jacket he had taken out of a Datsun in Riverdale the week before, but Angel and the kids didn't have anything but their skimpy leather jackets. After a while Angel couldn't take it. "Let's get the fuck outta here before we freeze to death."

"We ain't goin' nowhere 'till they tip, man," Jose said.

"But they ain't got no reason to stop us," one of the kids said.

"The man sees four dudes like us walkin' down the street at seven o'clock in the morning, he knows we're into somethin'."

"Shit, man, you're paranoid," the other kid said.

"I'm movin' out," Angel said.

"You're stayin' here, motherfucker," Jose snarled. He pulled out that .22 starter pistol he had bought for fifteen dollars from Cookie on Fox Street. It was a rotten piece. Anybody who knew anything about guns would laugh in his face if he pulled down on them with this. He hadn't even tested the thing to see if it worked. If one of these kids decided to rush him . . .

But there was no fear of that. Angel and the two kids from the neighborhood knew all about Jose. He was "big time." Skinny, stringy-haired, ugly motherfucker that he was, he had a rep. He'd done time in Attica and Greenhaven, and there were rumors that he'd been the slave to some Mafia guy, giving him head, cleaning his cell—a jailhouse wife. It was hard to believe, especially since everybody was talking about how he'd cut up these two dealers from Harlem in the after-hours on 149th Street, and about how much heart he had. But then, when he got crazy, which he was now, waving that piece in their faces, his voice got real shrill like a chick's, and he flapped his arms around, and he looked like those insane drag queens who hung out in Crotona Park, which made him even scarier. Jose was hooked in with Hernando, who was the "sho' nuff" heavy dealer in the neighborhood. Hernando copped right from the source. He copped "pure" white smack. Even when he put it out on the street, it was three or four, when everyone else was getting two percent of that brown Mexican shit. Hernando's dope came from Iran or Afghanistan. Everyone said the Russians were sending it in to get the whole fuckin' country hooked, so they could move in.

"You'll freeze to death if I say so," Jose said. "I ain't goin' back to the joint 'cause some *chamaco* kid thinks he knows more than me. I'll blow your ass away right in here . . ."

Keep on talkin' and movin' that piece around, Jose was telling himself. Keep that front up. Next kid that opens his mouth give him a whoops right upside his head.

"*Mira*, what's this?" Angel said, pointing toward the street.

The hooker was crossing the street to the radio car.

"I told you assholes," Jose said in triumph. "Didn't I tell you something was goin' down? It's a drop."

"That chick ain't wearin' nothin'," one of the kids said.

"She's wasted," Angel said. "Look how she's walkin'."

"Look at her breath comin' out. Looks like she's smokin'."

"Nah," one of the kids said, "it's cause she's talkin' like this." He put his hand on his hips, and wiggled over to his friend, speaking in a throaty whisper. "Lemme suck your dick, cop. I'm gonna take it all, all of it . . ." Then, he stopped and looked quickly at Jose, who was staring at him with a little half smile.

"Hey . . ." Angel shouted.

The shots sounded like firecrackers. "She's offin' 'em," Angel shouted.

"Be cool, man. Be cool." Jose ran to the doorway as the hooker emptied her pistol into the police car. It was at least a block away, and he couldn't see who it was. "It's a hit," he said. "Get back against the wall," he snapped. The boys obeyed quickly. Jose ran to a window and looked out over

Charlotte Street. "She's probably got five guys watchin' her from a car somewhere."

"I didn't see nuthin'," one of the kids said. "I didn't see no car."

"Anybody know that bitch?" Jose asked.

"No, man, I didn't even see her."

"I ain't never seen no chick who looked like that around here."

"I didn't see her face, man."

Jose made them wait as the girl crossed back behind a building, and disappeared. They heard a car start, but didn't see it.

"She musta gone down Southern Boulevard," Angel said.

Guns, Jose was thinking. Clean, beautiful .38's.

"Hey, you . . ." Jose turned suddenly and grabbed the kid who'd been talking funny. He grabbed a clump of hair at the base of the kid's neck, and pulled his head back. "Go out there, and see if these two cops are dead."

The kid gasped in pain. "I ain't no doctor."

Jose almost pulled him back off his feet. He snarled through clenched teeth. "Just see if they ain't movin or makin' any noise, and wave to us if it's cool, you understand. Now go ahead, you little cocksucker, run up that block, or I'll burn your ass right here."

The kid took off running up the deserted street, his arms churning, looking around in panic. Angel turned to Jose, his eyes bulging fearfully. "*Mira,* Jose, there's gonna be five hundred cops here in a minute . . ."

The kid had reached the car, and was waving back to them. Jose shoved Angel toward the door. "Hey, man, you wanna get tight with my main man, with Hernando? Do you?"

"Yeah, but . . ."

"Run up that street, and get the guns off them two cops," Jose said. "Take 'em right outta the holsters and bring 'em back to me. You and your boys here . . ."

Angel was close to tears. "I can't do that . . ."

Jose shoved him again, and waved the starter pistol in his face. *Oye, maricon,* you wanna show me your *cojones?* You wanna be big time?

Angel nodded. He ran out of the building and up the street, followed by the other kid. Jose stepped out, and looked both ways up the street. There was nobody around. Not even a truck was passing. In a minute they were back, the guns hidden under their coats. They had taken the cops' wallets, too, and went through them, scattering cards and papers to the wind, and keeping the few dollars they found. Jose grabbed both guns roughly away from them. They were big police specials, so new that the barrels gleamed. *"El Tremendo,"* Jose said in admiration. "These ain't no Saturday Night Specials. You know if you shoot this motherfucker it's gonna go where you want it to." He smiled, and pointed the guns lazily at Angel and his friends. "Don't go tellin' nobody about this, man. Some stoolie'll think you're a cop killer, and bring the man down on you. And the cops won't believe that you just were walkin' by, and copped these two guns. They'll think you did it, man, and even if they don't they'll put it right on you anyway. And if you get me and my man into it . . ." He let the threat hang in the air until Angel piped up anxiously, "We won't tell nobody, man. Nobody."

"We promise, man."

Jose stuffed the pistols in the pockets of his ski jacket. "You don't have to promise, man, because I know you ain't gonna tell. One way or another, you dig?"

Jose walked up Southern Boulevard to his apartment on 174th Street. He kept his hands in his pockets, fondling those two tremendous pistols. He'd never felt this safe in his life. Nobody could mess with him now. Even if a cop car stopped to hassle him, he could just walk over real slow just like that bitch had done, and rip those suckers to shreds before they knew what was happening. Now he could throw that starter pistol away. No, better to keep it. Keep all the heat. You pull down on a dude with that nowhere piece, and then when he thinks he's gonna get over on you, you blast him with *El Tremendo*. BOOM, motherfucker, BOOM!

Jose passed the super on his way into the apartment. The super looked at the ski jacket, and shook his head. The man never said hello, never showed him any respect. So he knew Jose had copped the jacket. He wished he had one. I could back this motherfucker right down in the basement, Jose thought as he climbed the stairs. Make him get right down on his knees in a pile of garbage.

Jose heard the baby crying as he opened the door. His old lady was under the covers with him trying to keep warm, watching "Captain Kangaroo" on television.

45

"No heat today?" Jose said.

"The boiler's still broke," she said. "Where the fuck you been?"

"I put some goods out on the street," Jose said. "Forty bags with these kids from Jennings Street. Just to see what they can do."

"Throw that fuckin' jacket over here, will ya," she said. It was so cold he could see her breath in the air.

"In a second. I just gotta put somethin' away."

She got out of bed, carrying the baby. Suspicious bitch. She was wearing his long army coat. Ugly bitch. She'd been drinking that rum again, he could smell it on her.

"You been with another chick?"

He wheeled on her. He would have smacked her if she hadn't been holding the kid, and she knew it. That's why she hadn't let go of the little bastard since he was born. "I told you where I was. Puttin' some shit out on the street."

"How come it took so long?"

"Hey, bitch, what are you, the D.A.?"

"How come it took so long?" she screamed. Pasty-faced Irish junkie bitch: no *Latina* would ever yell like that at her old man. Maybe take a knife and cut his throat when he was sleeping, but never screech like a fuckin' alley cat. He hated when she yelled like that, because he knew the neighbors could hear it. It made him look like shit.

"Will you shut your mouth?"

"If you think you can leave me in this fuckin' dump all day . . ."

"I got into a hassle with the cops, okay?"

"You're full of shit," she said, shaking her head.

"It's true. One of these kids got high, man, and started noddin', you know, and I was tryin' to get the bags out of his pocket when these fuckin' cops roll up."

"So how'd you get out of it?"

Jose laughed nervously. Keep up the front. "You'll find out. Just turn on the radio in a couple of hours, and you'll find out."

She looked at him with contempt. What do all these bitches think they have that makes them better than men, he wondered.

"What's that supposed to mean?" she asked.

"That I blew them away, man," Jose said. "Both of them.

I had to do it. I ain't ever goin' back to the joint again. I'll kill every cop in the Bronx before I do that."

She just stared at him, her mouth all twisted up, shaking her head. "You fuckin' liar. You couldn't kill a cockroach."

"Yeah, well I just killed two of 'em over on Charlotte Street. You don't believe me, just turn on the radio."

She turned and headed back to bed. While she had her back to him he slid the two pistols out of his pockets. "That piece I copped from Cookie works pretty good, but it ain't nothin' compared to them guns I took off them dead cops."

She turned. She had her mouth all screwed up to say something nasty, but she just froze up when she saw the two pistols in his hand.

Jose walked right up to her, twirling the pistols between his fingers western style.

"What's the matter? All of a sudden you ain't makin' no jive-ass remarks."

"Where'd you get them?" she asked, backing away.

"I told you, didn't I? Now get outta here, and lemme get some sleep." He slipped the pistols under the pillow, and got under the covers with all his clothes on. Even the baby got quiet all of a sudden. She went out into the kitchen to huddle next to the stove for warmth. "Make me some coffee, while you're out there," he said, snuggling up and reaching under the pillows to feel the cold steel of the pistols. This was more like it.

10

It was party time at the Emerald Saloon. Even though it was seven-thirty in the morning, nobody but the help wanted to go home. It was too cold out there. You could hear the wind whistling up Westchester Avenue under the El. Pieces of cardboard and newspaper flew by like birds heading south. Old hubcaps and garbage can covers careened down the street

47

with every fresh gust. Besides, if there was anything worth while at home, the place would have been empty hours ago.

Long ago, in another time, the Emerald had been an Irish saloon. It was now one of the many properties of Spanish Pete, the numbers king of the area. The original green sign with the two shamrocks, now a bit weatherbeaten, was still outside; the original mahogany bar, a few chips knocked out of it by the heads of recalcitrant customers, remained, as did the grimy tile on the bathroom floor. But everything else was new, including the customers. Here, off-duty cops drank with numbers runners, dope dealers, hookers, and pimps. At four o'clock in the morning when, according to New York State law, all taverns must close, the Emerald was just starting to get busy. The prices went up as the window shades went down, and the place became an after-hours joint. The door was locked, although nobody knew why, anyone who knocked was promptly admitted. There were no bouncers. Lureen, the barmaid, kept order. She was a mountainous brown lady of indeterminate age and boundless energy who could waddle up and down that bar for twelve hours straight. "As long as they're standin' and spendin'," she said, which they always were. She knew everybody in the neighborhood, knew what they drank, and how much it took to get them happy, morose, maudlin, and finally dangerous. She could spot trouble brewing out of the corner of her eye, and could usually scotch it with a sudden, profane basso rumble.

At this time of morning, the place was peopled with the real die-hards, the ones who didn't want to go home. Throw them out, and they'd go to another after-hours, or wait in a diner until eight-thirty came, and it was legal to have a drink again. If there were no gin mills to go to, they'd go to a McDonalds, or a library. Hell, they'd sit in the park and freeze before they'd go home, this bunch would.

Most of them were cops with unhappy marriages. Some, like Charley Morgan, who was making a drunken spectacle of himself by the jukebox, had been separated and were living alone. Others, like Johnny Murphy, just couldn't make it home after work. Ask them why, and they really couldn't tell you. Home was just the very last place they wanted to be.

There were barmaids and topless dancers from other saloons, cynical, hard-drinking bitches, who sat there hoping romance would walk in the door. There were the hookers, who were afraid to go home because they knew they'd catch a beating from their old men for not earning enough. There were the junior racketeers, gaudily dressed, jewelry flashing, who were so full of cocaine they had to drink and talk the anxiety away. But mostly there were cops. Guys from the Four-One and the Four-Two, sitting at tables, smoking and drinking, eyeing the girls. Just killing time until they had to go to work again.

Murphy didn't socialize. He sat at the far corner of the bar barricaded behind his three packs of Marlboros, his over-flowing ashtray, which he wouldn't let Lureen empty, and his stein of lukewarm Budweiser. He didn't drink that much. Just sat there doing bar tricks, balancing a quarter on a pile of salt, building houses of wooden matchsticks and pieces of pretzel, folding a cocktail napkin so that it took off like a rocket when a lighted match was touched to it. Lureen couldn't understand him. He wasn't drunk, or unruly, didn't seem depressed. He just sat there night after night.

"That beer must taste like piss by now," she said. "How come you keep drinkin' it?"

"I figure if I drink enough you might start lookin' good to me," Murphy said.

She patted down her back hairs, and leaned in flirtatious-ly. "I start lookin' a lot better after a bottle of champagne, honey."

"You buyin'?"

"Sheeit . . ." Lureen poured her thirtieth shot of Dram-buie, and threw it down with a practiced flip of the wrist. "You cops are somethin' else. Why don't you go home to your wife?"

"Why don't you?"

"For all the good you been doin' her, she might be better off with me," Lureen said. "At least I'd wash the dishes every once in a while."

"Yeah," Murphy said, "that's what we need, a maid. How about it, Lureen?"

Lureen looked archly at him. "You couldn't afford me, honey." She looked over Murphy's shoulder. "And your boy Charley Morgan over there . . ."

"He ain't my boy," Murphy mumbled.

Lureen pretended not to hear. "They're gonna put him

in the home any day now. Hey, Morgan," she shouted. "Yo twinkletoes. That's right, I'm talkin' to you."

Murphy looked at Morgan in the bar mirror. He was trying so hard to have a good time, his veins were popping out on his forehead. For the last hour he'd been feeding the jukebox, stumbling around, waving his arms, shaking his hips, to the amusement of all. Then he'd grabbed a girl on her way back from the bathroom, a shy, Dominican chick who was sitting with Indio, a coke dealer. He wouldn't let her pass. "C'mon baby, you can dance," he said. "I know you can . . ."

Indio had that pained smile on his face. It was alright that his old lady was being hassled. After all, it was a cop. What were you supposed to do? It was alright . . . up to a point.

"Hey, John Travolta," Lureen called. "Why don't you cool it? It's late, and we all wanna go home."

Morgan waved irritably at her. "So go home. I know where the booze is." The girl tried to slip by him, and he grabbed her by the waist, lifting her off the floor and turning her around. "C'mon baby, shake it, shake it just one time for me . . ."

Indio half rose in his seat, and looked angrily at Lureen. She called down the bar to Murphy: "Hey Murf, gimme a hand with this white boy."

"Just tell him to go home," Murphy said.

"Well, shit, what you think I've been doin' for the last hour?" She waddled down the bar, and leaned in confidentially. "He's comin' on to Indio's old lady. That little dude'll pull down on him, I know he will."

Murphy slid off the stool, and put his cigarettes in his pockets. "I hate people who can't handle their own beefs."

"I'll take care of Indio," Lureen said. "But I ain't messin' with no cops. They shoot you in the back, and say it was self-defense."

"Yeah, and they pay you two-fifty for your watered booze and look the other way when you deal loose joints outta here . . . Hey Morgan," he shouted, before Lureen could answer him back.

Morgan staggered back, peering through the booze blur, trying to place that familiar voice. "Murf?"

Murphy walked over, getting between him and the frightened girl. "Hey Murf," Morgan said, "we closin' this

50

joint again." It was a standing joke between them, at least as far as Morgan was concerned. They would sit for hours in the same saloon without exchanging a word, and then on the way out Morgan would shout it to Murphy. It was this big stiff's way of pretending to a friendship that didn't really exist.

"Yeah, they're rollin' up the sidewalks," Murphy said. "The help wants to go home."

Morgan looked around in drunken scorn. "They ain't got no homes. Look at 'em. They all live in the zoo."

"So they wanna go back to their cages . . ."

"Well, fuck 'em." Morgan turned to face Indio. "Fuck them and the horse they rode in on." And he turned back to challenge Murphy. "Right?"

"Anything you say, sport, only now let's go home."

Morgan squinted with drunken suspicion. "You tryin' to kick me outta here, Murphy?"

"You might call it that, yeah."

"Well, I gotta dance with this young lady over here, you understand?" Morgan turned and lurched for the girl. Murphy grabbed him by the shoulder, and spun him around. That wasn't the way to do it. Better to jump on him, hug him, make him think you're as drunk as he is. Just two Irish cops against the world—fuck 'em all, big and small—and walk him out of the joint nice and easy. But it had been a long night, and Murphy didn't feel like using psychology. So he spun him too hard, and Morgan almost fell over.

"Don't gorilla me, Murphy," he said, balling his big fist.

"Will you stop breakin my chops and just get outta here," Murphy said, losing his patience.

Morgan lowered his head like a bull about to charge. He was telegraphing this punch in from Jersey. He lunged out, swinging wildly with his left. Murphy had plenty of time to step back, but he could feel the breeze, and knew what it would be like if that punch ever connected. "Easy, champ," he said, "the only person you're gonna knock out is you."

Morgan came at him again, this time with the right. Murphy stepped aside, and Morgan went head first into the jukebox. A few of the low-lifes in the back started to laugh. Murphy gave them a hard look to shut them up, then bent to help Morgan up. "C'mon, Morgan . . ."

Morgan waved him away, and managed to stagger to his

51

feet. There was a bloody gash on his forehead. "I'm drunk," he said.

"Don't go jumping to conclusions," Murphy said. Now he felt sorry for this big drunken slob. He knew how the guy's wife had thrown him out, and was living with some bank teller. Morgan was just another burnt-out case. Murphy put his arm around him. "C'mon, let's get outta this dump."

"Yeah," Morgan mumbled, leaning on him. "Yeah."

The morning wind hit Murphy in the face like a broken bottle. He propped Morgan against a lamp post, and went back inside to get his coat. When he came back Morgan was pissing on the subway steps. "I really got fucked up, Murf," Morgan said.

Murphy slipped the coat over Morgan's shoulders. "You want me to drive you home?"

"Nah . . . nah . . ." Morgan shook his head, and fumbled with his zipper. "I leave my car here, they'll strip it in thirty seconds." He started off down the street. "I'll be alright," he said, over his shoulder. "And if I'm not, it's no great loss."

Murphy leaned into the wind, and made it to his own car. It was a long drive out to Mineola. He kept the radio on, and the windows open so he'd stay awake. When he pulled up in front of his house he turned off the radio, closed the windows, and fell asleep with his head on the steering wheel. Anything was better than going home.

It had been a bad night for Corelli as well. He and Murphy had responded to a signal 10–30, a robbery in progress at 11:30, just a half hour before they went off. And what did they find? Not a robbery, but a full-fledged rumble. Three guys were beating one poor schmuck to death with bats on the third floor landing of a building on Kelly Street. Murphy and Corelli had to fight the three of them all the way down the stairs and into the street. One of the guys fell and broke his leg, which meant they had to call a bus and go with him to the hospital, because he was a prisoner. Murphy threw another guy over the hood of the car to cuff him and one of the wipers snapped off, which meant they would have to put in a repair report. It took an hour to get everything done at Jefferson Hospital, and then another fifteen minutes to get Murphy away from some P.R. Emergency Room nurse who'd caught his eye. She had a nice body, but looked a little washed-out to Corelli; still, Murphy hung in trying to make conversation and getting the cold shoulder until Corelli finally got him out of there. Then, back to the precinct to fill out reports, get the prisoners printed, mugged, and locked up. By the time they got out it was two o'clock. And Corelli had promised Teresa he'd be at her house no later than twelve-thirty.

She lived with her family in Pelham, a nice residential area of the North Bronx, only a fifteen-minute drive from the Four-One. Corelli made it in five. The lights were off in the two-story brownstone. There was a faint blue glow coming from Teresa's bedroom. She was probably watching the late movie, sitting there in that pink nightgown she'd bought in Lohmann's last Sunday. ("For our wedding night," she'd said coyly, drawing the nightgown over her breasts.) Sitting there naked, the long black hair falling down her back, a few tresses arranged over her tits. Oh, those tits. Corelli drove three times around the block just thinking about them. The way they kind of stirred slightly under her blouse when she moved, or bounced when she ran down the block to greet him. Or just stuck out three miles in front of her when she wore a bra on Sundays, when he had to sit in that stuffy parlor and have demitasse with her father. Those tits. He couldn't believe that in 1980 a guy like him, who'd been all over the world, had only seen those tits once, and that was when she was taking off her bathing suit top to get her back tanned at Jones Beach.

He didn't dare ring her bell now, though, or he'd never get his hands on them. He knew Teresa's mother was lying awake just waiting to catch them. That nasty old bitch. She was jealous because her tits went down to her knees, and nobody wanted any part of them, least of all her own husband who was always asking Corelli if he knew any clean hookers in Hunts Point.

Corelli made a U-turn, and sped back to the South Bronx. Ida, the barmaid at the Garden of Eden on Tiffany Street, was working tonight. It wasn't too late to catch her. Talk about tits. Hers were so big she didn't have cleavage. And she was a hot mama as well. Corelli had met her when they busted an after-hours joint on Freeman Street. She had a .25 and an eighth of cocaine in her pocketbook when he searched her, but he let her go. "You're too pretty to go to jail," he told her. And she was, tiny with angry black eyes and long black hair, and a nice trim little body except for those tits. *Marone a mia.* Corelli had to admit it: he was a tit man.

She wrote her phone number on a pack of matches. "Come visit me any time," she said.

He was there that night, and she was ready. He'd hardly closed the door before she had his pants off, and was pulling him into bed. After the first time she came back to bed with a kitchen knife. "I like you," she said. "So don't fuck me over, okay?"

He shrugged. "Okay."

She shuddered whenever he touched her. When she really got going she would shriek and moan and carry on so much he thought she was putting on a show. But she meant it. That first night she scratched up his back so bad he had to go to the police surgeon to have it treated. After the second time he was lying on his back, hands behind his head, drowsy with contentment, when suddenly she rose over him, her hair matted down over her forehead, the tears of bliss hardly dry in her eyes. "You're real proud of yourself, ain't you?" she asked angrily. "You really think you're hot shit now. You think I'll come crawlin' any time you snap your finger. We'll see who comes to who."

And she went down on him with such passionate ferocity that he could hardly get out of bed. The next day, in the surgeon's office, the blood still hadn't gone back to his dick. "Just married?" the surgeon asked.

"No, I'm still engaged," Corelli said.

"You oughta tell your girlfriend to save something for the honeymoon," the surgeon said.

"This ain't from my girlfriend."

The surgeon nodded. "In that case, you'd better save something for the honeymoon."

Corelli started seeing Ida two or three times a week. He'd run down to the Garden of Eden as soon as the tour was over, and hang around playing poker dice with the bouncer until she got off. They didn't talk much, didn't do much of anything except screw. On the nights that Ida's mother stayed over, they'd do it on the hard marble floor under the stairs in her building. Sometimes they did it in the car, but Corelli was afraid she'd leave a piece of incriminating evidence under the seat—a hairpin, or a tube of lipstick. The other woman always liked to leave tracks; he'd already discovered that, to his regret.

After a few months of this Corelli began having dizzy spells. He had trouble urinating, and when he did it felt like he was pissing barbed wire. He went back to the surgeon, and got pills that turned his urine red, and a piece of avuncular advice. "Keep it in your pants a little more often, and you'll be fine."

So he cut down his nights with Ida, and then cut them out altogether. It had been three weeks since he'd seen her last. On the way to the Garden of Eden he kept thinking of that greedy look she got in her eye as she watched him undress, of her moans and sobs, the way she gagged and spat when she gave him head. Of her tits . . .

The barmaids in the Garden of Eden wore pink leotards and tights with high heels. Nobody looked better in that outfit than Ida. Her tits pointed straight ahead like footballs. But he could tell she was pissed off when he walked in, and his heart sank. It looked like he was going to get shut out tonight.

"Hey, big shot," she shouted over the jukebox. "Couldn't get it on with your girlfriend so you came down here, huh?"

A couple of cops from the Four-One were at the bar, laughing behind their hands. Corelli leaned over the bar right into her face. "Hey, bitch, don't go puttin' my business in the street."

"I been waitin' for you to come in here, motherfucker," Ida said. "Just waitin'. If you think I'm some kinda hooker you can just call up whenever you feel like gettin' your rocks off, you can forget it."

"Okay, I'll forget it." Corelli started away from the bar, but she wasn't finished with him yet.

"Six months I been hangin' out with you. You never took me nowhere . . ."

"Where the fuck can we go at five o'clock in the morning?" Corelli protested.

"You never bought me nothin'. Not even a cheap bottle of perfume."

"I bought you that coffee machine, didn't I?"

"Yeah, that's cause you like to have expresso in the morning." She was crying now, and Corelli noticed that hood Ramirez down at the end of the bar. He and Murphy had busted Ramirez the week before for beating up a guy with a baseball bat. And now he was out on bail, drinking, having a great time, and laughing at Corelli. Every mutt in the joint was laughing at him. Corelli grabbed Ida by the arm, and dragged her over to the service end of the bar. "Listen, you wanna say something to me, say it in private," he snarled. "You're making me look like an asshole in here."

"So, you did the same to me. I told everybody you were my old man, and then you don't show up for three weeks . . ."

"Your old man. I never told you that. You knew what my story was. I never promised you nothin'."

"I'm just as good as that tight-assed little chick you're gonna marry. I'm better than her. You told me so yourself."

"Yeah," Corelli whispered vehemently, "you're better in some departments, you know what I mean, but that don't exactly make you the marryin' type."

"Why not?"

Corelli laughed right in her face. "Why not? You kiddin', or what? I'm gonna marry a chick who works half-naked in a gin mill? Who walks around with a gun in her purse? Whose house is so dirty she has to get her mother over to clean it up once a week? I'm gonna marry a chick who's got nothin' in her refrigerator but an ounce of cocaine, which she got by being very nice to somebody, and it wasn't me . . ."

"You bastard," she screeched. She reached for the black-jack under the bar, but Corelli grabbed her wrist and twisted it back until she winced, and flailed out at him with her free hand. He shoved her back a few feet. "Next time I see you is when you come crawlin' back to say you're sorry." And he stormed out of the joint, first turning back to make sure nobody was looking at him.

As soon as he got in the car he was sorry, but it was too late to go back. He drove over to Arthur Avenue, the Italian section of the Bronx, where he still lived with his family. It was a lopsided three-story building he'd been living in all his life. The foundation hadn't been dug right, and it leaned slightly to the right, like the Tower of Pisa. His whole family, five brothers and three sisters, had been born and raised there. The only way you escaped was by getting married, which was what he was finally doing at the age of twenty-nine.

It was four-thirty in the morning when he got in. The lights were on in the basement where his father had gotten up to press grapes for his home-made wine. His younger brother, Bruno, the only other son left in the house, was in the kitchen checking his numbers slips. Bruno was a business administration major at Baruch College where he booked bets, and took numbers on the side. He sat at the table making his calculations on the pocket computer Corelli had bought him for Christmas.

"Jeeze, what a business, Andy," Bruno said. "Know what the number was today? Four-forty-four. Except for a little single action, I didn't get hit once. Eight hundred and thirty-two bucks clear profit, with no overhead. I wonder if bookies have a patron saint."

"You'd better hope they do when they bust your little operation and throw ninety days in Rikers at you . . ."

"C'mon, I'm workin' my way through college," Bruno said. "You want me to drive a hack and get my throat cut by some junkie?"

"That's not the point," Corelli said, but stopped as he heard his father's shuffling footsteps on the cellar stairs. The old man had purple stains on his hands and face. "Hey, look who's here," he said, and went to the stove. "You want coffee?"

The old man had been in America for almost fifty years, and still hadn't lost his accent. He was a mason, and he was built like a larger version of one of those forty-five pound cinder blocks he threw around with such ease. Every weekday morning since Corelli could remember, his father had gotten up at four, and gone to the basement to press the grapes and mend the barrels in which he made his wine. Then at six-thirty he would go off to lay bricks for nine hours, and back for dinner. Two hours later he was asleep in front of the TV. He was a happy man, and the old lady, who Corelli could hear stirring around upstairs before coming down to have coffee with her husband, seemed happy, too, although she'd never done anything more than cook and clean and pray for her nine children.

"You two guys been fightin' again?" the old man asked, standing at the stove with his back to them. You had to hand it to the old bastard. He always knew what was going on.

"It's like a slap in the face to me, him countin' his slips like that," Corelli said.

"Ah, he's just uptight 'cause he didn't get laid last night," Bruno said.

Corelli raised his hand. "You little bastard."

"Leave him alone," the old man said. He took Corelli's arm. "Come, come down to the cellar, and help me pour the juice into the barrels. I'm tellin' you, Andy, I got a beautiful load of grapes from that truck driver in New Jersey."

"They were hot, Pop. He stole 'em from the market . . ."

"Ah c'mon, whaddya you care? Big juicy purple grapes, is gonna make beautiful wine. And we'll have grappa, too."

Corelli followed the old man down the stairs. "My brother's a bookie, my father's a bootlegger," he said. "I could make a fortune shakin' down my own family and I'd never have to leave the house."

11

The driver's door of the radio car was open. Loomis's body, unbalanced by its own dead weight, was slipping slowly off the seat onto the sidewalk. People trickled out of the sparsely populated buildings across Southern Boulevard. As they hurried toward the subway, bracing against the cold, some of them saw the open door. The keener-eyed saw the bloody arm of the policeman, the upper body sliding slowly onto the sidewalk. They quickened their pace.

A super came out of a building on Jennings Street to walk his dog. As he looked up the street, Loomis's body tumbled out of the car onto the sidewalk. The super turned the other way.

There were some who had heard the shots. They drew their blinds, and waited for the sirens. It was eight o'clock. The two cops had been dead for almost an hour.

It had been a cold night at the Four-One. The fifty-two-year-old boiler had sighed, shuddered, and died somewhere around two. Desperate phone calls to Borough Maintenance had been to no avail. It was hard enough to get a plumber to Fort Apache at any time, but at two o'clock in the morning, you could forget it. At seven-thirty, by the time the eight-to-four crew began drifting in, the place was as cold as a dungeon.

"It's colder in here than it is on the street," Applebaum said.

"You wanna stand outside and test that theory?" Pantuzzi said.

Heffernan had hardly cleared the front door before he realized the heat was off. "Oh Jesus Christ on a fucking cross. I knew this was gonna happen. I was havin' breakfast, and the radio said it was the coldest day of the year. 'That's it,' I says to the wife. 'That means the goddamm boiler'll break down.' Well, I think I'm just gonna be sick today. My bursitis can't take the cold. You guys didn't see me." He turned and walked back toward the door.

"We never see you, even when you're here," Pantuzzi said.

"You oughta stick around today, Loot," Applebaum said. "The new boss is taking over. We already got eleven no-shows on the eight-to-four. He might take it as a sign of disrespect if his desk officer wasn't here to greet him."

Heffernan walked back to the desk, and lowered his tone. "Dugan's leaving today?"

"He's in his office right now packin' up his paper clips," Pantuzzi said.

Two rookies pushed through the door with a dark, demented man in a windbreaker and a pair of torn fatigues. "Oh, great, they got Porfirio," Applebaum said.

Clendennon, the twelve-to-eight desk sergeant, came out of the bathroom blowing on his hands. "I just pissed a frozen rope."

Now, two more cops came through the door, shoving a cuffed and a bleeding black youth in front of them.

"Don't worry, Loot," Applebaum said. "In a little while we'll have a full house. Everybody else who don't have heat will come here to get warm. Body heat'll raise the temperature."

"Charge?" Pantuzzi said, intent on his writing.

"Indecent exposure," one of the rookies said. The little man in the windbreaker giggled.

"On a night like this?" Applebaum said.

"Just showin' his face is indecent exposure," Heffernan said sourly.

Clendennon looked at the two rookies with disgust. "You guys collar a dicky-waver at seven o'clock in the morning in the South Bronx?"

"He was standing right in front of the subway station," one rookie said, defensively.

"Maybe he was hitchin' a ride," Pantuzzi said.

"Everybody in this house has come across Porfirio," Clendennon said, "but you're the first two assholes who ever busted him. Get him outta here."

"Too late for that," Pantuzzi said, raising his pen. "I already got him written up. Take him up to the squad to get printed."

"Oh, they're gonna love this up in the squad," Applebaum said. "Makin' them work on a flasher."

"If yiz don't come down in fifteen minutes, we'll send a rescue party for you," Heffernan said.

The two rookies looked at each other with trepidation. "Where's the squad, Sarge?" one of them asked Pantuzzi.

Without looking up Pantuzzi pointed up the stairs. "Next patient," he said.

Captain Dugan came out of his office. "Heffernan," he bellowed, "are you doin' anything about getting the boiler fixed?"

As cold as it was, Heffernan began to sweat. He became nervous, obsequious. "Well, I just got in, Captain, but I'll get right on the horn to Borough. . ."

"Yeah, sure," Dugan said. "I need a fuckin' pair of ice skates to get around my office." He walked to the desk, and the two cops yanked their prisoner out of his way. "Somebody get me a coupla cardboard boxes to pack my stuff."

"Sure, Boss," Applebaum said.

"We're gonna miss you, boss," Pantuzzi said, still not looking up.

"Yeah, like you miss the clap," Dugan said. "Maybe on my last day up here you guys could stop bullshittin' me." He walked toward his office, but then turned back with a vindictive smile. He was a stout, bald man with a fringe of white hair over a mottled head. His beady blue eyes roamed nervously. There were purple spots on his cheeks and nose that seemed to glow when he got angry. "Anyway, you had it easy with me. The new guy's gonna cut you to pieces."

He turned and looked at the prisoner, then snarled at the two cops. "You bring a collar into this house chewin' gum?" He shoved the kid. "Swallow that gum, mutt."

The kid spit the gum out on the floor by Dugan's shoe. Dugan punched him in the groin just below the belt, knocking the wind out of him. The kid fell forward. Dugan grabbed him by the back of the neck and threw him on the floor. "I want him to pick that gum up in his teeth, and swallow it," Dugan said, and walked angrily to his office, slamming the door.

"Hey, the boss has got talent after all," Clendennon said.

"That's the most work I've seen him do since he's been up here," Pantuzzi said.

Applebaum came out from behind the desk, and picked the gum off the floor. "You just assaulted a police officer, big shot. If you'd have hit him it would have been attempted murder." He stuffed the gum in the kid's pocket.

"Charge," Pantuzzi barked.

"I wanna call Legal Aid," the kid said.

"You have the right to make one phone call," Pantuzzi said. "Charge?"

Clendennon looked down at the sign-out roster. "Hey, we're missin' two guys. Those rookies, Loomis and Shoup."

"Maybe they didn't sign out," Applebaum said.

"No, I didn't see them come in. . ."

"They're probably gettin' piped over at Hunts Point," Heffernan said. "That's the first thing these fuckin' kids do when come on the job: get piped by some broad, and then they walk out on their wives."

"Can't get 'em on the radio, either," Clendennon said.

"Charge," Pantuzzi said patiently, waiting as the two cops lifted their prisoner off the floor.

Heffernan was looking over the chart. "You're gonna have to work the four-to-twelve, Applebaum."

"Whaddya talkin' about, Loot?"

"We got three sergeants out sick on that tour, so you gotta cover it."

Shaking his head, Applebaum took a bagel out of his satchel. Working an extra shift ruined his diet. He wouldn't eat anything that wasn't strictly kosher, which meant every restaurant and *bodega* in the area was off limits. In the morning his wife packed him four bagels to last him through the day. The first had a mountainous smear of cream cheese, and a sprinkling of crushed scallions on it. That was breakfast. The second was spread with *lekvar,* or prune jelly, and was consumed at about eleven, with a cup of Postum that Applebaum brought in a thermos. This combination immediately sent Applebaum to the bathroom, *Daily News* in hand, on a "submarine chase," as Pantuzzi called it. For lunch his bagel was stuffed with a mound of salmon salad that oozed out over the sides whenever he took a bite. And around three, to fortify himself for the long drive to Spring Valley, a suburb about forty miles away, he bit into a pumpernickel raisin bagel with margarine spread on so thickly it occasionally dropped through the hole and onto the desk perilously close to Pantuzzi's contest forms. Applebaum would have to space his bagels out over sixteen hours instead of eight. He was going to be a very irritable man.

"Anybody know who the new boss is?" Heffernan asked.

"Captain Dennis Connolly," Pantuzzi said. "Sound familiar?"

"He's from I.A.D., ain't he?"

"Story is he asked Borough for a command when he made captain. Everybody over there loved him so much they gave him the Four-One."

"I knew him," Heffernan said. "He was down in Headquarters for a while working on corruption investigations. I think he's busted more cops than anyone else in Internal Affairs."

"*Oy vay,* a Headquarters hero," Applebaum said.

"I give him three months up here," Pantuzzi said. "If I don't get a charge and a name on this prisoner I'm going to let him go on time served."

Clendennon came back to the desk. "We've located those missing rookies," he said.

12

The horn woke Murphy up. In his sleep he had leaned on it, and it had pierced his dreams with a million errant images. A traffic jam, Murphy desperate to get through. Murphy pressing the horn to get a double-parked car out of his way, blowing the horn to get his boy to the hospital, and finally the hollow echo of horn as he embraced that nurse, the skinny one with the sad eyes from the E.R. over at Jefferson Hospital. She just sat there as rigid as a psycho while he slid his hands down the front of her dress, and under it, feeling the slivers of warm skin under the runs in her panty hose. She reached over slowly, and tried to open the door. Her movements became more frantic, but her face remained impassive.

"Dad. . . Dad. . ."

Timothy was rattling the door, banging on the window. Little seven-year-old Timothy all bundled up, come to get his daddy out of the car.

"Jesus Christ." Murphy opened the door. "Hi, Timmy."

The kid was real serious. It looked like he was going to write Murphy a summons. "Mom sent me out to get you," he said.

"Well, I'll go quietly." He got out, and reached for Timmy's hand; the kid held it stubbornly at his side. Shit, Murphy thought, I wouldn't hold my old man's hand, either, if I found him asleep and leaning on the horn in front of the house. I'd think he was a bum, too, especially if that was all my mother talked about.

The guy from Sunshine Petroleum was filling up their tank. Mrs. Keighley, the next door neighbor was peering disapprovingly through her kitchen window. Oh shit, Murphy thought, I put on a show.

Mary was standing just inside the door where nobody

could see her. "If you're moving into the car, at least let me give you some curtains so you'll have privacy." Tears of rage glinted in her light blue eyes. Her hand shook so much she jammed it in the pocket of her housecoat. This is torture, Murphy thought.

"I'm sorry," he said.

"Oh, please." She walked into the kitchen. "Your two daughters had to pass their drunken father passed out in the car on their way to school. And so did most of their friends."

"I wasn't drunk." It was remarks like this that infuriated him, even when he was dead wrong and knew the only right thing to do was to get down on his knees and apologize. She knew he hadn't had a drink since Houlihan had been killed. Only beer, and that didn't count. He could drink a river of it, and hardly even get a buzz. Which she knew. But he had to be a drunk. It wasn't that he was tired, or just plain miserable. He had to be a drunk because that made her a fucking martyr.

"Well, you were certainly giving a good imitation." She poured herself some coffee, her hands still shaking. Jesus, it was awful. He knew she was as unhappy as he was. He wanted to say, "Look, Mary, this is no way to live. Why don't we just separate? What's the big deal, anyway? People do it every day. You want money? You want the kids? The house? You got 'em. Let's put this marriage to sleep." But she was too proud and too Catholic for that. She'd endure this agony forever, as long as it remained private. As long as they didn't fight in public, kept everything from the children, and put up a good front for the family, she'd stick it out. She'd take a tense, tedious marriage in which the spouses gradually drifted apart. If it had been good enough for her parents, it was good enough for her.

Charley Morgan doesn't know how lucky he is that his wife threw him out, Murphy thought. It should only happen to me.

Timothy sat down at the kitchen table, and frowned reproachfully at him. He was siding with his mother now. One day when he is big enough he might even punch me in the mouth defending her honor, Murphy thought. But then he'll get fucked over by some broad, and he'll understand everything.

"How come you're not in school?" Murphy asked him.

"He had a temperature this morning," Mary said. "With all the flu going around, I thought I'd keep him home."

To sit around and keep Mommy company while she drank coffee and watched the game shows. Sick, sick, sick.

She had those metal curlers in her hair. Her eyes were all puffy from crying. How she loved to cry.

"You look like the Bride of Frankenstein," he said.

"I am." She turned on the TV. The news was on. Murphy went into the living room, and lit a cigarette. There were enough rooms in this house for the two of them never even to cross paths. And as they got older, and the kids left, there'd be even more places to hide. He closed his eyes, and thought of that nurse. Funny, he'd never seen her before last night.

"Two police officers from the notorious Fort Apache precinct of the South Bronx were found shot to death in their radio car early this morning," the news announcer said.

Murphy got up and ran into the kitchen.

13

". . . The apparently motiveless killings were discovered at eight-thirty this morning when the officers Frederick Loomis and Donald Shoup failed to report back from their midnight-to-eight tour. . ."

Captain Dennis Connolly heard the news on his way to the precinct. His mouth went dry with excitement. His first day on the job, and already he was in the middle of something. There would be a flood of media coverage on this. The Four-One, his command, would be in the news for days. He'd have daily consultations with the Headquarters brass. The Chief of Detectives, Chief of Patrol, Chief Inspector, even the Commissioner—people he'd never gotten to know during his three years down at Headquarters. It was a stroke of luck, alright. Connolly's wife Kathleen had made a novena yesterday, and prayed for his success in the new job. It looked as though her prayers had been answered.

Connolly pulled over to a luncheonette, and called Lieutenant Reynolds, his connection at the Bronx borough office. "Get me everything you can on these killings this morning, Pete," he said. "I want to walk in strong, in case there's any press around."

He ordered coffee, and waited. It was cold-blooded, getting palpitations over those murders. He wasn't happy those two men were dead, but anybody would have to admit it was a great way to start in the job. He was absolutely golden. Nobody expected him to clear the killings, but if they were solved from his precinct he'd be a hero. Getting this command had been a good career move after all, although he'd had his doubts when he'd gone to complain to Deputy Inspector Fritsch, his boss at Internal Affairs.

"I've been down here at Headquarters for three years, and there's been no talk of a promotion," he told Fritsch.

Fritsch leaned back in his swivel chair. "And there won't be, either." He said it matter-of-factly, but there was a hint of satisfaction in his voice. Connolly knew Fritsch didn't like him. You never like the guy who does all your work for you. "You're up against a stone wall, Dennis. And the stone wall is me."

"How's that?" Connolly asked.

"I got twenty-six years in, and I'm gonna die in this chair. There'll be no promotions for me, I've made too many enemies. They don't need two Deputy Inspectors in the division, so it looks like that closed the door on you."

"I could be promoted and assigned somewhere else," Connolly said.

"Not out of Internal Affairs, you couldn't. In case you haven't noticed, we're not too popular around here. We're the shoo-flies, the cops who catch cops. Street cops hate us because all street cops are trying to get away with something. And every man on this job from the Chief Inspector on down has been a street cop. Get the picture? If you want to move, you'll have to do it from another department."

So Connolly had applied for a command. Months went by. He was passed over time and time again. Captains with much less seniority got the good precincts. And then the Four-One came through. The previous commander, Dugan, had done a good job of running it into the ground. His stats were the worst in the city, and now he was being forced into early retirement. They were throwing Connolly into the mess Dugan had made, saying: go ahead, big shot. You want a command. You got it.

Well, he liked that fine. He'd start from the bottom, the way he always had, and he wouldn't owe any favors; he'd be clean.

Connolly had researched the precinct, and had come up with the answer to its lackluster performance. Discipline and motivation: that's what was lacking, and that's exactly what Connolly intended to supply. Add to that the kind of scientific management Connolly had learned about in his night courses at John Jay College of Criminal Justice, and you had a definite formula for success.

Reynolds called back with the information. It was a typical South Bronx murder—no weapon, no motive, no witnesses. Only this time the victims were two cops. The Four-One squad had roped the area off, and had begun canvassing the area, but it had been superseded by a special citywide unit that had been created to investigate all assaults on police officers. The unit was headed by Detective Lieutenant Edward Dacey, who had been Connolly's classmate at the Police Academy seventeen years before. Dacey was as ambitious as Connolly, but he hid his careerism behind a gregarious, wisecracking manner. He made himself likable without making it look as though he were fawning. Still, he was a conniving bastard. He'd hog all the press and all the credit, if he got a chance.

Connolly got directions from Reynolds, and drove to the scene. He had made several tours of the precinct since learning of his assignment, but he still wasn't used to the rubble, the absolute desolation of the place. He couldn't see how the government had let the neighborhood degenerate without doing something about it.

At the scene, patrolmen were dutifully putting up barricades with signs that read CRIME AREA. Radio cars were cruising around looking for witnesses. Cops ambled in and out of the gutted buildings, while others kicked lazily at the dirt in the vacant lots, looking for clues. Detectives had a wino braced up against the wall of a building, and were gingerly going through his pockets. It didn't look like a very thorough or inspired investigation.

Connolly opened the spiral notebook he'd bought especially for the job, and made his first notation. "Juice up investigation at precinct level. Provide incentives, positive and negative."

Cars were triple-parked in front of the precinct. Connolly and a *Daily News* photographer's car headed for the same spot. The *News* guy wouldn't yield, not even when Connolly flashed the shield. He got out of the car to argue, and then backed off when he saw the bars on Connolly's uniform, which was packed neatly in a cellophane bag on the seat next to him.

Connolly had gone over the floor plan of the Four-One a hundred times. Sometimes, unable to sleep, he'd driven up here all the way from his house in Brooklyn, and parked down the block, just staring at it. But he had never been inside, and he was shocked when he entered.

The place was in complete chaos. People with no apparent business in the precinct were wandering around the desk area. In the muster room, a group of kids chased each other under the indifferent eye of a huge, blubbery sergeant, who was sitting on a bench talking to several young women who were rocking infants in strollers. The sergeant was wearing a skullcap fastened by a bobby pin to the back of his head, the kind religious Jews wore. In another corner some old men were playing dominoes, while a few feet down from them on the bench, a grinning, obviously retarded young man tapped softly on a conga drum. In the desk area, cuffed prisoners stood next to social workers and community people. The desk was besieged with people waving forms, some shouting in Spanish, others complaining about broken pipes, no heat, a stolen car. Babies shrieked in their mother's arms; a radio was blaring in the Community Relations Office.

The place was a mess. Paint was peeling off the walls. Huge chunks of plaster looked ready to rain down on this noisy mob. And, most bizarre of all, there were these Indian mementoes all over the place. Tomahawks, arrowheads, war bonnets, posters of Indians, and rubber spears were nailed to the walls. They were everywhere, except around the wooden monument with two gold plaques attached, commemorating the two police officers who had been killed on the premises.

Behind the desk a red-faced lieutenant yelled and waved his arms, trying to keep order. A dark, hawk-nosed sergeant sat imperturbably writing, never looking up once to check the chaos that was forming around him.

Connolly made another entry in his spiral notebook. "Security in desk area is nonexistent. Remove all nonessential personnel from precinct. Paint job. Sergeant with skullcap is not in proper uniform. Remove Indian bric-a-brac from walls."

Behind the desk on the steps leading to the second-floor squad room, a handcuffed prisoner was struggling with a burly policeman. "You flaked me, motherfucker," the prisoner shouted. Over by the phone another cop had a thin man in a cashmere topcoat by the hair. "You remember now?" the cop asked, as if for the thousandth time. The man shrugged, smiled, and shook his head. Without showing the slightest trace of anger or annoyance, the cop slammed the man's head against the phone. "You remember now?"

A thin ribbon of blood trickled down the man's temple. "I think my recollection is being refreshed," he said.

Connolly made another note: "All interrogation of prisoners should take place in detention pen or squad areas, away from the muster room."

Connolly picked his way through the mob to the front of the desk. The red-faced lieutenant had disappeared; only the hawk-nosed sergeant remained.

"Captain Dugan's office?" Connolly said.

Without looking up, the sergeant pointed to the right. Connolly looked over the desk; the sergeant was working on a scrambled word game from the *Daily News*.

"Don't you monitor the people who ask to see the Captain, Sergeant?" Connolly asked. "What if I was a lunatic with a gun?"

The sergeant still didn't look up. "Then you wouldn't be a police officer, Captain Connolly. Or would you?"

Connolly looked for the man's nameplate. It was supposed to be on the left breast pocket in plain sight, but wasn't there.

"What's your name, Sergeant?"

The sergeant put down his pencil, and gave Connolly a slow, mocking salute. "Kicking ass and takin' names, huh, Captain? Well, my name's Sergeant Anthony Pantuzzi. I got

69

twenty-two years on the job, and I'm ready to put in my retirement papers if I get a hard time from my new commander. I'll take the half pension before I'll take any crap from anybody. Captain Dugan's office is over on the right as close to the street as he can get." He fished his nameplate out of the drawer, and clipped it to his pocket . . . upside down.

"Thank you, Sergeant," Connolly said. As he turned away he made another quick note: "Pantuzzi." And he underlined it several times.

Captain Dugan's door was open, and Connolly could see the portly, bald man fussing in his office. He knocked on the door frame. "Captain Dugan?"

Dugan stopped and looked him over. "Connolly?"

"Yeah."

"C'mon in, and close the door."

Dugan gave Connolly a quick, perfunctory handshake, grabbing his fingers and squeezing them. "Welcome aboard."

"Thanks."

"You got a great day to take over. The place should be jammed with reporters any second now. Looks like Fort Apache's gonna make Page One your first day in command." Dugan bustled by Connolly with a cardboard box overflowing with papers. Connolly stepped aside, and looked him over as he fulminated.

"Members of the press, members of the community, members of the P.B.A. Everybody's a joiner up here. Everybody but the commanding officer. They always leave him out on a limb." He dropped the cardboard box on his desk. "You like press conferences, Connolly?"

Connolly shrugged. "They're part of the job."

Dugan gave Connolly a bitter look. "Yeah, well, after two years in this job you won't wanna talk to nobody."

"I'm not a big talker at any time," Connolly said pointedly.

But Dugan didn't get the message. Or didn't want to. "Word's around that you volunteered for this job."

"They offered me the command, and I took it. If that's considered volunteering. . ."

"A lotta guys figure they'll make a reputation for themselves up here," Dugan said. "Well, forget it. You'd do better walkin' a beat in Beirut that you will in the Four-One."

This conversation was starting to degenerate. Dugan

was a defeated man. He was being forced into early retirement, a few months before a new contract went into effect with higher salaries and better benefits for captains. They had brought up an old bribery complaint against him. They didn't want to fatten his pension any more than they had to. Somebody up there really didn't like him. There was reason to feel a little compassion for the guy. It was tough to put in thirty years on a job, and then get screwed. But, looking around this precinct, it was clear that Dugan deserved it.

"You're supposed to have some background material for me," Connolly said.

"Got it right here." Dugan pointed to an ink-smudged manila folder on his desk. "Block by block run-downs, ongoing investigations, trouble spots, community contacts, personnel evaluation. . ."

"I'm interested in the ratio of rookies to veterans," Connolly said.

"I didn't get that specific. . ."

"I'll probably want to reshuffle the radio car assignments," Connolly said. "Two rookies in a car is always a mistake."

"Oh, sure. . ." Dugan nodded feverishly. "I'm gonna end up bein' blamed for those killings this morning. . ." He pointed angrily, and took a breath. Connolly could feel a tirade coming on.

"And I'll be blamed if they're not cleared," he said quickly. "Now, how about corruption?"

"Yeah, I understand that's a specialty of yours," Dugan said. "Well, lemme tell you this: every man on the job in my precinct is clean."

I could really lose my temper with this guy, Connolly thought. Just like I could have really gone to town on that sergeant out there. They want me to blow. They're all going to provoke me.

"Your precinct has the highest absentee record in the city, Captain Dugan. It has the most disability claims, the highest percentage of men on sick call, the least convictions per arrest, the lowest ratio of arrests to reported crimes. But you want me to believe that there are no men on the take. . ."

"So maybe they toss a numbers runner for a coupla dollars," Dugan said. "Turn a pimp upside down for a little loose change. There's nobody gettin' rich up here."

71

"Nobody's doing much of anything, as far as I can see," Connolly said. "These men aren't motivated."

Dugan reddened. "Motivated? Where do you think you are, Connolly?" He pointed angrily out the window. "This is Siberia. Most of the men up here have been transferred. We got the connivers, the slobs, the shirkers. Guys who beat up the wrong guinea, or gave a diplomat a parking ticket, screwed a big-mouth hooker, shook down the peddler . . . You oughta know what we got. You sent a lotta them up here."

"Not me," Connolly said. "I don't believe in punitive transfers. A bad cop is a bad cop no matter where he is . . ."

"Then how did I get all these losers?"

"There are plenty of good cops in this house," Connolly said. "You're the one who's fallen down on the job."

"Me?"

"I checked your stats."

Dugan slammed his fist on the desk. "My stats. All of a sudden they belong to me. All of a sudden Dugan's the bad guy. Oh, that's the fuckin' limit . . ."

Connolly shrugged. As Dugan's anger rose he became calmer. "It's all there in black and white."

"That's the fuckin' limit," Dugan said, carried away by his righteous indignation. "You can let the politicians and the landlords and the fuckin' animals off the hook now. Just blame Dugan, that's the easy way. You got a neighborhood with seventy thousand people packed like sardines into broken-down old buildings, smelling each other's farts, crawlin' around like cockroaches . . ."

"If that's the way you characterize the people you were supposed to be dealing with . . ." Connolly began.

"See if you feel any different about them in a coupla months," Dugan interrupted. "You got the lowest per capita income, and the highest rate of unemployment in the city. That's Dugan's fault, right? Why ain't he out there gettin' all those people jobs? Largest proportion non-English-speaking population. Obviously, Dugan's the culprit here. Why ain't he out there teachin' these people English? One percent Spanish-speakin' cops on the force. Hey, Dugan, get your ass out in the barrio and recruit. You got families that have been on welfare for three generations. Youth gangs, winos, junkies, pimps, hookers, maniacs, cop killers. And that's my fault. As soon as I leave they'll disappear. You'll have fuckin' ballerinas

72

and sidewalk cafes; brownstones, little faggots walkin' their dogs. There'll be a fuckin' string quartet in the muster room. The most serious crime'll be some guy goin' around smellin' bicycle seats . . ."

"You finished?" Connolly asked coldly and quietly.

Dugan stood there, breathing heavily. He had shouted himself out of breath. One of his double chins was still trembling. "Yeah, I'm finished." He went to the coat rack and put on his uniform jacket. "I'm goin' to Florida. I'm goin' fishin'. Gettin' outta your way. So bring in your computers and your slide rules and your management techniques. This neighborhood'll bury you. There's enough dirt up here to bury every smart-assed cop in the city."

14

Jose couldn't sleep. He had to show Hernando the pieces.

"Where you goin'?" his old lady called after him.

"Shit, bitch, where does it look like I'm goin'? I'm goin' out." He jammed the two guns in his pockets, and hit the street.

Jose walked eleven blocks through the cold to get to Hernando's pad. All the while he was thinking about how he could get bullets for the guns. There was Cookie, the guy he'd copped the starter pistol from; he'd have .38 shells. But you had to be cool. You really didn't want anybody to know. If Cookie got busted he could buy himself a lotta time sellin' that information to the cops. Hernando would know. He could probably score the shells from his man downtown. Those foreign dudes had all kinds of fancy fire power.

Jose walked by a garbage truck that was parked by the vacant lot on Intervale. Three guys were sitting inside having coffee. I could wheel on those motherfuckers, Jose thought. Blam, blam, blam, three dead garbage men. Inside the truck a powerfully built red-headed guy cleaned a small spot on the heat-fogged windshield. "That's Ruiz, ain't it, Tony? The guy Hernando works with."

A swarthy, thick-necked man in a mohair overcoat played with his diamond pinky ring. "They were bunkmates in Attica." He hummed "The Anniversary Waltz." "Jose's his jailbird wife."

"Well, shit, somebody's gotta keep the cell clean," the red-headed guy said.

"I wouldn't want to be in the same cell with you, Nolan, you slob. You'd be leavin' your candy wrappers and dirty fuckin' socks all over the place. . . ."

"Hey, Tony, why don't you take a suck outta my ass . . ."

The slight, dark man between them stirred nervously. This banter went on all day long. Nolan and Fabrizio thought it was cute. They thought they had a regular comedy act going for them. They didn't take anything seriously. And why should they? They were only back-up. He was the under-cover. He had to get in with these people, win their confidence, make the buys. He had to put his life on the line; they didn't.

Julio Mendoza had been an undercover narcotics cop for seven years. He was perfect for the job because he wasn't much different from the drug dealers he was supposed to bust. He was a street kid out of Spanish Harlem, spoke Spanish like a stone *jibaro,* and knew as much about dope as any dealer in the world. He could sit and talk about dope for hours. He loved it; dope was as much a part of his life as it was of the guys who dealt it. Unlike most of the under-covers, including the Spanish cats, he wasn't adverse to par-taking himself, although that was strictly against department regulations. How could you pass yourself off as a big-time dealer if you didn't taste a little of the shit? The smarter dealers were wary of people who didn't use drugs themselves. Julio would snort a little coke or smack, if offered. He'd let himself get high and crazy with the dealers he was working on, and that always got him over. He made more collars than any other undercover on the job. He was a star, but they treated him like a messenger, sending him around the five boroughs on the tough investigations, into situations where only a Rican could penetrate. As far as they were concerned he was just another spic, nothing special. Anyway, it got him twenty-four thousand a year plus overtime and expenses. And once he got on a case, once *he* was inside on some dealer they really wanted, then he ran the show, and all the white assholes had to back up.

Nolan passed Mendoza a photograph of Hernando. "This is the guy. Hernando Rivera. He's been working as a counselor in the detox center over at Jefferson Hospital."

It was a mug shot. The guy had a bushy Afro and a scraggly beard. His expression was casual, his eyes dead. A killer.

"He's got most of the addicts working for him," Nolan said. "He passes the shit to them when they come in for consultation, and they move it for him. The kid Jose's been putting it out too. Jose does a lot of street dealing. Hernando never goes out, and won't talk to strangers. They even put a policewoman from Puerto Rico on him, but he didn't go for it."

"Maybe he'll go for Chino," Fabrizio said. "Maybe he likes boys."

Mendoza was called Chino because of the slight Oriental cast to his features. He was a pretty boy, and that helped. He had his shiny black hair styled every month, and always dressed well. Sometimes these dealers had old ladies who really ran the operation. Mendoza could bat his long, curly eyelashes, rap with them in barrio Spanish, dance a little salsa. If the chicks dug you, everything was cool. A lot of the dealers had done heavy time, so you had to figure they'd been into a little butt-fucking in the joint. They would never talk about it, never make a move. And being pretty didn't hurt when you were dealing with a faggot.

"So what's my move?" he asked Nolan.

"Just get next to him," Nolan said. "The guy's hard to penetrate. You'll have all the bread you want. Make as many buys as you have to. We're in a holding pattern with Hernando."

"What are you waiting for?" Julio asked.

"We wanna bust him on his birthday," Fabrizio said.

"They didn't tell you anything about this?" Nolan asked.

Mendoza shook his head. Why tell the spic? All he had to do was go in on the dude; he didn't have to know anything.

"We're on loan to the Drug Enforcement Administration

on this squeal," Nolan said. "They got a Rumanian diplomat they think is bringing the shit in from Afghanistan. They think he's hooked in to the KGB, and they want to make a major espionage case on him. This fuckin' thing goes all the way up to the CIA. Satellite photographs of opium processing plants, wiretaps on the Embassy."

"And how does this go all the way down to a street dealer in the South Bronx?" Mendoza asked.

"Hernando's hooked in with the Garcias, the Cubans in Washington Heights, and they've been copping from this Rumanian dude. The D.E.A.'s got a man inside on the Garcias, and they're covering most of the dealers who work with them like this Rivera."

"It's a big case," Fabrizio said. "We'll get a lot of ink when the busts go down."

"I won't get nothing," Mendoza said. "I'm undercover."

"You'll get a medal," Fabrizio said. "And the thanks of a grateful populace."

"Just don't go to sleep on this Rivera," Nolan said. "Everybody says he's a killer."

"The stools won't go near him," Fabrizio said. "They're scared shitless . . ."

"The D.E.A. has their man in the hospital now," Nolan said, "so you can see how important this guy is to them."

That tripped a few alarm wires in Mendoza's head. "You mean there's another undercover on this case?"

"Yeah, a D.E.A. guy. I told you."

That was bad. Mendoza didn't like working with other guys, especially Feds. It only meant splitting the credit, and doubling the risk.

"What's this dude's name?"

Nolan shook his head. "Couldn't get it."

"What if I bump heads with the dude, and I don't know who he is?"

Fabrizio cocked his fingers into the shape of a gun. "Boom, that's what."

"I don't like working with the Feds," Mendoza said.

"What are you worryin' about, you're with us," Nolan said. "We're your back-up. You'll never even see the other people . . ."

"Until the President invites us all down to the White

76

House to give his personal thanks for our fine patriotic work," Fabrizio said.

Nolan hit Mendoza playfully in the arm. "Hey, Chino, don't worry. We'll be on you like white on rice."

"Except when we go off to get piped," Fabrizio said.

It was true, they were good. Mendoza had worked with these two clowns before, and felt safe with them. They had good instincts, and they weren't afraid to go through a door if they had to. Nolan was a sergeant in the unit. He had been investigated several times on bribery allegations, but nothing ever stuck. Fabrizio, his partner, wore four-hundred-dollar suits and drove a new Caddy, as if daring his bosses to prove something.

"Like I said, you'll have a lot of buy money on this case, Chino," Nolan said.

Fabrizio looked out of the window and whistled softly.

"I don't think you'll have to account for all the buys you make," Nolan said. "I don't think anybody will ask you to. There's always a lot of loose money floating around on these Federal squeals . . ."

"I don't think they even give a shit," Fabrizio said.

More alarm bells went off. The approach was too crude, too obvious. Were they trying to set him up? And how about this mysterious guy, was he on the job just to watch Mendoza? Was this whole thing just an elaborate trap? You never knew.

Mendoza drummed impatiently on the dashboard. "Let's get outta here before I get clocked with you two assholes," he said. This was a strange case. He'd have to be real careful on this one. Real careful.

15

A black banner hung over the door of the precinct. All the men had fixed thin strips of black crepe to their shields. The chaotic activity had not diminished—with all the reporters and mobile units around, it had intensified—but the precinct seemed subdued. Cops walked in and out of the building with tense, thoughtful expressions. There was none of the wisecracking or jocularity that usually prevailed at the change of hours.

The locker room was unusually silent. Some of the men had arrived for the four-to-twelve without having heard about the killings. Others had spent the whole day thinking about them. A collection box had gone up for the families of the rookies. Arrangements were being made for mass cards, car pools to the funerals. There was little talk about who had done it, or why. When Murphy came in, the locker room was dead silent.

"The President's comin' up here again?" he asked, going to his locker. "All these fuckin' reporters around I couldn't find a place to park my car."

Morgan was slumped against the radiator, head in hands. Murphy shook him. "Hey, Morgan, don't take it so hard."

Morgan waved irritably. "Take what hard? I'm hung over."

Eddie Finley shoved his off-duty revolver in his belt.

"What's this," Murphy said, "the gunfight at the O.K. Corral, or what?"

"With these fuckin' cop killers around, I'm gonna be ready," Finley mumbled.

"Don't make no difference how many guns you got, you still only have two hands," Murphy said.

Things were loosening up a little. Corelli, who had been sitting in front of his locker trying to figure a way to get out

78

of the job, looked gratefully at Murphy. "A comedian," he said. "They coulda used you on the *Titanic*."

George Patterson, a big, black cop made impeturbable by twenty years in the Four-One, came around the corner. "Murphy don't need no hardware," he said. "All he has to do is breathe on the suckers, and they give up without a fight."

"Yeah, well if you can't get your man with six bullets, you better go out there with a tank."

"That's a great idea," Corelli said. "We should suggest that to the Commissioner. Radio tanks for high-crime areas."

The men had been issued bullet-proof vests several months before. They were cumbersome, but effective for the limited area they covered. They were strapped over the chest, leaving the back unprotected. Murphy had thrown his in his locker the first day, saying, "If I put one of these on, some sucker'll come along and shoot me right in the balls. That's the kinda luck I have." And now, as all the men put on their vests, he still disdained his.

"I mean we don't know who the fuck's out there," Finley said.

"The Dispatcher says there was no record of any radio call to or from their car," Gerry Donahue said. "Looks like an unprovoked attack."

"Unprovoked?" Murphy looked to heaven for guidance, and said with a quavery Irish brogue, "God, will ya help me with poor, dumb Oirish clucks?" He shoved his uniform shirt in Donahue's face. "See this, Gerry? This is a provocation, you know what I mean? In some quarters it's considered a mortal insult. You don't have to do anything but put it on."

"I know that . . ."

"It looks like the sixties to me," Finley said. "I been sayin' it for months now, right, Charley?"

Morgan looked up, bleary-eyed. "Well, you better not say it tonight. I want a little silence in the car out of respect for our departed colleagues, and for my fuckin' swollen head."

"All these fuckin' groups formin'. They were demonstratin' by the construction project on Kelly Street last week, remember, Charley? People carryin' fuckin' signs . . . down with this; this guy's a racist; don't kill our children. You know, them same kinds of signs we saw around Columbia in 1968." Finley looked worried. "I'm tellin' ya, the shit's gonna start all over again. Fuckin' bomb-throwers. Only this time they're gettin' fuckin' guns from the Cubans. They got fucking bazookas, it's gonna be an all-out war."

"Jesus," Patterson said, "let's all go home and hide in the closet."

Corelli took out his comb. "Man, you must be fun to live with."

"He's a barrel of laughs," Morgan said, getting up slowly and stretching.

"You'll see," Finley said doggedly. "You'll see. These guys were killed for no reason, and that's terrorism."

"Anybody know these guys?" Corelli asked.

"Loomis is the black kid we broke in, wasn't he?" Donahue asked Patterson.

"Yeah. He just got outta the Academy. The other guy, too."

"Shoup was his name. Another rookie. The squad guys said they still had their coffee in their hands when they bought it. Head and face, almost point-blank range."

Corelli looked inquiringly at Murphy. "It does sound like a hit, doesn't it?"

"Maybe they pulled a guy over, and were writing him a ticket," Donahue said.

"They coulda called some wino over to the car, and he pulled down on them," Patterson said.

"It was probably one of their wives," Morgan said.

"Now there's a solution that makes some sense," said Murphy. "I mean, if they were checking a plate they would have called it in, wouldn't they, so there'd be a record. And who ever heard of a wino banging out two cops with a gun."

Corelli snapped his finger. "I got it. They caught the Cubans unloading a truckload of bazookas and antipersonnel . . ."

"Fuck you, Corelli," Finley snarled.

Corelli turned slowly and raised his eyebrows in mock surprise. "I beg your pardon."

"What the fuck do you know," Finley said, squaring off, his freckled fists clenched at his sides. Corelli just looked at Finley with amusement. He had been hanging his jacket up. Murphy knew that if Finley made one more remark or moved an inch closer, he'd get that metal hanger right across his face. He moved between the two men, and snatched the hanger out of Corelli's hand.

"Yeah, what do you know about it? Look at this guy." He snatched Corelli's white jacket out of his locker. "Beau Brummel over here. They could be droppin' A-bombs on the Bronx, and you'd still be figurin' out what kinda jockey shorts went with your tie."

Murphy gave Corelli a quick, cautioning look. Corelli caught on, and went with the joke. He pushed Murphy away, and snatched his jacket back.

"Jealous, jealous, typical bust-out cop reaction. A man has a little style, a man tries to rise above his circumstances, and you gotta knock him."

"I got something you can rise above," Patterson said.

"That's just what we need up here, a cop with style," Murphy said. "Guy wears the same blue coat every day of his life . . ."

"Whoa, slow down, Jack, I ain't no twenty-year man like you. Take a look in that locker, take a look at those threads. I'm dressin' for a success." He thumped his chest. "I got plans for this carcass, and they don't include draggin' it all over the Bronx."

"Here he is, ladies and gentlemen, the million-dollar mouth," Murphy said. "If it wouldn't be askin' too much, Mr. Mouth, just what kind of plans do you have?"

Corelli shoved Murphy playfully. "Would you mind not breathing Budweiser on my cashmere over here? Thank you. Now, as to my future, when I cruise up here in my Bentley . . ."

Murphy leapt up suddenly and grabbed Corelli in a bear hug. "Quick, grab him. Take the needle out of his arm. He's startin' to dream again."

Corelli struggled free. "Hey, muh fuh, I ain't no junkie . . ."

"Abbott and Costello over here," Morgan said sourly.

"Jou's on first, baby," Corelli said.

"Fuckin' asshole," Finley muttered as they walked out.

"Hey, Finley," Corelli called. He ran toward the door, but Murphy jumped in front of him.

"He said it quiet so you wouldn't hear it. So don't hear it, okay?"

"That hump gets on my nerves," Corelli said.

"He's an empty suit, don't even think about him. He thinks the Russians are gonna strafe Southern Boulevard."

"If that's what twenty years on this job gets you," Corelli said.

"The guy's brain-damaged from alcohol," Murphy said. "Him and that nuclear scientist he rides with. I'll tell you one thing, I'd hate to be selling loose joints in their sector tonight. 'Cause they're gonna be kickin' ass out there, thinkin' everybody's a cop killer."

Corelli studied himself in the mirror. "I'm a good-lookin' guy. How'd I get hung up in this job?"

"There weren't any openings in the Sanitation Department," Murphy said.

16

Hunger smoldered in Applebaum's huge bulk. Like a fire in the hold of a ship, it burned steady and unquenchable. There was nothing to do but endure it. Applebaum thought of those two golden, toothsome bagels in his satchel. Gritting his teeth, he forced his attention to the men shuffling into the muster room for inspection before turning out.

There was a lot of work tonight. A lot of complaints to be investigated, in addition to all the stuff that would come in during the night. Look how these guys *shlepped* in. You'd think it was the end of the tour, instead of the beginning. "Let's get a move on, awright," he said.

"What's your hurry, Sarge?"

"He doesn't like to stand on his feet too long," Murphy said. "The doctor told him it draws the blood away from his brain."

"Look, Murphy, this is the second time I'm doin' this today, awright? So hold the jokes for a second." The men gradually assembled in a formation in front of him. Some of them were still wearing their civilian pants, others hadn't buttoned their shirts or put their ties on. If the new boss saw this . . . There was a light burning behind the frosted glass of his office. He could come out any time. "Form into ranks, will ya," Applebaum said, and waited until they did, ignoring their hurt looks.

"Okay." He looked down at his clipboard. "We lost two guys on the eight-to-four today. Shot almost point-blank with a .32. The same gun used on both of them, and it's clean, so there's no help there. Their guns and shields were taken. We found their wallets in a lot down the street with the money missing, but robbery cannot be considered the motive. Nobody's gonna murder two cops to get what's in their wallets."

"Amen," Corelli said.

"So you got no motive, no witnesses, no technical evidence of any kind—prints, clothing fragments, nothin' at all. A big zilch. Now there's a special unit under the command of Lieutenant Edward Dacey—" Applebaum said the name slowly and carefully. "—they'll be movin' into the squad for a coupla days. So what we gotta do is canvass our sectors, hit the stoolies, the bars, the *bodegas*. Any information should be turned over to the squad, or to one of Dacey's guys, whoever isn't watchin' TV at the time. You know it's just not a good idea to let the folks think it's open season on cops. We're movin' targets, those of us that move. There's a coupla guys in this house, me included, who've been on the job long enough to remember when a cop killing was almost unheard of. Now, we got about ten a year in New York, but that still don't make it an everyday thing. Not to me, anyway. Let's really work on this one a little, awright."

Applebaum took a weary breath. "I feel like I'm doin' a command performance. We had a rape of an eleven-year-old girl on the day tour. Suspect described as black male, six foot six, two hundred and forty pounds, still at large. The Sex Crimes squad has sent over a name and a mug shot on a possible suspect fitting that description. It's over at the desk. We got complaints on a crap game in back of St. Anselmo's Church. The sisters called it in. They say the perps keep promising to move, but it's been a week, and the crowd's gettin' bigger. The sisters also think these guys might be sellin' a little grass in there, which wouldn't exactly send me to the hospital in shock. Check it out, and bust it. The sisters will finger the organizers for you. Track star workin' Jerome Avenue. Skinny black kid with felony shoes and a World War I aviator's cap, snatchin' purses over in front of the bank, and takin' off into the park across the street. Cock fights in the basement at 843 Wilkins. There was a call from the A.S.P.C.A. that they were fightin' dogs up there, too." Applebaum took another breath. He'd gotten a stitch from talking so much. "Now, as some of you probably know, Captain Dugan is retiring. He's been replaced by Captain Dennis Connolly."

There was a stirring in the ranks at the mention of that name. Applebaum looked warily back at the Captain's office. The door opened, and Connolly came out as if he'd been crouching by the keyhole waiting for his introduction. He walked across to the muster room, and stood in the doorway as Applebaum concluded.

"We were gonna throw a racket for Captain Dugan, but with the different tours and all, it just didn't work. So we set up a collection to buy him a going-away present. Any of you guys wanna contribute, there's a kitty on the desk. Okay, there's a lotta TV guys outside and all. Remember the standing rule: we don't talk to reporters unless we get clearance from the commanding officer."

"But I was all set for my screen test, Sarge," Murphy said, grinning defiantly at Connolly.

"So do it for silent movies," Applebaum said. He slapped the clipboard against his hip. "Let's go to work."

The men shuffled by Connolly, who leaned against the wall, arms folded, looking intently into the ranks. He saw quite a few familiar faces. There was Donofrio, who had been the silent partner in an after-hours joint in the Village. Charles Morgan, the big, rawboned guy; there had been an investigation on him several years before—a bribery complaint from a narcotics informant. And Murphy, the smartaleck, the guy whose partner was shot in a stickup while he was passed out in the bathroom. There were others as well; the names had jumped out at him as he went over the roster. There had been investigations on many of the men in this precinct, ranging from drunkenness and neglect of duty to racketeering, and even murder. He had the cagey ones up here, the guys who had beaten the raps, and had been transferred to the Four-One as the best alternative to suspension and criminal prosecution. They were the ones who would do the least amount of work, but would cover themselves so well you could never catch them shirking. A few of the men saluted him as they passed. The rookies averted their eyes out of timidity. The wise-asses like Murphy ignored him.

Sergeant Applebaum wandered past Connolly in a daze. He was doing complex calculations on how long he would have to wait to have the fourth bagel if he had the third one at five-thirty. There was a kosher deli way up on the Grand Concourse, probably the last one in the Bronx. Maybe he could shoot up there . . .

"I see you're working a double shift, Sergeant," Captain Connolly said.

Applebaum sighed. "Yeah, you know with all this flu around, you get a lotta guys out sick." Over on Bathgate Avenue there was a guy who sold kosher chickens . . .

"But you don't get the flu?" Connolly asked.

"Nah, I think it's my diet. I bring everything from home, and I don't eat in public places. That's where most germs are transmitted." So big deal, what was he going to do with a raw chicken? Maybe he could take it to that restaurant on Prospect Avenue, and have them boil it for him. No, schmuck, their pots weren't kosher, he'd have to buy them a new one.

"Don't disappear yet, Sergeant," Connolly said.

Applebaum followed the Captain to the desk, brooding about the dearth of delicatessens and appetizing stores in the Bronx. He could remember when there was one on every street. You could go in and buy whitefish, pickles out of the barrel, anything you wanted. Bakeries with fresh *chalah* on Friday nights, and honey cake. You'd walk down Southern Boulevard drooling. And it was all *shomer shabos* one hundred percent *glatt kosher.*

"I'd like to get this place painted, Lieutenant," Connolly said briskly.

Heffernan was startled by the request. "Well, that's kind of a problem, Captain," he began apologetically. "You see, painters and maintenance people in general don't like comin' up here. I'm havin' a helluva time gettin' the boiler fixed."

"Well, maybe we can get some people in the community

85

in to do it. Talk to the community relations officer about it, and give me a progress report tomorrow."

Heffernan looked at Applebaum in puzzlement. What the hell was a progress report?

Connolly pointed to the Indian adornments on the wall. "What's all this?"

Heffernan tried to smile, tried to make light of what he knew was a flagrant violation of department regulations. "Well, you know this nickname we kinda picked up . . ."

"Fort Apache. I know," Connolly said.

"Well, the men got a little carried away with it, you know. I guess it makes 'em feel special . . ."

"It's become a tradition here, Captain," Applebaum said. "The men put all this stuff up. Every time somebody goes away on vacation, he brings back a little souvenir . . ."

"Have it taken down," Connolly said. "It makes the place look like a fraternity house."

Applebaum winced and shook his head. "I'm sorry, Captain, but maybe that's not the best idea in the world."

"I'm sure it's not," Connolly said. "I'm sure I'll come up with plenty of better ones. We all will. But for the time being I'd like to discourage the nickname, and all the implications that surround it. I'd like this precinct to become just plain Four-One, clean, orderly, well-staffed . . ." He stopped in mid-sentence as he realized the two men were staring at him in astonishment. "We can start by getting all civilians and nonessential personnel out of the precinct."

"Can't do that," Applebaum said with a firmness that annoyed Connolly.

"Excuse me, Sergeant?"

"People come in here for protection, especially the old folks," Applebaum said. "They come in here to get warm when there's no heat in their buildings. On welfare check day they come in here to get a lift home so they don't get mugged with all their money. The place is like a fort to them, a place of refuge in hostile territory."

"That's fine," Connolly said. "I want it to continue to be all those things. But our first priority is handling the business of the precinct: getting prisoners booked and into detention, for one thing; answering legitimate complaints, for another; getting a smoother transition in the change of tours, en-

86

forcing dress discipline among the men, cutting down on absenteeism."

"But this isn't an ordinary police station, Captain," Applebaum said.

Connolly looked deliberately up at Applebaum's natty plaid yarmulka. "It will be, Sergeant. It will be."

17

The press was barred from the precinct during the change of tours to prevent any eavesdropping on the sergeant's instructions. In high crime precincts, where suspects were addressed in less than respectful language and even manhandled on occasion, it was best to keep proceedings out of the public eye. So the reporters were left to freeze at the entrance to the building. They pounced with pencils and mikes poised on the departing tour. Avid for details, background, color—anything that would add a little variety to the same story that had been running all day—they chased the cops to their cars, badgering them with the same familiar questions.

"Did you know the two victims?"

"Any progress in the case?"

"How does it feel to go out on patrol after two of your buddies have been murdered?"

It was a good story. The public gasped over a cop killing. If two cops with guns were vulnerable, then nobody was safe on the streets. And they wanted to keep it alive; if not with hard facts, then with color—mourning cops, a tense community, background on the precinct, human interest . . .

The spotlights went on, and the cameras started rolling as soon as the cops hit the street. Murphy dashed out of the building, head down, pushing through the clamor. Corelli hesitated, waiting to be approached, until Murphy beckoned him angrily.

"What's the matter with you all of a sudden?" Corelli asked, trotting over to the car.

"It's a fuckin' circus," Murphy said, getting and slamming the door.

"Hey man, a cop killing's a media event," Corelli said.

Murphy gunned the motor. "They love it. They'll put a black border around the pictures, probably get those yearbook shots from the Academy. Inspector's funeral with all these humps standin' around in their dress uniforms . . ."

"I still don't see what you're so pissed off about."

"Everybody loves it, asshole, don't you see that? Everybody loves it when a cop gets killed." Murphy leaned on the horn to clear a path through the congested streets. "Even the cops. They strap on the extra guns, start feelin' sorry for themselves, the 'we risk our lives on the street and nobody gives a fuck about us' routine."

"Well, shit, it breaks up the day. You don't expect anybody to really suffer over two guys they didn't know. I mean you're sorry they bought it and all, but it really doesn't change much . . ."

"You know how much extra work we're gonna have because of these fuckin' reporters," Murphy said. "The kids'll be settin' fires all over the neighborhood just so they can see their street on the tube. I don't care if it's twenty below, everybody'll be out on the street doin' their thing for the cameras. And these fuckin' reporters: who'll be buyin' loose joints, who'll get raped in a hallway while looking for local color, whose car'll get ripped off, who'll wander into the wrong saloon to make a phone call and get whacked on the head . . ."

"It's typical of the Department that they don't let us talk to the press," Corelli brooded. "Jealous bastards, they know guys like us would be stars, overnight sensations . . ."

"There you go pullin' your prick again," Murphy said.

"No, really, can you see me on the tube? I mean I know how to handle it, real subdued and serious." Corelli cleared his throat and composed his features. " 'We believe that the perpetrator accosted the dowager in the vestibule of the edifice.' They'd probably offer me a job on the spot. Andrew Corelli, police analyst for WCBS . . ."

"They might let you be a urine analyst," Murphy said, "but there's not much demand for that on TV."

"Yeah, yeah," Corelli said. "You're puttin' me down, but you really don't have any faith in yourself. With those blue eyes, and that touch of gray at the temples . . ."

"Why don't you touch this . . ."

"You're a star, Murphy, you Irish clodhopper. Take you out of this uniform, and put you in a nice pin-stripe suit. Shit, with your good looks you'd be ballin' every anchor lady in town."

"Not with my luck," Murphy said. "If it was raining anchor ladies, I'd get hit with Walter Cronkite."

"Luck, luck. With you it's always luck. I'm tellin' you, guys like us got a potential that we just don't realize. We get intimidated or something, I don't know what it is. Some of them reporters are ugly bastards, did you see 'em? Guys my age, you know, making fifty, sixty grand a year already, and they just started. Me, I'm sittin' with my twenty-three K over here, waitin' for the fuckin' P.B.A. to get me thirty-cents every two years. I can look right down the pike and tell you what I'll be makin' in twenty years. I could do that job just as well as any of those guys."

"So do it," Murphy said.

"Shit, all you gotta do is walk around with a mike, and ask questions. You don't even have to know how to spell."

"So do it. Go down to the TV station and apply for a job. That's all it takes."

"I'll get to it in my own good time," Corelli said.

"You're full of shit. You spend your time reading all this crap. What's this one?" Murphy grabbed the book out of Corelli's hand, and read the title. *"Dress for Success.* Another self-help hustle. You don't learn nothin' from these books."

Corelli grabbed the book back. "That's where you're wrong. Adornment is crucial . . ."

"Why don't you adorn this?"

"It's true. People don't realize that they are giving out a certain kind of message with their clothing."

Murphy fingered Corelli's uniform. "You call this dressing for success?"

"I'll be outta these pajamas in a couple years, don't worry about it."

Murphy pointed out of the window. "How about that fashion plate? What's his message?"

A tall black guy wearing a white fur coat and a wide-brimmed black hat had a black chick pinned against the wall of a building, and was slapping her in the face.

"Based on my years of experience, I would say that man is a pimp," Corelli said.

"And the chick?" Murphy asked, pulling the radio car to the curb.

The girl was dressed in a skimpy gold lamé outfit. She seemed more concerned with her blonde wig than her face, and kept adjusting it with every slap she took.

"Looks like an anchor lady to me," Corelli said.

"Well, let's see if I get lucky," Murphy said. He hit the siren once, but the pimp didn't seem to hear it.

"This guy loves his work," Corelli said.

They got out of the car. It was one of those streets where inhabited buildings stood next to gutted ones; new cars were parked next to abandoned wrecks, making it impossible to tell if the neighborhood was coming up or going down. A white El Dorado with a black vinyl top, wire wheels, porthole windows, chrome fixtures, and Alabama plates was parked in front of the building. They walked right up to the pimp who was still swinging and cursing, oblivious to their presence. Murphy tapped him lightly on the shoulder, and he wheeled around. He was light-skinned, with a thin mustache and a glittery cocaine stare.

"You'd better take it off the street, my man."

The pimp smiled and backed up. Corelli moved around behind him. If he couldn't see both of them he wouldn't try anything.

"It's cool, fellas," the pimp said. "I mean, this bitch has been giving me a lotta static, you dig. She's a treacherous bitch."

"Aren't they all?" Murphy said.

The pimp backed up a little further, trying to get Corelli in view. At this point he didn't know if he was going to be arrested, shook down, or beaten up. It was nice to keep him in suspense.

"I mean, you know the game. I put the chick to work, and she don't come back with nothin'. And she used to be the

90

main hole on the set. Cars stoppin' short. Dudes always tryin' to cop her from me. Now she ain't worth shit . . ."

"You wanna take up a collection for this guy, Andy?" Murphy said.

The girl had slid to the ground, her wig flopping over her eyes. Corelli helped her up. "You alright, beauty?"

She smiled and primped. "I'm fine, baby. Fine." She smiled through her swollen lips. "You wanna come party with me, baby?"

"You see," the pimp said. "The bitch is nuts. She's been smokin' that angel dust. That shit'll make you crazy. I can't deal with her."

"Just take it off the streets, blood. We like a nice clean sector," Murphy said.

"Yeah, yeah . . ." The pimp backed up. "I don't know you, do I?"

"We don't sit in the same pew," Murphy said.

"Yeah." The pimp reached into his coat pocket, and Corelli grabbed him in a bear hug.

"Hey, man, be cool," the pimp said, trying to struggle free.

"No fast moves, motherfucker," Murphy said. "You oughta know that by now."

"Shit, I was just lookin' for my wallet," the pimp protested.

Murphy reached into the coat pocket and came out with an alligator wallet. "You see," the pimp said with a sly look. "I just wanted to show you guys my driver's license. I mean, shit, I'm a businessman. I don't shoot cops. I got a better way of dealin' with 'em."

"You do, huh?" Corelli slid his fingers admiringly along the pimp's coat sleeves. "Nice coat. How'd you like me to cut it open, and let all the rats out?"

The pimp pulled his arm away angrily. "This coat's worth more than you make in a year, motherfucker."

"He knows your name," Murphy said to Corelli.

"I told you I was famous."

Murphy walked over to the El Dorado. "This pimpillac belong to you?"

"That's a El Dorado custom," the pimp said, highly insulted. "It's legally parked."

"Uh huh." Murphy broke one of the headlights with the butt of his gun. "Defective lights."

The pimp screamed in agony. "Get your hands off that car."

Murphy ripped the windshield wipers off. "No windshield wipers, that's another violation." He grabbed the pimp by his ample fur collar, and threw him over the hood of the car. "You don't buy me, dirtbag, you understand?"

"Okay, okay," the pimp said.

Murphy knocked his hat off. "You try to grease me again, and I'll turn your head like a doorknob," he shouted. He slammed the pimp against the hood.

"Hey Murf, slow down," Corelli said, alarmed at his sudden and unusual outburst of temper.

Murphy threw the pimp to the ground. "Get your shit off the street, and keep it off, sucker."

"Hey, Murf, you wanna start a war or what?" Corelli said. "My boy got the message."

Muttering, the pimp rose slowly and retrieved his hat. He looked around to see who else had witnessed his humiliation. Only the girl in gold, who sat against the wall of the building, licking her finger and wiping it on her skinned knee. Only her.

Corelli walked Murphy back to the car. "Lighten up on the dude," he said. "You know he'll give her ten for every one you gave him. You act like you've never seen a pimp before."

"Fuckin' scumbug," Murphy said. "He thinks he can own me for a coupla bucks."

"Like he owns a lotta other cops," said Corelli. "He's just doin' business, that's all."

Murphy watched the pimp enter the building. The girl got up and limped after him. "And we are, too, right?"

"We're livin' in a world we never made, my man."

"That don't make it any easier to live in," Murphy said.

18

His name was Style. "I don't *have* style," he told his girls. "I *am* Style." His trademark was black and white— black-and-white car, clothes, and girls. He had three girls in the Bronx, working Hunts Point during the day and the Bronx Zoo at night, but his star was down on Lexington Avenue in the Fifties. Little Randy: he'd met her wandering around the Port Authority three o'clock in the morning the summer before. She was a runaway from St. Louis. Sixteen years old, real blonde hair, cartoon tits that looked like they'd been siliconed to death—the johns loved them jugs, especially on a little girl like this—but were real like everything else on her. Some chicks are natural for the life, and she was one of them. You could put her in cut-off jeans, clogs, and a leotard, and walk her down East 86th. You could give her the hot-pants and the spiked-heels act on Eighth Avenue in the Forties. It didn't matter. Anywhere this chick worked, it was like a revolving door, johns going in and out so fast you needed a computer to keep track of them. Style had bought her a few nice dresses—black and white went great with her blonde hair—and brought her into a hotel bar on 51st and Lex. It cost him five hundred a week to keep her there, but shit, she made that in an hour. Just give her a Quaalude, wind her up, and let her go. The chick was hollow. She had no insides, had no conscience. Style had moved her in with him downtown. He didn't want these old bitches poisoning her mind.

Style wanted to cut the whole Bronx scene loose. Three washed-out crybaby bitches giving twenty-dollar blow jobs. Shit, they were more trouble than they were worth. And now this fuckin' useless junkie, stealing his car, and making him look bad right out on the street. He pushed her through the

93

darkened hallway, and threw her into the elevator. "Get in there, bitch."

She stumbled and hit her head against the railing. Her wig was askew, her nose bleeding.

"You're a mess, you know that, Charlotte?" he said. She sat there sucking on her thumb staring blankly at him. "You old now, too old."

Tammy was waiting by the elevator, nervous and full of excuses. "We couldn't stop her, Style. You were sleepin', and we were afraid she was gonna hurt you."

Style shoved her out of his way. Big, flabby, gray chick, it made him sick to look at her. She wasn't good for nothin' more than humpin' truck drivers, and neither was that stringy black bitch, Lonnie, who was standing by the door.

Style yanked Charlotte out of the elevator by the arm. "You gonna catch a whuppin' now," he whispered in her ear.

Charlotte lowered her eyes and smiled. She did a slow walk down the hallway, hips swaying, heels clicking. She could still shake that moneymaker.

"Careful, Style," Lonnie warned. "She gets crazy . . ."

Charlotte turned to smile at him. "I'm just snakin'."

"Push her in here," Lonnie snarled. Tammy rushed by Style and pushed Charlotte into the apartment. Lonnie stepped away from the door, and hit Charlotte in the face with an umbrella handle. "Bitch," she shrieked, hitting Charlotte repeatedly. Charlotte stood there taking the blows as though they were drops of rain, until her knees started to buckle.

Style hung his coat in the closet, taking his time, recovering his composure. Let the girls take care of it. The less he had to do the better. They had her pinned face down. "Don't let her fuck up the rug," he said. He was still proud of the pad, even if the bitches weren't happening. It was black and white right down the line. White walls, black sofas and chairs, a zebra carpet, wall to wall; and he'd taken the extra pieces, and thrown them over the bar. A nice mirror in a thick silver frame behind the bar. He would spend more time up here if these bitches didn't bring him down so bad. As it was, one night a week was about as much as he could take.

Style was wearing the white zoot jacket that came right down to his hips, black shirt with wide cuffs that tapered at the waist, the white pants with a heavy peg, and white suede shoes. Like those jitterbug World War II dudes, everything was loose. Style walked slowly into the room, rolling his sleeves up.

"Look, Style," Lonnie said, pointing to a bloody welt on her cheek. "I tried to stop her last night, and she cut me with one of your razor blades. Look." The blood shone against her black skin.

Style stood over Charlotte, and shook his head. "You fucked up, Charlotte."

Charlotte tried to get up, but Tammy kneeled on her back, pressing her face into the rug. "She's been smokin' that angel dust," Tammy said. "This dyke dealer over on Freeman Street gives it to her. She don't know what she's doin' anymore."

"Is she workin'?" Style asked Lonnie.

"We ain't seen her for days, Style," Lonnie said.

"Bumpin' pussy and gettin' high, huh, Charlotte? You goin' right down the sewer, ain't you?" He went to the closet and took out a coat hanger. "Get me some cotton outta the bathroom," he told Lonnie.

"You nuts, Charlotte," he said. "We're gonna take you down to Bellevue, down to the nuthouse. Only dope you'll get there is aspirin."

Lonnie brought back the surgical cotton, and he wound it around the hanger. It was the best way to beat a bitch. You could hit them in the face, and it wouldn't leave any marks. You hit them in the back, in the knees, and the backs of their legs. They'd be walkin' funny for a few days, but you could put them to work that night.

"Takin' my car," he said. "Don't you know there's an energy crisis?"

Charlotte moaned and dribbled bloody spittle on the rug. "Put somethin' in her mouth, she's fuckin' the rug up," Style said.

Lonnie ran into the kitchen. She came back with a towel, and shoved it in Charlotte's mouth.

"Take her in the bathroom," Style said.

"Why don't you just put her out, Style?" Tammy begged. "Look at her, she's crazy."

"Yeah, I'll put her out," Style said. "That dumb bitch used to be the best hustler in New York City, you know that, you fat, sloppy piece of trash?"

Tammy started to blubber. "Why you gettin' on my case. . . ?"

"Make you two look like shit when she was in her prime. Nobody passed this motherfucker by. She could pull anybody. Pull 'em out of goddamn Cadillac goin' seventy-five on the FDR. Put her in the fuckin' graveyard, and the motherfuckin' corpses would be jumpin' out the ground."

"Well, she ain't what she was," Lonnie said defiantly. "She cut me, and I want you to put her out."

"You tellin' me what to do, bitch?" Style slapped Lonnie with the hanger.

She retreated, holding her cheek. "No, Style . . ."

"Now take the bitch in the bathroom like I told you."

They twisted Charlotte's arms behind her back, and dragged her away. Style knew she would have to go. He hated to lose a girl, but she wasn't earning, and she was making trouble with the girls who were. He'd end losing all three of them if he wasn't careful. He'd come up to the pad one day, and they'd be gone.

What a shame, Style thought. Even drugged-out and crazy like she was, the chick had it. She had what it takes, and it broke her heart to give it away. It wasn't in the body. Every chick had a body. And it wasn't in the act, because flirting came naturally to all these bitches. It was something from the inside, something magical. It was like she sang a song, and they all came running. Or dropped a smell on them, like a bitch in heat. Little Randy had it. And Charlotte, she was just as big a star in her day. Hell, she still was, she hadn't lost a thing. You could clean her up right now, and put her out on the street, and there wouldn't be a man out there who'd pass her up. It was really too bad she had to go.

19

As Murphy had predicted, it was a busy day. The cop killing was like a rock dropped into a stagnant pool; it made waves long after its initial impact. All the legit criminals closed up shop for the day as press and detectives roamed the neighborhood. Street action in numbers and drugs had stopped. The hookers were still pounding their shivery beat at Hunts Point at four-thirty, but even they disappeared when the radio cars cruised by and started asking questions about the killings.

Detectives, canvassing the area, wandered into bars and *bodegas* where numbers were taken, knocked on apartment doors where drugs, stolen property and guns were being sold. As far as the pros were concerned, it was a quiet day. The amateurs had the whole neighborhood to themselves.

Murphy and Corelli answered three family disputes. A woman had slashed her husband when he wouldn't let her talk to a camera crew. A man had come home to watch the midday news, and had found his wife in bed with the super. A numbers guy, staying home for the first time in years, threw his wife out of the house so he could play cards with his friends.

The crazies were incited by the unaccustomed hubbub in the streets. Winos chased the cops and reporters around with their solutions. A Vietnam vet, well-known in the neighborhood, who lived quietly with his parents gobbling prescription tranquilizers from the Bronx V.A., went berserk and attacked a television reporter. It took six cops to subdue him. They surrounded him, and when they were sure nobody could see, Patterson knocked him cold with his blackjack. It turned out the guy had gone crazy at the sight of the TV cameras; he hadn't seen them since his hitch in Vietnam.

Filthy Freddie, a raggedy bum who lived in the garbage

cans on Westchester Avenue, managed to find himself a kitchen knife and began menacing passersby. Nobody realized how big he was, because nobody had ever seen him standing up. Nobody realized how mean he was, either, because he was usually anesthetized with Night Train, the fifty-cents-a-pint wine he subsisted on. An old man tried to chase him with a broom. Freddie cut a chunk out of the old man's arm with the kitchen knife. By the time Murphy and Corelli arrived, an angry crowd was pressing in on Freddie. They backed the people away, called an ambulance for the old man, and stood there trying to figure out what to do.

"Are we gonna have to shoot this poor bastard?" Corelli said.

"I hope not," Murphy said.

The sight of blood on the knife had plunged Freddie into a frenzy of violent movement and incoherent shouts. He slashed the air with the kitchen knife, screaming back at those who cursed him.

"Lemme see if I can out-nut him," Murphy said. "Cover me."

Corelli took his hat off, and hid his gun behind it. Murphy slipped his blackjack up his sleeve, and went into his act. He flipped his hat around, dropped to one knee, and started barking like a seal. "Freddie," he called, screwing his face up and sticking out his tongue as if he were having a fit. "Freddie, help me," he croaked in hoarse, imbecilic tones.

Freddie paused in his slashing, and looked at Murphy.

"Freddie." Murphy rolled over on his back, and held his arms out. "Freddie, help me." Murphy turned over suddenly and began gagging, his face getting purple. Corelli moved forward a few steps, lifting his hat so the gun pointed right at Freddie's chest.

Murphy coughed and spat a huge lunger at Freddie's feet. Freddie's jaw sagged; he stared down at it in puzzlement, the knife slowly lowering.

Murphy came up in a semicrouch. He spread his arms out, and beseeched the heavens. "Oh God, help me."

Freddie's eyes went skyward as well, and Murphy came out of his crouch. He grabbed Freddie's wrist with his left hand, and cracked him on the temple with the blackjack. The side of Freddie's head opened like a piece of rotten fruit. He went over with his legs sticking up in the air.

"That was some clam you laid on him," Corelli said.

Murphy wiped his chin.

"I knew smoking Camels was good for something."

They had hardly gotten Freddie tucked into the ambulance when a signal 10–54 came over. "Report of a man on the water tower at 9004 Tiffany," the Dispatcher said. "Threatening to jump. Emergency Service Units are responding."

It was seven o'clock and dark by the time they got to Tiffany Street. They could barely make out a figure standing on the water tower seven stories up.

"Looks like a chick," Corelli said, squinting up at the roof.

Murphy turned to the crowd of freezing bystanders. "Anybody know this woman?"

"Wait, wait . . ." A flowery, spectral creature came out of the darkness of the lobby. It had dark, shoulder-length hair, and was wearing a lacey white nightgown under whose gossamer folds were two muscular arms covered with tattoos.

"It's a fuckin' drag queen," Corelli said.

Some of the kids in the crowd began quacking, and screaming, *"Pato, pato,"* the Spanish word for duck, which was Puerto Rican slang for fairy.

The creature showed her bright vermilion nails and hissed like a cat, then covered her face and sobbed dramatically. "Why don't they let us live? Just let us live."

"You know this guy?" Murphy asked.

"Carl Peterson," she said in a suffering monotone. "He's my roommate." She cupped her hands and screamed up to the roof. "And I hope he jumps and breaks his stupid neck."

Murphy took her by the arm, but she pulled away with sudden strength. "You gotta remember these guys are men," he whispered to Corelli.

"You can't arrest me," the drag queen said, backing away.

"Who's arresting you?"

"They'll kill me in prison," she shrieked. "They'll rip me into pieces . . ."

"Look . . ." Murphy took a few conciliatory steps forward. "What's your name, anyway?"

"Raquel," the drag queen said shyly.

Corelli snorted and turned away.

"Listen, Raquel, we just want you to come up on the roof and help us convince Carl to come down," Murphy said.

"I don't care what happens to him," she said. "He's a thief, and he's a prostitute for all the bums on the block." She looked up at the roof and screeched, "He's disgusting. I don't want him in my house anymore."

"C'mon Raquel," Murphy said, "don't you wanna kiss and make up? If Carl jumps he'll make an awful mess."

"They'll be cleaning his guts off the sidewalk for days," Corelli added.

"You'll be sorry then," Murphy said persuasively. "But it will be too late. It's always too late when we lose a loved one. And then we're sorry."

Tears shone in the drag queen's eyes, and she looked at Murphy as if she'd found a kindred spirit. "It's true. We had a bad fight."

Murphy took her by the arm as if he were escorting her to the prom and walked her into the building. "What about?"

"He took my Donna Summer wig."

"What's this?" Corelli asked, fingering the Dynel strands of the wig she was wearing.

"Oh, that's Chair."

"Chair?"

"Yes, Chair." She tossed her hair back. "You know, the singer."

Murphy poked Corelli. "Chair, you asshole. My partner doesn't know too much about music."

Raquel looked fondly at Corelli and licked her lips. "You have pretty eyes."

"Thanks," Corelli said. "You're kinda cute yourself."

"Oh, don't make fun of me," Raquel said, brushing the Dynel off her forehead. "Don't be cruel."

"I'm not," Corelli said. "I mean it."

By now they were in the elevator. "This could be the start of a very beautiful friendship," Murphy said.

"Don't," Raquel said crossly. "You'll make me cry if you make fun of me."

Corelli closed his eyes and took a rapturous sniff. "Chanel?" he asked.

"No." Raquel smiled shyly. "Windsong, by Matchabelli."

They climbed the rickety metal stairs to the roof, and pushed open the door. The night was cold and clear. For a moment there was a lull in the wind, and they could see clear across the ravaged rooftops of the Bronx to the Hudson River and the Lower Manhattan skyline, even across the river where the lights of suburban New Jersey twinkled and where people, secure in their warm living rooms, watched news reports about murder in the South Bronx.

There was a figure dressed in a shiny green jumpsuit standing on the edge of the roof, hands clasped prayerfully.

"Carl," Raquel shrieked.

The figure in green turned, and shook its fist. A sudden blast of icy wind obscured its words. Murphy and Corelli threw their hats back through the door.

"Stay away," the figure warned, stooping like a diver ready to take off.

"Carl," Raquel shrieked, "I hope you break your stupid neck."

"Too late to apologize," the figure said.

Crouching against the wind, Murphy and Corelli approached the jumper, each coming at him from a different side.

"Carl, you don't want to die, do you?"

The figure turned and Murphy saw its face in the moonlight. It was a man, slashes of rouge across his dark cheeks, crimson lipstick, mascara laid thickly around his eyes. His features were twisted as if he were in pain.

"Yes, I want to die," he said as if he had just thought of it. "I hate my stinking life."

"I hate you, Carl," Raquel shrieked.

"Carl, let's see how the wig looks," Murphy said.

"It's a vermin pit, and everybody in it is full of shit," Carl said. He reached into his shirt, and took out a black afro wig.

"You pig," Raquel shouted, advancing angrily on Carl. "You put my wig next to your stinking body . . ."

"I am an artist," Carl shouted. "I can do whatever I want."

"Puta!" Raquel screeched.

"Raquel, you're not helping," Murphy said. He looked down on the street. Emergency Service hadn't arrived yet, but the crowd had gotten larger and people were clapping and urging Carl to jump. Corelli was moving around the water tower, trying to get behind. Murphy couldn't stand

101

heights. He knew in a minute or two he'd be crawling along that ledge trying to coax Carl down. Shit. Why not just light a cigarette, and let the faggot jump if he wanted to? He was right, life was a pit, everybody was full of shit.

"Look, you see," Carl said, pointing downward, "they love me . . ."

"They'll love you even more with the wig on, Carl," Murphy said. Get his mind off it. Get him to follow orders. If he obeyed once, Murphy could talk him off the ledge. "C'mon Carl . . ."

"Is Tom Snyder here yet?" Carl called, swaying dangerously over the parapet as he searched the crowd below.

"He's downstairs, Carl," Murphy said. "He's waiting for you downstairs."

"You're lying," Carl hissed.

"No, Carl, he's in the hall downstairs with the cameras and the lights. He wants to talk to you . . ."

Corelli was moving stealthily along the ledge about fifteen feet away from Carl. The thing to do is get him around the knees, and pull him back down on the roof. Not the upper body, because you might go over with him. Murphy wracked his memory to see if he and Corelli had ever handled a jumper in their six years together, to see if Corelli knew what had to be done.

"Tom," Carl called.

Murphy got on the ledge. "Tom wants to talk to you, Carl. He's waiting downstairs."

Carl's jumpsuit flapped like a broken awning in the wind. He jammed the wig on his head, adjusted it, smoothed it down a bit. "I'm coming down, Tom," he cried.

"Carl!"

Both Murphy and Corelli lunged forward, but Carl stepped calmly off the roof. "Do you think Tom will let me sing on his show?" he asked.

20

'Carl got giddy in the elevator. He could hear the shouts of the crowds as they approached the ground floor.

"For God's sake fix my wig," he said to Raquel. "They're waiting."

"It's not your wig," Raquel said, but fixed it anyway. "He's on an acid trip," Raquel confided to Corelli.

"Bad girl, bad girl/I'm such a dirty bad girl," Carl sang.

"You wish," Raquel said.

An ambulance was waiting outside. The Emergency Service truck had arrived and dispersed most of the crowd, but Carl wasn't disappointed. As soon as the flashing lights from all these vehicles hit his face he was on.

"Turn down the lights now baby/'Cause tonight is here to stay."

The few stragglers who had braved the cold to see Carl gave him a cheer, and he entered the ambulance singing.

Raquel stood on the curb waving and crying as if Carl were going off to war. "Don't put him in jail," she begged Murphy. "They'll kill him in jail."

"He won't go to jail, Raquel, don't worry about it," Murphy said. "He'll just be under observation for a couple of days, and then he'll be back here stealing your panties."

"Observation? Oh God, just tell him it's an audition, he'll love it."

Murphy and Corelli followed the ambulance to Jefferson Hospital. Carl was still singing as they strapped him to a stretcher, and carried him into the Emergency Room.

"Last dance/Last chance/For love . . ."

"It's not too bad tonight," Corelli said, looking around the Emergency Room.

"Psycho/Psycho/Over here," Murphy sang.

A nurse looked up from the admissions desk, her glance

going pointedly from Murphy to Carl. "Where?" she asked.

Corelli nudged Murphy. It was the same chick he'd come on to before. She was tall and thin. You couldn't see her legs from behind the desk, but Corelli remembered that they were pretty good. You couldn't see her tits, either, but that was because she didn't have any; at least not the way he liked them. She was dark, and had coils of lustrous black hair tucked neatly under her cap. Pretty face, but a little hollow around the eyes, as though she'd been out partying the night before.

Murphy didn't notice any of those things. He was looking at the curve of her neck, the sturdy yet delicate set of shoulders. He looked at her fingers, long and slender, her neatly trimmed nails. He had never even noticed these things in a woman before. And her expression . . . Corelli said she looked blown-out, as though she'd been on a heavy binge, but that was wrong. It wasn't fatigue, it was sadness. Her eyes were so luminously sad that Murphy could almost see the tears welling up in them. It made him sad as well, and he wanted to clown around and cheer her up, to get a smile out of her. But the look she gave him was so scornful he didn't dare try.

An agitated Puerto Rican intern came out of one of the treatment cubicles.

"What happened?"

Murphy checked out his nameplate. "We got a jumper here, Dr. Perez."

The intern shook his head. "You know we don't have psychiatric facilities."

"So sedate him, and ship him to Bronx State in the morning."

"Where's your medical degree?" the nurse said.

"I keep it home in a little jar . . ."

The nurse walked around to Carl on the stretcher. "What's his name?" she asked Corelli.

"Carl."

"How come the girls always like you better than me?" Murphy joked.

The nurse bent over to talk to Carl, who had become suddenly quiet. "Think you can wait here while we get a treatment room ready for you, Carl?"

Carl looked at her and shook his head. "I'm all messed

up," he said in a plaintive, masculine voice. Gone was the lisp, the posturing, the gaiety. Carl had gone gray under his makeup. The nurse looked up at Corelli.

"Are you going to arrest him?"

"Nah, it's an aided case."

"Okay, so we can take his history and sedate him," she told the intern. She patted Carl's hand, and he smiled weakly.

"The magic touch," Murphy said.

The nurse ignored him and walked back behind the desk.

"You're trying too hard," Corelli said.

"At my age you can't be cool." Murphy walked back to the admissions desk. "Hey *muneca* . . ."

The nurse shook her head wearily. "Do I look like a *muneca* to you, man?"

"Yeah, a little doll. That's what it means, right?"

She pointed out to the reception area. "Look, I got a room full of sick people," she said. "I don't have time to play around with you."

"Okay, let's play around later," Murphy said, leaning over the desk. He touched her hand. It was cool and dry. She didn't jerk it away, but just sat there, waiting. "Come out for a drink with me after work," he said.

She still didn't take her hand away. "Two hundred cops ask me out for a drink every night, so why should I say yes to you?"

Murphy smiled and tickled her palm. " 'Cause you say yes to all the others."

It didn't get a rise out of her. She just smiled back, and said, "I guess that makes you the first cop in the Bronx I say no to . . ."

She was going to make him take his hand away. He did, retreating awkwardly, fumbling for a cigarette. The nurse pointed to the No Smoking sign. "Light it outside," she said.

Corelli stood by the entrance, laughing. "Man, that chick sure beat the shit outta you."

"Which shows how much you know," Murphy said. "The broad's nuts about me."

They walked to the car, dodging two attendants carrying a little girl, screaming and bleeding, on the stretcher. Patterson and Donahue were huffing along behind them.

"What happened to the kid?" Murphy asked.

"She wouldn't listen to mom's new boyfriend, so he slashed her with a bottle opener," Patterson said.

"Oh Jesus." Murphy turned to look back at the girl. She looked about four or five.

"Think I'll try that on my kids," Donahue said. "Nothing else seems to work."

"Jesus Christ," Murphy said. He hated to see the kids getting abused, especially the little girls. The tears of helpless children were the worst sounds he'd heard in all his years on the job.

"C'mon," Corelli said, yanking him away, "we'd better get something to eat. You're gonna need your strength for that nurse tonight."

21

"What'll it be, Puerto Rican, Puerto Rican, or Puerto Rican cuisine?" Corelli asked.

Murphy managed a lame smile. "Decisions, decisions . . ." He knew his partner was trying to keep the banter going, the jokes, the put-downs. Silence in a radio car made the time drag. But you couldn't pour your heart out, either. Nothing killed a good partnership faster than the truth.

Both men knew everything there was to know about one another. Corelli knew Murphy was unhappy at home, and that he stayed out almost every night after work. Murphy knew Corelli was miserable on the job; that he felt he had no future; that his impending marriage seemed to lock him into the P.D. for the next twenty years. He knew about that crazy barmaid, Ida, knew Corelli hadn't even gotten a sniff from his betrothed. They discussed these things, but always with that saving tinge of humor or insult, keeping the conversations frivolous.

Corelli was worried about Murphy, but would never admit it. Murphy had seventeen years on the job, fourteen in the Four-One. It was starting to get to him, just as it got to all the veterans. He had lost his cool with that pimp today, then he came on too desperate with the nurse. And he had stared at that kid like he'd never seen an abused child before. Now he was looking out the window as they drove down Jerome Avenue, looking at the cross streets with the boarded-up buildings, the bums warming their hands over trash can fires. Corelli knew what he was thinking. What the fuck am I doing here? he was thinking. The next step was, he put in his papers. He could get half pay. Or he faked an injury, and got off with three-quarters, tax-free. Or he went berserk one night and put his service pistol in his mouth.

Corelli reached out and nudged Murphy out of his reverie. "Hey, wake up."

Murphy stretched, and grunted with pain. "I'm gettin' too old for this fuckin' job."

"C'mon, you're just a kid."

"I'm gonna be forty-one, Andy. That's too old to be ridin' around playin' cowboys and Indians in the Bronx."

"Ah, it keeps you young."

"Look who's stickin' up for the job all of a sudden."

"Hey," Corelli said. "Make me a better offer. I'll be outta here so fast my uniform'll still be sittin' behind the wheel."

Murphy's eyes got vague as he reminisced. "You wanna know the smartest move I ever saw on this job? It was when I first came on. I was still on foot patrol. There was a guy in the squad, Jerry Donnelly, big fat slob of a guy. Man, and the things they used to do to collars in those days. Hang 'em outta the window until they gave up the information, put their legs up on the fingerprint table, and smash their knees with bats. Everybody got a workout in the squad. Finnegan, another wild man, once decked a D.A. because he thought he was a bookie. You had to walk in flashin' your shield, because if they didn't know you, you were in trouble. Anyway, one night they called a 10–13 over on Webster Avenue. Donnelly and some other guy had gone in on a Rastafarian grass dealer, and there had been an awful fracas. The Rasta barricaded himself in the apartment, and put three shots through the door . . ."

Corelli yawned deliberately. "This story better be good because it sure is long enough . . ."

"What do you care, it's killin' time. So anyway this Rasta throws three through the door, and one of 'em hits the wall about an inch from Donnelly's head, and by the time we get up there he's sittin' down on the landing a million miles away. I mean his fuckin' mind was workin'. So we cleared the building and pumped a few rounds through the door ourselves, and the guy came out, holding his hands to be cuffed. Donnelly's partner, Tony Mancini, runs up and kicks this Rasta right in the nuts, and slams him in the head with his blackjack. Now the poor bastard is lyin' on the floor, semiconscious." Murphy began to shake with silent laughter. "Donnelly gets up, and walks over to him. Now you gotta remember, we knew he was a mean bastard—he showed no mercy—and we thought he was gonna cremate this guy. So he walks over. The guy's layin' right by the stairs. Donnelly walks over, takes a look at the guy, takes a deep breath, and throws himself down the stairs."

"He threw himself down the stairs?" Corelli said in disbelief.

"Yeah, yeah," Murphy said, shaking his head, and wiping tears of mirth out of his eyes. "One of them steep walk-up stairs, too. That fat bastard bounced like a sack of potatoes all the way down. Then he lay there waitin' for us to get to him. His leg was twisted under him, and he was sobbin' with pain, but he grabbed me by the collar. 'You saw him, right?' he says. 'You saw him push me down the stairs, didn't you?' I was just a kid, you know, and I couldn't figure it out. But my partner, Houlihan, he came runnin' down. 'Yeah, Jerry,' he says. 'We saw what that cocksucker did.' So Donnelly kinda smiles and says, 'Thanks fellas,' and passes out."

"Sick bastard," Corelli said.

"He was sick, all right. Broken leg, fractured wrist, fractured skull. But he never spent another minute on the job again, and he got his three-quarters pension, tax-free. There was no hearing, no investigation, we didn't even have to testify. He just got it." Murphy pointed like a schoolmaster, like the brothers in Catholic school had done when making a crucial point. "And that young man made the smartest move I've ever seen anybody make on this job."

"That ain't sayin' much for the job," Corelli said.

"It ain't exactly a commercial."

Corelli spotted that purse snatcher they had been briefed

about, the black dude with the sneakers, the leather jacket, and the aviator's cap sliding into a doorway on Jerome Avenue. Murphy saw him, too.

"We're about to do another smart thing," Corelli said. "We're gonna drive right by this sucker."

"Wait a second, he's casin' the Bingo Parlor." Murphy checked his watch. "And it lets out in about a minute."

Corelli blipped the siren, and the kid came out to take a look. Murphy waved. The kid waved back. A few doors down a group of elderly women came out of the bingo parlor. Corelli pulled over to the curb. "Skinny bastard," he said.

"I hope we don't have to chase him," Murphy said.

Corelli waved to the kid. "The big, bad policemans are here, so don't commit a violation."

The kid waved back, and started walking down the block right behind the old ladies. A few of them stopped to bundle up, and the kid moved so smoothly it looked for a moment like he was just going through the crowd. He stripped four handbags off the ladies' arms as easily as if he were shucking corn, and took off across the street before Murphy and Corelli realized what he had done.

"That sonofabitch, right in front of our fuckin' faces."

One of the ladies teetered and fell on the sidewalk as the others screamed for help.

Murphy opened the door. "They said he runs through the park. Get around to the other side. I'll chase him to you."

Corelli screeched into a U-turn, and called in a 10–30 as Murphy ran across the street. The kid was running up the stairs to the park, taking three and four steps at a time. Murphy followed doggedly. The cold seared his lungs. His holster flapped against his thigh. He saw a patch of black ice ahead of him, but couldn't turn away fast enough, and skidded a few feet before grabbing onto a lamp post. Lousy reflexes, he thought. Old fart . . . gotta stop smokin'.

Most of the lights were broken in this part of the park, and Murphy had to navigate the darkness, following the rhythmic flap of the kid's sneakers. He managed to get his flashlight off his belt without breaking stride . . . not bad . . . The kid was about fifty feet in front of him, and widening the gap. Murphy clamped his hat down on his head. He only had to move fast enough to keep the kid in the beam. The kid looked back and grinned. The bastard wasn't even breathing hard. He hurdled a park bench, and ran down the hill toward the handball courts. The footing was tricky down there. Murphy played the beam in front of him to make sure the kid wasn't running him into a ditch. When he raised it the kid was gone. Instead, the beam caught three guys standing against a tree. They looked guiltily at him, and took off. A fuckin' drop, Murphy thought. He ran toward the handball courts. He caught the white flash of a sneaker sole. The kid was running back up the hill toward the Tremont Avenue exit. Murphy's knee buckled, and he had to stop for a second. He took a few deep breaths; it felt as though he were sucking razors into his lungs. Then he started off up the hill, past the benches over the path to another row of benches. Murphy climbed gingerly over a bench. The flashlight hit a boy with his pants down, and a chick with long hair crouched between his legs. She screamed. Christ, a blow job in twenty-degree weather, Murphy thought. He looked toward the entrance, and saw the track star trapped in the light of the lamp posts at the edge of the park.

Corelli saw him, too. He had parked at the exit by the handball courts, but he saw the track star and was trying to head him off. They were racing, Correlli on the outside, the track star on the inside of the park. Corelli could move. He ran with his head up, arms churning. The track star sprinted with long graceful strides; he didn't seem to be straining at all. He got to the entrance a few steps ahead of Corelli, vaulted a parked car, and dashed across Tremont Avenue, disappearing in the darkness.

Murphy managed to make it outside the park. Corelli was leaning against a parking meter, catching his breath. Murphy was doubled over with a pain in his gut. He wanted to drop to his knees, and crawl the rest of the way. "I think I'm gonna puke," he said.

Another radio car came down Tremont. Morgan and Finley got out laughing.

"Better call a bus," Morgan said. "These guys are gonna need oxygen."

"That fuckin' track star," Murphy said. "Anybody got a cigarette?"

Morgan gave him a Marlboro. "Why didn't you just chop the bastard?"

Murphy took a deep drag. "Shoot a purse snatcher, right? They'd fuckin' crucify me."

"So you say he attacked you," Finley said. "We'd back you up."

"You know the prick's holdin'," Morgan said. "And if he's not . . ." He took a cheap flick knife out of his pocket. "You lay the old flake on him."

Murphy coughed up a huge gob of phlegm, and shone the flashlight down on the sidewalk to see if there was any blood in it. "So that's how it's done, huh? Listen, Morgan, I know how to flake a guy just as good as you do, okay? And I know when to do it, too."

Morgan shrugged. "You'll get a heart attack before you'll ever catch a nigger, Tarzan."

Finley laughed and thumped his chest. "Awhooo, awhooo." And they walked back to their car.

"What's the matter with Morgan?" Corelli asked.

Murphy spat. "He thinks I'm a liberal."

22

On Prospect Avenue, amidst the darkened, caged storefronts, the hollowed buildings set far back on the broad sidewalks, the aqua lights of *La Borriqueña* gleamed like a beacon. The restaurant was on the corner of 163rd Street, on a block where patrolmen walked in threes—nervously. Yet, its owners, two brothers from Santurce, acted as if they were running a star operation on Madison Avenue. They raised their own blue claw crabs, buying them at the fishmarket, then placing them in a neon-lit tank in their window and fattening them on fresh corn, the way the old fishermen in Puerto Rico did. They brought in South American wines exclusively for their customers, and served full-course meals twenty-four hours a day so the cops, firemen, politicians, and crooks—all of whom kept irregular hours—would always

111

have some place to bring their girlfriends. The waiters wore tuxedos, perhaps a bit casually, but they discussed the meals with great seriousness. The food was so good that even an Irishman like Murphy, who'd had nothing more exotic than pork chops and mashed potatoes for most of his life, could end up eating cold octopus salad with *yuca*, a turniplike legume, yellow rice, and red beans with great appetite. Outside, the sirens wailed, and occasionally one heard the sound of screams and shots. The windows looked out on the intersection of 163rd and Prospect, affording an occasional view of a fight, a crowd, a body in the gutter. Inside, the diners were oblivious, at least for the moment, to the turmoil on the streets. The jukebox murmured *salsa*, or heartfelt Latin *canciones*. Everybody minded their own business, and ate.

Corelli parked across the street out of deference to the owners; a radio car sometimes scared away prospective customers. A girl stood shivering on the corner. She couldn't have been more than fifteen. Up and down the street people stood in small groups, smoking, talking, occasionally walking out into the middle of the road, and looking.

"Waiting for the connection," Corelli said.

Murphy nodded. "Haven't seen that for a while."

"Smack is back, Jim. I don't see why they just don't legalize it, and stop makin' all these scumbag dealers rich."

"Because if they legalize it, the same scumbags will get three times as rich, and instead of ninety thousand junkies, you'll have nine million."

"Yeah, but at least we won't have to bust them."

Murphy pointed up and down the street. "I ain't bustin' anybody. Are you?"

Felipe came out from behind the cash register to greet them. His brother, Raul, ran out of the kitchen, drying his hands on his apron, his forehead shining with perspiration. They shook hands, clapped backs—a big greeting. It was done every time Murphy and Corelli came in, to alert the other customers to the presence of the cops, and to let them know that these cops were friends of the house so there was no need to eat and run.

Murphy and Corelli chose a table by the window so they could watch the car. They felt all eyes upon them as they took their jackets off, placed their hats and walkie-talkies on the side of the table, and adjusted their gun belts so they'd be more comfortable. There were at least thirty people in the room, and they knew that all conversations had stopped momentarily while a few unkind or disdainful sentiments were aired.

Tito, an elderly waiter with a white mustache, a frayed tuxedo, and an elegant manner, brought Corelli a bottle of Coca-Cola half filled with rum. Murphy had a beer poured in a Seven-Up bottle. "Something for a cold night," he told Tito. "*Un asopao de gandules.*" It was a thick soup made with chick peas, red beans, pieces of beef, and rice.

Tito laughed and clenched his fist. "That will make you like this all night with the women."

"I'll have one, too," Corelli said.

"It'll only make you fart," Murphy said.

Across the street, Chino stood hunched in a doorway, watching. Those two white bastards were really living it up in *el barrio,* sitting in a nice warm place, eating good. Meanwhile, he was out on the street freezing his dick off. And for what? A coupla thousand a year more plus a gold shield. Sure, they gave the Ricans the gold, they gave them the grade. And then they made them catch fucking pneumonia to earn it.

Chino had been standing there for hours, just like those junkies, waiting for Jose to show. He wanted to make contact, to get the show on the road. He wouldn't sleep until he'd gotten a line on this case. He'd even gone out without back-up. If he couldn't handle one street dealer by himself he might as well turn in his shield.

He spotted Little Toni, an informer he'd used many times, standing across the street by the phone booth. She was waiting to cop for herself, and her old man, a paraplegic named Ronnie, a black cat who'd been paralyzed in a Harlem shoot-out several years before and now sat in the house watching TV with a sawed-off on his lap. Toni was a real down *Latina,* all right, standing out there in the cold taking care of her man. He had to respect her for that. He had to scare her a little, too, to get what he wanted. Hunching into his jacket, his hands thrust into his pockets, his head down, Chino crossed over to Toni.

"*Como 'ta Mami . . .*"

Toni was cool. No quick movements, no running away. She knew. Nobody on the street was paying any attention, but everyone would know if she made a wrong move. So she didn't move. Only her eyes betrayed her fear. As many times as you use them, as much as you pay them with dope or money, you have to keep the stools afraid. You can never let them know how much you need them.

Chino put his hand on her upper arm, as if he were about to make a pinch. Her panic excited him. He'd always been curious . . . A nice chick, real young. Nice and skinny, he liked them that way. She couldn't be getting too much at home, not with her old man paralyzed. Even the junkies like to do it once in a while. They give great head when they don't nod out with your joint in their mouths. "You waitin' for Jose, Toni?"

"I'm just waitin' to cop, Chino," Toni said neervously. "I ain't nothin' more than a customer, Chino . . ."

"Cuidada flaka, take it easy, that's all *I* want to do. I wanna cop from him, that's all. You get me next to the dude, and you're out of it."

"I don't wanna do nothin' with these cats," Toni said nervously. "They're bad. They don't like women . . ."

Chino whispered softly in her ear. "Hey, baby, did I ever lie to you? Did I ever break a promise?"

Toni shook her head.

"Okay . . ." He gave her another shot of warm breath. "You just tell him you used to cop from me down on Eldridge Street, on the Lower East Side."

Toni pointed down the street. "He's coming."

It was that same stringy-haired *maricon,* strutting down the street, feeling his power. He disappeared into a building, and came out a few seconds later. Counting the bread right out on the street like that. Showing off. This asshole was going to be real easy.

"How much you got?" Chino asked.

Toni showed him two crumpled twenties clutched in her fist. Just enough for two spoons. He slipped her another forty. "Here, this'll keep you out of the cold for a while."

"Oh no, Chino, it's too much. He'll get suspicious . . ."

"Let him think you turned a trick with me. Shit, use the bread to buy food, I don't care what you do with it."

114

Toni slipped into the phone booth as Jose approached. He stopped when he saw Chino, and his hand went into his pocket. Right to the heat, finger on the trigger. Toni picked up the receiver as if she were talking, and slipped the folded bills into the coin return. Then, she stepped out, and Jose was supposed to go in and pick up the receiver, taking the money and slipping the bags of dope into the coin return. But he grabbed her when she got out of the booth, and pulled her into the shadows.

In *La Borriqueña*, Murphy lit an after dinner cigarette, stirred his expresso, and watched a dope drop taking place about ten feet from the radio car. Corelli was talking a mile a minute. Another one of his get-rich-quick schemes—this one was to buy a pet shop in New Rochelle, and specialize in exotic animals—monkeys, snakes, etc. Meanwhile, right across the street, a guy was getting rich quick right in front of their faces, just like that track star.

"The thing has incredible potential," Corelli said. He picked up that jargon out of those books he read. *How I Made a Million in My Spare Time, Conquer Yourself, Conquer the World, Building a Business From the Ground Up.* The kid was desperate, confused. "It's an untapped market," Corelli said. "But there are enough people who want exotic animals and fish to make us fuckin' millionaires. We could do it mail order, send these fuckin' things all over the world."

"Sure as long as you're the guy who pastes the stamps on the boa constrictor, you got a deal."

As Murphy watched, this guy came back out of the building with that poor little chick. He went right to the dude standing by the phone booth, and gave him the old soul handshake. Yeah, there were some people in this world who knew how to do business.

23

They finally put Charlotte out in the cold. Style had beaten her until his arms were tired, trying to get her to say she was sorry for taking the car and slashing Lonnie. But she wouldn't say anything. She just lay on the bathroom floor, biting down on the towel they'd shoved in her mouth, growling like a rabid dog, her eyes wild and vengeful.

Style pronounced the final judgment. "The bitch is nuts." He was afraid to let her up, afraid she'd attack him. Bitch gets crazy like that, she gets strong. Style had to let her go.

With each of the girls twisting an arm behind her, they threw Charlotte out into the hallway. Style threw her purse out after her. "Anything you got in there is yours," he said. "You on your own." And he slammed the door.

Charlotte tore the sodden towel out of her mouth, and threw it against the door. "Motherfucker," she screeched, and then in low, menacing tones, "I'm gonna kill your ass, too." Her back was stiff from the beating. Her legs ached. Her ankle went out from under her when she tried to walk, and she had to hold onto the wall for a while. Peepholes clicked in the gloomy hallway as the other tenants checked out. After a while the blood stopped pounding in her head. "Motherfucker," she mumbled. "Kill him too . . ."

Murphy and Corelli saw her staggering down Wilkins Avenue. "Isn't that Goldilocks?" Corelli asked.

Murphy took a closer look. "Yeah. Looks like that pimp didn't kill her after all."

"You don't kill a piece of flesh like that. You slap it around a little and put it right back on the street where it can earn."

"Hey, you'd make a pretty good pimp," Murphy said.

"I've had a few offers."

"That little barmaid. . . ?"

Corelli poked Murphy angrily. "Ida ain't no hooker."

Murphy laughed. He had his partner going. "If she ain't, she's missing a golden opportunity with the sheer number of guys she's bestowed her favors on . . ."

"There's that double standard again," Corelli said. "A guy can screw his brains out, and he's a stud, right? A big man. A chick wants to enjoy herself, too, and right away she's a slut . . ."

"Double standard, huh? You wait until your wife tells you she wants to fuck the plumber, and then talk to me about double standards . . ."

"Jesus Christ, this chick can hardly walk." Corelli pointed at Charlotte. "He beat her bowlegged. Nice lookin' head. Nice tits . . . You know, I always wonder if these hookers enjoy screwin' at all . . ."

"I don't know. I like takin' a shit, but if I had to do it twenty times a day seven days a week . . ."

Corelli opened the window. "You fart thirty times a day, and you still like doing it . . ."

Murphy lit a match. "The Carbon Murphoxide form of suicide. The perfect crime. Lay a fart, light a match, and your troubles are over."

"Whew." Corelli stuck his head out of the window. "Only a sick fuck like you could compare sex with defecation."

"Defecation, the man said. What do you compare it with, beauty and poetry? Is that why you do it in dirty hallways and on top of roofs and anywhere else you can wave your dick without gettin' caught?"

Corelli sucked in the cold air. His partner was in better spirits, and that was worth a few farts. He looked up the street for the hooker, but she was gone.

"Hey, where'd that chick go? I wanted to interview her."

"Four-One Ed K," the radio squawked.

"Another fuckin' call." Murphy picked up the mike. "Four-One Ed . . ."

"Respond 4290 Fox Street, Apartment 3E. Girl having a seizure."

"A fuckin' poet," Murphy said. "Is her purse being seized? Or her pussy . . ."

It was a four-story walk-up next to a vacant lot. You could look at it, and tell there hadn't been any heat or hot water since winter began. Half the building was welfare, the

117

other half squatters. A group of men huddled around a trash-can fire, their grim faces caught in the light of the flames. "These guys ain't winos," Murphy said.

"It's probably warmer out here by the fire than it is in their apartments," Corelli said.

Murphy nodded to the men. *"Donde está la enferma?"* he asked.

They shrugged, shook their heads. *"No sé."*

"Quién es?" Murphy walked over to the stoop, standing clear of the entrance to the building, and peered up into the gloomy hallway. "I hate goin' into a building like this with cop killers runnin' around."

"So we wait for the bus," Corelli said.

Murphy tried to read the building. Some of the windows were boarded up; the faint light of squatters' fires shone behind others, and in others were the flowered curtains of the inhabited apartments, desperate attempts to make a home.

"Ah, fuck it," Murphy said, "there's nothin' here."

They climbed the rickety stairs, Murphy walking slowly ahead, Corelli behind him, walking backwards up the steps, just in case. 3E was in the rear. A little boy stood in the hall. "Over here," he said sharply. A tough kid, about the same age as Murphy's son Timmy, only centuries older. He had his hands jammed in the pockets of a tattered pea jacket. Probably had a flick knife in one of those pockets. "My sister's sick," the kid said, leading the way.

An elderly couple sat in the kitchen by the stove. Candles were burning in the living room. Pictures of saints lined the walls.

"My grandmother's tryin' to make white magic to help my sister," the kid said. The old man got up, drawing his jacket around him. *"Esperas alli,"* the kid commanded. The old man sat down.

"Where are your parents?" Murphy asked.

"My father don't live with us anymore," the kid said. Not a word about the mother. Murphy didn't push it.

A fifteen-year-old girl was lying under a pile of blankets in a bedroom, sobbing softly. "She was throwin' up and coughin' blood all day yesterday," the kid whispered. "She wouldn't let me take her to Emergency, so I called the cops."

Murphy approached the bed. The girl turned away, shaking her head. "No, no . . ."

Corelli opened the window, and leaned out to get better transmission on his walkie-talkie. "How we doin' on that bus for 4290 Fox Street?"

"What's her name?" Murphy whispered to the boy.

"Nina." The boy moved closer to the bed. He looked at his sister curiously, without emotion. "What's wrong with her, man?"

"I don't know." Gently, Murphy pulled off the blankets. "Nina, how old are you?"

The girl hid her face.

"She's fifteen," the boy said.

Murphy tried to open the girl's coat. She whimpered and pushed his hand away. He felt around the dampened sheets. "Oh shit, her water broke." He leaned over the girl, and smoothed the hair off her clammy forehead. "You walked around for three months with your coat on, right, Nina? I guess you were lucky it's winter, but now your time's up. You gotta have that baby, Nina. If you let me help you everything will be all right." He straightened up and took off his gun belt, draping it over the bed post. He put his hand on the boy's shoulder. "Go outside, and keep your grandparents outta here. Even if they hear the screamin', keep 'em out." He looked at his hands. "Shit, I gotta wash up."

Corelli felt his dinner coming up. Just the thought of a pregnancy made him nauseated. Murphy left the room, and Corelli heard him telling the boy to put a pot of water on the stove, so he could wash his hands. The girl lay on the bed, her legs spread, writhing and clutching her face. Some broads carried on like that when they were getting laid. The thought disgusted Corelli. He leaned out of the window, and hit the walkie-talkie. "C'mon, we got a fuckin' maternity case over here."

Charlotte found her way to Gloria's building, and leaned on the buzzer until Gloria came out to open the door. "I got people here, honey. I told you, it's not good when I got people here." Gloria was a worrier. Her hair had turned snow-white during her first week at Bedford Hills prison, making her look like a woman in her fifties when she was only thirty-two. She was stout and swarthy, and from the back she could have been somebody's grandmother. She knew that the kids on the block called her *"La Vieja,"* and *"Abuela."*

But they were real nice to her when they wanted to get high.

"If I take you inside, you gotta promise you won't hassle nobody," Gloria said.

Charlotte smiled. "I ain't botherin' nobody." She took Gloria's hand, and pressed it to her breast. "Style threw me out on the street."

"Did he hurt you? Did he beat you, baby?"

"Ain't nobody can hurt me," Charlotte said haughtily. "I'm the one doin' the hurtin'."

" 'Cause I'll kill him, baby, I swear I will." Gloria's hand trembled as she stroked Charlotte's face. "I'll kill that nigger if he ever lays a hand on you. Now you come on inside with me. I'm taking care of you from now on . . ."

Two kids were nodding on the mattresses in Gloria's living room. A tall, skinny, black kid with a pilot's cap sat against the wall staring into space. He looked up in amazement at Charlotte. She smiled down flirtatiously at him. "Tuck your feet in, turkey," Gloria said, kicking him in the shins. The kid giggled, and drew his bony knees right up to his nose. "Don't pay attention to these junkies, baby," Gloria said. She hustled Charlotte into the bedroom, and locked the door from the outside. "I'll be right in, baby. I got something for you. Just relax."

Everything Gloria owned was crammed into this small room. She wasn't stupid enough to leave anything in the living room where those junkies could get to it. An electric heater glowed in the corner. Gloria had found a nice blue wallpaper with a floral pattern and put it up, covering the walls with posters of all her favorites, Farrah and Cheryl and Linda Ronstadt plus the really great centerfolds from *Penthouse* and *Oui*. She had this beautiful chest of drawers she had picked right out of the garbage on the Grand Concourse. The color TV. Plus a big sawed-off that she kept under the bed to blow away any motherfucker who intruded.

"Just relax, Charlotte," she said through the door. "I'll be right back."

Charlotte put out the light, and warmed herself in front of the heater. The heat felt good against her bruised legs. Her eyes narrowed to feline slits; she smiled, comforted by visions of blood and carnage. When Gloria returned, Charlotte was lying nude on the bed, the red glow of the heater traveling up and down her body like a lover.

120

Corelli had gone outside when the ambulance and the paramedics showed up. The girl had been screaming. Murphy was leaning over her with his hand shoved up her . . . Oh, Jesus—Corelli couldn't take it. "Push, Nina, push," Murphy was saying. And then there was silence. The old folks hadn't known what was happening, hadn't dared ask. But when they heard that thin, anguished cry, they knew. And their faces closed.

A few minutes later Murphy stuck his head out of the door. "It's a girl," he said.

Corelli went into the room to help the attendants get the girl into a wheelchair stretcher. "You're actin' like the father," Murphy said.

"That's the one thing I can't take."

They had given the baby to her mother. "Probably the last time she'll ever see it," Murphy said. One of the paramedics was sponging her forehead. The baby was quiet in her arms. She looked at it in confusion, and gave it up readily to the paramedics. The baby started crying as soon as it was transferred.

"Fuckin' amazing," Corelli said. "She wants to be with her mommy."

"She'd better forget about that idea," Murphy said.

24

The Emergency Room was crowded now, mostly with the very young or very old, all victims of the cold. Patterson and Donahue had brought a stabbing victim in, and were trying to find a doctor. The victim, a kid in his twenties, sat motionless on the stretcher, holding his arm in the air with the makeshift tourniquet they had fashioned for him. Jefferson was known as the best place to be treated for a stab wound; the doctors there worked on so many they became experts. But the victim was unimpressed with the type of medical care he was about to get. His face was yellow under the crackling fluorescent lights, his eyes dim. He seemed to be lost in thought. And then his mouth opened, and he fell off the stretcher. The crack of his head against the cement floor cut right through the cacophony of shrieking babies, quarreling spouses, and P.A. announcements. He was dead by the time they got to him.

Donahue came running out of the Chief Resident's office. "Jesus, did we lose him, Eddie?"

The paramedics were lifting the kid back onto the stretcher, and hustling him into surgery where the residents would try to get his heart going again.

"Shock," Patterson said. "Some people just aren't the type to fight with knives."

The intern, Perez, had greeted Murphy and Corelli when they brought the girl and the baby in. "You guys tryin' to take my job?" They put mother and daughter in a treatment room to await admission to Maternity. "Better take the baby away," a passing resident said. "Sometimes the mothers go berserk and hurt the kids in a situation like this."

Murphy felt like popping the resident. Snotty Jew bastard! But he was right, Murphy had seen it happen. So they took the little girl upstairs, making sure she had an I.D. bracelet with her mother's name on it. Nina lay on a stretcher staring at the ceiling. There was no one to hold her hand; she'd have to wait until one of the social workers was available to offer their professional brand of comfort, while they took information for the mountain of forms that had to be filled out. Her little brother had come down in the radio car with Murphy and Corelli. He stood like a sentry outside the treatment room, his hands jammed in his pockets, chewing gum ferociously.

"See if you can get your grandparents to come tomorrow," Murphy said.

"Yeah," the kid said, indifferently.

Murphy grabbed him. "It's important. You don't want your sister to feel like a *puta,* do you? Call everyone in the family. See if you can get Moms on the case, too, okay?"

"Yeah."

"Got any idea who the father is?"

"I know who it is. I'm gonna kill the motherfucker, too."

"What's his name?" Murphy asked.

"'Richie Conte, he works over at the supermarket on 149th Street. He thinks he's slick, but I'm gonna cut his ass . . .'"

"Richie Conte . . ." Murphy made a great show of writing the name in his memo book. "Okay, now that I know his name, if anything happens to this kid, I'm gonna come personally and lock you up, you understand?" That was the easy way. Let the kid off the hook, let him save face. "You wanna do something for your sister, then take care of her, and get her out of this mess, and stop thinkin' about cuttin' people, or you'll end up in the joint, and everything will really be messed up."

The kid just nodded. He wasn't paying attention, and there was no way to make him. You didn't listen to cops, you lied to them, stalled them—anything to get them off your back. Besides, he was too young. How can you ask a ten-year-old kid to do anything but show up at school every day?

Murphy wandered out into the hall to smoke a cigarette. The nurse, who had been watching him talk to the little boy, called Corelli over. "What's the matter with your partner?"

"Just 'cause he ain't hittin' on you anymore, you think something's the matter."

"He looks like he's gonna pass out," the nurse said.

"Postoperative depression," Corelli said. "He just delivered a baby."

The nurse went out in the hall. Murphy had unbuttoned his tunic, and was slouching in a bridge chair, a cigarette dangling out of the corner of his mouth.

"You all right?" she asked.

"What do you care?"

"They said you delivered a baby . . ."

"Yeah, it was my seventeenth in fourteen years up here."

"Seventeen, you could almost be an obstetrician. Well . . ." She turned to go. "Congratulations, anyway."

"For what? For bringin' an orphan into the world."

"For saving a life," the nurse said.

Murphy waved his cigarette. He felt drunk, but he was just very, very tired. "Temporarily, baby, that's all. The mother is in disgrace. I don't care how many social workers talk to her, she'll probably never get over this. The kid gets put up for adoption right away, you know, but first she's sent from one foster home to the next, and maybe ends up in one

123

of those institutions. So congratulations ain't exactly in order for any of us."

The nurse folded her arms, and looked down at him for a long time. Murphy fidgeted under quiet scrutiny. He could usually tell what broads were thinking, but this one was a mystery.

"You need a drink," she finally said.

"I need a nurse," Murphy said.

She turned to head back to the Admissions Desk. "You supply the booze, I'll supply the nurse," she said over her shoulder.

"You askin' me out?" Murphy said.

"Maybe," she said, her back to him, still walking.

"Two hundred nurses ask me out every day," he called after her. "Why should I say yes to you?"

She turned. She was smiling. "Because you say yes to all the others." Then, she turned away from him again. "See if you can find your way back here at midnight."

25

Connolly heard the laughter through his office door, and knew immediately what was going on. Ed Dacey was entertaining the press. He hit the intercom, and got Applebaum at the desk.

"Sergeant, could you ask Lieutenant Dacey to step in here a moment. You come in, too."

He watched them through the smoked glass of his office door, the pear-shaped waddle of Applebaum, and Dacey's chic, well-tailored silhouette. Connolly patted his own bulging middle. Ed Dacey had always kept in shape. He had taken up tennis when the rest of the guys were still going bowling once a week. The scuttlebutt around Headquarters was that he played in a doubles group with the Commissioner once a month.

There was a jaunty knock. Dacey was a real comedian. "Come in," Connolly said.

Dacey peeked around the door. "Any policewomen in here? Only under the desk, eh, Dennis?"

Dacey looked like every movie-goer's idea of a detective. Tall, a touch of gray at the temples, well-dressed, a handsome Irishman with thick, black brows over roguish, blue eyes, a smooth square jaw. "Clark Kent," they had called him at the Academy.

"Really burning the midnight oil on this one, aren't you, Ed?" Connolly said.

"I'm hangin' in with the press," Dacey said. "We wouldn't want them wandering unchaperoned around *this* precinct, would we? They might come across a skeleton in the stairway, or maybe even a Puerto Rican who cut himself shaving."

"Well, what are they all waiting for? The story's over."

"Something might break, Dennis. I've got them convinced that the considerable might of the Police Department has gone to work on this . . ."

"Which is what I wanted to talk to you about," Connolly said. "I'd like to get the whole precinct involved in this case."

"Fine with me," Dacey said. "Just as long as you know that all the publicity will be given to my unit. That's not me talking, now, it's the way Headquarters wants it."

"Publicity is not my primary concern," Connolly said. "We're turning the tours out with specific instructions to canvass their sectors."

"That might cut into their cooping time a little."

Connolly ignored that. "And if there's any way, bring our squad in. I know you've excluded them."

"The purpose of my unit is to relieve the squads of this investigative burden. They're already loaded down up there, anyway, and to lay this squeal on a guy who already has three other cases is criminal in itself. Now, I have six good detectives working full-time on this investigation. Isn't that better?"

"It would be best if you could consult in some way with our squad people."

"I've consulted. We've got no technical evidence, no witnesses, no obvious motive. So now it's a question of waiting for the stools. Or just gettin' lucky."

"Sounds like thumb-twiddling to me, Ed. I think we need a more aggressive program."

Dacey reddened. "Oh, I agree, Dennis. I agree. I'd like to take a couple of obvious suspects off the streets right now. Bring 'em in the squad room, close the door, and hang 'em out of the window by their ankles until they told us what we wanted to know. But we can't do that anymore, can we, Dennis? Thanks to the new regulations that guys like you put into effect."

"Brutality was never an effective method of solving crimes," Connolly said.

"Bullshit," Dacey said. He loosened his tie, and leaned forward. "You were never a detective, so you don't know. In the old days, before you I.A.D. guys started telling everybody how to behave, we had a foolproof way of getting information. You know what we did, Dennis? We went onto a block where we knew a numbers guy was operating, and we told him, 'You're closed until we get some information on this homicide. If we catch you doing business we'll pinch you, and we'll drop a few bags of heroin in your pocket just to make it a little harder on you!' In a couple of days we'd have the information we wanted, and the guy would go back to work."

"That's blackmail," Connolly said.

"But it worked every time. So we let a policy guy slide to get a murderer, is that a bad deal? Only now we can't do that. I.A.D. says a police officer must immediately apprehend any criminal, or face departmental charges."

"Those rules were put into effect to stop corruption."

"But they stopped good police work, too, and that's what hurt. We're not all Sherlock Holmes, you know. We get a cop killing with absolutely no clues like this, then we've got to get information from the neighborhood. We've got to get some people in here to spill their guts."

Connolly cleared the papers away from a map of the precinct he had put under his glass desk top. "You keep saying it was motiveless. But this particular block is one of the highest crime sectors in the precinct."

Dacey sighed wearily. "I've done my homework, Dennis."

"Just thinking out loud, Ed, that's all," Connolly said. "There's been a lot of small-time drug traffic in these buildings, according to arrest reports. Stolen cars are stripped there. These officers could have stumbled upon a felony in progress."

"Then they would have at least ditched their coffee, and gotten out of the car to investigate. The Interruption of Crime in Progress Theory is definitely out in this case."

"So what's left?"

"Two possibilities . . ." Dacey ticked them off on his fingers. "One, a random, motiveless attack by an insane individual, who might or might not strike again. That's canceled out by the fact that the officers' guns, shields, and wallets were methodically stripped from them. That was a little too rational for most maniacs."

"And . . ."

"The theory that this was a political hit, like the kind we had in the sixties. A planned, paramilitary act of terrorism, which will be repeated. That's what we're working on now."

Connolly thumbed quickly through the stack of memos on his desk. "I've got a list of community groups, government agencies, intelligence reports . . ."

"We're going through that now," Dacey said.

Connolly turned to Applebaum, who'd been looking from one man to another like a spectator at a tennis match. "Of all the political groups up here, which one do you think is the most capable of violence?"

"I don't know," Applebaum said. "I never really thought about it. You could ask Martinez, the Community Relations Officer."

"We already did," Dacey said. "He mentioned the South Bronx People's Party."

"Know anything about them?" Connolly asked Applebaum.

"Disco revolutionaries," Applebaum said, shrugging them off. "They got federal money to set up a storefront on Fox Street. They preach armed revolt, and make a lotta hate-cop noises, but they spend most of their time ballin' white chicks from Scarsdale."

Connolly looked over at Dacey. "Are you following up on this?"

"Sure. Might even make a little trip to Scarsdale."

"I want some action on this case, Ed," Connolly said.

"Then come up to Scarsdale with me."

127

"I'm serious. If it's terrorists, I don't want them picking my men off while you make jokes with the press."

Applebaum rose quickly. "I'll get back out to the desk."

"You stay," Connolly said. "Lieutenant Dacey has got to get back to work."

Dacey didn't like being rebuked in front of a sergeant; he didn't like being thrown out of the office. "You're in a bad neighborhood for quick solutions, Dennis. You got a lotta bad people with rap sheets, about twenty thousand. Which means you got twenty thousand potential cop killers. Takes time to toss 'em all."

"Just start with the South Bronx People's Party," Connolly said calmly. "And keep me informed on your progress . . . Close the door on your way out, please. Thanks for your time."

Connolly turned to Applebaum even before Dacey was out of the office. "I want to change the image of the precinct, Sergeant. I think we can convince Headquarters to mount a publicity campaign to get this Fort Apache stigma off our backs."

"That's a good idea, Boss," Applebaum said, thinking all the while about how he could get transferred out of this precinct.

"I want all the desk sergeants to go through the 61s, the accident reports, aided cases, etcetera, at the end of the day," Connolly said. "See if you can pick out some act of heroism or civic duty that was performed by the cops. Or the citizens. Any citizen coming to the aid of a policeman . . ."

"Up here?"

"I'm sure it happens, Sergeant, so let's find it. I want to turn things around in the Four-One. I want the public to know that everybody up here is trying to improve conditions."

"Yes, sir."

The four-to-twelve had checked in, and the men were dressing when Applebaum came into the locker room with his clipboard.

"Anybody do anything heroic today?" he asked.

"Yeah, I came to work."

"I ate Puerto Rican food."

"For real, for real," Applebaum said. "The Captain wants to change the image of the precinct."

"So let him move it to Park Avenue."

"Murphy delivered a baby tonight," Corelli said. "That's pretty heroic, ain't it?"

"Only I delivered it to the wrong address," Murphy said.

"I always thought you looked like a stork," Patterson said.

"Looks like you're our first hero," Applebaum said, writing on the clipboard.

"Hey, Sarge, how would you like to eat my foreskin?" Murphy said angrily. "Don't write me down for nothin'."

"C'mon," Corelli coaxed, "let 'em put your name in the paper. Your wife'll see how hard you're workin'."

"I don't want her to know I'm workin' at all," Murphy said. "I want her to think I'm screwin' around." He tapped his forehead. "Reverse psychology."

Corelli turned away with a shrug. "The man's a genius, what can I tell you?"

Applebaum kept writing. "Captain told me to go through the day's work, and find all the heroic, public-spirited acts his officers performed, which is what I'm doin'. You don't wanna be part of the program, you explain it to him." Applebaum hitched his pants up, gave Murphy a poisonous look, and waddled out.

"I think you hurt his feelings," Donahue said.

"Fuck him . . ."

Corelli mimicked him. "Fuck him, fuck this, fuck that, you have a very limited command of the English language."

"You missed one," Murphy said. He grabbed Corelli by the back of the neck. "Fuck you!"

Corelli pulled himself free. "Hey, don't wrinkle the fabric, all right?"

He was wearing a white shirt with a wide collar, tight black pants that tapered at the waist, and he was carefully brushing a suede jacket that he had gotten for thirty dollars from Armando on Eagle Street.

Donahue slammed his locker door. "Will ya look at this guy. You know you take more time gettin' dressed than my wife, Corelli?"

Corelli bent slightly to comb his hair in the mirror on his locker door. "If that's a proposition, I'm already engaged."

"The man's got a heavy date tonight," Patterson said. "Which means the man's gonna score."

"The man's seeing his fiance tonight," Murphy said. "Which means the man's gonna get shut out."

Corelli advanced on Murphy with his fists clenched playfully. "Back up, Jim, you're talkin' about the woman I love."

"Love?" Murphy hooted. "You know what a Catholic school boy means when he says he's in love. He means he ain't gettin' any *cho cha*."

"No *cho cha* for de keed?" Donahue said.

"No *cho cha?*" Patterson said.

Murphy flicked an imaginary piece of lint off Corelli's jacket. "Not even a *cho* . . ."

Corelli looked Murphy up and down with disdain. "You scruffy Irish potato eater, what do you know about style? I'm givin' out a heavy message with these clothes."

"What's that?" Patterson asked.

"The message is . . ." Corelli dropped to his knees on the bench, and clasped his hands prayerfully. "Take me . . . please take me . . ." He sobbed feigned tears. "Three years we been goin' out. I'm gettin' lower back pain from all this anxiety."

"Aw, the poor baby," Donahue said.

"Please take me," Corelli moaned. "Somebody . . . anybody."

"We're gonna need a padded patrol car for this guy," Murphy said.

"Take it slow, Casanova," Donahue said on his way out.

"Don't get your zipper stuck," said Patterson.

Corelli called after them, "Go home, peasants. Go home to your humdrum, ordinary lives. I'm on the trail of love and adventure."

Donahue's cackling laugh resounded in the hall.

"And as for you," Corelli said, winding up as if he were going to paste Murphy, then slowing down and patting him patronizingly on the shoulder. "Try not to drink out the whole brewery tonight, okay, kid?" And he swaggered out.

Murphy smoked a cigarette and brooded about the nurse. Big tough cop, huh. He was getting palpitations at the thought of seeing her. Maybe it would be better to go home. Surprise Mary. Maybe catch her in bed with the oil truck guy. What a relief that would be. Murphy went into the bathroom, and checked himself out in the mirror. A broken-down cop, wearing a field jacket and a pair of baggy corduroys. What kind of message was he giving out?

26

By the time he got to the hospital, Murphy had a chip on his shoulder. He was convinced he was being set up; that cunt of a nurse had asked him out just so she could turn him down. Plus she was ten minutes late. He'd give her another five, and then cut out.

Then he saw her walking quickly down the driveway, wearing a black beret and a cloth coat, and he was overwhelmed by that same sadness he had felt before. How could she wear such a thin coat? She'd catch pneumonia. Murphy pushed the heat up in his car, and got out to wave to her. She waved back, and started running down the drive, but stopped as a big, black dude wearing a fur cap and a loden coat called her back for what looked like an urgent conversation.

"I didn't think you'd come," she said when she finally got down to the car.

"I had to break a date with Charley's Angels," he said, holding the door for her.

"I hope you don't regret it. Ooh, it's nice and warm in the car."

The black dude had followed her part of the way down the drive, and now stood there staring angrily at Murphy. Murphy stared back. "Who's that guy?"

"Oh, that's Frank," she said. "He's an orderly in the hospital."

"I didn't take him for a brain surgeon," Murphy said. He kept staring back at the guy. He'd stand there all night before he'd turn away. Nobody was going to mau mau him. The

131

guy finally nodded like he was remembering Murphy's face, turned, and bopped back up the drive.

"If I'm breaking up a little twosome here . . ."

"You couldn't care less," she said. "But don't worry, you're not. Now, are we gonna have that drink?"

"Sure . . ."

Murphy took her to the Emerald. As soon as he hit the door he knew it was a mistake. Morgan and Finley were at the bar with some of the younger guys off the tour. Morgan was holding court, telling the story of the stiff in the East River for the five millionth time.

"Two hundred pounds of chain around the body, and it still rose to the surface."

"It was the gases in the abdominal cavity," Finley said, belching.

It was crowded and smoky. Murphy thought he might get by them undetected, but Morgan saw him and weaved over.

"Hey, cowboy." He looked the nurse up and down, and gave Murphy a lewd wink.

"Hey, tough guy," Murphy said, maneuvering past him. "Let's go to the table in the back," he said, grabbing the nurse's arm and steering her through the dancers.

"Now he's goin' out with nurses, huh?" Finley said.

"Makes sense," Morgan said. "He catches something from her she can always cure it." He said it loud enough for Murphy to hear it, but Murphy made no response. "Let's send the happy couple a drink," he said, going back to the bar.

Murphy chose the last table in the rear, closest to the jukebox. "I like to sit with my back to the door," he said holding a chair for the nurse. "Okay?"

She shrugged. "Knock yourself out."

Lureen came out from behind the bar. She was wearing a bright red backless leotard, under which her breasts jumped like cats in a bag.

"Date night?" she asked with a scornful smirk.

Murphy ignored her. "What are you drinkin'?"

"Bacardi and Coke."

He looked up at Lureen. "Me too."

She raised her eyebrows. "No beer? What is it, your birthday?"

"Make 'em doubles," Murphy said.

The nurse lit a cigarette. "You won't get me drunk," she said.

"Wanna bet?"

"My money's on the lady," Lureen said.

Murphy glared at her. "You wanna join us?"

Lureen put her hand between those enormous breasts, looking like an offended dowager. "Well, excuse me," she said, and flounced off.

"Quite a lady," the nurse said.

"I don't understand it," Murphy said. "Every night she gives me the cold shoulder. Now, all of a sudden, she wants to talk."

"She's jealous," the nurse said.

"Oh, if you two have something goin' . . ."

The nurse slapped his wrist. "Of you, jerk . . ."

"Hey," Murphy raised a warning finger. "You can't call me a jerk until after we've gone to bed."

"I'd probably call you worse than that."

"You'd call me every day," Murphy said.

Lureen arrived with the drinks. "That'll be six dollars, C.O.D.," she said, still smarting from Murphy's rejection.

"Six bucks? What is this, the Waldorf Astoria?"

"You asked for doubles, Mr. Sport."

"I can pay for my own drink," the nurse said, reaching for her purse.

Murphy grabbed her hand. "Nah, it's okay." He put a five and a single on Lureen's tray. "Keep the change."

Lureen slammed Murphy's drink in front of him. "This is the one with the arsenic," she said.

Murphy raised his glass. "Here's to a long life and a quick death."

"I'll drink to that," the nurse said.

Even through the Coke the booze went down harshly. Murphy knocked back another swallow, just to get in practice. He could feel it irrigating the dry parts of his brain. Oh yeah, he was definitely going to get in trouble tonight.

"Boy, I feel smarter already," Murphy said. "You see, it's been a while since I had hard liquor."

"Oh yeah, what's the occasion?"

"Well, Isabella . . ."

"How'd you know my name?"

"I saw it on your name tag. Isabella Ortiz, R.N. Good detective work huh? What does the R.N. stand for, Rape Now?"

"Real Nasty," she corrected.

"I'm not surprised. Well, anyway, the occasion is this little date we're havin', if you must know."

"You mean you don't do this every night?"

"How about never?"

"Why not? You married?"

"Yeah," Murphy said, ready for a fight or a walk-out. "Does that make any difference?"

"If I was your wife, it might," she said.

"But you're not."

"That's right. So I don't care if you're a grandfather."

"We're just two ships that pass in the night," Murphy said.

The nurse raised her glass. "I'll drink to that, too."

Murphy drained his glass, and waved to Lureen. "The S.S. Isabella."

She returned his challenging stare. "That's right."

Lureen came by with the drinks. Murphy put the money on the tray, and she stuffed it quickly into her bosom. "Oh, by the way, this round was on your friend and colleague, Mr. Morgan. And I'm keepin' the change."

"That's petty larceny, you know," Murphy hollered after her. He took the nurse's hand. "So, mysterious lady, tell me something about yourself."

She took her hand away. "Why?"

" 'Cause that's what's you're supposed to do on a date, isn't it?"

"I guess so, but I don't like talking about myself. Let's start with you."

"I don't like talking about myself, either," Murphy said defensively.

"So we'll talk about two other people. I got it. We'll talk about that barmaid . . ."

"Hold it, I got a better idea," Murphy said. "I'll tell you about yourself, you tell me about myself, you understand? And the person who's right buys the next round."

"Okay," she said. "You start."

"Square business?"

"Tell it like it is."

134

"Okay." Murphy took the nurse's hand and gazed into her palm, nodding sagely. "Poor family. A lotta brothers and sisters. You're the oldest. You've got a brother in the joint. Your mother's sick, in and out of the hospital. You got a scholarship to nursing school and you did real good, but you can't get a job anywhere else." Murphy looked up at her, brow furrowed. "Or maybe you feel you have to stay in the barrio. How am I doing so far?"

She stared impassively at him, and shook her head.

"Poker face, huh? Okay. You smoke a little reefer, fool around a little. You oughta get married, but there's not much of a selection around this neighborhood. You spend too much time alone. How am I doing?"

"You finished?" she asked.

Murphy searched her palm. "I guess so. You go now."

The nurse sipped her drink. Her eyes behind the glass were angry, her hand trembled slightly. "You come from three generations of cops," she said, pointing with the swizzle stick. "Your grandfather, your father, your brothers are all cops. It's a good thing there are some lady cops, or you wouldn't have a sex life . . ."

"Hey, you can't accuse me of ballin' lady cops," Murphy said, good-naturedly.

"I'm not finished yet," she said. "You get drunk every night. You think all men are thieves and all women are sluts. You don't trust anyone but your partner." She broke off and looked questioningly at him.

"Looks like the drinks are on me," Murphy said.

"No," she said, "this is my round."

Ezio's Pizzeria was closing, but Corelli banged on the door, made a fist, flashed his shield, and finally got him to open up. He had gotten a bottle of cheap chianti on Southern Boulevard, but he needed the pizza. Teresa loved pizza. "Sausage, meatballs, mushrooms, anchovies, pepperoni, dandruff, throw a little bit of everything on there," he told the cook.

He drove out to her house. The light in her bedroom was on. He parked at the end of the block, so if her snoopy sister came home she wouldn't recognize the car. He'd planned everything. Tonight was definitely going to be the night.

135

Couldn't ring the bell because the whole, fucking, ugly hunchbacked family of hers would show up at the door. They'd eat his pizza, drink his wine, and wait for him to leave. They loved to break his *coulliones*.

He went through their garbage can, and came up with a can of Tab. Nice and empty and light—it wouldn't make too much noise. Tiptoeing to the top of the steps, he flipped the can against Teresa's bedroom window. It fell to the street with a tinny clatter. What a fucking racket. But still no Teresa.

He tiptoed back down to the garbage can, and got a nice big veal bone, which had been picked completely clean. That had to have been Teresa's mother: the woman sucked up food like an anteater. Gripping the bone at the end like a boomerang, he threw it against the window. It sounded like a fucking grenade. Any second now there'd be a radio car with two cops laughing their asses off . . .

The window opened. Teresa leaned out. Corelli ran to the top of the steps, brandishing the pizza box. "Teresa, look, I got pizza. Pizza . . ." That would get her down almost as fast as a diamond engagement ring.

In a second a light went on behind the door. Teresa opened the door a crack. "Andy, for God's sake, it's after midnight."

"I didn't come up here for a time check, Teresa." He pushed the door open, pinning Teresa to the wall with the pizza box. "Just let me come in for a minute." She was wearing that pink nightgown and no bra, so he could see her tits moving around like burglars behind a curtain.

"Andy, for God's sake," she whispered desperately, "my parents are sleepin'."

"I sure hope they are, otherwise I'll have to get three more pizzas."

"It's late . . ."

"I told you I was comin'," Corelli pouted.

"Yeah, I know, but I got tired."

"Aw c'mon, Teresa, if you don't wanna do nothin' how come you're wearin' that nightgown?"

"You want me to wear a cop's uniform to bed?"

"Just let me come in for a second. Please, please . . ." He gave Teresa a whiff of the pizza, then dropped to his knees. "Just a second, baby. I won't do nothin' wrong . . ."

She smiled down indulgently and tousled his hair. That

was the one thing about him she couldn't resist, his hair. She loved to comb it, play with it. Well, tonight he'd give her something else to play with.

"Okay," she said, "you can come in, but don't get crazy."

Corelli closed the door gently. "We're just gonna eat the pizza, I promise."

After an hour and about five drinks, Murphy got philosophical. "You know what's wrong with hangin' out in bars? You run out of conversation long before they run out of booze."

"So what do you do when that happens?" the nurse asked.

"You go home."

She lived on Evergreen Avenue in a renovated building a few blocks away from the devastation. Murphy left the motor running, and draped his arm casually over the back of the seat, barely touching her hair.

"Well, the moment of truth has arrived."

She shook back her hair, letting it fall over Murphy's hand. "Yeah. Well, thanks for the drinks."

"Any time."

"I guess I oughta be flattered that you're not making a move. Means you respect me."

"I don't go to parties where I'm not invited."

She opened the door. "You want an engraved invitation?"

Murphy reached around and closed the door. "What's this, a walk-up?"

"Afraid so," she said. "And I'm on the fifth floor."

"Well, let's get on that stairway to paradise."

"I don't think paradise is ready for you yet," she said. "Let's go to your place."

"I don't think my wife would understand. I'll tell you what we can do, though. We can join hands, and walk off into the sunset."

"What?"

"The Sunset Motel."

Murphy got on the highway, and drove across the Throgs Neck Bridge into Queens. The Sunset Motel was a cheater's place near Kennedy Airport. There were no traveling salesmen, no tourists, just errant spouses sneaking off for a quick one. The bar was dark, the lights in the parking lot were never on, and the desk clerk made a point of not looking at the guests.

The nurse waited in the car while Murphy registered. A gloomy red light flickered over the office door. A few men stood in line at the ice machine. Murphy came out walking jauntily, twirling the key around his finger. "Room 302. We ought to play that number tomorrow."

"Let's see how lucky it is for us tonight," the nurse said.

They got out of the car. "The Sunset Motel has seen better days," the nurse said.

"So have most of the people in the Sunset Motel," Murphy said. He reached for her hand, but she danced away, coquettishly.

"You got any other names aside from Murphy?" she asked.

"Don't get personal," Murphy warned.

"Remember you said that when we get to 302."

Murphy lunged and threw his arm around her shoulder. "John Joseph Vincent the Third. Satisfied?"

"Big name," the nurse said.

"Big man," Murphy said.

She stepped away and looked at him appraisingly.

"We'll see about that."

Murphy fumbled with the key. "I always have trouble finding the hole," he said. She made him nervous, just standing there watching. When she wasn't smiling or talking, her expression became sad again, as if everything else were only a momentary distraction from the great burden she carried within.

"There." Murphy finally got the door open, and made a courtly bow. "You want me to carry you over the threshold?"

"Save your strength," the nurse said.

The room didn't help you forget you were at the Sunset Motel. The bureau was chipped, the carpet frayed. There was one small closet, which was all that seemed necessary for a place where nobody stayed for more than a couple of hours. An old Admiral TV was on a rickety cart. There was a box of paper cups in the bathroom. The nurse threw her bag on the bed and went into the bathroom.

138

"Hey, they got one of those vibrating beds here," Murphy said.

She closed the door. "They never work."

"Aha," he said. "So you've been to places like this before."

"No, I'm a virgin. You're the first man I've ever been with."

"I can go down and get a bottle from the bar," Murphy said.

"If you need it."

Murphy was insulted. "I don't need nothin'."

She came out of the bathroom, holding her shoes and stockings, her uniform folded neatly over her arm. She draped it over the TV and dropped her shoes by the bed. She was just as naked and natural as if they had been married for twenty years. Murphy was startled.

"Isabella." Her name came out choked and ardent. She bent over to pull the covers back from the bed. "Put out the light if you're bashful," she said.

Teresa ate four pieces of pizza and had three water glasses full of chianti. And she was still hungry. "You want a piece of fruitcake? My mother made a great fruitcake."

"Your mother is a fruitcake," Corelli grumbled as Teresa went out into the kitchen. He had been lying there on his side on the floor of the living room watching her eat. She had turned the TV on; it was the first thing she did when she walked into any room with a TV. He'd have to remember to keep the TV out of their bedroom. She came back with the whole fucking fruitcake, and made him eat a piece. It was the real Italian kind, which tasted like somebody had stuck a few slivers of candied fruit on a chunk of cement. Her lips still glistening from the pizza, Teresa devoured the cake. She chewed like a dog, her jaws snapping fiercely. Oh, those glistening lips. He could picture them wrapped around his cock, those eyes bulging in avid surprise. Sure, giving head would be the last thing a chick like Teresa would do; but he would train her. It wouldn't take long. She'd take it all, and rub it on her tits.

"Oh . . ." Corelli groaned and rolled over onto his stomach.

"What's the matter, you sick?" Teresa asked.

."Yeah, yeah, I got a little *agita*. C'mere and sit on my back."

"You got gas?"

"Yeah, just sit on my back." He felt those warm thighs bestriding him, "That's it." She giggled and bent down, letting her breasts graze his back. "Feel better now?" That fucking cockteaser, he would get her for this. Stick two pillows under her ass, and shove it right in, no matter how much it hurt. Make her face China, and stick it up her ass until she screamed. Thrust it all the way down her throat until she gagged. Oh yeah, baby, payback is a bitch. What goes around comes around, and your day is comin'.

He reached around, and touched her buttocks. "Andy," she warned. His fingers strayed downward toward the forbidden area, sneaking in through the back door. She lay still, waiting for them to arrive, holding her breath. And then when they did, she sat up suddenly, and slapped his hand.

"Andy!" She jumped off him, and sat on the couch. "Not here. Not with my parents . . ."

"They're sleepin', Teresa."

"No, my father comes out every night for *brioschi*."

"Oh shit." Corelli rolled over onto his side. "If your father's stomach gonna screw up my sex life . . ."

"Andy." Teresa patted the cushions. "C'mere . . . please."

Pouting and putting on a great show of injured pride, Corelli sat next to her. She put her arm around him, put the other hand on his leg, painfully close. All he had to do was turn, and she'd have it right in her hand. Fucking cockteaser!

"Don't you think I want to?" she asked with adolescent seriousness.

Corelli looked away. "I don't know, do you?"

"I do, I do. But can't it wait until we're married."

"Wait?" Corelli took her hand. "You forget, I'm a cop. Any day I go to work could be my last."

"Oh, Andy, don't say that!"

"It's true. Why today I almost . . ."

Andy!"

"Five guys opened fire on us in . . ."

"Andy." She put her hand over his mouth. He smelled the pizza on her fingers. Her hand slid down to the bulge in his pants. "Promise you'll be quiet."

140

"Put your hands up," he whispered in her ear.

She raised her hands, and he slid the nightgown right over her head.

"Andy." She pushed him back, and kissed him, flicking her little tongue around inside his mouth. His hands closed slowly over her breasts while she unzipped him notch by notch.

From the very first moment Murphy knew it was going to be all right. He could fall over himself, be clumsy, come in twenty seconds, it wouldn't matter. He didn't have to perform, to fulfill any fantasies she might have about cops. This was going to be different.

They made love quietly, surely, as if they had been doing it for years. Afterward, she held him within her. She hugged him tenaciously, her thin arms surprisingly strong, and wrapped her legs around him. Later, she went into the bathroom, emerging with a wet towel, which she placed gently on his face, wiping the sweat off, kneading his cheekbones, sponging his neck, shoulders, and all the way down his body. Outside the cars roared by on the highway. Inside the radiator clanked and hissed. Those were the only sounds he heard. He lay back, his hands behind his head, watching her. She covered every inch of his body, slowly, patiently. Not like those broads who gave you a couple of half-hearted scratches when you asked for a massage. Then she rose up over him, her hair cascading over her shoulders. She was amazingly hard and soft—slim, sturdy shoulders, soft breasts that almost disappeared when she stretched her arms back. Her ribs stood out so prominently he could run his fingers down every one of them right to the shocking softness of her belly, the sharpness of her pelvic bones, the smoothness of her thighs. Hard and soft. Soft and hard.

Murphy's watch glowed on the night table. It was two-thirty. There was plenty of time. She nestled under his arm. He brushed the damp strands of hair off her forehead.

"You sleeping?" he asked.

"No, just thinking."

"What about?"

"You."

Murphy reached for a cigarette. "And what's the verdict?"

She laughed. "Does there always have to be a verdict?"

"There always is, ain't there? You like me, you don't like me. You think I'm good, you think I'm lousy. That's the way life is, right?"

She took a puff of his cigarette. "You've been a cop too long."

"Seventeen years."

"That long?"

"I'm an old man."

"Oh, I know that," she said playfully.

"Uh huh," Murphy squeezed her. "When you walk outta here bowlegged you can tell me how old I am."

"Mira, popi chulo over here," she said in a tremulous Spanish soprano. "Oh *popi, popi,* let go, I can hardly breathe." And then back to her natural voice. "If I walk out of here bowlegged, they'll have to take you out on a stretcher."

"What's a *chulo?"* he asked.

"A great lover."

"I fit that description perfectly."

"To a T." She took his head in her hands and shook it. *"Mira el conquistador.* You get it off with a chick, and right away you're ready to conquer the world."

"Yeah, us men are all alike, ain't we?" Murphy said. "We can all be replaced by a fourteen-inch electronic dildo."

"Mmm . . . sounds good," she said. "You don't happen to have one on you . . ."

He rolled her over, and tried to pin her arms. She fought back, giggling, but finally yielded. *"Ai, ai,* you hurt my wrist."

"I got an electronic dildo for you right here," he said.

She gave him a sly, wanton smile. "Well, let's take a look at it."

It was tough doing it on the couch, but Teresa was afraid to go upstairs. They'd have to pass her parents' bedroom, and the door was always open. The couch was covered in cellophane, and Corelli's arms and ass kept sticking. Teresa was surprisingly nimble. She handled it as though she were in the back of a car. She was a real make-out artist. She knew exactly how to maneuver. Corelli hadn't spent that much time in the back seat with her, so she must have learned it some-

142

where. She scrambled all over him as though he were a hill in Crotona Park. It was tough getting in; Corelli had to get on his knees on the scratchy carpet, and put her legs around his neck. He hadn't wanted to go down on her right away—"tame it with your dick before you claim it with a lick" had always been his philosophy—but she was tight and dry and nervous, and he could feel the skin shredding off his cock. She squealed like a stuck pig, and pushed his head in so close he was afraid he'd have to breathe through his ears. Then, she wouldn't let him out; every time he raised his head she pushed it back down in a reproving moan. That greedy cunt. He'd get even with her for this, too. When she finally came, you would have thought the house was on fire. She yanked on his ears, jumped and jiggled and screamed bloody murder. What happened to everybody having to be quiet? he thought. It was just a trick. The whole fucking family was in on it. The parents were probably crouching by the stairs, ready with the flash bulbs and the shotgun. That little teeny-bopper sister of hers, Angie, the one who slept in the bedroom in the back, was probably right outside the living room door jerking off with a salami. And Tony, the married brother, the *gavone*, who tried to pass himself off as a wise-guy just because he drove a private garbage truck, was out front with a baseball bat in case Corelli tried to split. That scumbag: he'd end up getting his ass kicked one of these days. Yeah, the whole family was in on this little scam. They wanted to make sure he was really locked in. Sure, perfect timing. A month to post time. A lotta guys chicken out in the final days, so they give him a little taste of the forbidden fruit and now he couldn't back down. Served him right for getting involved with these mountain guineas. They were shrewd, you had to give them that, but they couldn't run his life. He would cancel the wedding the day before, if he felt like it. Shit, he wouldn't show up at the church if he wasn't in the mood. But first he was going to shove it in so hard she'd wake up the whole neighborhood.

There! He spread her legs and plunged. Oh, beautiful; it was like sticking it into cold cream. Her eyes widened. She shook her head and nibbled on her finger.

"Oh Andy . . ."

She slid down on the couch until she was almost standing on her head. Fucking broads. They sat around and did

143

nothing all day long, but when they got into bed they were acrobats.

"You like it, Teresa," he said pushing harder.

"Andy!" She got a shocked expression on her face as if somebody had just dropped dead.

"Andy!" She dug her nails into his arms, and started rocking back and forth.

"Andeee . . ." She put his hands on her breasts, and arched her back. Her whole body was trembling. She wiggled and pushed as though she had an itch she couldn't scratch. And then she froze. She looked quizzically over his shoulder as if someone had come into the room, and gave out with such a shriek, he thought there was a burglar behind them.

He put his hand over her mouth. "Teresa, cool it."

But she was gone. Out of control. He could feel it himself. Jesus Christ, she had one of them talking pussies. They were one in a million. It opened and shut like a clam. And opened and shut, and opened and shut. Jesus Christ!

Teresa finally calmed down. She looked at him adoringly, and put his hand over her pounding heart. "Feel, Andy, feel that."

Corelli pushed up to get a better angle. He was going to explode, light up her insides like an aerial bombardment, like a fucking bolt of lightning.

"Yes, Andy, yes, baby," she urged, stroking his nipples. "Yes, now . . ."

He pumped harder and harder, and all of a sudden she stopped.

"Andy wait, please wait."

"What?"

"Andy, don't. I don't have anything. No protection."

"That's all right," he pleaded. "It's only a month away."

"No, no, please wait. I'll do it for you, I promise." She squirmed away from him, and he was out, humping the air. He felt a shooting pain in his rectum. That prostatitis again. That fucking cockteaser, he'd murder her for this.

She dropped to her knees next to him, and pushed him up onto the couch. "It's all right, honey, I'll do it. I'll do it for you," she whispered. She got between his legs and kissed it. God, she's a freak, he thought. She went all the way down on it, gurgling with glee. Up and down, up and down. He lay back waiting for the end. "Oh, do it, baby. Do it."

144

And then suddenly he was out again. He could feel the cold air. What happened?

Teresa reached under the couch, and produced a white handkerchief as if by magic. She wrapped the handkerchief around him and thrust it between her breasts. "Oh Andy, Andy . . ." She moved forward and backward, forward and backward. His joint was wrapped up as tight as a mummy. Forward and backward, backward and forward. Fucking cunt, she'd pay for this. He'd shove it down her throat, he'd . . . Oh Jesus, not this way. Oh shit! Shit, shit. Jesus, Jesus. Shit! Ah fuck it . . .

And then it was over. She sat between his legs, resting her head on his thigh watching his dying member with a smirk. Then she got up, gave him a quick, businesslike kiss on the forehead, and ran off to the bathroom.

Corelli checked the couch for blood. Nothing but a lot of slime. Her mother would be sitting on cooze for the next few weeks, that was something, anyway. Maybe, virgins only bled when the man came. Nah, that couldn't be. There had been other virgins, too, who hadn't bled. Or were they virgins? Maybe they had lied, too. Maybe all women were liars; it wouldn't surprise him.

And how about that handkerchief, the way she had it stashed in the couch and everything. How many times had she pulled that trick? Corelli picked it up gingerly. It was monogrammed, her father's initials. That was great. He'd come here to ball his old lady, and ended up coming in her father's handkerchief.

Corelli dozed on the couch. He knew he had to get up, and get out of there, but his limbs were like lead. All the wine and the excitement had really put him away. If he could just make it outside, the cold air would wake him up. Soon enough his bachelor days would be over, which meant that he'd be able to screw and sleep in the same bed. Corelli stretched contentedly. She was a freak, all right, a hot little mama after all. So what if she knew her way around a little? But the way she ate, after five years and a couple of kids she would be as fat as her mother, the flesh sagging off her like baggy stockings. She would sit in bed with a box of cookies, and watch TV. Ah, so what, she was a good kid. People were supposed to get fat as they got older. She would cook him macaroni every night, and they'd get fat together.

"Andy . . ." She was back on the couch next to him, stroking his belly. She wanted to do it again, right? Only what was she going to do this time, slam the door on it?

"Andy," she whispered insistently.

"What?"

"I'm glad we did it. Are you?"

"Glad we did what?" he mumbled sleepily.

"Wise guy." She slapped him sharply on the back, then snuggled under his arm. "Andy?"

"What now?"

"Did you enjoy it?"

"Yeah, it was all right."

She sat up, hurt. "Just all right?"

Corelli yawned. "Yeah, you know, there wasn't enough pepperoni on it and the anchovies tasted like shoe leather."

"Andy . . ." She slapped him on the back of the head. "I didn't mean the pizza. I meant me."

"Oh, you . . ." Corelli said. "Well, you were okay, but there wasn't enough pepperoni, and the anchovies tasted like shoe . . ."

"Shut up." She slammed the cushion down on his face, and climbed on top of him, managing to knee him in the groin while she was at it.

"Get offa me," he said, now fully awake. He lifted her in the air, and held her.

"Ouch, I'm gonna have black and blue marks." Then she squeezed his biceps. "Oooh, you're strong."

"Yeah, I'm strong." He put her over his knee, and gave her a resounding smack. "And I'm telling you something right now. After we're married, if I ever find a handkerchief under the couch I'm gonna give you a beating you'll never forget."

They held each other for a long time without speaking, immersed in their private thoughts. Then she laughed softly, amused by something, and kissed him.

"John Joseph Vincent Murphy the Third."

"You called?"

"J.J.," she said. "Yeah, J.J. That's what I'm gonna call you from now on."

"Murphy will be just fine if you don't mind."

146

"Okay, Moiphy," she said, imitating a Bronx accent. "Murphy, Murphy, the Irish cop on the corner."

"That's me." he said.

"How can an Irish cop work in a neighborhood like the South Bronx?"

"You think I can't understand these people? Lemme tell you a secret that no Irish cop will ever admit. The Irish are a lot like the Puerto Ricans."

"You won't find too many Puerto Ricans who'll admit that, either," she said.

"Well, it's true the Irish are the Puerto Ricans of England. They like to drink and dance and sing and make love. I'm talking about the ones on the other side. Something happened to them when they got over here. They became a bunch of tight-assed priests and bank tellers. Maybe they started making money for the first time, and it went to their heads. But back in the old country they get pushed around, people tellin' jokes about them and all. They don't even have their own country anymore, at least not all of it. That's amazing, come to think of it. They're more like the Puerto Ricans than I thought . . ." He broke off at the sound of her regular breathing. "I talked you to sleep, didn't I, baby?"

She murmured, and turned over, kicking the covers off. The room was like a furnace, the radiator blasting away. Murphy got up to see if he could turn it down; it was too hot to touch. It didn't make much difference. It was four o'clock, and they would have to leave soon anyway. He would let her sleep for a while, and then . . .

Murphy lit a cigarette. He played the match along her body, the legs so long, and . . . The match burnt Murphy's finger. He shook it out hurriedly, and lit another. He had seen something.

There was a cluster of tiny marks on her calf, along the vein. It was almost nothing; Murphy's attention had only been drawn because he'd seen those marks before in greater abundance on people's arms. A few tiny puncture wounds, and further down her leg, almost right to the ankle, there would be a few more. Murphy lit another match and sought them out. And then between her toes, also. Those who wanted to avoid detection injected between their toes. Maybe she did, maybe she didn't. Maybe she got down every day, snorting sometimes, skin-popping when she had a little more time, even hitting the main line once in a while. It didn't make a difference, because it was the last time he was going to see this chick.

Murphy stroked the nurse's hair. She smiled in her sleep, and reached for his hand, kissing it and pressing it against her cheek. He shook her gently. "Isabella, Isabella, get up. I gotta go home."

27

ALL DISABLED VEHICLES MUST BE DRIVEN OFF THE HIGHWAY.

It was a nightmare Arthur Michaelson had every time he drove by that sign. His car would suddenly, inexplicably overheat or stall, and some implacable cop would be standing by the exit waving him off the safe highway into the jungle of the South Bronx.

And now it was coming true. Just before he hit Jerome Avenue on the Cross Bronx Expressway he heard that metallic racket, and his car started to wobble. He had a flat. His rim was riding the road, going over the bumps and the potholes. If he rode on it too much longer the tire would be useless, but he couldn't pull over. There was that sign. They would come and tow him off, he'd seen them do it to the other cars. And once they towed you, forget it; the front end was never the same, everything got knocked out of shape. So, he pulled off at the exit, and rode all the way to Washington Street on his crippled rim.

Arthur Michaelson had been making this trip for years. This was the quickest way to get home to Great Neck unless he wanted to take the train, and you could just as easily get mugged in Penn Station at this hour as you could anywhere else. Arthur owned a restaurant in the garment district, and he liked to stay until closing, lingering at the bar, watching the checks, doing the totals. If he let the help run the joint they'd take every fucking nail out of the walls—he had learned that the hard way. Besides, this way he trained his wife to expect him in at about five every morning, on the off-chance that if anything did come up with one of the waitresses, he would have a built-in excuse.

It was usually a pleasant drive. There was no one on the road at that time of morning. In the warmer months he could see the blackened buildings of the South Bronx rising out of the dawn. Now, in the winter, they were only dark shapes. He could remember what it had been like living in the Bronx as a kid—the stores on Burnside Avenue under the El, Third Avenue and 149th, where his mother dragged him for special orthopedic shoes, the synagogue on Tiffany Street where he'd had his bar mitzvah. It was a reflective time for him. Riding home to a house full of aggravation, a wife who no longer interested him, a son who never came to visit, a daughter who wouldn't stop smoking pot, he thought of the simpler days of his childhood. What had Mama always said? "We had nothing, and we wanted for nothing." Those days were certainly gone forever.

Knock wood he had never had trouble on the road. He bought a new Caddy every two years; now it was a Seville. He paid for the luxury, and the dependability. He wanted to make sure he got where he was going and back without any trouble. Was that too much to ask when you forked over twenty-one thousand dollars? New tires; they hardly had eight thousand miles on them, and look where they'd stuck him.

Arthur Michaelson hadn't set foot in the Bronx in years. Not since he and his brothers had moved their mother out of her Morris Avenue apartment into the nursing home in Riverdale where she died six months later. There were no landmarks, everything was torn down. He had to peer up at the street signs to see where he was. Jesus, it was frightening. Trash-can fires burned in vacant lots, dark figures standing around them. They would take one look at the Seville, the cashmere coat, and they would cook him. All those gutted buildings. There were probably guys with knives lurking in every one of them. But he had to stop. It wouldn't get any better the further he drove, and he would ruin the axle if he kept going. He had to stop.

Arthur pulled over to the curb, and took his revolver out of the glove compartment. He had gotten a permit for it two years before when his place had been held up, and hadn't even fired it once. But he jammed the gun in his coat, ready to use it at the slightest provocation.

It was colder than a witch's tit. The wind stabbed through his coat. He buttoned it up to the neck and pulled his calfskin gloves on. He hadn't changed a flat for years, didn't know how to begin. Oh yes, chock the opposite wheel. Arthur found a jagged piece of rock on the sidewalk, and bent to place it under his front tire. There wasn't a soul around. Not a soul. Still, it was better not to make any noise. Don't drop the fucking jack, or anything. Do it quietly without drawing any attention.

"Hey lover, you wanna go out?"

He turned in terror, the rock raised over his head. A black girl in gold shimmered in the darkness. Her heels clicked on the sidewalk as she walked toward him.

"You don't wanna hit me with that, do you, honey?"

Where the hell had she come from? There weren't any other hookers around. She seemed to be alone. Arthur dropped the rock, and reached into his coat pocket for the gun.

"You wanna come party with me?" she asked softly.

It was a fucking mirage, it had to be. Here was this gorgeous girl standing there with nothing on but this gold lamé outfit. Shit, she was practically nude.

He took out the gun. "Are you alone?"

She laughed. "Alone? Baby, I'm the last woman on earth. Ain't nobody left but me. And you the last man."

She came closer, holding out her hand. Just another tacky hooker, that's all she was. Built, oh yeah, with the kind of body Arthur Michaelson had never been as close to as he was now. But he could see the smudges on her arms, the cheapness of her wig. Not that it really made any difference.

"How much?" he asked.

"Too much, baby. If I was sellin' it you couldn't afford a kind word, you dig. I'm givin' it away. It's free. Like me."

She took his hand. Her touch was warm. Stepping gingerly, she led him up the steps of an abandoned building. I'm crazy, he thought. I'm crazy. But he followed her into the building over the cracked parquet floor of what had once been the lobby, through an empty doorway into a room,

150

The debris was knee-deep. A mattress stood against the wall. There was a rickety chair in the middle of the room. Arthur could see his car through a hole in the wall, unlocked and vulnerable out there on the street. I'm crazy, he thought. Out of my mind. But he let her unbutton his coat.

"I'm gonna do it to you, baby," she whispered. "I'm gonna do it like nobody can."

She sat him down on the chair, and knelt between his legs. "Ain't nobody can do it like me," she whispered.

He leaned back as she unzipped his fly. Her hands were so warm. He could feel her breath.

There was a stirring. He looked down. She was rising slowly. Her eyes were as cold as a cat's. A razor gleamed between her teeth.

Before Arthur Michaelson could scream, she sprang up and drew her lips across his throat, cutting it from ear to ear. The blood gushed like water out of a fire hydrant. He watched through death-dimmed eyes as she spit the razor out, and stepped away. Then he sighed at all the blood on his cashmere coat.

28

Connolly couldn't sleep. Every time he closed his eyes, that crowded desk area flashed into his brain. The clamor, the chaos, all those desperate faces. It was only his first day, and he had a million conflicting impressions. One moment he felt an incredible surge of confidence—he would institute rational programs, discipline the men, set up quotas, reach out into the community, change the image of the precinct. He would turn the place around so quickly it would make their heads swim at Headquarters.

Then, in the next second, his optimism would deflate as he thought of the hopelessness of it all. The neighborhood was shot, and would take years to rebuild. The people were either despairing, enraged, or apathetic. Life was a series of petty frustrations for everybody up there; it was impossible to break the vicious circle. The cops in his command were cynical. Morale was low. They were just trying to get through the day with as little aggravation as possible. The murders of the rookies had lit a fire under them, but it wouldn't last. The investigation would drag on—no suspects, no arrests—and they would lapse back into their old habits again. Or the murderers would strike again. There would be a reign of terror. He would be inundated with transfer requests, the sick list would get longer, the newspapers would sensationalize the whole thing. The precinct would never lose its stigma. Somewhere in Florida, Dugan would be sitting with his fishing rod laughing vindictively.

Kathleen moaned in her sleep, and passed her hand over her forehead. She would wake up with a headache for the fourth day in a row. The doctor had suggested the eye mask, and also a cup of camomile tea before bedtime. Anything but those pills. Connolly had made her watch him flush the Valiums and the Seconals down the toilet. It would be painful, but it was necessary. A few more months with those pills, and she would have to be hospitalized. So now she slept lightly, near the surface of wakefulness. She awoke exhausted, haggard, wincing with headache, looking as if she were about to shriek with uncontrollable rage at any second. But with great effort she remained docile, even cheerful at times. You could sense the hysteria boiling underneath the calm. Her hair had thinned; blue veins showed on her cheeks and temples. Even now she was so sensitive that his wakefulness disturbed her slumber. His breaths, the way his body shifted; it was better for him just to get up, and let her sleep.

Connolly eased off the bed, and out of the room. He went downstairs past the children's rooms to the kitchen. The house was empty now. That was part of the problem. The doctor had explained it to him, then the police surgeon, then Father Buckley. Denny Junior was at Notre Dame; he had broken his leg in an intramural rugby game, but wouldn't let them come down to see them. Kathleen had worked and planned for months on Maureen's wedding. Then, at the last minute, she and her boyfriend had decided they wanted a different ceremony, completely outside the church, and had gone off to Boulder with a few friends. That was four

152

months ago; except for one postcard they hadn't heard from her, since. "The entry into middle years is a difficult period of adjustment for a woman," Father Buckley had said. "A woman without a career, like Kathleen, devotes her life to her children, basically. And then one day they leave her. She has no resources. Her husband is buried in his work . . ."

Buried in his work. Connolly sensed the rebuke in those gentle words. It was true enough. From the day he had put on the rookie's uniform, he had been obsessed with the Police Department. It was like no other job in the world. They gave you a badge and a gun and absolute power over your fellow man. "You are the guardians of civilization, of the American way as we know it," Mayor Robert Wagner had said at his graduation from the Academy. That wasn't just empty rhetoric, either; it was true. Without cops there was anarchy. They were a buffer between the constructive and destructive elements of society. As corny as that sounded, it was true, goddammit. What could be more rewarding, more deeply satisfying than a job of such importance? He had never understood the cynicism of most of the men he had met on the job. How could they cheapen themselves by malingering or taking graft? When he was first assigned to the Internal Affairs Division, he had been shocked by the cases he came across. Cops taking bribes from drug dealers, or even selling dope themselves. Cops shaking down storekeepers, tow truck drivers, abusing their sacred mandate for a couple of bucks. He had pursued them relentlessly, running every complaint, no matter how trivial, to the ground. Some were outright criminals, others were sick individuals whose values were warped, and others, like that Murphy, were good cops with bad attitudes. It was an attitude problem that had caused Murphy to lay dead drunk in a bathroom while his partner was shot to death. The man's record was good. He and his partner had more collars than any other team in the command. He had leadership potential, but he had remained in the Four-One all these years without trying to better himself. Men like that were incomprehensible to Connolly.

Connolly sat down at the kitchen table with his reports. He had put in a good fourteen-hour day, getting that crap off the walls, reading Dacey the riot act, making his presence felt in general. Yet, when he left at midnight he could almost feel the precinct starting to sag back into its stupor. If he could only motivate the men. Punitive leadership was never effective for very long. The men soon found a way to get around any sanctions. They made it a point to foil the commander. No, they had to be motivated in some positive way. A quick collar in these murders would be helpful, especially if it came on information supplied from within the ranks. Dacey's detective logic was repugnant to him. Trade one crime off for another. If there were people with information in the neighborhood, there had to be another way to get it out of them.

Of course, it was simple. Connolly put down the reports, trembling with excitement. There was a more direct and completely legal method of intimidation. It was known as arrest.

29

It was Applebaum's week to work the four-to-twelve. But when he got to the precinct he almost turned around and went home, convinced he had made a mistake. It looked like a Sunday morning after a summer Saturday night. Radio cars were parked at crazy angles in front of the precinct. Cops were horsing prisoners into the house. Veterans who wouldn't make a collar in a national emergency were dragging two and three guys out of their cars.

Applebaum looked at his calendar watch. No, it was Tuesday, all right. He stuck his hand tentatively out of the window. It had warmed up a little, but not enough to explain this craziness.

Inside, the precinct was a madhouse. Applebaum saw a few big numbers guys, the aristocrats of the neighborhood, in cuffs. And they were mad.

Augie "Joe Strunge" Bilardo was berating Tom Hennessy, a mild-mannered pot-bellied twenty-year man, who usually pulled his car to the Tiffany Street pier and watched the gulls for the duration of his tour.

"You think you're gonna get a bigger taste by pinching me, scumbag? Well, forget it, you're out."

And even stranger yet, Hennessy was trying to pacify him.

"Augie, I'm sorry, really. I had to, okay, but I'll take care of you, don't worry . . ."

Pantuzzi sat at the desk patiently writing up all the collars.

"What did they do, put LSD in the Budweiser around here?" Applebaum said.

Pantuzzi pointed toward the Captain's office. "Your presence is required, Seymour."

Applebaum fought his way to the locker room, and got into his uniform. Something told him to shave as well. Murphy was in the bathroom, bleary-eyed and irritable. "What the fuck's goin' on?" he asked.

"I don't know," Applebaum said, hurrying out. Then, hit with a second thought, he turned back. "Hey, Murphy, your brothers have a little grease downtown, don't they?"

"Maybe."

"Do you think they could pull me a transfer? I'll go anywhere, any house, any detail . . ."

Murphy rubbed the yarmulka on top of Applebaum's head. "How many members are there in the Emerald Society, Sarge?"

"About eighteen thousand."

"Well, that means about eighteen thousand guys'll get the jobs they want before my brothers start doing favors for rabbis."

"I'm not a rabbi, Murphy."

"Besides, what do you want a transfer for? I thought you liked it up here?"

"I got premonitions." Applebaum tapped his forehead. "Bad premonitions."

Applebaum went back downstairs and tapped timidly on Connolly's door, hoping he wouldn't be heard, and could sneak away to a quiet corner to eat his first bagel of the day. But Connolly's voice ended that pipe dream.

"Come in."

Connolly was at his desk going over the roster. Heffernan

155

stood behind him. He flashed Applebaum a quick look of foreboding and shook his head slightly.

"We're making some changes, Sergeant," Connolly said. "I'm not satisfied with the production up here."

"Production?"

"Number of arrests per man per tour," Connolly said. "So starting today we'll switch three of the most productive teams on each tour onto anticrime. Plainclothes, unmarked cars, no specific sectors."

"I don't think that'll really make much difference, Captain," Applebaum said. "The people up here know a cop when they see one. A coupla white guys drivin' around in a beat-up old Plymouth aren't going to fool anybody."

Connolly looked at Applebaum in amazement. "You are the most argumentative subordinate I've ever come across, Applebaum."

Applebaum didn't flinch or apologize. "Just trying to give you the benefit of my thirteen years' experience up here, Captain."

"If I need it, I'll ask for it. Now what you can do is suggest three radio teams we can put on this new assignment."

"Well, Murphy and Corelli are pretty responsible."

"Responsible?"

Heffernan made a face and raised a warning eyebrow, but Applebaum blundered ahead.

"Well, I mean they answer every call in their sector."

Connolly's knuckles whitened around his pencil, but his voice stayed calm. "Every officer in this precinct is supposed to answer every call in his sector, Sergeant. If he doesn't, the sergeant in charge has to write up a complaint."

"I know, sir," nodded Applebaum mechanically. He wasn't in that office. He wasn't listening to this Nazi. He was meditating. The Talmud says, "He who is abused and turns away, spares himself further abuse." Applebaum turned away. From now on he would dedicate himself to getting out of this precinct. Everything else would have to take a back seat.

"I suggested Lynch and Sullivan for this detail, Seymour," Heffernan said, trying to change the subject. "They're young guys and ambitious and all."

"Ponce and Nieves would be good, too," Applebaum

156

said. "They're the only Spanish guys we've got on the tour. At least they'd look more natural in the neighborhood."

Connolly looked them up in his personnel file. "I don't care about their nationality, just as long as they're productive."

Applebaum nodded, and said, "Yes, sir." He wasn't going to argue anymore. He wasn't going to do anything but get out of this precinct.

"All right, Sergeant, Ponce and Nieves are a good choice. Announce it to the men today at the turnout. I've gotten three unmarked cars from Borough. We'll also need at least two vans for prostitution arrests."

"And for the cockfighters, too," Heffernan said, eager to explain and smooth things over. "One of the problems we have is the sheer number of men involved when you bust a cockfight."

"Then let me see if I can squeeze a few more vans out of them." Connolly reached for the phone. He gestured impatiently. "All right, that's all."

Outside Connolly's office, Applebaum grabbed Heffernan. "We gotta break this hoople in, Loot."

"Forget it, Seymour." Heffernan pointed out into the chaotic desk area. "See that? This tight-ass is makin' a career move on our backs, and there's nothing we can do about it. He started this anticrime thing on the eight-to-four. Made a speech, too; he'll probably make one on our turnout as well. He wants arrests, he says. We'll be up to our fuckin' eyeballs in paperwork inside of two weeks."

"So then we gotta leave the sinking ship," Applebaum whispered urgently. "Do you have any grease to get me a transfer?"

"If I could, don't you think I would have used it myself?" Heffernan said.

Applebaum clutched his arm desperately. "I'll pay, Loot. I'll pay plenty to get outta here."

"Who wants us, Seymour?" Heffernan straightened Applebaum's tie. "You're a fat slob with a funny hat, and me? I've been up here so long I'm part of the furniture."

"Okay, okay, you're right. I'm a slob, and you're a has-been."

Heffernan was taken aback. "You don't have to put it so bluntly."

157

But Applebaum was in no mood for niceties. "So that means if we can't get out, then we have to get him out."

"It's the man's second day on the job, and you're trying to get him out," Heffernan said. "Give him time, he'll screw himself. They're all waitin' for him to fuck up anyway. That's why they put him up here in the first place. Give him time."

"No, no, you don't understand." Applebaum walked away, shaking his head. "There's no time."

Fifteen minutes later Applebaum faced the four-to-twelve. He had to shout over the din at the desk area. The men from the previous tour were still trying to get their prisoners booked. They were on unauthorized overtime, which meant they probably wouldn't get paid, and they were mobbing the desk, yelling at Pantuzzi to hurry up. Pantuzzi was doing a double tour, and was in absolutely no hurry. No amount of cajolery or abuse could speed him up.

"All right," Applebaum shouted after roll call. "The boss wants production . . ."

"Production?" Patterson said. "What's that?"

"Let him make a movie if he wants production," Finley grumbled.

The men were agitated. They had been talking to the guys on the eight-to-four. It seemed that Connolly had made the Lieutenant run a uniform inspection and most of the men had been caught in irregularities during roll call. No ties, no hats—one guy had even been caught wearing brown shoes.

"Arrests is what he means," Applebaum shouted. "So we're taking a few anticrime units out of each tour. You guys'll be plainclothes, unmarked cars, Lynch and Sullivan, Nieves and Ponce, Murphy and Corelli . . ."

"Corelli don't have no plain clothes," Murphy said.

Applebaum sagged. He was going to get *tzures* from these guys, with all these new programs. "So let him wear a tuxedo, what do I care. The idea is to make a lot of good collars, okay? That's production."

A few of the men looked over Applebaum's shoulder. The Captain was standing in the doorway. "May I have a moment, Sergeant?" he asked.

Applebaum stepped back and Connolly moved forward to address the men. The noise in the desk area abated as he

158

started to speak. Even the prisoners wanted to hear what he had to say.

"The Department isn't good at official introductions, so this is it. I'm Dennis Connolly, the new commander. In the weeks to come I hope to get to know each of you men personally, to discuss your duties and your plans for the future . . ."

"I don't believe this asshole," Corelli whispered.

"Somebody better wake Morgan up," Donahue hissed between his teeth. They all looked down the line at Morgan, who was dozing against the wall, still drunk from the night before.

"For the time being, however, I'll have to be more impersonal," Connolly was saying.

"If he starts to snore, shove him," Patterson said.

"I'm going to be making some innovations in procedure, and I want to explain them all to you myself," Connolly said. "Now . . ." He stopped, waiting until he had everyone's undivided attention. Morgan started to slide down the wall, but Finley grabbed him in time.

"Two distressing situations exist hand-in-hand, and I think we can take steps to resolve both of them. The first is the murder of the two rookies. I happen to feel, and I'm sure you all agree, that a cop killing must be cleared immediately, even if extraordinary measures must be taken to clear it. We have to reestablish respect for the police in these areas, and the best way to do that is to show that we take care of our own."

"He's going," Murphy whispered as Morgan started to slide again. Finley and two guys in the back line grabbed him, but his nightstick slipped through his fingers, and bounced three times off the hard floor before it came to rest and began rolling down the slight incline toward the wall. Morgan was awake now and alert; he smiled sheepishly at Connolly.

"Pick it up, Patrolman," Connolly said quietly.

Morgan retrieved his nightstick, and staggered back to the ranks.

"Nightsticks aren't required on radio patrol," Connolly said.

"I find it to be an effective weapon," Morgan mumbled, trying to look serious and businesslike.

"What did he say?" Murphy said, smothering a laugh.

159

Connolly looked sternly at the men. "If I may continue." Again he waited for silence. The men shifted awkwardly under his scrutiny. "Another problem we have in policing this community is our disregard for many of the crimes that are committed here. Victimless crimes, the press has taken to calling them. The people up here don't agree. Captain Dugan had on file scores of letters from community and church groups protesting the presence of prostitutes in certain areas, the blatant practice of cockfighting, dogfighting, and other forms of gambling . . ."

"I never seen no dogfighting, did you?" Corelli whispered.

"Wherever it is, I got twenty on the Doberman," Patterson said.

"All of you know of criminal situations that exist," Connolly said. "Up until now you've looked the other way. People in the community think that you've been bribed, which may be true in some isolated cases. But the majority of you are either too lazy to enforce the law, or you've taken it upon yourselves to decide what is a crime, and what isn't. Well, that isn't your job. Everything from double parking to homicide is a crime, and is dealt with in the penal code. Your job is to enforce that code, and nothing else."

"Corelli had a penal code once," Murphy whispered. "Couldn't get a hard on for weeks."

Corelli tried not to laugh, but he hadn't stood in line like this for a lecture since somebody dropped cherry bombs in the toilet at Holy Name grammar school, and the monsignor had lined them up to make them confess. Somebody had broken him up then, and he had gotten in trouble, and it was happening again.

"What did you say, Murphy?" Connolly asked calmly.

Smart cocksucker, Murphy thought. He knew we were kiddin' around all the time. "I only said that if a cop goes around with his nose buried in the penal code in any place in New York City, let alone the Forty-first precinct, he's gonna make a lot of collars that won't stick, give out a lot of summonses that'll make a lot of people mad at him. He's gonna be one busy little police officer."

"Which is exactly what I want him to be," Connolly said. "Now if you're averse to a little hard police work, you can stay in and clean out the shithouses until your retirement."

160

"Thank you, sir," said Murphy with a perfectly straight face.

Corelli had almost managed to compose himself, but this set him off again. He bit down hard on his lower lip as Connolly continued.

"Starting today, I'm gonna want you men to make arrests. I want you to go through your sectors, hitting every criminal activity you're aware of, making arrests on complaints you would generally ignore. Every suspect we bring in will be questioned by the squad for any information on the murders. We'll bring them in, book them, toss them, and see what they spit out. And we won't stop until we get a lead. You can see how I hope to combine my two objectives, improve day-to-day precinct operations, and clear the murder with one program." Connolly paused to see how they were taking it. Some, like Morgan, were feigning attention, trying to look serious. Murphy stared straight ahead with that bored, cynical, heard-it-all-before cop look, just waiting for him to finish. His partner Corelli seemed to be having a coughing fit, or was he covering up a fit of laughter?

"Now I don't expect something for nothing from you men. I don't expect instant motivation. So I'm offering a deal. You collar someone who gives us useful information, and you get a week added to your vacations . . ."

There was a noticeable stirring in the ranks at this offer. The men looked at Connolly with real interest. "Two leads, two weeks, and so on. Call it bribery, call it dedicated police work . . . Just get out in the streets, and bring in those cop killers. I won't question your motives. That's all."

He turned back, but Murphy's voice stopped him in his tracks.

"Would you mind explaining what you mean by a lead, Captain?"

This son of a bitch was a barracks lawyer, a troublemaker. He would have to be gotten rid of. "I would think a police officer of your experience would know what a lead was, Patrolman Murphy."

"Well, sir," Murphy said, with mock thoughtfulness, "would it have to be a lead that led directly to the apprehension of the murderers? Or perhaps a piece of general information that when combined with other pieces of general information resulted in the identification of the suspects . . ."

"Don't split hairs with me, Murphy. You and every other man in this house knows that the solution to these crimes is out there in the street." Connolly could feel his voice rising. He planted his feet and lowered his head like a bull about to charge, but managed to fight off that hot surge of anger. Stay in control, he told himself. You must stay in control. "What I'm telling you to do is go out and get it. Every piece of relevant information will be rewarded." He stared straight at Murphy. "Any questions?"

There was a silence. "All right, Sergeant," Connolly said. "Put 'em to work."

"Better get out those travel folders," Donahue said as the men headed for their cars.

"Wonder what Bermuda is like this time of year?" said Patterson.

"You'll never find out," Murphy said.

"Why not?"

"Because this was all just a trick to get us to make collars, so his stats'll go up, that's why."

"Ah c'mon," Corelli said, "you gonna be paranoid all your life?"

"You think he's gonna get permission to add a week or two on to thirty guys' vacations, asshole?"

"It's an incentive program," Applebaum said, passing them by. "It's been done in other houses."

"There, you see," Corelli said. "Now who's the asshole?"

"He's smart," Murphy said. "I gotta give him that . . ."

"Hey, the great Murphy bestows a compliment," Corelli said.

"He gets out there, and talks our ears off. He knows cops have a short attention span. After about five minutes their minds begin to wander . . ."

"Speak for yourself," Patterson said.

"Oh, right, I forgot you were a nuclear physicist in your spare time. For the rest of us dodos the technique is perfect. He talks and talks and the only thing we remember is arrests and vacation time. We forget about all the fine print."

"Man, you are the most paranoid motherfucker," Patterson said.

Corelli slapped him five. "Ain't he, though. I'm telling you the man's got a problem."

"My problem is I'm surrounded by assholes," Murphy said.

"Then you must be a piece of shit," Morgan said, coming out of his stupor.

"Please, no profanity," Corelli said. "This is important. The man has a basic conflict with authority which stems from an unsatisfactory relationship with his father . . ."

Murphy grabbed him by the collar. "C'mon, Dr. Joyce Brothers, let's go fight crime."

"Can I make a weewee first?"

30

The men hit the streets with a vengeance. They went right to the felony areas in their sectors. The blocks around Hunts Point and the Bronx Zoo where the hookers cruised. The sneaker warehouse on Simpson that was burglarized almost every other day, the moldering tenements that were constant targets for arsonists. Each team had a few special locations. Some had a big-numbers banker working out of an apartment, or a garage in which stolen cars were stripped. Some knew about a block near the subway where the muggers lurked to catch the people coming home from work. Most of these would be cheap collars, and, like Murphy said, they wouldn't stand up. In some cases the perps would make the low bail, and just split the neighborhood, not bothering to make the court appearance, and waiting a few weeks until the bench warrant had been issued and their old hangouts checked before they returned to recommence their operations. Most of these people wouldn't know anything about the killings of the rookies, but the smart ones would catch on that information could buy them out of the pinch, so they would start making things up. Which was fine with the cops. The boss had said he wanted arrests and information. Well, he would get them both. And the men would get their vacation time; he would have to give it to them whether the information checked out or not.

But they found the streets unusually quiet. The eight-to-four shift had been there before them, motivated by a similar deal. The hookers who worked the market had either been collared or chased off the streets. For the second day in a row, street business in numbers and drugs had been curtailed, this time by the rampage of the eight-to-four tour. Bars and *bodegas,* where you could place a bet or buy a loose joint, were suddenly very respectable.

The cars roamed the streets like predators, pouncing on every infraction they saw. A few hapless junkies were caught in the net. Donahue and Patterson drove up the stairs into Crotona Park and sped, with sirens wailing, right up to the handball courts to catch a guy dropping off a few bags of dope. Morgan and Finley had been watching a guy selling loose joints out of a Sabrett frankfurter stand on Westchester Avenue for several weeks, trying to figure out whether to pinch him, shake him down, or just give him a workout and chase him out of their sector. Now, they collared him. There were five pounds of grass in the cooker where the hot dogs usually were. Morgan and Finley vouchered three for evidence, and saved the other two. Later on in the evening, when a stoolie sent them to a building on Boone Street where he said they were selling grass and angel dust in the hallway, they flaked the guys they found there with the remaining two pounds.

Ponce and Nieves cruised the area looking for fancy cars. They finally saw a metallic silver Coupe de Ville and a tan Continental double parked in front of a hardware store. It had to be a drop, a meet—something. They sat around for an hour, and when nobody came out, they called a 10–13, the assist to patrolmen signal, into the precinct, and hit the hardware store with guns drawn. Four mafia guys were sitting around a table in the back going through a pile of numbers slips. They looked up, mildly annoyed at this intrusion. Sirens throbbed in the distance as several radio cars sped to the officers' assistance, but the four men put up no resistance.

"You got a warrant?" one of them asked as they cuffed him.

"No."

"Then this pinch won't stand up."

"We know."

"Is this a shakedown?" another guy asked.

"No."

"Well then, what the fuck are you wasting our time for?"

"Just doin' our jobs, mister. Just doin' our jobs."

Murphy and Corelli had started out in a dirty gray Plymouth with no shocks, one of the unmarked vehicles the Borough had supplied. "Fuck it," Murphy said, "we're gonna need something bigger than this." They returned to the precinct, and picked up an asthmatic old police van.

"Let's go on the pussy posse, first," Corelli said.

They drove over to the Hunts Point market where at least twenty or thirty hookers could be found every day, taking a ride around the block with the truck drivers, or the businessman who stopped off for a quickie before heading home to Westchester. There wasn't a soul around. The truckers sat forlornly in the cabs of their semis; a few late-model sedans cruised up and down the street.

"The other guys must have taken them all off the streets," Corelli said.

Murphy squinted out of the window. "They'll be back. The night shift, you'll see. The pimps'll send 'em out."

They drove around for a while.

"It's dead," Corelli said.

"Yeah . . ." Murphy turned down Wilkins Avenue. "There's a guy in a phone booth selling bags. I see him almost every day."

The guy wasn't there. A few junkies were standing in the lot across the street, each of them alone, standing apart from the others. They stood there blowing on their hands, smoking, shrugging in their thin jackets, waiting for the connection.

"Poor bastards," Corelli said.

Murphy thought of the nurse. She could be standing on some corner somewhere. Or was she ballin' a doctor to get it?

"I wonder what happens to these fuckin' people," Corelli said. "They don't all die or go to the joint."

"Did you ever see an old junkie?" Murphy said.

"I don't know," Corelli said. "If they're not young, and

blowin' their noses and scratchin' their faces while they try to sell somebody a TV, or if they ain't layin' dead in a pad somewhere with the point still in their arm, I can't recognize them."

"Me neither," said Murphy. All the years he'd been a cop he would never have thought that a girl like her . . .

"Looks like we're gonna have to collect some favors if we wanna get any time off," Corelli said.

Murphy floored the van and skidded into a U-turn. The junkies in the vacant lot watched impassively. "Let's hit Armando first."

Armando ran a hot clothing store out of two apartments on Eagle Street. He had the best designer brands, Pierre Cardin, Yves St. Laurent, Bill Blass, suits, blazers, and slacks hanging on racks around the apartment. "Factory rejects," he blithely called them, and that was good enough for the cops who shopped there, paying forty dollars a suit, and twenty-five dollars for the Bally shoes that he had in boxes stacked to the ceiling. The only drawback was you had to arrange for your own alterations.

Corelli, the clothes horse, was a steady customer. "I hate to do this," he said.

"Think of all the weeks added to your honeymoon," Murphy said.

"Ah, he owes me a favor anyway, all the suits I've bought off him. Maybe we oughta call him first, so he can get somebody to move some of his inventory for him."

They pulled over. Corelli jumped into a phone booth and came back a minute later.

"He's cool. I told him he was gonna have to take a pinch. He says we should come over. Maybe, just to make amends, I'll buy a pair of shoes or something."

"I'll bet that fat fuck's heard something about the killings," Murphy said.

"Hey, be nice, will ya? That's my haberdasher you're talking about."

"The guy's a fuckin' fence, Andy," Murphy said.

"Who's he hurtin'?" Corelli said. "Those fuckin' designer clothes cost too much anyway. You just don't like him because he don't carry any Lew Magram leisure suits."

Armando left the door open for them. He was on the

phone when they came in. "I'm just calling my lawyer, fellas. Be with you in a second."

Armando was a fat, swarthy Cuban with rings on every finger and a gold chain around his neck. His apartment was jammed with clothing racks and shoe boxes. He was watching a soap opera on a huge color TV.

"I gotta get some guys over here to move some of this stuff," Armando said. "You know I don't want you to seize the whole joint . . ."

"Oh no, oh no," Corelli said apologetically. "We just have to take a rack. You know we wouldn't be doin' this at all if it wasn't because of this lunatic new commander we got . . ."

"Yeah, I heard about him." Armando offered cigars, which both men shook off, so he lit one for himself. "He's bustin' the whole neighborhood."

Murphy prowled the apartment. Suits, shirts, shoes— expensive stuff. In one of those shoe boxes he wouldn't be surprised to find a couple of ounces of pure heroin. Armando had quite an operation, all right. Seven years in the same location, and he had only been arrested once before. Rumor was that he'd been a big drug dealer who had cooperated with the D.E.A., and was given this as a reward. There was no doubt he was under somebody's protection. His was the ideal place for a stickup. Yet in a neighborhood full of people desperate for money, it had never been hit; at least, not officially. Through the years an occasional dead body or two had popped up in the vacant lot across the street, or down the block under the El, all stripped clean of money and identification, all shot neatly in the back of the head. Who knew, maybe Armando had a few wise guys as partners. Maybe a few cops.

"Know anything about those cop killings yesterday?" Murphy asked, turning suddenly on Armando.

Armando puffed placidly on his cigar. "Nah, nothin'. I'm real sorry about those two boys, though." He winked at Corelli. "Shit, cops are my best customers."

Murphy took one stride, and knocked the cigar out of Armando's mouth. "I can't hear you with that turd in your mouth, Armando."

"Hey, Murf," Corelli protested.

Armando got up to confront Murphy. "You'd better watch your hands, mister."

Murphy shoved him back down. "Sit down, tons of fun, and don't try to tell a cop what to do."

Corelli stepped between them. "Hey Murf, you crazy or what?"

"I think he knows something, Andy," Murphy said. "I think the fat fuck heard something yesterday."

"I didn't hear nothin'," Armando squealed. He tried to get up, but fell back over the chair, and landed heavily on the floor. Murphy sidestepped Corelli and kicked him in the side. "You're lyin', Porky."

Armando clutched his side and whimpered, "Get him off me, he's nuts. I didn't hear nothin', I don't know nothin'. I got a bad heart. This guy's gonna kill me."

"Lay off him, Murf," Corelli said through clenched teeth.

"Why don't you go talk to that creep across the hall if you want to get something on this case," Armando whined.

"Who's this?" Murphy asked.

"That prick across the hall in 1B." Assisted by Corelli, Armando labored to his feet, and brushed himself off. "He's been dealin' guns outta there for weeks. I've been watin' for somebody to bust him."

"Dealin' guns?" Suddenly, Murphy's attitude changed. He put his arm around Armando's shoulder and pinched his quivering jowls. "Why didn't you drop a dime on him yourself, cutie pie?"

" 'Cause I didn't know who he was connected with," Armando grunted resentfully. "He walks around here like he owns the joint. He brings chicks in and out. Acts real mean, like he's stoned on downs all the time. Blasts his fuckin' stereo at all hours . . ."

"Didn't he ever hear of the good neighbor policy?" Murphy patted Armando's cheek. "You know, I think you are gonna have a heart attack. Now why don't you just arrest yourself, and take a little walk out to the van in front. We'll bring you some company in a little while."

"Don't tell him I gave him up," Armando said, suddenly frightened.

"Don't worry," Murphy said. "We'll tell him we're from the Bureau of Noise Control."

Murphy and Corelli stepped out in the darkened hall, and walked stealthily toward 1B.

"What were you pickin' on that guy for?" Corelli whispered.

Murphy hissed back vehemently, "He's got a fuckin' attitude. I don't like seein' a dirtbag like that rollin' in dough while I can hardly make the rent every month."

"He's takin' the risks, ain't he? He don't have no cock-knockin' Civil Service job like you do, you know . . ."

Murphy was astonished. "You actually respect a guy like this . . ."

"So what if I do?"

"I guess that's just part of your Italian heritage."

Corelli raised his voice angrily. "Don't go gettin' ethnic with me, potato head, or I'll slap the shit outta you."

"You couldn't slap the shit out of a squirrel."

Armando came out of his apartment buttoning his overcoat. "I'm going to the van now," he announced with a hurt look.

Murphy waved him out of the door, and turned back to his partner. "You wanna take this gun dealer outta here, or you wanna fight?"

Corelli headed for the door of 1B. "I'll deal with you later."

"Hold it." Murphy grabbed Corelli's arm. "The guy ain't blastin' his stereo."

"So?"

"So maybe he's just sittin' behind the door with an M–60."

"In that case I think I'd rather fight," Corelli said.

"Funny man." Murphy walked down the hall under the stairs to the garbage cans. He brought one back, and dumped a load of garbage in front of the door, muttering as he spread it.

"All I want is a little respect from these mutts, you understand? I don't want them treatin' me like an equal. This guy's too familiar. He's just a fat, fuckin' fence when you come right down to it, I don't care who he knows."

"All right, all right, all of a sudden you want respect. I mean I've known you to take a few dollars in your time."

Murphy dropped a match on the pile of trash. "I don't

care. I'm still better than these guys. So's any cop, any schmuck with a shield as far as I'm concerned."

The garbage started to burn, sending a cloud of black, acrid smoke into the air. Murphy and Corelli stepped on either side of the door, their pistols out, their arms over their noses.

"Fire," Murphy called shrilly.

"Fire," Corelli echoed, imitating a woman's voice.

"*Fuego,*" shrieked Murphy.

"Nice touch," Corelli said admiringly.

By now the garbage was starting to crackle as flames shot out of its soggy mass. The door to 1B opened suddenly. Murphy and Corelli sprang forward, and a thin, nude girl with black hair right down to her buttocks came running out, screaming in panic. She was followed by another nude girl, this one a little heavier, whose huge breasts bounced so much they threatened to topple her into the fire.

"This guy does all right," Corelli said. A tall wiry dude wearing black bikini underpants and waving a .357 Magnum came sprawling through the smoke, coughing and cursing. Murphy and Corelli stepped back so they wouldn't catch each other in a crossfire.

"Freeze, motherfucker," Murphy shouted.

"Don't turn around, hands up, faggot," Corelli shouted.

The gun dealer turned his head, and Corelli slapped him with the barrel of the gun. "I told you not to turn around, faggot."

The dealer's head lolled back, and his knees buckled. Murphy grabbed the gun out of his hand before he fell. Corelli stamped on the fire as Murphy cuffed the semiconscious dealer. "Where'd those broads go?" he asked, squinting through the smoke. When they got out into the street with their prisoner, the girls had disappeared.

"Did you see the knockers on that second one?" Corelli said. "Hey, you." He shook the gun dealer, who was just beginning to come around. "Tell me that chick's name, and I'll go inside and get you a pair of pants and a coat. Or else you're gonna ride to the precinct in the altogether."

Chino had set himself up for the buy. It had only taken a few hours of conning Jose, feeding him Cuba Libres, and dropping the names of all the big dealers from the Lower

170

East Side that he knew. He told Jose about their Rolls-Royces, the beautiful chicks they hung out with, the discos they secretly owned, all the land they had bought in P.R. Sure, he knew them. Hadn't he busted them all? A kilo of "pure" heroin. Three hundred and fifty thousand bucks. Not the biggest buy in history, but imagine carrying a suitcase with thirty-five hundred hundred-dollar bills down Eldridge Street at three o'clock in the morning. Guys on roofs with high-powered rifles. Two back-up teams on both corners of the street. Undercovers slouching in doorways. Everybody watching you, waiting for you to make the buy. Walking down the hairiest block on the Lower East Side, looking like any ordinary street hustler. Only with three hundred and fifty Gs. And what if a couple of guys had decided to take him off? They would have had the shock of their lives as thirty cops descended on them. But nobody bothered him, and he walked right into the back room of Juanito's Tavern past all the muscle at the bar, the guys with the Magnums and the 9-mms in their belts, where the three dealers were waiting. They were the biggest, and they were cool. Chino respected them. They dressed conservatively, were soft-spoken, never made threats. And they had the goods. A cellophane bag of white powder that they dumped on the table, after they'd counted the money and checked to see if it was counterfeit. They had a scale, but Chino, playing the paranoid dealer to the hilt, had brought his own. And he weighed the dope carefully, thinking all the while, I came in with three and fifty Gs, but I'm walking out with about four million. I'm a fucking star. There wasn't a sound in that room. They watched him fiddling with the scale. And then he was gone. There was a handshake, a promise to keep in touch, and he was out that door with a kilo of "pure." Right through the bar and onto the street. Nolan and Fabrizio hardly let him clear the door before they hit the joint. They took everybody —the bartender, the porters, even the super of the building who just happened to be having a beer at the bar. Over thirty cops piled into that saloon. They caught the three guys in the back room splitting the bread. It was a dream bust. There were two inspectors and a Fed from Washington in a trailer monitoring the operation. The reporters and TV guys got there almost as fast as the paddy wagons. They laid out the dope, the weapons, and the money for the cameras. Everybody's name got mentioned in the papers. Except Chino's. He got a handshake from the inspector, and a plaque, a fucking plaque from the D.E.A., signed by the President. A three hundred and fifty thousand dollar buy, and they give him a plaque which his mother put up on the mantle next to his high school graduation picture.

And as for the targets, the dealers they had spent so much time and money to apprehend: the Cruz brothers managed to get their bail reduced to two hundred and fifty thousand cash. Suarez had a homicide warrant on him, so his bail stayed at half a mill. The three of them made the cash bail as easily as if they were buying a movie ticket. Then, with teams of men on round-the-clock surveillance of them, they all disappeared. For all Chino knew, they could be a block away from him right now. Or they could be in Brazil buying *haciendas*, getting ready to spend the rest of their lives in the lap of luxury while he was out here freezing his ass off on this fishy job.

Jose pointed outside. "Hey man, don't you see what's going down out there? You hear them fuckin' sirens. The cops are goin' bananas up here, man." He leaned forward, his eyes bulging. "They been on a rampage, man, bustin' everybody they see. Takin' people off the street and plantin' shit on 'em. You open your mouth and they club you down. I mean these motherfuckers ain't playin', Jim."

"People get popped up here every day," Chino said.

"Not like this, man. They took the biggest numbers guy up here. They chased the fuckin' hookers off the street. They never do that."

Chino sat back, and gave Jose a hard, disbelieving look. "Yeah, well if your boy's as cool as you say he is, we can do business anyway."

"My boy's so cool that he split, man, that's how cool he is. The motherfucker is gone. I went by his crib before to pick up some shit, and there was nobody home. He took the stash, the scales, the bread, the pieces, everything. Now I gotta go out there and cool all those motherfuckin' junkies out there 'cause I ain't got a bag to my name."

"So that means you're out of business," Chino said.

"No, man, it means we're gonna be bigger than ever. Because when everything cools down, my man's gonna be the

172

only dude who's holdin'.'" In his excitement Jose inadvertently touched Chino's wrist. He drew his hand away as if it had been burnt. You didn't touch like that, not when you'd done time, because that meant you were a faggot. "I'll take care of you in a coupla days. Get you to meet my boy, Hernando. I already told him all about you. Just let this shit cool out first . . ."

"How come the fuckin' man's freakin' out all of a sudden?" Chino asked.

"I don't know. Maybe it's 'cause of those two cops who got iced the other day." A mysterious look spread over Jose's face, and he lowered his voice. "I could tell them something about that. Motherfuckers went where they didn't belong, you dig?"

A real punk! Now he was coming on like he'd killed those rookies. "I don't give a shit about the cops, or what's goin' on up here, or anything else," Chino said, staring Jose down. "I came up here to buy dope, and if I can't do it I'll go somewhere else."

"You'll do it, you'll do it, man. I'll get you weight just like I promised. Here . . ." Jose wrote his number on a napkin. "Call me tomorrow morning. I'll tighten you up tomorrow morning, man, I promise."

Nolan and Fabrizio were sitting in a van across the street. Chino shook his head slightly as he came out of the bar, indicating that he hadn't copped. Nolan and Fabrizio made a U-turn. Chino walked all the way down the hill on Prospect until he was sure no one could see him. The van was parked on the corner. Nolan was eating a Twinkie.

"What happened?"

Chino hopped in back of the van. "He's afraid to deal. Says the cops are bustin' everybody."

"They are," Fabrizio said. "You see these fuckin' radio cars tear-assin' around? It's like the Keystone Kops."

"They got a new commander," Nolan said. "Guy used to be with I.A.D. He figures the only way to lower the crime rate is to arrest the whole neighborhood." He laughed and spit crumbs on Fabrizio's cashmere coat.

"You are a vulgarian, you know that, Nolan," Fabrizio said.

"You been sittin' here cuttin' some of the meanest farts from that fuckin' sausage sandwich you had for lunch, and you call me a vulgarian. You smell like the Love Canal at low tide . . ."

"Still got the money?" Fabrizio asked Chino.

"Sure I got it. I'll hold onto it until tomorrow."

Fabrizio lit a cigar.

"Oh Jesus," Nolan said, "now you're really gonna stink up the joint."

"Hold onto the money for the rest of your life, I don't care," Fabrizio said.

Nolan threw his Twinkie wrapper out of the window. "It would have been funny if you would have made the buy, then walked outta the joint, and one of these guys from the Four-One comes over to toss you."

"What would you do?" Fabrizio asked.

"What do I think? I'd ditch the fuckin' dope. I ain't gonna blow my cover unless I absolutely have to."

"You'd be in trouble with no dope to voucher, and out the twenty-five hundred," Nolan said.

"Trouble? I took the proper action to protect my cover, and his whole fuckin' operation. There wouldn't be any trouble."

And then it dawned on him. They were suggesting a scam. Use this new campaign in the Four-One to their own advantage. I say I made the buy, I saw a radio car on my tail, I ditched the dope to avoid blowing my cover. Twenty-five hundred split three ways is over eight hundred bucks apiece. A nice score. Too nice. Too easy. This job was starting to stink more and more.

Lieutenant Dacey had gotten the dossier on the South Bronx People's Party from the Bureau of Special Services, the political intelligence arm of the Police Department. They had infiltrated the organization the year before, and their undercover had filed regular written reports.

"There are five pictures on the wall of party headquarters," he wrote. "After some research this agent has been able to identify them as Karl Marx, Vladimir Lenin, Kim Il Sung, Fidel Castro, and an as yet unidentified Hispanic male, who might be Che Guevara. The agent does not wish to ask, for fear of showing his ignorance and compromising his cover story.

"The program of the South Bronx People's Party is clearly to indoctrinate the youth of the area in Communistic principles. The leaders of the group are—" There followed a long list of names which Dacey didn't bother to peruse. The report was almost a year old, and the personnel had probably changed since then.

"There are lectures given in the Communistic theories of Karl Marx and Friedrich Engels, his associate," the report continued. "Also, there is constant talk about what the policies of American Imperialism have done to the countries of the Third World of Africa and South America. There is a karate class that is conducted in Crotona Park during the warm weather, and lectures on urban guerrilla activity, with special emphasis on weapons training. Most of the people here seem to believe that armed revolution in America is about ten years in the future. They also think that the CIA and FBI are making preparations to assassinate all potential revolutionary leaders . . ."

"I wish to fuck they were," Dacey murmured under his breath. His driver, Seidman, looked over inquiringly. "What did you say, boss?"

"If you were supposed to hear it, you would have," Dacey said. "Do you know where the South Bronx People's Party is?"

Seidman picked up a list on the car seat. "It's in here somewhere."

"All right, let's go," Dacey said.

The phones had been ringing in the tiny storefront of the South Bronx People's Party all day. Something was going down. The cops were pulling everyone off the street, and taking them to the precinct where detectives questioned them about yesterday's murders.

"It's the beginning," said Andre, the head of the education department.

"The repression?"

"Yeah," Andre said. He got on the phone to other groups in Brooklyn and Jamaica. Yes, now that he mentioned it, they had noticed an increase in police activity.

175

"They'll use these murders as a pretext," Andre said. "And then they'll round everybody up."

There were four of them in the office. Shields, Pena, and Salazar. Along with Andre, they were the nucleus of the group. Andre was the oldest. A large black man with a shaven head, he'd been a corporal in the Special Forces contingent that invaded Cambodia. Although he had totally repudiated his five years as a mercenary for American imperialism, he still favored the fatigues and field jackets of the American Armed Forces, and even wore his beret on occasion. The others had adopted his style. It made for a simple but strong image in the community.

"But why today, why now?" Shields asked.

"Something must have happened somewhere," Andre said. "Something more serious than just a street riot. A real insurrection somewhere."

"There's nothing about it in the paper," Salazar said, holding up a copy of the *New York Times*.

Pena reached for the radio. "Let's put on the news."

Andre laughed harshly. "You motherfuckers are never gonna learn, are you? Did Hitler publicize the Blood Purge? Did they put out a press release before the Palmer raids in 1923 when they rounded up every radical on the East Coast?"

"No, Andre . . ."

"Well, if the structure's been hit. Say in Washington, or L.A., or even City Hall right downtown about ten miles away there's a news blackout on, and we don't know nothin'."

"All we can do is guess," Shields said.

Pena flicked on the radio. "And try to make an analysis out of what little intelligence we receive from the outside world."

"So now they're plucking people off the street," Shields said. "You think they'll start hitting organizations next? You think they'll hit us?"

Andre looked out of the window. "They're just about to."

Dacey had called Cordero and Russell in for back-up. A black and a Puerto Rican; it might help break the ice with these guys.

Party headquarters was in a low slung, one-story tarpaper

on Webster Avenue. There was a hand-lettered banner draped across the store window. It looked peaceful enough. Dacey got out of the car, and walked across the street, waving for Cordero and Russell to join him.

Inside, Shields had run to the filing cabinet in the inner office where they kept the weapons. He came out with the sawed-off shotgun, and stationed himself by the door.

"Forget it, man," Andre said. "We haven't got enough ammo to wage much of a fight, and besides, this place is indefensible. They could pour so much fire in here that they'd incinerate us all without even having to hit us, you understand, so put that piece down . . ."

But it was too late. In approaching the building, Dacey had seen Shields standing in the doorway holding the shotgun. "Man with a gun," he shouted, and dove into a doorway for cover. Cordero went down so fast he slipped on the ice, skidding halfway across the street on his back, but coming up with his pistol out. Russell was crouched on the blind side of the building, under the window. Seidman was behind the car.

Dacey shouted to him. "Call in a 10–13 to the Four-One." Seidman opened the passenger door of the car, and crawled in to the radio.

"Just take the bust," Andre was advising his colleagues. "I'll get out and organize a demo. We'll see if we can use this as an organizing tool."

"Yeah, but we may never get out of that goddamn precinct."

"I'll get you out," Andre said. "The Four-One's been attacked before. Only this time there'll be angry mobs inside the buildings as well as in the street."

Andre slipped out the back window into the yard. He climbed over the fence, and went up the block to the headquarters of J.A.P., the federally funded JOBS ACTION PROJECT. The tiny office was crowded with young men filling out applications for training programs. The director of the project was an ex-police officer named Clarence Stone, a burly, middle-aged black man with a perpetual look of anger and frustration. He was yelling into the phone, "Don't ask me why I'm so hostile. Just get my people the work you promised." He slammed down the phone.

"We're being raided, Clarence," Andre said.

"What do you mean?"

"The cops are making an unprovoked attack on our headquarters. Something's happening, man. It looks like the fascists are making their move."

"Oh man, don't hit me with that ghetto paranoia," Clarence said. "Not today."

"It's true, Clarence," Andre said.

Clarence went out into the front room. All the benches were filled with job seekers, and he had to step over men who were squatting on the floor laboring over their applications. He looked out of the front window, and saw Cordero and Russell, their pistols drawn, Cordero screaming into a walkie-talkie. Clarence turned angrily to Andre.

"All right, Andre, don't bullshit me. What did you do?"

"We didn't do shit, man. I'm tellin' you, they're makin' a move."

A few of the applicants looked up.

"What's happenin', man?"

"What's goin' down?"

The men went to the window. Clarence looked worriedly around the room. "I'll call Borough Headquarters," he said, going back into his office.

"Look out there," Andre said. "Look how the man is persecuting your brothers."

"What'd they do?"

"They worked in the interests of the oppressed classes, that's what they did," Andre said.

Clarence stormed out of his office. "What are you trying to do, start a revolution?"

"I'm trying to get my fucking rights, and the rights of my brothers, Clarence," Andre shouted. "Is that all right with you?"

One of the men pointed out of the window. "Hey, look how they're beatin' up on that dude."

Dacey had inched over to a spot behind the door, just out of the line of fire. Meanwhile, Russell had backed up to a phone booth on the corner, and called the Party. "You people come out nice and slow with your hands up," he said to Pena.

"Fuck you, man," Pena shouted. "We didn't do nothin'." And he slammed the phone down. "Motherfucker wants us to come out with our hands up," he said.

"Oh shit," Shields said. He kicked the door open, and stepped out into the streets, his hands at his sides. "You motherfuckers think you gonna get away with this, huh?"

Dacey leapt out of the doorway, and kicked Shields in the groin. Shields went down on his knees. Dacey jammed his gun in Shields's ear, and dragged him by his coat collar out of the doorway. With the wind knocked out of him, Shields struggled for breath, but Dacey mistook the wild flailing of his arms for resistance, and smashed him with the butt of his gun. The gun went off, shattering the wintry calm. Shields went face down on the pavement; it looked as though he had been shot.

Pena and Salazar backed into the office. "They shot him," Pena cried.

"Get the fuckin' guns, man," Salazar said. "If we gonna die, we'll die fighting."

At that moment three cars from the Four-One and one Emergency Service van came speeding around the corner.

"Hit the store," Dacey screamed, pointing to the storefront. "Hit it!"

Cordero and Russell, followed by the uniformed cops, rushed the storefront, catching Pena and Salazar as they headed for the weapons cache. They shoved them against the wall. "Spread 'em," Russell shouted, kicking Pena's legs apart.

"You think you're gonna stop the movement just like this," Pena said, as they frisked them. "It's the wave of the future."

"You're helpless against it," Salazar said, as they buffed him. "You can kill us, but four more will rise up to take our places."

The men in the Jobs Action Project ran out into the street to see what was happening.

"Looks like a fucking invasion, man."

They heard the shot and saw Shields fall.

179

"They shot that dude."

"Just shot him for no reason."

More men came out into the street, coatless, their breath coming out in angry puffs. They walked toward the action down the block, wary at first, but growing in conviction as they went.

The police saw them coming, and called in another 10–13. Then another as some of the men starting shouting.

"What did you shoot that man for?"

"These guys ain't doin' nothin'. Why don't you let 'em go?"

The cops formed a flying wedge around the detectives and their prisoners. "Get them into the radio cars, and let's get the fuck out of here," Dacey shouted.

The men in the front ranks started arguing with the cops.

"What did you shoot that man for?"

"Just cool it, nobody was shot."

The cops backed away toward their cars, hands on guns. The two Emergency Service guys were wearing flak jackets and holding shotguns.

At the back of the group of men, Andre started a chant. "Let the brothers go. Let the brothers go."

It was picked up by some of the men, then more, until it was a full-throated, rhythmic shout. "Let the brothers go . . ."

Other police cars arrived as Dacey and his men threw their prisoners into cars, and zoomed down the block, sirens screeching. The men confronted the new arrivals, shaking their fists. "Let the brothers go. Let the brothers go."

31

Murphy and Corelli cruised the streets with Armando, the fence, and the gun dealer cuffed together in the back seat. Murphy wanted to wait until after six to go back to Hunts Point for the hookers. "We'll have to bust old Tony's cockfight, too," he said. "And this sonofabitch." He pointed out of the window. "Remember him?"

It was the track star, the purse snatcher who had led them such a merry chase the day before. He bopped along unconcernedly, crossing right in front of the van.

"Run him over," Corelli said. "It's the only way we'll get him."

Murphy honked the horn. The kid gave him the clenched fist greeting. "I think he's stoned," Murphy said. "Maybe that'll slow him down."

"He's probably stoned on speed," Corelli said.

Murphy turned down Kelly Street and pulled about twenty feet in front of the kid. He opened the door, and the kid passed him in a blur. Murphy jumped back in the van, and gunned the motor.

"Forget it, will ya?" Corelli said.

"Can't. Fuckin' kid's makin' an asshole out of me."

"If you chased everybody who made an asshole out of you, we'd never get any work done."

Murphy slid into a skid on Intervale, and the van made two complete turns before he managed to steer out of it.

"Let me off, I'll take the subway," Corelli said.

The track star cut down a narrow street, and Murphy followed.

"Hey man, you're goin' the wrong way," the gun dealer complained.

"So make a citizen's arrest," Murphy said. It was one of the many little streets in the Bronx that stopped abruptly in

181

a dead end. This one ended in a little circular vest-pocket park. Murphy jumped out and squinted through the dusk. "Kid's a magician, too," he said.

They sat on this quiet back street for a while, and listened to the calls flooding the radio. Crime in progress signals, assist patrolman signals—everybody was very busy out there. Every few minutes they would hear the sound of a siren somewhere in the neighborhood. A few signal 10–50's, reports of disorderly persons, came over the radio. By the time Murphy had finished a cigarette and gotten underway, the signals had changed to 10–51's, which meant roving bands of people.

"Sounds like a parade," Murphy said. "Is today a holiday?"

They drove over to the market. Murphy pointed in gleeful triumph at the solid row of late-model cars parked on the street. "I told you we'd catch the night shift." He cut the lights of the van, and pulled up behind the last car in the row. He turned the volume on the loudspeaker up full blast. "Alright, music lovers," he said, "everybody out. Yes, this is a raid." Car doors flew open, and girls came tumbling out, pulling their skirts down, buttoning their coats. Corelli dashed out after them. He shone his flashlight on his face, and doffed his cap. "This way, ladies." One of the girls, a blowsy bleached blonde, took off down the street. Corelli ran after her and caught her by the arm. "Wrong way, baby," he said gently.

She tried to pull free. "I can't go. Please let me go, please . . ."

"C'mon, the rest will do you good," Corelli said, trying to get his arm around her. "Anyway, your old man'll get you out . . ."

"He won't." She opened her coat to reveal a huge pregnant belly. "He says I ain't earnin' enough." She started to sob. Mascara ran in sooty tracks down her face. "He won't never come for me."

"Bring her over, Andy," Murphy called.

The johns' cars were peeling away as fast as they could pull up their pants and start the ignitions. Murphy ran over and helped Corelli drag the hysterical girl to the van. He shook her roughly. "How far gone are you?"

"I don't know. Please let me go."

Murphy stood there looking at her, shaking his head.

"You wanna have your baby out here on the street, do you?"

"I gotta get back."

"How dumb can one person be?" Murphy twisted the girl's arm, and shoved her into the van. "Get in there. You're going to the hospital whether you like it or not. How old are you, anyway? Never mind, I don't want to know."

Andre stood out in the freezing street shouting about police repression, resistance of the working classes, trying to keep the men from the Jobs Action Project from scattering, trying to feed their rage and frustration to the point where they could act in concert as a revolutionary force. He had read somewhere that once workers freed themselves of the bourgeois individualism of the capitalist society and combined in a group, no longer thinking of acting for themselves alone, but for the movement, they experienced an exhilaration they never knew existed, greater than anything the capitalist system could provide—even drugs, liquor, or sex. If you could move them into positive action, they would never return to their old ways; they would be yours forever.

Andre was a forceful speaker. He had the example of the unjust, brutal seizure of his associates, the frustration felt by ablebodied men who couldn't get work, the hint that dark forces were poised to strike them all down. He proposed a march to the precinct to free the three men who had been arrested, and was astounded when the men roared back their assent.

Clarence was standing in the doorway, arms folded, listening. "You're gonna get your ass shot off, boy," he said to Andre. "The Four-One ain't no place to get political."

"We're gonna overrun Fort Apache, Clarence," Andre said.

Clarence went back into his office. "Not today, you won't."

Tony Novia had been running cockfights in the basement of a tenement on 162nd Street for twenty years. He was a wizened little man in his early sixties. Everyone on the block called him "Jefe;" even the gang kids deferred to him. A favorite winter sport of the neighborhood was guessing just how much money Jefe had salted away, and where it was.

Murphy and Corelli had run out of handcuffs so they

183

had to take three of the hookers into the building with them. They walked all the way down the hall to the stairs that led to the basement, and then down a dark, narrow passageway. The girls balked, and wouldn't go any further.

"I knew this wasn't no pinch," an enormous black girl said. "If you takin' us to some kinda party or somethin', we wanna get paid."

"You're going to jail, Mama, don't worry about it," Murphy said. "But first we're taking a little detour."

Down in the subbasement the cement floor had been sledge-hammered in, and a pit dug in the dirt. Red bulbs strung along the walls gave the place a festive air, while three naked white bulbs cast a harsh light over the fighting area.

About thirty men were clustered around the pit yelling and waving money as two roosters strutted and pecked at each other. They were so intent on the fight they didn't even notice the cops.

Murphy banged his blackjack on a steam pipe. "Alright, sports lovers, this is a raid."

Jefe came out from behind a pile of crates. "Hey, Murf, what are you botherin' me for?"

"Alright, line up over there," Murphy instructed the men, then turned confidentially to Jefe. "You've got to take a pinch, boss, I'm sorry. You know we been good to you, right?"

"That's right."

"Left you alone. Never asked you for nothin'. Well, it's pay-back time, Jefe, understand?"

"Put a muzzle on those birds, and let's get outta here," Corelli said. "I feel like the walls are gonna cave in on me any minute."

"Any of you guys got knives, guns, narcotics, stolen credit cards, ditch 'em now," Murphy announced. "You'll have to stand a search in the precinct, and anything you got will be held against you."

Objects rained down on the cement floor as the gamblers discreetly rid themselves of illegal commodities.

"Hey, Murf, you can't take the birds," a trainer named Pepe said. They had pulled the roosters apart to stop them from doing further harm to each other, and now the birds, their talons tied with metal bands, their beaks bound shut, their bright eyes murderously watchful, ruffled and leapt in their trainers' grasps.

"Gotta bring 'em in as evidence, my man."

"But these are good birds, Murf," Jefe said. "The A.S.P.C.A. comes and takes them away."

"We spend a lotta time and money on these chickens, man," another trainer grumbled. "Take me if you have to. I'll get out in a coupla hours, but they'll keep my chicken, man."

Murphy and Corelli exchanged a quick look. Jefe had a full house, more men than they had anticipated—policy guys, car strippers, maybe a dealer or two, all the people whose businesses had been closed down by the busts. They had been pretty docile up to now, but they could get restive, or downright rebellious. Then there would be a problem.

"Okay, we'll work something out," Murphy said. "You can leave the roosters."

There were a few appreciative mumbles. The mood had definitely improved. The men marched agreeably through the hallway, and up to the street. "There won't be enough room in the van," Corelli said. "We'll have to call for back-up."

"And have other guys claiming our collars?" Murphy said. "No way, Jose. We're gonna bring these people in ourselves if we have to march them up to the precinct."

The rear door of the van was open. Halfway down the block they caught up to the gun dealer and Armando, rolling and fighting in the gutter.

"I tried to stop him, I tried to stop him," Armando cried, his torn shirt and battered face eloquent testimony to his story. "I didn't want to escape. I didn't want to go nowhere."

The gun dealer could hardly walk. The effort of dragging the three-hundred-pound Armando down the block had brought him to the brink of collapse. His wrist was raw and bleeding from the handcuffs he shared with Armando. His free hand was swollen from pounding Armando's face.

Corelli pointed back to the twenty-odd people standing patiently around the van. "This ain't gonna work, Murf. We'll have to ditch some of these folks."

Murphy shook his head doggedly. "Captain Connolly wants arrests, he's gonna get 'em. Remember those old cartoons when thousands of elephants and giraffes come runnin' out of this little house? That's what the fuckin' Four-One's gonna look like."

A city bus turned the corner. Murphy ran out in the middle of the street. "Police business," he told the driver. "We're making one unscheduled stop," he told the dozen or so passengers. "Everyone please move to the rear so we can get our prisoners on."

Corelli marched the prisoners onto the bus. "I've always wanted to drive one of these things," he said.

The driver slid out of his seat. "Be my guest," he said. "I've always wanted to drive a police car."

Murphy pointed to the van. "Be our guest."

Corelli opened and closed the bus doors a few times and put the bus in gear. "All aboard," he called.

"Wrong vehicle," Murphy said.

"Ah, stop being a party-pooper, Murphy." Corelli maneuvered the bus out into traffic. "Anybody know how to sing 'Ninety-nine bottles of beer on the wall'?"

32

The march was getting bigger. It was turning into a full-scale demonstration, an insurrection. Andre didn't know where the people were coming from, as cold and late as it was, but each time he turned around there were more of them, marching in step, chanting in unison: "Let the brothers go. Let the brothers go."

The marchers turned up Southern Boulevard past a store front where a community theatre group was rehearsing.

"What's goin' on?" an actor called to one of the marchers.

"We're marchin' to the precinct. We're gonna get the brothers out of jail."

The head of the group got on the phone to his friend at a veterans' counseling service on Freeman Street. "They're protesting this wave of arrests," he said. "Everybody's going to congregate at the Forty-first precinct."

"We'll be there," his friend said.

Then he called the shop steward at the Jefferson Hospital,

who went around drumming up support for the march in the various community service departments. He spoke to Hernando in the detox counseling section. Hernando wasn't impressed.

"What you gonna do when you get there, stand out in the cold, and sing songs?"

"We're trying to draw attention to this fascist behavior, man. We've already called the press . . ."

"So I'll watch it on 'Eyewitness News'," Hernando said.

Frank, the Emergency Room orderly, who seemed to spend more time in Hernando's office than he did at his post, was even more disdainful. "We went through the marching shit all through the sixties, and what did it get us?"

"It got us out of Vietnam," the shop steward said.

Frank turned away in disgust. "I oughta know better than to talk politics with white people."

Hernando laughed. *"Vaya,* bro, you're right about that."

"Well, it's a beginning," the shop steward said defensively. "We've got to get a little activism happening in this community."

"Activism?" Frank balled a big, black fist. "When you're ready to attack that precinct, and not with slogans or picket signs, but with guns and bombs, you come back to me, man. When you want to really get down, and do something real, I'll be here. But I ain't freezin' on no candy-ass fuckin' picket line."

Hernando cheered him on. "Alright, Frank, speak on it, speak on it to the man."

The marchers, now over a hundred strong, were joined by members of a parent-teachers group that happened to have been meeting in St. Anselmo's. Everybody picked up the chant, "Let the brothers go. Let the brothers go." Motorists honked in support and joined the chant. People came out of stores and bars, waving and shouting. A few drunks staggered along on the sidewalk. A group of kids came out of a community center sponsored by the Bronx Diocese, and joined the march, shouting and clapping. The anger of the original protesters was diluted by the shouts and laughter of the new arrivals.

Pete "Spanish Pete" Calandrino, the numbers boss of the area, was sitting glumly in the Emerald Bar as the marchers went past. "What's that?" he asked Lureen.

"How do I know. I been here all day."

"They're marching to the precinct," one of the runners said. "Protesting all these arrests in the neighborhood."

"That's a good idea," Spanish Pete said. Five of his runners were sitting around the bar. "Go out there and join the march," he said.

"Join the march?"

"It's freezin' out there, boss."

"Join the march," Spanish Pete said quietly. "It's for a good cause."

The boiler had finally been fixed at around six-thirty, and the heat came on with vengeance, as if making up for the two days it hadn't been functioning. With all the cops and prisoners milling around, the cigarette smoke hovering in the air, the place became an inferno.

Applebaum wiped his streaming forehead. "Before, I was in a freezer, now I'm in a turkish bath."

He had gone behind the desk to help Pantuzzi process the arrests. Every cop on the tour had come in with prisoners. Somebody had even collared Porfirio the flasher, but now nobody would acknowledge the arrest so Porfirio wandered around the desk area exposing himself to the hookers, policewomen, secretaries, and Community Relations clerks. Occasionally a passing cop would admonish him to "keep it in his pants." But when Murphy and Corelli came in escorting seven hookers, he went running over with his coat open, and had to be evicted from the precinct.

Angry prisoners were protesting their innocence, demanding Legal Aid, threatening to sue for false arrest. Three kids had their angry mothers. A drug addict shivered uncontrollably on a bench, and had to be covered with police overcoats.

Applebaum, who had been writing up the arrests, looked up and slapped his forehead as Murphy and Corelli brought their crew up to be booked. *"Oy gott,* we're gonna be here all night with this group." He tried to shout over the din. "All you guys book your people, then move 'em up and try to keep them quiet." Just line 'em up and try to keep them quiet." He looked hopelessly at Heffernan. "Is there any way we can speed this mess up?"

Heffernan looked down at Pantuzzi. "Tony?"

Pantuzzi shook his head, and kept on writing. "Don't look at me. I'll just keep writing the arrests up until midnight, and then I'm going home. I don't have any suggestions. I haven't had any suggestions for twenty-two years."

Dacey had taken over the Youth squad room to interrogate his prisoners. He closed the door, and put a man outside. "Don't let anybody in. We want to be alone." His sleeve had been torn, and he had twisted his ankle while trying to cuff Shields. Detective Russell's back and elbow were badly scraped. Cordero had a purple swelling under his eye. Three other detectives from Dacey's special squad had come in the room with them. The three prisoners, still cuffed and defiant, had been manacled to chairs.

The detectives sat across from them, putting forms into typewriters. They seemed bored, oblivious to the rage of Dacey and the other two injured detectives.

"Name, please," one of them asked Shields.

"I ain't tellin' you my name, man," he shouted.

"We ain't tellin' you nothin' until you tell us why we've been arrested," Salazar said.

"You were charged with resisting arrest, assaulting a police officer, possession of a dangerous weapon, obstructing the activities of a government employee . . ."

"You guys started the shit," Salazar said. "You attacked us."

The detective patted him on the shoulder with crocodile sympathy. "We're allowed to. You're not. If we tell you to come with us you have to come."

"They're not too bright," Cordero said. "They don't understand."

"We understand plenty, pig," Shields sneered.

"They're not too sociable, either," a detective said.

"You got us in here on a frame," Shields said. He twisted around to confront Dacey. "You're gonna set us up for that cop killing."

Dacey walked over and put his hand on the back of Shields's chair. "We would like to talk to you about that," he said evenly.

"We didn't shoot your cops, man," Pena said.

"We wouldn't waste our bullets," shouted Salazar, writhing frantically.

Dacey took two quick strides, and grabbed Salazar by the

189

collar. He lifted him up off the chair and slammed his head against the wall. Salazar's feet were still manacled to the chair. He fell over, taking the chair down with him, twisting his ankle and screaming in pain.

Dacey lifted him up by the hair. Salazar's eyes bulged. "You wanna go to war with me, tough guy?" Dacey snarled. "Do you? I've got seventeen assaults and five assassinations of police officers to clear. I'll nail your ass to the precinct wall if you hassle me, understand?"

"Leave him alone," Pena said. "He's an epileptic."

"He should have thought of that before he opened his mouth," Dacey said. He slipped the blackjack out of his pocket, and held it over Salazar's head.

"Don't hit him, man," Pena said desperately.

"Epileptics should be real polite," Dacey said. "Epileptics should answer people's questions."

"We didn't kill no cops, man," Shields said. "We were at a teach-in on nuclear power at Sarah Lawrence yesterday. We were there all day. Go check it out. We got five hundred witnesses."

"You wanna go up against five hundred honky college girls, man?" Pena said.

"Now leave him alone," Shields said.

Dacey helped Salazar up, fixed his collar, and patted him on the cheek. "Feeling better now? Now maybe you'll be a bit more cooperative. If you give us your names we'll be able to verify your alibi. We'll even let you call your lawyers. And once you've been cleared of that, you'll only be facing three other major felony charges."

Connolly had seen Dacey's men hustling the South Bronx People's Party suspects into the precinct. It looked like there might be a break in those cop killings, so perhaps Headquarters wouldn't object to a little extra expenditure. He called in Heffernan.

"I'm going to authorize overtime for the men on the eight-to-four and the four-to-twelve, so they can process the suspects."

"We're backed way up, Captain," Heffernan said. "It's like Grand Central Station out there. I don't know how we're gonna get the next tour out."

"Oh well, we have until midnight," Connolly said, trying to calm his harried lieutenant. The man was upset. He had dark blotches under the armpits of his shirt, his hair stuck out at crazy angles as though it had been electrified. He had probably never worked so hard in his entire life. "This will all settle into a routine in a couple of days. We'll work out procedures."

"You'll need a hundred more men if you want to run the house like this, Captain."

Pantuzzi opened the door. "Knock, knock," he said.

"What is it, Pantuzzi?" Connolly asked.

"We seem to have a bit of a riot building up, sir."

"Where?"

"Right here in the Bronx, sir. I wouldn't bother you if it was in Philadelphia."

Connolly pushed his way through the crowds in the desk area, with Pantuzzi and Heffernan following.

"It all started when that Special Investigations squad went over to the South Bronx People's Party," Pantuzzi explained. "They started agitatin' after the arrest, and built up quite a crowd. We had three 10–51s, and a few 10–13s. None of the guys out in the street want to take a shot at stopping the crowd. So, anyway . . ." Pantuzzi sounded exhausted, as if he hadn't done this much talking in all his years on the job, and didn't like it. "The crowd's headin' for the precinct."

"How many are there?" Connolly asked.

"It's only estimates, of course," Pantuzzi said. "But there seem to be over a hundred."

"Call every available car in off patrol," Connolly said. "Call Borough for back-up. I want a 10–46 called in, plus Emergency Service with riot control equipment."

A signal 10–46 called for the rapid mobilization of forty police officers, eight sergeants, and one lieutenant.

"That's overkill, Captain," Heffernan said. "On a street as narrow as this there won't be any room for all these guys."

"We're going to block off both ends of the street," Connolly said. "No unruly, unlawful mob will be permitted in front of the precinct." Connolly called to Applebaum. "Sergeant, you will be in charge of the inside of the precinct. Line the prisoners up in the muster room. See to it there are no disturbances."

Moving with astonishing quickness, Applebaum started herding prisoners into the muster room. "Alright, everybody

191

in here," he shouted. "All you guys bring your prisoners into the muster room to await processing."

Connolly went outside, and looked up the street.

"They're coming up Southern Boulevard," Pantuzzi said, appearing at his arm.

He could hear the faint, ghostly sound of the crowd, chanting. "Let the brothers go. Let the brothers go."

"Are all the keys out of these vehicles?" Connolly asked, pointing to the police cars.

"I'll get someone to check," Pantuzzi said.

"Captain . . ." Applebaum came running out of the station. "Borough's on the phone. Inspector Krieger."

Krieger. He was the Borough Commander. "Tell him I'll call back," Connolly said. "Heffernan," he shouted. Pantuzzi looked at him keenly, startled by the strain in his voice, then slouched back into the precinct as Heffernan rushed out.

"Yes, Captain?"

"Put a couple of men out here on guard. Two by the door, two on either side of the precinct. Do we have police barricades?"

"Maybe down in the basement."

"Well, go down and get them, for Chrissake," Connolly said. "Barricade the precinct on both sides of the building. Get somebody up on the roof to check for snipers. I want the detectives in on this as well."

"Yes, sir."

Connolly turned back into the precinct, and saw Dacey coming down from the squad.

"N.G. on those revolutionaries we got," he said. "The only thing they shoot is beaver."

"We've got a major riot building up because of your handling of this arrest," Connolly said. "I've had to call Borough for reinforcements."

"What do you want from me?" Dacey said. "We went in to question them, and they pulled guns on us."

"Why didn't you consult with my Community Relations people?" Connolly asked. "These people obviously have a large following in the community."

"Yeah, well, they can follow these cocksuckers right to Central Booking, Dennis. They assaulted three police officers, and resisted arrest, and were found in possession of deadly weapons."

192

"Don't shout at me, Ed," Connolly said coldly.

Dacey's voice went down, but his face stayed red. "You're the commander of this precinct, Dennis. Now I don't give a fuck if the whole Bronx attacks this house, I want my prisoners held and transported. So if you're thinking of releasing them . . ."

"I'm not releasing anybody," Connolly snapped. He turned and walked angrily toward his office. "Get me Inspector Krieger at Borough," he said to Pantuzzi.

Dacey turned and dashed up the stairs toward the squad room. Pantuzzi looked after him. "He's calling the Chief of Detectives, the Captain's talking to Inspector Krieger. They're each gonna blame the other for what happened."

Heffernan smoothed his unruly hair. "And for what's about to happen."

33

Andre felt a sense of power. Marching at the head of this rhythmically chanting mob, he had the merest inkling of what it must have been like for Lenin when he addressed cheering throngs that stretched right to the horizon. Or for Fidel when he made his triumphal march into Havana. It was the power of the masses, the people. Led by him, yet leading him at the same time. The demonstration had grown. Whenever he looked back, there were more people joining the march, picking up the chant. Occasionally, there was the tinkle of broken glass as somebody threw a rock through a store window. The merchants on Southern Boulevard hurriedly closed shop, drawing iron fences in front of their windows. Some kids overturned a car, and set it on fire. Andre heard the sirens all around him. The cops were mobilizing for a confrontation.

Andre turned the corner onto Simpson Street. There were barricades in front of the station house, a couple of Emergency

Service trucks parked on the sidewalk. Cops were rushing out, and taking posts on either side of the building. They were all wearing crash helmets. Some of them even held shotguns.

Andre had no plan; he never thought he would generate this much support, never anticipated such a reaction by the cops. He could think of nothing better than to bunch his people together across the narrow street and demand that his brothers be released, hoping that the people inside would start a demonstration of their own.

More police cars sped the wrong way down Simpson Street. Cops wearing helmets jumped out, and ran into the station house. More cops came out, and took posts at the barricades. This proved it: the Establishment was going to war with the underclasses. And what if they opened fire? What if he had led all these brothers and sisters into a trap?

Connolly watched the demonstration form from his office window. There seemed to be one leader—the tall black man who stood in the middle of the street, shaking his fist and leading the chant. "Let the brothers go. Let the brothers go." Neutralize him, and the demonstration would dissipate.

He called the Emergency Services sergeant in. "How many people do you estimate are in that mob?" he asked.

"A hundred, a hundred and twenty-five."

"Do you think we have enough manpower in case they rush the precinct?"

The sergeant looked surprised. "I don't think they're gonna attack us, Captain."

Connolly walked out of the office, and beckoned to Heffernan. "I want a half-dozen men at the door here, Lieutenant, and stationed around the desk."

Sergeant Martinez, the Community Relations Officer, stopped Connolly at the door. He had a worried look, and he spoke with controlled calm. "Captain, I see a couple of people out there that I know. Maybe if I just went out and talked to them and got a dialogue going I could . . ."

"If they want to talk, this isn't the way to do it," Connolly said.

"I agree, but if I just went out and reassured them about those three prisoners. That they weren't being beaten to death in here. A lot of people have misconceptions about cops . . ."

Connolly dismissed this impatiently. "We're not responsible for their misconceptions, Sergeant. These people are not legitimate representatives of the community."

Martinez's restraint was beginning to crack. "They live here, Captain."

"And because they do I will not dignify their action with any recognition other than a warning." Connolly walked to the door. "You can help the people you know out there by telling them to disperse immediately, Sergeant, or face arrest."

Martinez turned away angrily. "Crazy motherfucker," he muttered.

Connolly walked out into the street in his shirtsleeves. The chant was growing louder as more stragglers joined the demonstration. Connolly could hear it coming from the prisoners inside as well. "Let the brothers go. Let the brothers go."

He turned to a patrolman on guard. "Go inside and tell Sergeant Applebaum to keep those people quiet." He walked out and confronted the tall black leader of the mob across the barricade.

"Are you the leader here?"

"Ain't no leaders here, man," the black man said. "Only one soul with a million voices."

"You are interfering with the operations of a police station," Connolly said.

"You are interfering with the lives of my people," the black man shouted back.

"That is a violation of the law," Connolly continued. "And if you don't cease your activity I will place you under arrest."

The black man shook his fist in Connolly's face. "You let our brothers out of your dungeons, and we'll go."

Connolly checked the time. "I'll give you five minutes to disperse."

He turned back toward the station house. "We ain't goin' nowhere until we get our people out," the black man shouted after him.

Heffernan was waiting at the door of the station house. "I've given them five minutes to disperse," Connolly told him. "Issue gas masks and tear gas to all the officers on guard."

"Captain, we've had these things before," Heffernan said. "On a cold night like this you know you can outlast them. If you just let them blow off steam they'll go away after a while."

195

"I don't want to outlast them, I want to overpower them," Connolly said. "If they haven't dispersed in five minutes we'll release tear gas into the crowd. Tell the men. Also tell them that anyone attempting to rush the barricades is to be beaten back with appropriate force and arrested."

Connolly ran through the desk area to the muster room, where some of the prisoners were still defiantly chanting. "I want quiet in this room," he shouted. "Anyone caught making any noise in this room will be charged with disorderly conduct."

"You can't stop us from talking, man," a prisoner shouted. "We know our rights."

"We'll sue you for false arrest."

Applebaum lumbered over apologetically. "These guys spend so much time in court they know more than lawyers."

"Take the name of anyone who makes a sound from now on," Connolly said.

Pantuzzi appeared at the door. "Borough calling again, Captain."

Connolly rushed into his office and closed the door. Murphy and Corelli, who were stationed by the door, watched in amusement. "He's as happy as a pig in shit," Murphy said.

Heffernan stood by the door, checking his watch every few seconds.

"You can give them five days now, Loot," Corelli said. They ain't goin' anywhere. Once you start playin' school yard with these people, you gotta go all the way."

"At least he could have made an announcement on the bullhorn," Heffernan said.

"I hope my car's alright," Murphy said. "Lemme go outside and take a look."

Murphy went out into the street, and hopped a barricade. A few kids were sitting on the hood of his car, chanting and clapping their hands. Murphy grabbed the biggest one. "Hey, what's your name?"

The kid shook him off angrily. "I didn't do nothin'."

"I know, and here's your reward." Murphy took out a five-dollar bill, and shoved it in the kid's pocket. "Now, what's your name?"

"Felipe."

"You wanna make ten more, Felipe, make sure nobody fucks with this car, okay?"

"Yeah, sure, we'll take care of the car."

"You just come to the station house when all this blows over, and ask for Murphy."

"You better be there, man," Felipe said.

"What do you think I got the uniform for, Hallowe'en?" Murphy said. "I'll be there."

He trotted back toward the station house. Heffernan was standing in the doorway shouting through a bullhorn, his words lost in the wind and the cries of the demonstrators. The Emergency Service cops had put their gas masks on, and lowered the tear gas rifles. Under the sputtering streetlights they looked like spacemen who had just come out of a flying saucer and were moving slowly through unfamiliar territory. The crowd surged toward the barricades. People appeared on the roof of an abandoned building across the street from the precinct. Murphy heard the explosion of the tear gas rifles. Cottony puffs of smoke appeared in the air and coalesced into one acrid cloud.

Murphy covered his eyes with the back of his hand. Mace was murder on a cold, damp night like this. It condensed, and fell like stinging rain, getting in your eyes, your nose. Another volley from the guns rose up in the air. A shower of debris fell through the thickening air—rocks, bottles, crashing down on the cops behind the barricades, driving them back. Roofs were the worst place to be when there was mace in the air. It rose slowly until a gust of wind blew it into your face, and you had to find your way downstairs, blind and screaming with pain. It was better to be low, as low as you could get. Or inside.

Crouching, covering his face, Murphy headed back toward the station house. The crowd had begun to disperse. People were running wildly, clutching their throats, gasping for breath. Murphy was caught in the path of the fleeing mob. Even the wind was against them; it changed direction, and sent the clouds of mace in hot pursuit.

Murphy couldn't fight his way through the mob; it was like trying to swim against the current. He retreated back to his car, and sat in the back seat with the windows closed, watching as people dropped to their knees, some spitting and vomiting, others staggering, crazy with pain and fear.

The gas settled like a fog on his car windows. People stumbled blindly into the car, bouncing off it and onto the street, some lurching away, others lying in the gutter semi-conscious, trampled by the fleeing demonstrators.

Through the haze on his windshield, Murphy saw a figure with a gas mask and a white shirt. Two gold bars shone on his shoulders. It was the Captain, right out in the middle of the street, barreling through the crowd, probably coming to order him back into the station house.

Murphy stepped out of the car and was almost bowled over by a dark figure. He grappled with the man, jamming his forearm into his Adam's apple, hooking the man's ear with his thumb and jerking him off balance. In a moment the Captain was upon him, his voice almost muffled by the gas mask. "Hold him, Murphy, hold him."

The guy was strong. Murphy tried to turn him face down over the hood of the car. He squinted tightly, keeping his eyes as narrow as possible to avoid the mace. Connolly came up and kicked the man in the back of his knee.

"Motherfuckers," the man shouted as he went down. "You'll have to kill me." He swung out wildly, and hit Murphy in the groin.

"Get him back to the station house," Connolly said.

Murphy tried to twist the man's arms behind him, but the Captain yanked him up by the collar and sent him sprawling out into the gutter. "Get him back into the precinct house," he shouted gruffly behind that mask. "Didn't you hear me?"

"Let me cuff him first," Murphy said. "I can't fight the bastard all the way back to the house." He pounced on the writhing man, and twisted his wrists. "Don't fight me, mother-fucker, or I'll break your fuckin' arms," he shouted.

The man let up a bit, and Murphy got the cuffs on him. "Get up," he said, lifting the man under his arms.

"My eyes," the man screamed.

"Mine too," Murphy said, pushing him toward the station house. "The sooner we get inside, the better off we'll be."

The Captain came up and grabbed the man's arms. "Let's go, Murphy."

A bunch of cops with gas masks came up the street to meet them.

"Murf," one of them shouted, and threw Murphy a gas mask.

They stepped over the bodies of marchers who had been

overcome by the tear gas, through a gap in the barricades, and into the station house. Connolly whipped off his gas mask and pushed the prisoner to the desk where Pantuzzi sat, as bored as ever.

"Sergeant, book this man for incitement to riot, assaulting a police officer, resisting arrest, criminal anarchy, disturbing the peace . . ." He turned to Murphy, who was wiping his eyes with a wet handkerchief that Corelli had given him. "You men give your names as arresting officers. Bring the prisoner to the squad room when he's been booked."

The prisoners in the muster room had begun to chant defiantly, "Let the brothers go. Let the brothers go."

"I got all their names, Captain," Applebaum said. "The only way we can shut them up is to shoot 'em or bribe 'em."

"You think you can hold me here now?" the black man shouted at Connolly. "You jive-ass motherfucker, we're gonna tear your dungeon down. Tear it down."

The prisoners in the muster room picked up the chant. "Tear the dungeons down. Tear the dungeons down."

"A new tune for the Top Forty," Applebaum said.

Connolly turned back toward his office as Murphy and Corelli shoved the black man up against the desk.

"Hey man, we don't want you in here," Corelli said. "You just cool it, and let us book you, and you'll be out on the street in a couple of hours."

"Think the revolution can wait that long?" Murphy asked.

"It'll wait," Andre said defiantly.

"Well, alright, then. Give the nice sergeant your name, and we'll get you a little Murine."

Connolly called Heffernan into his office. "Take a detail out there, and bring in all the injured people," he said. "We'll see if we can give them temporary treatment until the ambulances arrive from Jefferson Hospital. Also, bring the barricades back in, and let's see what we can do about getting this place back to normal again."

Heffernan and his men brought eleven people into the station house, among them four young women and two kids, who looked about eight or nine. They had burn blotches on their faces, contusions on their heads and bodies where they had been trampled by the others. The children were crying hysterically, the adults seemed dazed. One of the women was twitching from shock. They sat her down on a bench next to Andre, who had been booked and was waiting for Corelli to come back with a wet towel for his eyes.

The prisoners in the muster room cheered the injured, shouting, "Tear the dungeons down. Tear the dungeons down." But the injured took no notice.

Murphy was in the bathroom immersing his face in warm water. Corelli watched worriedly.

"You alright, Murf?"

"Yeah, yeah, go take care of Andre. The poor bastard thinks he's gonna die."

Corelli heard the ambulance sirens as he came out. Andre was bent over on the bench, running his fingers gingerly over his red, tearing eyes.

"I'm blind," he said, as Corelli sat next to him, and began to sponge his eyes out.

"You'll be okay in a couple of hours," Corelli said.

The prisoners in the muster room kept the chant going. "Tear the dungeons down. Tear the dungeons down."

Dacey came downstairs from the squad room, and looked in at them. "You're gonna need a bus to take all these people to Central Booking," he said.

"We'll just release 'em all when the Captain goes home," Pantuzzi said.

Andre's arms and wrists were beginning to hurt from the handcuffs. The pain in his eyes had penetrated to the back of his head. His face was throbbing. He hardly heard the cheers of support from the other prisoners. He just kept repeating over and over again, "I'm blind, I'm blind . . ."

34

At the end of the four-to-twelve, everybody headed for the bars. They were all too keyed-up to go home. Even the veterans, who had learned to take everything in their stride, had to wind down with a couple of drinks. Even Corelli, who fled the precinct as if it were being bombed every night, was going to hoist a few over at the Emerald.

But not Murphy. "I don't feel like tellin' war stories tonight," he told Corelli.

"You just gonna go home?"

"Why not? I've got a six-pack in the refrigerator. It'll be quiet in the house. I go to a saloon with you guys and all that smoke will irritate my eyes. One of the guys, Morgan or somebody, will get real pissed, and there'll be a fight. Nah, I'm goin' home."

Murphy got in his car and drove straight to Jefferson Hospital. He didn't think once of the resolution he had made never to see her again. It was just common sense to avoid junkie chicks. They couldn't be trusted, and they would end up ripping you off one way or another. They were deceptive, like all junkies. They could be charming if they had to. Like all junkies. And they were great liars . . . Like all junkies. If you let them play on your sympathies or affections, they would take you for everything you had.

Murphy drove right to the Emergency Room driveway. The shift was just breaking. She came out in a group. That big, black orderly was with her, and a couple of Spanish dudes he'd never seen before.

Murphy got out of the car, and let her see him. She detached herself from the group.

"Back for seconds?" she asked.

"Guess I can't stay away."

"Well, you can practice tonight. I've already got something on."

"So break it."

"Can't . . . not tonight."

Murphy reached for her hand. "Look, I don't wanna come on heavy."

"Then don't . . ."

"But we had a real crazy day today. I just feel like talkin' . . ."

"You comin', Isabella?" the black orderly called harshly.

She turned and waved. "In a second. I know you had a hard day," she said to Murphy. "We had all your victims in here. We had a hard day, too." She turned to go, but Murphy pulled her back.

"You don't wanna go with them," he said.

"Hey cop," the black guy said, running over. "Why don't you just let the chick go if she wants to?"

Murphy ignored him. "I really want to talk to you, Isabella."

"Don't you know better than to stick your fuckin' face in where you're not wanted?" the black guy said.

Murphy stepped away from the nurse. "Why don't you mind your own business, sucker?"

"Why don't you go out and celebrate all the little kids you beat up today, motherfucker!"

The nurse turned to pacify him. "Frank, it's okay. I'll be with you . . ."

"I can beat up a big kid, too, if I have to," Murphy said.

"Whoa Frank, whoa man." The little Spanish dude stepped between them.

"Lemme do him, Hernando," the orderly said.

"Yeah, Hernando," Murphy said, "let him come."

Hernando turned with a wide, ingratiating smile. "Hey look," he said to Murphy, "we all had a tough day, you know. Everybody's a little uptight. This man's a cop, Frank," he said to the orderly. "He ain't gonna lose, man. Cops don't lose, man." He spoke in a hoarse, persuasive tone. He was the dealer. Murphy could toss him right now. He'd probably find enough dope on the dude to send him away for fifteen to life. But the case would be thrown out for illegal search. It wouldn't make trial. They'd dismiss it in pretrial hearing. ("What made you suspect this man was a heroin dealer,

Patrolman Murphy?" "Well, it was the way he manipulated the people around him. The way he spoke, and looked. It was just a feeling I had." "Did you have any concrete evidence?" "No." "Dismissed.")

"If Isabella wants to go with the man, let her go," Hernando said.

"No, no," the nurse said. "Wait for me." She touched Murphy's cheek. "I never thought I'd see you again," she said. "I'm sorry."

"Sure." Murphy got back in the car, and watched her walk down the block with the others. She didn't look back.

Murphy drove out to Mineola. It was beginning to snow. The flakes swirled lightly on the highway, blown into shifting patterns by the wind. Murphy's eyes were stinging from the strain of focusing on the road. It would take a few days for all that gas to get out of his system. He pulled over to the side of the expressway, and lit a cigarette. The windows were closed, the motor was running. All he had to do was finish his cigarette, lean back and close his eyes. In a couple of minutes it would be over. He would be out of the race. Murphy in the fourth. Scratched.

He leaned back and closed his eyes. How come it's so easy to die, and so hard to live? There had to be a reason. How come you get so drowsy and comfortable, and you can almost feel someone leading you down into the restful blackness?

"Shit!"

The cigarette had burned right down to his finger. Murphy leaned against the handle until the door opened. He fell out of the car. He staggered over to the side of the road, and vomited in a snow drift.

Chino had given Jose the number of a bar on the Lower East Side. He drank about ten screwdrivers, and snorted coke to keep himself sober. Every time he went to the bathroom to tighten up, the barmaid smiled knowingly. She was a pretty little *mamita,* stylish, too, with her short hair and designer jeans. Nice ass, swinging back and forth. The coke made you concentrate on things like asses and lips, and the way she wrapped her fingers caressingly around the neck of the bottle when she poured drinks. She liked him. She knew he was holding. He had everything she wanted. The blow would open her eyes. Eighty-seven percent Bolivian, and so fresh you could smell it as soon as you opened the tinfoil. It was part of half a pound that had gotten "lost" in a seizure of seven keys he had made a few months before with two guys from the Task Force. The other two were married men, and had sold their pieces. He had kept his to party with. It came in handy when you were trying to score with these young foxes. The first thing they always asked was, "You got any coke?" This Bolivian was speedy blow. It made their little hearts go pitter-pat.

Just before the last call, the phone in the booth rang. The barmaid swung around to answer it. "Chino?" she called. "Oh, it's you," she said coyly when he came to answer the phone.

It was Jose. "Can you make it on up here?" he asked. "My man says he's back in business."

Chino rolled about a half a gram into a dollar bill, and stuck it under his drink as a tip. This way he knew she would remember him the next time he came in. And if there were any I.A.D. guys on his case, he could always say he was working on the joint. There wasn't a saloon on the Lower East Side that didn't have something going down.

There were no cabs on the Lower East Side at this time of night, and even if there were, they would never stop for a lone Hispanic male. Chino walked up to 14th Street, and all the way across to the West Side. He was numb with cold by the time he got on the I.R.T. The train was almost empty, except for a few people obviously going home from work— waitresses, night watchmen, private policemen. Everybody looked down at their shoes; eye contact on the subway could be fatal. At Forty-deuce a bunch of rowdy black kids got on. They walked through the cars shouting, smoking cigarettes, checking out any potential victims. Chino put his hand in his pocket and stared straight ahead. Couldn't sleep because they would think you were a wino, and try to roll you. Couldn't show fear because they would think you were holding. Chino didn't have his gun or his shield. All he had was this ratty switchblade, and twenty-five hundred bucks that he had brought to cop the eighth. It would be really great if these kids tried to take him off. Nolan and Fabrizio would never believe he had been mugged on the subway; they would think he had fabricated the story to keep the bread for himself. They would make things real tough for him after that. He would never be able to trust them at his back again. So he stared straight ahead, his hand on the knife, knowing that if these kids started something he would have to cut them.

Above 96th Street there wasn't a white person left on the train. Above 149th, the train was deserted except for him. Chino could remember going to Brooklyn with his whole family to visit his uncle, and coming back to the Bronx on the subway at one o'clock in the morning. His mother and his sisters chatting away. His father reading the Sunday *News,* and passing him the funnies. The train would be full of people, mostly black and Spanish. There were no cops, no fights. Even the drunks were harmless. How long ago was that— twenty, twenty-five years? B.H., before heroin.

Chino got off at Simpson Street, and walked to Hernando's building. The fourth floor, Jose had said. As he approached the apartment he could hear the sound of rubber bands snapping. They were packaging tomorrow's bags in there, quarter grams wrapped in glasseine envelopes. Chino knocked softly.

Jose came to the door weaving and smiling. "Come on in, man." He was real high. He had that look that some junkies got, as if their features had been pasted on at weird angles. Nothing on his face made any sense.

Jose slapped Chino five. "Okay, bro, you made it up here. Come over here and meet the man."

Hernando was working under a red lamp, cutting the dope. He was a little dude with a wild curly Afro-style hairdo, and a scraggly beard. Good dresser—leather jacket with a suede collar, leather pants, cowboy boots, probably Tony Lemas, probably with a twenty-five stuck into one of them.

"Hernando, man," he said, offering his hand.

"Chino."

"My man says you want to cop weight," Hernando said.

"That's right."

"Well, we got weight. You got the bread?"

"I got the bread."

"Well, all right." Hernando turned away from his work, and looked Chino up and down. "You the man?"

"Yeah," Chino said. "You're under arrest."

Hernando hiccoughed, and Chino realized he was high. Which made him dangerous. The junkies who didn't nod behind the smack were the ones you had to watch out for. The ones who functioned on the shit were into another metabolism. They were paranoid, cunning. Hernando's eyeballs had that high gloss, and he hiccoughed. That was the only sign he was high. All of a sudden Chino wished he had called his back up.

"You got a gun?" Hernando asked.

"Not with me," Chino said.

"You carry all that bread without a piece?"

"If I'm gonna be ripped off, the gun will only get me killed," Chino said. He knew he was being tested, that a wrong answer might be his last.

"Take off your clothes, man," Hernando said. "With all these fuckin' cops runnin' around I gotta be sure."

Chino always went undercover without his gun or his shield. Sometimes, if he thought there might be a bust, he carried his police I.D. card in his sock. It was always good for a Spanish cat to have proof that he was a cop; they usually didn't take his word for it.

"I'm glad you got heat in here," Chino said, taking off his shirt.

"We got everything here," Jose said.

It was a nice pad. Wall-to-wall red carpeting, beaded curtains, comfortable leather furniture, a stereo—a big color tube. The man lived good.

"What's this, a strip search?" Chino asked, slipping out of his pants.

"We ain't gonna look up your asshole, if that's what you mean," Hernando said. "Even if you want us to."

"And what would you do if I turned out to be a cop?"

Hernando took the pistol out of his boot. "Blow you away, man," he said quietly.

Chino stood up straight, nude except for his socks, an oversight he hoped would be passed over. "And what if there were twenty cops outside the door?"

"I'd blow as many of them away as I could," Hernando said. "Because I ain't goin' back to the joint, man. You ever been in?"

Chino nodded. "I did a nickel at Lewisburg."

"Federal," Hernando said. "I'm talkin' about hard time upstate at Attica or Greenhaven. Just as soon get a little hair on the walls right here, get it over with . . ."

"Meanwhile, I'm standin' here with my balls hangin' out," Chino said.

Jose giggled. "He's clean, man."

"Yeah." Hernando lit a Pall Mall. "Okay, bro, you can put your pants on."

"Now can we do business?" Chino asked, slipping quickly into his shoes.

"Sure, man. You wanna take a look at the goods?" Hernando stepped away and let Chino sit down.

It was a table with a mirrored top. There was a strainer, a spoon, and a woman's nylon stocking. And two piles of white powder, one at least ten times larger than the other.

Hernando put a triple-beam scale down on the table. "You trust my scale?"

"For the time being," Chino said.

"*Vaya*, let's go." He took a cellophane bag off the table, and carefully spooned a pile onto the scale, adding, subtracting, and weighing until it came to three and a half grams.

"This shit any good?" Chino asked.

"Take a look, man. It's pure white like the snow. My boy just did it. Look at him."

Jose was sitting on the sofa, leaning forward to watch them, his eyes slowly closing, his head sinking onto his chest.

"The shit's good, man," Hernando said. "You can hit it seven, eight times, and them junkies'll still be comin' to you with their hands out. It's right off the boat. You can't get no better skag in the world. Take a taste, go ahead, if you don't believe me."

"Not out of my stash," Chino said.

Hernando chuckled. "Help yourself, baby. I got enough."

Chino had been dreading this. On top of the booze and the blow, and the fourteen hours he'd been up and moving around, even a one and one of this *shmeck* would put him away. Hernando took a metal ruler, and separated two thin lines of powder from the smaller pile on the mirror. He handed Chino a metal straw. "Try it, you'll like it," Hernando said.

What a fucking job, Chino thought, putting the straw to his nose, and bending over the neat white lines.

35

The story was on the front page of the *Daily News*. POLICE CAPTAIN GASSES PROTESTORS. In the *Times* the headlines read POLICE BATTLE DEMONSTRATORS IN THE SOUTH BRONX. And the *New York Post* trumpeted COPS QUELL BRONX RIOT.

The station house was mobbed with reporters for the second time that week. The TV guys waited outside with their cameras. They besieged Connolly when he arrived in the morning, firing questions about the new arrest program, the community reaction, etc. He tried to brush past them, but they blocked his way, shoving mikes in his face, flashbulbs popping in his face, everyone shouting at once.

"If we can just have you for five minutes, Captain . . ."

"Captain Connolly, is it true that this is your first command?"

"How do you respond to the charges of some members of the community that you are a racist?"

That stopped Connolly in his tracks. He turned coldly to the reporter who had asked that, a black girl who worked for one of the smaller radio stations in the city.

"As I understand it, a racist is someone who makes discriminatory distinctions on the basis of race," he said. "I don't do that. I arrest criminals no matter what their race. I hope the law-abiding people of this community will come to see that in time, and will support my efforts."

"Why won't you let us bring our cameras inside the station house? What are you hiding?"

Connolly pushed his way to the door. "I'm not hiding anything. I'm also not putting on a TV show. I will not have the operations of this precinct obstructed in any way."

With that he pushed his way through into the station house, leaving the reporters to marvel at his attitude.

"He's an old-fashioned book cop."

"A blast from the past."

"He's the story. Not the neighborhood or the riot or the cop killings. This guy is the story."

Connolly had all three newspapers sent in, and read their versions of the previous day's events. Unable to get information from the precinct, or from the Police Department press office, which usually handled such stories, the papers had relied solely on the accounts of various community groups, and on interviews with members of the march, who claimed they had been gassed, beaten, and arrested without provocation. The cops were characterized as "storm troopers" in one story; in another it was alleged that they took off their name tags when they "waded into the mob, swinging their billy clubs." The *New York Post* claimed fifty people had been treated for smoke inhalation and various injuries. That was not even a distortion, it was an outright lie. Connolly had counted eleven people. But they had willfully, knowingly inflated the figure. And there was no one to stop them.

Through his office window Connolly watched the growing mob of press people in front of the precinct. It had snowed the night before, and they stood ankle deep in slush, shivering, blowing on their fingers, but running toward any cop or community resident who appeared on the street. They grabbed Dacey as he got out of his car, and got him to stand still long enough for an interview.

Connolly hit the intercom, and got Coughlin, the day desk sergeant. "Go out there, and tell me what Lieutenant Dacey is telling the press," he said.

This wasn't the amiable Dacey, the personality boy. His expression was grim. He pointed several times toward Connolly's office as he spoke.

Coughlin came in when the interview was over and Dacey had entered the station house. "He really let you have it, boss."

Connolly looked down at his call sheet. He had messages from the Borough Commander, from Headquarters, from the heads of community groups. "What did he say?"

"That your policy of using arrests as a means of getting information on the killings was counterproductive. That it had probably driven the killers further underground, and that it would make their apprehension that much more difficult."

Coughlin related all this with relish. Sure, they loved to see their boss in the doghouse. That was the only satisfaction they got out of their jobs. Word had obviously reached them. If Dacey, the master politician, had the nerve to repudiate him publicly, they all had to know. He was going to hang for this. He was going to take the rap.

Connolly called Inspector Krieger at Borough Headquarters first.

"I've got a pile of messages from every civil rights group in the city on my desk, Dennis," Krieger said. "You really caused a furor with your new incentive policy."

"It was simple enforcement," Connolly said. "I want the law enforced in this precinct as it is in every other."

"There's no such thing as simple enforcement, Dennis."

"Everyone arrested was committing a crime, in the judgment of my officers," Connolly said. "I just can't see how people can get all worked up over it. I'm trying to clean up their neighborhood."

"Well, they don't look at it that way," Krieger said. "To them it looks like repression, racism. And because it is their neighborhood we'll give them the benefit of the doubt. We're going to cancel your incentive program, Dennis. And in the future if you have any innovative ideas, please call me first. You got my ass in a sling down at Headquarters with this as well."

"What am I supposed to tell the men? Stop arresting people?"

"You don't have to tell them anything," Krieger said. "They'll know." His voice cracked in annoyance. "And for Chrissake don't use tear gas on innocent people."

"They weren't innocent," Connolly said angrily. "They had been warned that they were in violation of the law. They were causing a disturbance, and threatening the security of my station house. The Four-One has been fired on before, and I wasn't going to let it happen again. If you want to remove me . . ."

"That decision isn't up to me," Krieger said. "But if it was, you'd be pounding a beat in Staten Island right now." And hung up.

There was a message from Chief Inspector Foley at Headquarters. He was the second in command to the Commissioner, a career cop with forty years on the job, famous for his shrewdness and self-preservation. His name had been linked with several corruption scandals, but he had always managed to wiggle out of trouble. They had even started a file on him in I.A.D. once, but the folder had stayed empty without one report or investigation so they finally threw it away.

Foley spoke in a soft, familiar voice, as if he'd known Connolly for years. "What are you buckin' for, Connolly?" he asked. "You wanna run for Congress or something?"

"No, sir . . ."

"Well, there's gotta be a reason for you tryin' to get all this publicity. Advancement in the department can't be it, because Sonny, you're about as dead as Kelsey's nuts as far as that goes. You can't go around beatin' up on minorities in New York."

"I didn't look at them as minorities," Connolly said.

"Then you're blind as well as stupid. We've got a race relations problem in this city, and cops with tear gas don't help to resolve it."

Connolly's mouth went dry. "If you want me to put my retirement papers in . . ."

"Fuck your papers," Foley said. "I ain't makin' a martyr out of you."

"If it's a question of transferring me . . ."

"You're too good to be true, Connolly," Foley said. "Just as honest and forthright as they come. Well, that's great. You'll stay exactly where you are until further notice. I'm only calling you because the Commissioner asked me to. Being a political appointee who never spent one second in a police uniform, he respects what you did yesterday. He doesn't know what a useless pile of collars you accumulated, that you alienated the men who work for you, and the community you work in. He thinks your police work is just fine, but your politics need a little brushing up. He just wanted me to explain that we're trying to keep attention off the high crime areas in the city. It hurts us, hurts the image we're trying to promote as the new, improved, New York, safe for tourists and investors. It clashes with the city's big publicity campaign. He just wanted to explain all this, I guess, because he would really give you a medal if he had his way. He's the Commissioner, but he's not a cop, and he doesn't know what a horse's ass you are."

Connolly's hand was shaking when he hung up. Deader than Kelsey's nuts, Foley had said. So what if the Commissioner sympathized; commissioners came and went. It was guys like Krieger and Foley who decided on promotions. And as of today, they were his enemies. He was finished. Just when he thought his career was really beginning it was over.

Coughlin knocked and peeked in. "There's a delegation from the Community Board here to see you. They say Inspector Krieger told them to come."

About ten people crowded into Connolly's office, and hastily introduced themselves. There was a priest, a minister, a man from the Hunts Point Merchant's Association, the local assemblyman, two women from the redevelopment board, a few young men from various agencies. They spoke quietly, and with great precision, but Connolly caught flashes of anger in their eyes. He had more chairs brought in, got them coffee and tea and extra ashtrays. They spoke the need to promote a more positive image of the South Bronx, and he agreed. They said that there was still a great deal of misunderstanding between the police, and the people. He agreed. They intimated that there were certain plans afoot to encourage massive foreign investment in the area. The Japanese were looking at the possibility of building an electrical parts plant on Charlotte Street; a consortium of Arab investors had been approached about backing a middle-income housing project. Tax deferrals and other advantages were being offered manufacturers who would build factories here. It would mean thousands of jobs, a revitalization of the area, they said. But the important thing was not to scare anybody off, not to make them think the area was a den of thieves and drug addicts . . .

Connolly nodded and agreed. After a while their words and faces blurred into one another; he couldn't hear what was being said, or see who was saying it. He just sat there nodding, thinking all the while, "I'm finished, I'm finished."

With no official command from Connolly, the word spread through the ranks: the incentive program was off. The men grumbled. All that work had gone for nothing. There would be no extra vacation days after all.

"I'm takin' my vacation tonight," Morgan announced.

"You'll have to commit a triple homicide on the fender of my car to get me to make a collar."

It was a slow, restful night. Murphy and Corelli cruised for hours without a call. The streets had frozen over, and everybody was staying inside. This usually meant a night of family disputes, as families were stuck together, too many to a room. But the radio was quiet. The neighborhood was recovering from the great spasm of excitement it had endured the day before.

During their meal period, Murphy called the Emergency Room at Jefferson Hospital, and asked for Isabella Ortiz.

"This is your secret admirer," he said.

"What is it now?"

"I can't live without you."

"Wanna bet?"

"If I can't see you tonight, I'll kill myself. I'll drive off the Tiffany Street Pier, I'll eat a box of thumbtacks, I'll drink a quart of motor oil . . ."

She was laughing. He loved that sound. "I thought you did that every night."

"To avoid controversy, why don't we meet at a neutral place," he said.

"Who says I'm going to meet you?"

"How about the Emerald at twelve-thirty?"

"I'll be there," she said.

A little after midnight Murphy pulled up in front of the Emerald and waited. In a few minutes he saw her get out of the bus, struggling against the wind and the slush, and go into the bar. He had to drive seven blocks to find a phone booth that worked, but he finally got Lureen behind the bar.

"Do me a favor, baby. You know that nurse I came in with the other night?"

"She's here now," Lureen said.

"I know, that's why I'm calling. Tell her I'll pick her up on the corner in five minutes."

"What's the matter, you too good to drink in here all of a sudden?"

"What do you mean all of a sudden? I just want to keep it discreet, you understand?"

"Yeah, sure. Well, you can call me Cupid from now on."

"You'll need a pair of diapers and a bow and arrow for that," Murphy said.

He circled back toward the Emerald. She was waiting for him on the corner.

"What's all the sneaking around for?" she asked getting into the car. "You ashamed to be seen with a Puerto Rican girl?"

"Ashamed? Shit, I'll take you to the Waldorf-Astoria right now."

"I wouldn't want to be seen with an Irish cop in the Waldorf-Astoria."

"That's what I thought." He stuck his finger through a hole in her cloth coat. "You can't go around like this in this weather."

She snuggled next to him. "So buy me a mink?"

"Maybe I will if you're real nice to me. Maybe I will."

He drove over to the Howard Johnsons in Yonkers. "How civilized," she said, "he's going to feed me first."

"You've got to keep your strength up."

He made her eat a huge chocolate sundae. "I'll get fat, and you won't like me anymore," she said.

"I don't like you now," he said. He grabbed her hand. "Animal lust is all I feel for you."

"Ooh, I think I am going to need my strength tonight."

They drove to the Sunset Motel. "Let's get room 302 again," she said.

"But the vibrassage didn't work."

"Maybe they fixed it. C'mon, don't you have any sentiment in your soul?"

He asked for 302.

"What's the special attraction?" the clerk asked, handing him the key.

"The cockroaches put on a show in the bathroom," Murphy said. He looked at his watch. "And I'd better hurry up before I miss it."

She undressed quickly and jumped into bed. "C'mon," she said, making her teeth chatter, "it's freezing."

He put out the light as he undressed. "You shy?" she teased.

"I like to keep things a little mysterious," he said.

"You weren't so mysterious the last time."

"Yeah, well I was with a different person. And so were you."

"That's a little too deep for me."

"Forget it." Murphy got into bed, and she wrapped herself around him.

"Oooh, you're so warm."

"That's from years of putting antifreeze in my body."

"Feel how cold my feet are," she said, rubbing them against his ankles.

"Poor circulation," he said.

"Brilliant diagnosis, doctor. And what's the treatment?"

He kissed her cheek, her neck, the hollow between her breasts. Astonished at his own ardor, he slid under the sheets and kissed her thighs, the backs of her knees, the places on her calf where he had seen the puncture marks. She stroked his hair, and the back of his neck while he laid his cheek along the warmth of her thigh and whispered "I love you" in a voice so low and muffled that no one could possibly have heard.

Murphy got home at four o'clock that morning. It had started to snow again, which gave him a built-in excuse. The overtime, the bad weather, the roads. Not that Mary would ask him anything. She would be asleep, curled in a tight little ball at the very edge of the bed when he got in. No wonder she woke up with a headache every day.

The outside light was on. The dinner dishes were stacked neatly in the washer, leftovers all wrapped up in tinfoil in case he wanted a snack, garbage tied up in hefty bags—it was his job to put it out. Just another happy American marriage, that's what it was.

Murphy tiptoed upstairs. He peeked in the girls' room, then at his son Timothy, sleeping with his fists clenched, snarling wetly into the pillow. The kid was a brawler. His teachers had sent notes home several times. Mary wanted to send him to a Catholic school where he would get more discipline. But Murphy knew nothing would get that rage out of his system; it was in the genes.

He sneaked into his bedroom, undressing in the dark for the second time that night. It was so quiet he could hear Mary's little wisps of breath. Quiet . . . quiet . . . after all these years of sneaking around he was real good; he would make a great cat burglar as soon as his twenty years was up. He lay down gingerly, hardly making the springs creak, and closed his eyes.

"You bastard."

It was an otherworldly hiss, as if that headless bundle next to him wasn't his wife at all, but some vengeful imp.

"Mary?"

"Get out of my bedroom."

He leaned over to see her face, put his hand on her shoulder, but she turned quickly, scratching his wrist. "Don't touch me," she shrieked.

"Mary, for Chrissake . . ."

She swung at him, her nails raking his face. "Get out," she shrieked.

"Mary, keep your voice down." He rolled off the bed, away from her flailing arms.

"You stink from that prostitute," she screamed. "I won't have you in my bedroom. Get out."

He stumbled through the darkness. "Okay, Mary," he said softly. "You're right, you're right, okay . . ." He had to find his off-duty pistol. He heard too many stories of berserk wives shooting their husbands with their off-duty guns. "Mary, the kids. You're gonna wake the kids . . ."

"I don't care. I don't care about anything anymore . . ."

There it was on the back of the chair, where he always put it.

"I just want you out of here. Get out."

"Okay, okay, I'll sleep on the couch." Murphy backed out of the bedroom. "Try to keep your voice down, honey, please."

"You bastard," she cried. "You filthy bastard." She leapt off the bed, and slammed the bedroom door so hard plaster rained down from the ceiling.

Timothy was up, rubbing his eyes. "Dad?" he called.

"It's alright, Timmy. Go back to sleep, it's alright."

His daughters were sitting up in bed. He went into their room. "It's okay, kids. It is."

They stared at him. Their father in his underwear, holding his off-duty pistol. They were old enough to understand. Murphy went cold with shame. "It's okay, girls, really it is." He backed out of the room, and went downstairs where he sat on the sofa, trembling and holding his off-duty gun until dawn.

36

Connolly opened the newspapers the next day to find that he had become a hero. The reporters had dug up every scrap of information they could find about him, his department record, his family life, his philosophy of law enforcement, and produced a portrait of a dedicated and much-misunderstood police officer. The *Times* managed to find somebody at Headquarters to air an opinion. This unnamed source characterized him as a "stickler for the law . . . Dennis is inflexible when it comes to corruption. He'll run down even the smallest transgression. I'm afraid he doesn't have much sympathy for human nature." And the *Times* editorialist jumped all over this quote. "Perhaps we need more inflexible sticklers in the Police Department," the lead editorial read. "Perhaps we have come to a point in the history of our city—and our country—where we must return to a more demanding interpretation of the laws and ethics that we were founded upon."

The *Post* trapped the Chief Inspector in an embarrassing quote. "We've cancelled Captain Connolly's incentive arrest program," he said. "I'm afraid he still has a lot to learn about being a cop in the South Bronx."

"Maybe Chief Inspector Foley can explain to the people of this city what the difference is between law enforcement in the South Bronx and any other area," the *Post* lead editorial commented. "We were under the mistaken impression that every citizen in a democracy was supposed to be treated equally. It seems that the Police Department has other ideas on the subject."

The *News* had gotten Kathleen on the phone. Although she swore to her husband that she had spoken to the reporter for less than a minute, a complete family portrait of the Connollys was right there on page three. Connolly read about his son at Notre Dame, his newly married daughter—Kathleen

217

had left out the part about her hippie wedding—and his long-suffering, self-sacrificing wife. "It's been hard," Kathleen was quoted as saying. "Dennis devotes more time to his work than to his family. But he's so committed to it and, after all, it is so important, that we've always understood."

In tears, Kathleen denied saying that. "You know how these people can twist things around, Dennis. I know I told him how hard you worked. He just made the rest up."

But it sounded too much like Kathleen, that sweet regretful way she had of laying the blame on him, to have been the invention of a malicious reporter. Besides, the *News* loved her for it. And him, too.

"Are we crazy?" the editorial demanded, "or is this the kind of public servant who should be encouraged and rewarded instead of slapped down by his superiors and condemned by the people he's trying to help?"

The story hit the wire services, and the precinct was flooded with calls. Every city that had a decaying urban area wanted a hero like Connolly to come in and reclaim it. They wanted instant wisdom, a couple of magic words, a little inspiration. Connolly couldn't give it to them. He sat in his office with the door closed, wondering what to do. He knew how the Department hated publicity. How could he convince them that he hadn't engineered all of this? The few words that he had shouted at the reporters now shouted back at him in bold type: "I'm not running a TV show, I'm running a precinct." He wasn't even sure he had said that; he had only wanted to get those idiots off his back. But now everything he had said and done seemed so self-serving and calculated. He emerged from all these stories as a stiff-necked, careerist prig. It hadn't happened that way. He wasn't like that. But how could he convince them now? He could only hope that things would quiet down, and they would let him do his job.

The men in the precinct read the stories in disbelief; some were amused, some enraged.

"We break our asses, and he gets all the fuckin' credit," Morgan raved in the locker room that afternoon.

Even Patterson was upset. "It looks like we were all goofin' off until he got up here."

"Now that fuckin' asshole's gonna get to be Commissioner," said Donahue.

218

Murphy laughed bitterly at all of them. He laughed loudly, and too long. His eyes were red and his face haggard, as if he hadn't gotten much sleep the night before. The men were uncomfortable under his mocking look, but said nothing.

"Commissioner? That jerk will be lucky if he ain't out pounding a beat in two weeks. You guys have been on this job ten, fifteen years, and you don't know shit from Shinola. You all might as well be rookies the way you talk . . ."

"Lookit the big expert over here," Morgan said. "You gonna tell us how things work . . ."

Murphy cut him off angrily. "The guy's finished, and he don't know it. You don't know it either because you're just as stupid as he is."

Morgan slammed his locker shut. "What are you, a big fuckin' brain all of a sudden?"

"He made the bosses look like assholes," Murphy said. "They made statements, and the papers nailed them. You think Foley will ever forgive him?"

"Foley will have to retire now," Donahue said. "The Commissioner will go with Connolly, Murf. You'll see."

"It don't matter if the whole Headquarters staff goes," Murphy said. "They'll make sure he stays here for the duration. No promotions, no honors, the poor bastard won't even be allowed on the Captains' Association boatride." Murphy put his off-duty pistol in the locker. "I could almost feel sorry for the guy, but I'm just too busy these days worryin' about myself."

Andre's eyes were still red and smarting from the mace. He and his three friends had been released on their own recognizance after a famous Civil Liberties lawyer volunteered to take their cases. Now he sat in the South Bronx People's Party headquarters with a wet towel over his eyes while Shields read the newspaper stories aloud.

"Motherfucker invades the community, and they make him a hero," Pena said.

"I guess that proves what you were saying, Andre," Shields said.

"They're gettin' ready to come down hard on the people," Salazar said.

"They've already begun," Andre said. "The next step has to be resistance."

219

Spanish Pete read the stories, and immediately called a politician of his acquaintance.

"Is there any way to get rid of this Connolly?" he asked.

"We're trying," the politician said. "We're trying."

Chino had waited a day before calling Jose for another buy. The heroin he had scored from Hernando was pure. According to lab reports, it was identical to the dope the Garcia family was dealing around town, the dope this Rumanian was bringing in from Afghanistan. The word was to go easy, make a few more small buys, then ask for a half key, or a load big enough to get one of the Garcias up from Washington Heights to meet him. The next step in the plan was to bust the Garcia envoy, and flip him out as an informer to catch the Rumanian. Chino could imagine the contingent they would have for that collar—CIA, FBI, D.E.A., N.Y.P.D., all falling over each other to get the headlines. Meanwhile, he, the lowly undercover who had put the whole thing together, wouldn't get a mention. Well, this time things would be different. If he pinched a Russian spy he was going to get his name in the paper. Julio Mendoza—and spell it right, motherfucker.

Chino called Jose at four in the morning. Wake him up, scare him, catch him off balance. "Sorry to get you so late," he said.

"That's cool, that's cool," Jose mumbled groggily.

"My people want to do some more. Can you give me a price for a bigger number?"

"Not over the phone, man."

He loved this little bit of pointless caution. All these low-level guys liked to play it real cool over the phone just to show how professional they were. They didn't know that if there was a tap on them that meant there was a court order, and if there was a court order there was a team of agents working on them, and if there was a team of agents they were as good as busted no matter how cool they were on the phone.

"I'll meet you in that bar again," Chino said, playing along, and not mentioning the name of the bar.

"Two o'clock, man. I'll be there."

Chino tried to sleep, but without a Valium it would be impossible. He was too keyed up. It was the same way on every case, the excitement and anticipation. A trank would only make him lose his edge, and he didn't want that. Not now, not when the whole thing was heading for a showdown.

At nine o'clock in the morning Chino had gone into D.E.A. headquarters to ask for enough money to buy an ounce of heroin. He was taken to see a thin, white-faced young man in a dark suit.

"How much will you need for this purchase?" the man asked him.

"This quality dope goes for twelve thousand an ounce. I always like to negotiate with these guys. They get suspicious if you give up that kind of money too easily. So maybe I can get it down to eleven."

The man opened a black attache case on the desk. "Here, just to be on the safe side."

And he gave Chino thirteen thousand dollars in cash. "You may also have to pay more," he said, looking steadily across the table. "Sign this voucher, please."

37

Two days after the riot the sabotage began.

It started with little things. Cops would leave the radio cars for coffee, and return to find their tires flattened. Private cars parked around the station were vandalized—windows broken, antennae ripped off, red paint poured over the hoods.

Then, the false alarms started. Several cars responding to a report of a fight on Westchester Avenue were attacked with rocks and bottles from the platform of the elevated platform; the bombers got away on a passing train just as the cops rushed on to the platform. False complaints started coming in to the Four-One at the rate of five an hour. Cops were rushing, guns drawn, into *bodegas* that weren't being held up, checking out burglaries that had never happened, searching for bodies in the frozen rubble of Charlotte Street and finding dead rats.

Anonymous phone calls and letters poured in, offering clues in the killings of the rookies. Dacey's men had to follow them up, just as the police had to respond to every call. False alarms were called in to the fire station. In a neighborhood where real fires were so common, this became a serious hazard. There had always been the occasional prank to contend with, but this was sabotage—organized, orchestrated, and escalating.

Some of it seemed to originate from people who knew the inner workings of the police department. The desk got a call one day from a man who identified himself as Chief Inspector Foley. They put him through to Connolly.

"What the hell is going on up there, Connolly?" the man shouted. "Why haven't you people responded to the plane crash?"

"What plane crash?" Connolly asked. "We've had no report of . . ."

"The commuter plane that crashed in the water just off the Tiffany Street Pier. We've got thirty people in the water waiting to be rescued. Now I want every available car you've got over there immediately."

Connolly gave the order, and every car on the tour sped to the Tiffany Street Pier, scaring the hell out of the few bums who were sharing a pint by a fire on the otherwise peaceful pier. One of them got so rattled by this sudden onslaught of police that he fell in the river, and two cops had to jump into the freezing water to pull him out.

On that same day three different callers reported a severed hand in the gutter on Boone Street. Again several cars were dispatched to locate the hand, and if possible, its owner. Whenever they got to one location, someone called and said it was further down the block. Applebaum ended up crawling under a pickup truck, and coming out covered with frozen dog turds. "I think," he announced solemnly, "that we can officially classify this as a false alarm."

The men were confused, frightened. They came back from their tours with wild tales from street informants. There were rumors that Russian-trained assassins were assembling to launch a major sniping attack on the cops.

"This is gonna blow," a worried Finley predicted one night. "They're settin' us up for something."

Most of the men agreed. They called in the P.B.A. delegate. Some of them advocated an immediate wildcat strike unless the city promised to send the National Guard into the neighborhood until conditions returned to normal. Others said the precinct should be temporarily closed to give the neighborhood a chance to cool off. These proposals were impractical and impossible to implement, the delegate said. They couldn't even be presented in good faith to Headquarters.

"Well, what can we do, then?" a policeman asked.

"You can petition for an increase in manpower," the delegate said.

"That's great," Murphy scoffed. "Cops asking for police protection."

"Officially, that's the only thing I can think of," the delegate said.

"And unofficially?"

The delegate shrugged. "Hey, look, it's the flu season, right? People are dropping like flies."

So the sick roster grew. There were lines outside the police surgeon's office. The number of men who had aggravated old injuries and were now applying for a disability retirement was amazing.

The dwindling ranks were augmented by T.P.F. cops, and by men drawn from the slow, tranquil, middle-class precincts of Queens and Staten Island. Suddenly, police officers who hadn't drawn their guns in ten or fifteen years found themselves ducking bricks and bottles and taking verbal abuse in this strange neighborhood. They complained loudly about their new detail. If the guys assigned to Fort Apache were afraid to work there, why should they?

Connolly sat in his office waiting for the call from Inspector Krieger relieving him of command. It never came. They were waiting, he decided, letting him get in deeper with the absenteeism, the sabotage, the community discontent. Well, until the axe fell he had to run this precinct. He put up a notice that all men on sick call would have to submit a doctor's verification of their illness, and warned that any man found malingering would be suspended forthwith without pay or benefits. He called the Internal Affairs Division and began an investigation of all the false complaints. He met with community groups, and asked them to help stop the sabotage.

"If any of you have any influence among the people who are doing this, please try to convince them to stop. It would certainly be in the interest of the community as a whole."

"It's not just one group that's doing this, Captain," a social worker said. "The idea just kind of spread through the neighborhood."

"The people are going to war with you, Captain. You've torn up their neighborhood, and they're fighting back."

"It's like a gang war. The cops against the people."

They looked blandly at Connolly, but some could hardly conceal their delight at his predicament. They were secretly pleased by what was happening. He'd get no cooperation from them.

"If it is, in fact, a gang war," Connolly said, speaking in measured tones, "they should remember that my gang has twenty-eight thousand members with all kinds of sophisticated weapons. We won't be driven out of this neighborhood."

Taveras, the local assemblyman, nodded, clicking his pencil against his teeth. "I think a lot of people would be mollified if you just got out, Captain. Most of this would probably stop the day you left."

"It will stop before then, Assemblyman," Connolly said. "I promise you that."

Murphy came to work every day, disdaining the men on sick call. "These bastards are showin' their yellow streaks for the world to see," he said. "I like to hide mine."

"Bullshit," Corelli said. "You'd rather get hit with a brick than sit home with your old lady."

Murphy scratched his head in puzzlement. "How can a guy who knows so much about marriage actually walk down the aisle himself?"

Corelli bumped his head gently against his locker. "What do you want me to do? Everybody's supposed to get married, and have kids."

"Not a faggot like you," Patterson said.

Corelli bumped a little harder. "Everybody gets married," he said doggedly. "They have kids, get fat, fuck around, and break up. If you don't follow that pattern, you get in more trouble."

"That's a new way of getting your three-quarters pension," Murphy said. "Bangin' your head against the wall."

"That's the Italian way," Morgan said.

The last few days Morgan had been silent and morose. He sat by his locker clenching and unclenching his fists, nodding at times, as if he were engaged in an interior monologue. Everyone steered clear of him. His occasional black looks and insults indicated that he was looking for a fight. Nobody responded to him but Corelli. Corelli was getting married; he didn't care about anything anymore.

"What's the Irish way?" he challenged Morgan.

Morgan tapped his temple significantly.

"Does that mean smart or crazy?" Patterson asked.

"If it's the Irish way, that means it's crazy," Murphy said, and poked Corelli. "I said it before you did. I'm allowed."

Morgan looked at them with contempt. "You guys havin' a good time?"

"Pretty good," Murphy said. "I just wish it would warm up a little so I could go to the beach."

Morgan rose slowly and walked over to Murphy. "You're a panic, you know. A real, fuckin' panic."

Murphy smiled innocently. "Why, thanks, Godzilla. You're pretty scary yourself."

Morgan nodded. His bloodshot eyes were out of focus. Murphy wondered how many days he'd been drinking, how many more days it would take for his brain to turn off altogether. "You ain't that much smarter than me, Murphy," he said. "You're a cop, too, so how much smarter can you be?"

He walked slowly out of the locker room. The men stared after him waiting until he was out of earshot.

"Now there's an advanced case of alcohol psychosis," Corelli said.

"I don't know," Murphy said. "He's got a pretty good point there."

38

Charlotte was swathed in golden silk. It was wrapped in tight folds around her, the shoulders bare, the front cut all the way down to her navel; so tight it whispered when she walked; so cool against her body, her breasts swelled, the nipples hardened. I'm ready for love/I'm ready for love.

They were screaming for her. The lights were so bright she could hardly see out into the audience. Opening night, and they were screaming. Anxious, pasty-faced men in tuxedos wiping their sweat-darkened hair and leaning over onto the stage. Cool, brown dudes in white suits with wide shoulders, the jewelry glittering off their fingers and necks, clapping and smiling. C'mon, baby, do it to it. Get down.

Yeah, yeah . . . she could sing. Sing so good she brought them to their knees. All the booking agents and the producers; the kids standing outside screaming her name. Charlotte, Charlotte . . .

"C'mon, baby, please get up. C'mon, Puss . . ."

Gloria shook Charlotte gently. "Think you can get dressed, baby? Think you can take a little walk? I got the man coming over, and he don't like strangers around. Especially chicks. Hernando don't like chicks. C'mon, baby . . ."

Gloria helped Charlotte out of bed. "We'll get something warm for you," she said, going to her closet. She came back with a sweater and a pair of woolen slacks, but Charlotte already had her golden outfit on.

"I don't wear that shit," she said. "I'm a golden girl."

Gloria slipped a coat over her shoulders. "Here, this will keep you warm, baby." She slipped a twenty-dollar bill into one of the pockets. "Go over to Anita's Bar on Hoe Avenue. She'll take care of you. I'll come down later and pick you up, okay, baby? I'm sorry, lover, really, but it's better this way for both of us . . ."

Charlotte just looked at Gloria with contempt. Sorry? What was this ugly bitch talking about? She allowed herself to be bundled up, and walked down the stairs.

"Now you go right to Anita's," Gloria said when they got to the door. "I'll come for you in a little while." She kissed Charlotte on the lips. "Don't get lost on me, baby . . . Please."

Get lost? "Ain't nobody lost," Charlotte said as she started down the street. She walked across 165th to Hoe Avenue. With every step she took the cheers got louder. Charlotte smiled languidly. She threw off the coat. Men rushed by her shouting. The street was full of people screaming her name. *Charlotte, Charlotte.* Lights were flashing, ushers held back the crowd. She smiled, and they all went crazy. They opened a path for her. Two men waved her on. She could sing, sing so good she brought them all to their knees.

And so, smiling radiantly, ignoring the shouting cops and firemen, the rain of debris that was falling, Charlotte walked right through a riot on Hoe Avenue.

It had begun with a fire. Some kids had dragged a dozen tires out of a lot, and set fire to them in an abandoned apartment at 4450 Hoe Avenue. Soon the acrid smoke blackened the sky for blocks around. The boys tore chunks off the splintering banisters and fed the fire. The villainous wind picked up a spark, and suddenly the whole floor was ablaze. The kids were trapped. A few ran up to the roof. Others stood at the window screaming for help.

The news spread through the neighborhood that a bunch of kids were trapped in a burning building on Hoe Avenue. Every mother whose son wasn't home got hysterical and ran to the site. The smoke was so dense you couldn't see three feet in front of you. The cops had set up barricades. Fire apparatus were arriving in front of the building, and firemen with axes and portable extinguishers were rushing in. The women attacked them, pulling at their sleeves, crying, begging the firemen to save their sons.

Morgan and Finley arrived on the scene, and called in a 10–13, the assist patrolmen signal. "Get these fuckin' people away from my men," a fire lieutenant shouted to them. They posted themselves in front of the building, and started chasing people away. "Alright, get back, get back over there, give the firemen room . . ."

A woman came at Morgan. "Is my boy in there? I want to know if my boy is in there."

Morgan put his hand on her chest, and pushed her away. "Just get back, lady, and let the firemen do their job."

"But my boy—" She rushed him again.

"Get back, lady," Morgan shouted. He put his big hand over her face this time, and pushed hard. She lost her balance and fell backward onto the sidewalk, but was up almost immediately, crying, "Please let me see my son . . ."

A few kids in the crowd baited Morgan. "Hey, man, what did you hit that lady for?"

"She wants to see if her kid's in that building, man. Is that a crime?"

Morgan pushed the woman away, and went after the kids. "You got something to say?"

They backed up a bit, but looked at him defiantly.

"You like hittin' women, man, is that it?" one of them said.

"I like hitting anybody," Morgan said. He grabbed the kid closest to him by the jacket, lifted him off the ground with his left hand, and punched him in the Adam's apple with his right. The kid went down, clutching at his throat. Finley grabbed another kid. He stuck his gun in the kid's ear. "Alright, motherfucker, you wanna play? You wanna get your fuckin' brains blown out?"

The boy went stiff with panic. Others in the thickening crowd yelled at the cops. "Leave those kids alone." "They ain't doin' nothing."

Finley shoved his captive to the ground. "It's a fuckin' riot," he shouted.

Another radio car pulled up. Hennessy and Pace, a rookie with two weeks on the job, jumped out, and were greeted by a wild-eyed gun-waving Finley. "It's a fuckin' riot," Finley screamed.

Hennessy jumped back into the car, and called in another 10–13. Pace backed up, looking around in bewilderment. Morgan and Finley had thrown the two kids over their car, and were cuffing them together. Hennessy was under the steering wheel shouting into the microphone. People were screaming and shaking their fists. A rock zoomed out of the darkness, whistling past Pace's head and hitting a fireman who was just emerging from the burning building. A woman was on the ground thrashing hysterically in the grasp of several young girls who were trying to comfort her. "My son, my son, they're killing my son." Pace thought she was the mother of one of the prisoners Morgan and Finley had taken. "Why are they doing this?" the woman cried. "Why won't they let me see my son?"

She seemed to be looking at Pace. He felt he had to answer. "Your son broke the law, lady."

One of the young women charged him angrily. "What law did he break? Is getting trapped in a burning building a violation of the law?"

"If you're a P.R. it is," a young man shouted.

"If you're P.R. you have to stay in the building even if it's burning," someone answered.

"That's the law, ain't it, Officer?"

There was angry laughter. Pace looked out over the restless, milling mass, into those grim, derisive faces. They seemed to be moving in on him, backing him toward the burning buildings. He took out his pistol and shouted to Hennessy. "It's a riot, a fuckin' riot."

All the cars on patrol were called to the scene of the fire. Sirens could be heard all over the neighborhood. The smoke hovered over the buildings, providing perfect cover for those who took to the roofs to bomb the cops.

Murphy and Corelli had to nose their car through the hostile crowd. Some shook their fists and shouted, others pounded on the hood. Murphy leaned on the horn while Corelli held up his shield.

"I think the shield's a mistake," Murphy said.

Corelli put it away. "Let's make believe we're TV repairmen." He opened the window and shouted, "Did somebody call that their TV was burning down?" And then he closed it. "My God, did you hear that profanity?"

"I wonder how this started," Murphy said. "Just seems like an ordinary fire to me."

Corelli closed his eyes and slumped forward. "I think I'm getting shell-shocked. All I want to do is go home and sleep for about three weeks."

"Try going home and sleeping one night," Murphy said.

"Think I could get a three-quarters pension if I shot myself in the foot?"

229

Murphy pulled the car in behind a fire truck. "Just hang out in that burning building for a while. They'll put you off the job."

A fireman was doubled over at the curb, retching into the gutter. "Half a day?" Corelli said as they passed.

About a half-dozen kids were lying on stretchers gulping oxygen from valves held to their mouths. Firemen were bringing more kids out of the building. Flames darted out of the upper stories. Patches of frozen water glittered on the sidewalk.

Pace was on the hood of his radio car, waving his pistol and screaming, "Keep away, keep away from me, you motherfuckers." A crowd had gathered around the car. Rocks and bottles seemed to be coming from every roof on the block.

Heffernan stood in the middle of the street with a group of cops. "Let's disperse that crowd around the radio car," he shouted. "We've got two men down over there with prisoners."

Moving in a wedge, a dozen or so cops hit the crowd around the car, pushing, shoving, wielding saps and billy clubs, shouting "Let's break it up," "Make room, make room," "Move outta the way."

There were at least fifty people surrounding the car. They didn't yield easily.

"Lady with a baby," Corelli shouted, pushing his way through.

"*Daily News,*" Murphy said. "Excuse me, *Daily News* . . . press."

A man in the crowd grabbed Murphy. "They beat up on an old woman. You gonna put that in the paper?"

"Page one," Murphy said, plowing through.

Morgan and Finley had four kids cuffed together and lying face down in the gutter. Blood was streaming down Morgan's face. He was kneeling on the back of one of his prisoners. Finley was waving his gun at the taunting crowd. "I'll kill you," he shouted. "I'll kill all you motherfuckers."

"What the hell happened?" Murphy shouted to Morgan.

"We came out on this fire, and they started bombin' us from the roofs. These mutts attacked us."

"How'd you get hit?"

"Fuckin' brick went right through the windshield. I went over and caught a rock right on the fuckin' head." Morgan's face was contorted with pain. "What the fuck is the matter with these animals? Even when you come to help them, they try to kill you."

"Next time we'll just let all you cocksuckers burn to death," Finley shrieked at the crowd.

Heffernan fought his way through, and shouted up at Pace. "Come down from there, Patrolman."

"Keep them away from me," Pace cried. "Just keep them away."

Heffernan's tone became more gentle. "I'll keep them away, I promise."

Pace got off the car, sobbing. "It's not my fault. I didn't do anything."

Heffernan looked inside the radio car, and rattled the door. A shamefaced Hennessy emerged from the back seat where he had been hiding. "I was unconscious, Loot," he said. "I got hit with a brick."

The fire lieutenant rushed over. "I got three men down already," he said to Heffernan. "They're blitzin' us from the roofs."

Heffernan turned to Donahue. "Get back on the radio to the precinct. We need more men. Tell them to call another rapid mobilization." He looked around at the men. "We're gonna have to clear those roofs. Each of you pick a building. Use your own judgment. If it's just kids, get 'em off there, you don't have to collar them."

"I wanna get the mutt who did this," Morgan snarled, pointing to his head.

"Just get them off the roofs," Heffernan said impatiently. "We're not gonna be able to hustle ten or twelve collars through this mob." Everybody stood around hesitantly, none of the men wanting to break rank and venture out into the streets in twos. "Well, c'mon," Heffernan said, banging the hood of the car. "Let's clear those roofs."

"Oh shit," Corelli said. "Now I'm gonna get tar all over my new coat."

"At least let's pick a building with an elevator," Murphy said.

"The one on the corner," Corelli said. "I know a chick who used to live there."

They ran, heads down, across the street. A bottle crashed a few feet in front of them. Corelli put his hands over his head. "We could always keep going, you know. Right down to Anita's Bar for a little drink."

They pushed through the people at the entrance to the buildings.

"How's the roof?" Murphy asked the super.

He didn't want to talk in front of the tenants. "It's cold this time of year."

Murphy understood. "Let's go."

They took the elevator to the seventh floor. "You got a girl named Vera Morales still livin' here?" Corelli asked the super.

He smiled regretfully.

"I know," Corelli said, "it's cold this time of year."

They ran up three steep flights of stairs to the roof entrance. At one point Corelli stopped, and sat down on a step. "You know what always bothered me about this job? We run into these jackpots. We're in a big hurry, you know. I mean you'd think we were goin' to a buffet or a whorehouse or somethin'. No, we're runnin' to collar some mooks with bricks."

"So that's what bothers you about this job," Murphy said.

"Yeah, among other things."

Murphy ran up the rickety metal steps to the door, and called down to Corelli, who was still sitting shaking his head. "You'll be happy to know that this is a party. There's food, booze, and beautiful broads right behind this door, and you're the guest of honor."

Corelli looked up skeptically at the super. "Is he bull-shittin' me or what? Am I really the guest of honor?"

The super looked from Corelli to Murphy in confusion.

"Tell him he's the guest of honor," Murphy said.

"You're the guest of honor," the super said.

Corelli jumped up with a whoop. "Well, in that case, let's go." He ran up the stairs, and tried to push the door open.

"Bastards must have barricaded it," Corelli said, breathing hard.

"What do you expect?" Murphy said. "It's a private party."

When they finally stumbled onto the roof they were confronted by a very serious, very frightened teen-aged kid holding a brick. Murphy took out his pistol, and held it loosely, pointing at the ground. "Mine's better than yours, son," he said. "Mine's got bullets."

The kid dropped the brick and stepped out of their way. Three more kids were leaning over the ledge of the roof, dropping fragments of masonry onto the street.

"Freeze," Murphy shouted.

They turned, still holding the rocks, looking uncertainly at one another. Corelli dropped to one knee, pointing his pistol at them in the straight-armed two-handed grip favored by TV cops. But his finger wasn't on the trigger.

"Hands up," Murphy shouted.

"Tell 'em not to go into their pockets, Murf," Corelli shouted, feigning hysteria. "I'll blow them away if they go into their pockets."

"Better do as he says, fellas," Murphy said, approaching them. "He's new up here, and he gets rattled real easy."

"Tell 'em to do what I say, Murf," Corelli shrieked, waving his pistol crazily. "I'll kill 'em, I swear it."

"Take it easy, Andy," Murphy said soothingly. "These are smart boys. They're gonna cooperate. Aren't you, guys?"

They were kids, not more than sixteen. Clear-eyed, well-dressed, they weren't junkies or crazies. So why? Murphy felt like asking. Why are you up here dropping bricks on total strangers?

"Why don't you guys just put your hands down on the ledge, and spread your legs out," he suggested conversationally.

"Search 'em Murf, search the bastards," Corelli shouted.

Murphy had to turn away for a second to stifle a laugh. Corelli was overdoing it a little. "I'm going to, Andy," he said. "Just take it easy."

Corelli caught the mirth in his voice, and began to shake with suppressed laughter. "I'll shoot 'em right in the balls, Murf."

One of the kids began to tremble with fear. "Calm down, son," Murphy said. "He doesn't mean it."

"We didn't do nothin', man," the kid said.

"What are they sayin', Murf?" Corelli screamed. "Are they makin' wise remarks?"

"Everything's under control, Andy," Murphy said. "You

guys just better shut your mouths or I won't be responsible for what happens."

He patted the kids down, and found a flick knife, a couple of joints and a Trojan lube.

"You gonna bust us?" one of the kids asked in a quavery voice.

Murphy grabbed him by the hair, and twisted his head back. "That's what you want, ain't it, you little dirtbag? You wanna be a big hero in the neighborhood. Well, too fuckin' bad." He kicked the kid's legs out from under him, and did the same to the other two. "Now get up, and get off this fuckin' roof," he shouted, yanking one of them by the collar, grabbing another by the seat of the pants and throwing him against the water tower. Corelli lunged for one kid, who jumped away in panic, and fell against the door.

Murphy chased them waving his arms. "I ever catch you little pricks on a roof again, I'm gonna blow your fuckin' brains out."

"I'll shoot you in the balls," Corelli shouted, laughing. "Man, that sure puts the fear of God into 'em."

Murphy walked to the edge of the roof, and looked down. "I can remember when no kid would dare raise his hand to a cop, let alone throw a brick at him."

"I can remember when subways cost fifteen cents," Corelli said. "We've made a lotta progress since then."

The wind blew a rift in the smoke, and Murphy could see a boy and a girl on the roof across the street looking down at all the activity. Corelli put his hands to his eyes, and squinted at them.

"Has he got his hand on her tit?"

"You would see that," Murphy said. "At least some things never change. A freezin' night, a fire, a riot, and this kid's up on the roof tryin' to cop a feel."

"It's the best time for it," Corelli said. "Nobody will ever suspect them. It's like when I was in school, and we'd have to get under our desks for a Civil Defense drill. That's when we'd make out like bandits, and the sisters never knew what was happening."

"It's a cheap date," Murphy said. "Go up on the roof with a coupla sodas and watch a building burn down." He pointed out over the roofs at the Manhattan skyline. "Plus you got the greatest view in the world."

"And a full moon, too," Corelli said, "when the smoke clears."

The door to the roof flew open, and Murphy saw two cops leap out, their pistols drawn.

"Who's that?"

"Morgan and Finley, ain't it?" Corelli said.

Murphy walked to the other end of the roof for a better view. "I thought they were on the same side of the street as us."

"They must have cleared their roofs. Those boys have talent."

"Look at the assholes," Murphy said. Morgan and Finley were prowling the roof, crouching, flattening themselves against the walls of the water tower. The young girl ran behind a shed as the boy turned to see who it was.

"They think they got a roof full of mad bombers," Murphy said. He cupped his hands to his mouth and shouted, "Morgan, hey, Morgan."

"He can't hear you with all this racket goin' on," Corelli said.

Morgan and Finley turned a corner and saw the boy standing against the ledge. He put his hands up and walked toward them, while his girlfriend cowered behind the shed.

"Smart kid," Murphy said. "Talk your way out of it."

Morgan raised his gun hand and backhanded the kid. Finley stepped behind the kid, and grabbed him as he went down.

"What the fuck are they doing?" Murphy shouted.

Corelli turned away. "The old tosseroo . . ."

Murphy ran to the other end of the roof, shouting, "Morgan, you asshole. Hey, Morgan."

Corelli grabbed him by the arm. "C'mon, Murf, let's get off this fuckin' roof. I'm catchin' pneumonia."

Murphy pointed across the street. "You see what he's doing?"

Morgan and Finley were pushing the kid back and forth between them, pummeling him, pistol whipping him.

"Yeah, yeah, I see. The guy got hit with a rock. He's a little *stoonada* to begin with, you know."

Morgan punched the kid, driving his head against the wall. The kid struggled fiercely in Finley's grasp, breaking away for a moment. But Morgan was on him in two steps, grabbing him by the shirt, throwing him down, stomping him. They picked the boy up. He was unconscious, his body flopping like a rag doll. Morgan lifted him high over his head, and carried him to the edge of the roof.

"Hold it, Morgan," Murphy shouted.

"They're only gonna scare him, Murf," Corelli said.

Still holding the boy, Morgan walked to the part of the roof that overlooked the alley between the two buildings. He looked down at the street, and then, reaching back, he threw the boy off the roof.

"No . . ." Murphy shouted in anguish. He turned and grabbed Corelli. "Did you see that?"

Corelli looked him right in the eye, and shook his head. "Who, me? No, I didn't see nothin'."

"They threw that kid off the roof, Andy."

Corelli's expression didn't change. "What kid? I didn't see no kid. I didn't see nothin', Murf. Did you?"

39

Murphy wouldn't go into the station house. He sat out in the car chainsmoking, lighting one Marlboro off another. Corelli had been through a lot with Murphy. He had seen him scared, seen him angry; in six years he had learned to recognize his partner's alterations of mood, but now there was an expression on Murphy's face that he couldn't read.

"You okay, partner?" he asked.

Murphy wouldn't look at him. "What do you mean, okay?"

"You're not gonna do nothin' crazy, are you?"

"Like what?"

"I don't know. That's what scares me."

Except for the hand that brought the cigarette mechanically to his lips, Murphy was rigid. Corelli was afraid to touch him.

"I just don't want to go in the locker room while Morgan's in there, that's all."

"Hey, look, you can't avoid the guy forever."

"I'll be okay in a coupla days. But for now it's just better if I don't see his fuckin' face, okay?"

"Okay, okay." Corelli backed away from the car. "It ain't no skin off my nose. You do what you have to do."

He went in the locker room and changed quickly.

"What's this, no fancy threads?" Donahue asked.

"I don't feel very sartorial tonight," Corelli said.

Morgan looked over suspiciously. "Where's Murphy?"

Corelli turned angrily on him. "How the fuck do I know? He don't sign in with me."

Morgan gave Corelli a quick, apprehensive glance, then tried to make amends. "Slow down. I just wanted to know if he was alright."

Finley came out of the bathroom, white-faced and perspiring. He had thrown up twice since they got back. "Must be those pills they gave me at the hospital," he said, avoiding Morgan's scornful glance. Finley's arm had been cut by broken glass, and he had a crimson bruise over his cheekbone.

"They gave me the same pills, and I'm okay," Morgan said.

"That's 'cause you're washin'' them down with rum," Patterson said.

Morgan held up his hands; the knuckles were raw and swollen, and there were trails of dried blood from deep scratches on his forearms. "I took eleven fuckin' stitches in my head, and I'm okay." He nodded disdainfully toward Finley. "He's in shock."

"Sure you're okay," Donahue said. "You got hit in the one place on your body where there's no feeling—your head."

"What kind of pills they give you?" Patterson asked.

Morgan looked at the vial. "I don't know. Darvon, probably."

"Better not drink behind those pills, man. They'll put you away."

Morgan winced and touched the piece of plaster they had taped over his wound. "You mean I'll have a heart attack? Big fuckin' deal."

"If you wanna die, that's your business," Donahue said.

"I don't wanna die," Morgan said. "But if I don't wake up tomorrow morning that's okay too."

"There's a man with a cheerful outlook on life," Patterson said.

"Life sucks," said Morgan. He took a swig out of the pint of rum he kept in his locker. "The sooner it's over the better." He looked to Corelli for support. "Anyway, it goes by so quick. What difference does it make if you die now, tomorrow, or in thirty years. What difference does it make?"

Corelli turned away in disgust. Morgan's expression was craven and pleading, not at all the look of a man who cared nothing for his life.

Murphy hung around the desk after midnight. Corelli stayed nearby, afraid to leave him alone. The boy had fallen into a snowdrift between the two buildings, and hadn't been discovered yet. The girl wouldn't tell—not for a while, anyway. She had obviously been up on the roof against her parents' wishes, and she had to be afraid that the two cops who had thrown her boyfriend off the roof would come back and kill her if she talked. So, there was no news. Murphy loitered by the desk until Clendennon looked up impatiently. "You after my job, Murphy?"

"No, Sarge."

"Then get the fuck away from me before I call the Vice Squad."

Murphy drifted out of the room. Corelli found him in the bathroom a few minutes later staring at his face in the mirror.

"One of those books I've been readin' says you shouldn't look at yourself in the mirror for more than thirty seconds," Corelli said.

"Smart book," Murphy said. But he kept looking.

"Because after a while you don't recognize the person you're looking at, and you get scared."

"I recognize myself better and better, Andy," Murphy said.

"No, you see, you're wrong . . ."

Murphy raised a hand to silence him. "Nah, it's true. It's all on your face whether you like it or not. A coupla years ago when I took the kids to Florida I was sittin' by the pool talkin' to this guy. He came from British Columbia, the

238

other side of the world. How could he know anything about me, right? Anyway we were talkin' about jobs and all, and I bet him ten bucks he couldn't guess what I did for a living. 'That's easy,' he said. 'You're a policeman, a New York City policeman.' "

"Lucky guess," Corelli said.

Murphy turned away from the mirror. "No, Andy. Eighteen years on the job, and every second of it is printed on my face. All the scams, the blood, the drunken nights—I could walk into Grand Central Station, and everyone would know I was a cop."

"People believe what you tell them," Corelli said. "It's just a question of how good your hype is, that's all."

Murphy stared at Corelli with such intensity that he had to look away. "You can't hide the truth, Andy. It comes out . . ."

"Bullshit," Corelli shot back with quiet ferocity. "People get away with murder every day, and you know it."

"The truth comes out," Murphy said doggedly. "Look on my face tomorrow. You'll see it there."

40

The snow began melting the next day. By early afternoon the body of Cesar Quinones was revealed in the gray slush. He had multiple lacerations and contusions of the face and body, plus a fractured arm, and a broken neck that was officially listed as the cause of death. The detectives on the scene theorized that he had been beaten to death, and his body hidden in the snowdrift. There were no witnesses, no suspects. He lived with his grandmother, a sick woman who hadn't even known he was out of the house. He was fifteen years old, had no juvenile record, was unknown to the youth workers in the neighborhood, and was regular in his attendance at DeWitt Clinton High School. The police found no drugs on the body, none in his apartment, and the autopsy report found no evidence of narcotics in his system. After looking at all this information, the squad commander requested the Medical Examiner to see if the boy had been sexually assaulted.

The weekend brought no new clues. Because of the preserving effects of the snow and the cold weather, it was difficult to establish a time of death. The Medical Examiner reported that there were no traces of sperm in the boy's mouth or anus, no bruising or mutilation of the sexual organs, therefore no obvious evidence of sexual assault. The new theory in the squad was that Cesar Quinones had been killed in a brawl that got out of hand. His murderer or murderers had panicked, and hidden his body in the snow. The fight couldn't have taken place during the fire; there were too many people about. The obvious assumption was that the fire had been started to destroy the body, a common practice in that area. But then, how did the body end up in an alley across the street? The best explanation the detectives decided was that Cesar Quinones had been accidentally murdered in a fight with person or persons unknown. The two detectives who had been assigned the case returned to the exhausting work of canvassing the block, speaking to everyone in the boy's building, to the supers, the people in other buildings, the boy's friends. The solution to the case became a matter of legwork and luck.

Monday morning, bright and early, there was a social worker waiting on the bench outside Connolly's office. He wouldn't talk to the desk sergeant, and brushed away the lieutenant. "I wanna talk to the Captain, man, you understand, the Captain."

"You have to state your business first."

"Just let me say a few words to the Captain, man. He'll see me."

They brought him into Connolly's office. He threw his Human Resources Administration I.D. card on the desk. "I want to speak to you, Captain Connolly." He looked pointedly at the lieutenant. "Alone."

Connolly looked the card over. The man's name was Jerome Santiago. The picture matched. All I.D. photographs looked like mug shots; the subject had a grim, hostile stare. But this one was a faithful rendering of the man.

Jerome Santiago was a dark, wiry man with a grim, hostile stare. He spoke with exaggerated politeness, but his eyes betrayed his rage.

"Alright, Lieutenant," Connolly said. "I'll speak to Mr. Santiago alone."

Santiago waited until the Lieutenant had closed the door. He looked suspiciously around the office. "I suppose this room is bugged."

"The city can't afford to buy toilet paper, Mr. Santiago," Connolly said. "It certainly can't put electronic equipment in every precinct. Now what are these few words you have to say to me?"

Santiago drew his chair closer to Connolly's desk. "I have information about the murder of Cesar Quinones."

"That's a matter for the detective squad," Connolly said, reaching for the phone.

"Not yet it isn't," Santiago said sharply. "I know police procedures, Captain. I didn't come here by mistake. I want you to hear this first."

"Alright, Mr. Santiago."

"There's a girl I work with," Santiago said. "I work with her whole family, really. She called me at home yesterday. She says she was on the roof of Quinones's building with him during that fire. She says two cops came up, and threw him off. She saw it all."

"Does this girl have a name?" Connolly asked.

"We'll get to that later."

"How did she escape detection by these two policemen?"

"She hid behind a shed. She took me up and reenacted the whole thing. I believe her story."

"Why didn't she come forward with this right away?"

Santiago smiled bitterly. "For the same reason I'm coming to you first. She knows it's not safe to finger two cops for a murder. People go off roofs all the time up here, Captain, you know what I mean?"

"Can she identify these two officers?" Connolly asked.

"No, she didn't see their faces. But she saw the uniforms. She swears they were cops."

Santiago lit a cigarette without taking his eye off Connolly. Connolly pushed an ashtray across the desk to him. The story was plausible. Heffernan had sent men up to clear the roofs during the fire. It was an all too familiar case of brutality. Connolly had investigated several similar complaints when he was with the I.A.D.

"We'll have to have a signed, sworn affidavit from the girl . . ."

"You won't have nothin'," Santiago said fiercely. "This is a tip, Captain. I'm not involving that girl, not until the trial, if there ever is one. You go out and nail those guys, get other witnesses, get confessions, and then we'll bring her in. I don't want anybody to think that she's the only witness against them, you understand?"

"That's not good enough, Mr. Santiago."

"It'll have to be, man, because I'm not giving you her name, and I'll deny I ever had this conversation, if necessary. And . . ." He raised his voice. "If I am being taped, let me make it clear that I'll go to jail before I will ever reveal her identity."

Connolly considered this. It was unorthodox, not the way he liked to work. In effect, he was an accomplice to a felony—the withholding of evidence. But at the same time he had a golden opportunity to redeem himself with Headquarters. He would break the case. He would be seen as the man who had won the confidence of the community.

"Why did you come to me with this?" he asked. "You could have gotten the same guarantee of protection from the squad commander."

"Because I know you'll keep it quiet," Santiago said. "You made your rep hunting down cops. You know how to do it."

"You're no friend of the police. Why would you want it kept quiet?"

Santiago's anger hissed out like steam from a radiator. "I'm a friend to my people, man. They would hit the streets again if they heard cops had killed Cesar." Tears came to his eyes, and his voice trembled. Connolly had to look away, appalled by the anguish in the man's voice. "I don't want any more of my people gassed, or thrown off roofs, okay? I mean I tried to cool them out, but it just never works. When you're cold and hungry, and you know nobody gives a fuck about you, the last thing you want to do is listen to reason." Santiago stubbed out his cigarette. "I don't even know what reason is, anyway."

Connolly could feel the man's hatred, his despair. All

242

this excess emotion repelled him; he just wanted the man out of his office. He stood up.

"Alright, Mr. Santiago. You've got a deal."

Deal. The word was new to him. Deals meant collusion, corruption, compromise. And he was making a deal with a man he wasn't sure he could trust.

As soon as Santiago was gone, Connolly called the Bronx Medical Examiner's office.

"On the Quiñones case. Is there any way the boy could have been killed in a fall from the roof?"

"It's possible," the M.E. said. "The snow would have cushioned the impact enough to avoid the kind of injury one would normally sustain, but not enough to prevent the neck and spinal breakages that caused death. It's possible."

Connolly waited until the four-to-twelve tour came on, and called Heffernan into his office.

"You were in command of that detail over at the fire last week, weren't you?"

"Yes, sir."

Connolly kept his tone as matter-of-fact as possible. "I want a list of all the men you sent up on the roofs, and the buildings they were assigned to."

Heffernan's mind raced through all the possible reasons for this request. It was a beef, of course—a bad one. It was that dead kid. It had to be.

"I don't really know, Captain. I didn't make specific assignments. I couldn't tell you who went where."

Connolly was on home ground, having an encounter he'd had so many times before. Heffernan was naturally reluctant to implicate men he had known for years, but his loyalty would not survive a threat to his own career.

"Search your memory, Lieutenant, this is important."

"I'm sure it is, but . . ."

"You don't have to tell me right now. Take a few hours to think it over."

Heffernan gave him a pained, apologetic look. "I could think it over for years, and I still wouldn't remember who went up on the roofs and who stayed down."

Connolly delivered the threat gently. "A good officer is supposed to know how he deployed his men."

Heffernan stopped fidgeting, and returned Connolly's

look calmly. "I'm not a good officer, Captain, you know that. I'm barely competent."

"Well then, maybe you shouldn't be in command of so many men," Connolly said.

"I probably shouldn't," Heffernan said. "That's up to you. I'm sorry, Captain. I can't tell you who went up on those roofs."

Connolly nodded wearily. It was hard to coerce a man with no ambitions and no ideals, a man who was just putting in his time. "How many men responded to the fire?" he asked.

"Every sector on the tour ended up there," Heffernan said. "We had four 10–13s."

"Alright, then I'll have to see every one of them. Bring them in six at a time after the roll call."

Heffernan got up. "I'm sorry, Captain," he said.

Connolly nodded. "I understand." The man had nothing. No career, no self-respect—only that code of silence that bound all policemen. Strange how sluggish they all were in the performance of their duties, but how quick to pick up the slightest hint of suspicion against themselves; how quarrelsome and selfish they were during the normal course of events, but how solidly they stood together when one of them had committed a crime. Connolly knew the wall of silence and cunning he would come up against. He had broken through it before, and he would do it again.

A little after four o'clock Heffernan began to shepherd them into the office. Connolly looked every one of the men in the eye. By now the word had gotten around, he knew that. Each of the men had picked out his act, the role he played best, from indifference to outraged innocence. They were veterans and good at covering their asses, but Connolly knew that in those groups there were at least two murderers, and at least two more who knew who they were. That number would grow—it was inevitable. The men would solve the case themselves by a process of elimination, and then he would have to contend with a whole tour protecting two men. That was when they were at their strongest, because that was when they watched each other to make sure there would be no informing.

Morgan and Finley, Murphy and Corelli, Donahue and

Patterson: six of the stronger cops on the tour. Corelli was casual, Morgan sincere, Finley indignant, Donahue and Patterson took the whole thing lightly. Murphy sat in a corner of the office, separated from the others, even from his own partner, chainsmoking, eyes downcast. If this was an act, it was new to Connolly.

"I suppose you men know by now why you're in here," Connolly said. "We have several witnesses who say they saw two police officers throw Cesar Quinones off the roof at 1065 Hoe Avenue. I checked with the Medical Examiner, and he says the boy's death could have been caused by injuries sustained in a fall. Up until now the squad has not been able to establish a motive for the killing. In canvassing the block they came up with several people who corroborate each other's story." He looked around to see how they were taking it; he might as well have been talking about the weather. "Anybody got anything to say?"

They all looked up at him. Patterson broke the silence. "I didn't throw anybody off a roof. Did you, Eddie?"

Donahue scratched his head, pretending great thought. "What day was that again?"

"Don't try to cover this with jokes, Donahue," Connolly said sharply.

Donahue mumbled. "Sorry, Captain."

"Now, Lieutenant Heffernan has said that he dispatched men to clear the four roofs surrounding the fire," Connolly said, "but he doesn't remember who they were. Did any of you men go up on the roofs during the fire?"

"We went, Captain," a chastened Donahue said.

"Us too," Corelli said.

Connolly looked over at Morgan. He touched the bandage on his head. "We stayed down in the street, Captain," he said earnestly. "Both of us got banged up pretty good, you know, and we also had prisoners to watch."

"Alright," Connolly said, "we have every roof covered but one. I don't suppose any of you men went up to 1065 Hoe Avenue."

They shook their heads.

"Anything else?"

Finley raised his hand like a kid in school and blurted, "Maybe those so-called witnesses threw the decedent off the roof, and they're trying to lay it on us."

245

That was a normal reaction. "I've thought of that," Connolly said.

"Everybody's always lookin' to knock us up here, Captain," Morgan said.

"Especially up here," Finley said, warming up a little. "People don't appreciate cops up here. They blame us for all the problems in their lives."

"I'm aware of that," Connolly said. "I just want to go on record with you men as I have with the others on this tour. I'll go right to the wall with you on this. No politics or backstabbing. As long as I'm satisfied that you're innocent. And it's going to take a lot to satisfy me." He sat back and looked the men over. "Alright, that's all."

They rose slowly, tired old cops going out to a job they hated. A few of them mumbled, "Thank you, Captain." Murphy said nothing.

"Murphy," Connolly called.

He turned slowly. The other men slid by him through the door.

"Could you hang in for a moment?"

Murphy took a few steps into the office. His partner, Corelli, gave him a worried look. That's what it was. Connolly smothered a surge of excitement. There had been some kind of unspoken communication between the two men. He waited a few seconds after the door had closed.

"I didn't hear any denials from you just now," he said. "I didn't hear any suggestions, either."

Murphy looked out of the window. "I'm the shy type, Captain. I don't like to kiss ass in public."

"I'm not asking for that and you know it. I just want you to look me in the eye, and tell me you know nothing about that homicide."

"Sure, Murphy said, "I'll look you in the eye." He walked over and grasped the desk so hard his knuckles whitened. "How's this, Captain Connolly?"

Connolly wanted to hit him. He wanted to come up from his chair and clip that insubordinate bastard right under the chin. "Listen, Murphy," he snarled, "I know all about your family connections in the Department. Well, if you think the Irish Mafia's gonna get you out of a scrape with me you've got another think coming."

"How's this, Captain?" Murphy said. "Am I looking you

in the eye? Do you want me to put my hand in fire, and swear on my mother's grave?"

Connolly bolted out of his chair, and faced Murphy across the desk.

"I want you to tell me the truth."

"I didn't push that kid off the roof."

"And you don't know who did."

"Are you asking me or telling me?"

"Get out of here," Connolly said, through clenched teeth.

"Yes, sir." Murphy jumped back from the desk and stood at attention. He saluted Connolly with mocking, military precision, did an about-face, and marched out of the office.

Connolly felt a sudden jolt of pain in the back of his head. He sat down, wincing, and tried to compose himself, but all he could feel was rage. The room went dark with it. He gripped the arms of his chair. Rage at that insolent sonofabitch Murphy . . . rage at all those insubordinate, malingering, defiant sonsabitches. Rage . . . Connolly slammed his fists down on the desk. Those dirty, rotten, sonsabitches . . .

Murphy had trouble making it to the stairs. It was too crowded. No one would step aside. He shoved several people out of the way. They protested loudly.

"Hey, man, who you pushin?"

"Lighten up, man."

He stumbled up the stairs into the locker room where the men anxiously awaited him.

"What did he say?" Donahue demanded.

"Nothin', nothin'."

They crowded around him as he opened his locker.

"Why did he keep you back?" Patterson asked. "What did he say?"

"Nothin'," Murphy said. "He just wanted to tell me he was taking my name off his Christmas list."

"Stop clownin', will ya, Murphy, and tell us what happened," Morgan said.

Murphy ignored him.

"Murphy," Morgan repeated angrily.

Murphy slammed his locker door, and headed for the bathroom. Morgan pursued him.

"What are you, deaf and dumb all of a sudden?"

Murphy turned with murder in his eyes; he clenched his fists and moved toward Morgan, but Corelli jumped between them, and shoved Morgan away.

"Will you go to your room? The man don't feel like talking."

"I wanna talk," Morgan said.

"So talk to yourself like you always do." Corelli turned away from him, and put his arm around Murphy's shoulder. "C'mon, partner, let's go enforce the law."

41

Hernando sat at the cutting table under the red lamp, his hands folded at his chest, a little stub of a Pall Mall peeking through his fingers. His legs were drawn up under him, and he had the same drowsy half smile of contentment that Chino had seen on all those Buddhist statues in Nam. His eyes were narrowed to slits, but you could see the pupils rolling like marbles behind them. He took a long, slow puff at the cigarette, and nodded at his reflection in the glass.

"I knew you were after weight the first time I saw you," he said.

Hernando was stoned. He and his boy Jose had obviously taken a recreational dose. Jose sat on the edge of the couch, nodding. Every time it looked as though he was going to fall on the floor, his head jerked back and he began nodding again. Hernando had a stronger head than Jose, or maybe he hadn't reversed the point, drawing the blood out of his arm and letting the dope flow in to take its place. He wasn't a punk like Jose, so he would get high in a different way. The dope would affect his brain more than his body. He would get shrewd and persuasive. He would control all the people around him, get into their heads and read their minds. He would control the universe. Not a drop of rain would fall, not a cockroach would crawl without the okay from Hernando.

Or so he thought.

Chino was stoned, too. He had smoked a few pipefuls of Afghani hash, the black pasty stuff that was almost like opium, before he came up to the Bronx. He liked to get really wasted on hash before he set up a big buy. The drug sharpened his senses. It made him paranoid. He became aware of all the undercurrents, could read a threat between the lines of the most innocuous remark. He got into people's minds, and read their thoughts. He was totally on top of every situation.

Or so he thought. Now that Hernando was stoned as well, that Jose was in a long nod, that the windows were closed, and it was real quiet on the street, Chino realized there was absolutely no reality in the room. They could just as easily be zooming through space. Intergalactic shooting gallery. The three of them had cut the planet loose—their jobs, their families, everything that had gone before.

"We're dealing in abstractions, man," he told Hernando.

"How many times did you whack that ounce I sold you?" Hernando asked.

"I'm too wasted to talk business now," Chino said.

Hernando's smile broadened. "Business is all you wanna talk, man. Don't bullshit me. You ever spend a second without thinkin' about business? Now tell me, how many times did you whack that dope?"

"Six, man, six times," Chino said. "That's all it would hold."

Hernando started to laugh. "Hey, man, you're talkin' about the purest, whitest dope that ever came into this motherfuckin' city. The White Queen, man, that's what them old junkies down on 114th Street have been callin' it. The White motherfuckin' Queen. Six times?" Hernando's lashes fluttered, and his eyes flared open briefly. He bared his teeth and snarled. "You lyin', motherfucker. You cut that dope eight times, maybe nine. You got nine ounces out of that little old zee I sold you."

"Eight," Chino said. "We cut it eight times, okay?"

"Okay, okay." Hernando got sleepy again. "Ain't no point in lyin' to me about my goods, bro. I mean I know what I got. I got *El Mejor*. All them junkies out there in Jamaica went crazy behind this shit, didn't they, Chino?"

"How'd you know I'm dealin' in Jamaica?" Chino asked, looking around suspiciously. Hernando was just guessing, but he would play it up.

"Jamaica and Flushing and Jackson Heights and Corona. You're out in Queens, Chino, I know that. I know who I'm workin' with. You can move that shit real fast, can't you?"

"Not out there," Chino said. "There's a lotta people into coke."

"You can move that shit real fast out in Queens, man," Hernando said, gently reproving him. "Them niggers stand on the street, and people drive up in their cars. White dudes. Smack's gettin' real hip in them colleges with all them white kids. For seventy-five bucks them faggots get high. High . . . and they love it."

Chino put up his hands in mock surrender. "You're right, man. I'm movin' the shit pretty good out there. You're right."

"*Oiga me, coño,* I'm always right," Hernando said. "I have to be. If I'm not, it's my ass."

Then it's your ass, motherfucker, Chino thought. Because you're talking to a cop right now.

"So let's stop bullshittin' each other," Hernando said. "Money talks, bullshit walks. I know you got people behind you. So what are you looking for, a key?"

"You can get that much?" Chino asked, showing the proper respect. Flattery gets you everywhere with a little dude like this. Flatter him, and then flash a little money in his face.

"I told you, man, I can get you as much as you can pay for. I'll back a truck up to your pad, and unload it in hundred-pound sacks. I'll get you a railroad car, and ten guys'll have to shovel it out."

"I'll do a pound," Chino said.

"A pound," Hernando said, mulling it over. "Sixteen ounces."

"Can you give me a price?"

"You got your price, man. How much did you pay for one ounce? Twelve thousand times sixteen—" Hernando did the calculations in his head. "—that's a hundred and ninety-two thousand dollars."

Chino smiled and shook his head. "You gotta give me a better price than that."

"Why?"

"I'm buying in volume, man. Shit, everybody who buys in volume gets a discount."

"You gonna give those junkies in Jamaica a discount, man? We're talkin' about dope, not ladies' underwear."

"Hey, man, the ladies don't get no discount on their underwear either, you dig, but the guy who sells them does. That's business, bro. That's what we're talkin' about . . . business."

"Business," Hernando said, slowly, caressingly scratching his neck. "Business . . ." He seemed infatuated with the word. Now was the time to lean on him a little.

"You've never done this big a deal, man, so you don't know."

Hernando gave him that opaque, shiny stare that junkies always got when they were trying to think. "Hey, man, a pound of dope ain't shit, okay? I've done fuckin' keys right outta this pad."

"Then give me a price," Chino challenged.

Hernando lit another Pall Mall, and considered. He looked at Chino through the wisps of smoke. Time stopped. There wasn't a sound in that pad, not even a drip from the sink, or the clang of the radiator. Jose was passed out on the couch, his hands between his legs, his eyes closed, mouth open, a little trail of drool meandering down his chin. Outer space, Chino thought. I'm in outer space.

"I guess maybe you oughta meet the main man," Hernando said. "The man from Washington Heights."

"Let's go," Chino said.

"Be cool, spoon, be cool," Hernando said. "I'll have to talk to him first. You just don't go walkin' in on this dude."

"Then talk to him, don't be wastin' my time. I wanna get down."

Hernando chuckled sleepily, back in the driver's seat again. "You'll get down. You'll get your goods. Just let me tighten up the details. You come by the office at the Detox Center of Jefferson Hospital on Monday, and you'll meet the man."

"The hospital?" Chino protested. "Why not here?"

"My man don't like small rooms. He likes to talk business in public places with a lotta noise, a lotta people." Hernando took a few light years out for a coughing fit. When he finally calmed down, Chino realized he was laughing. "Hey,

251

man, don't look so suspicious, we're gonna do business. Don't worry, you ain't gettin' set up."

I'm no asshole, Chino thought. You are.

Murphy had inscribed a careful, drunken circle around the South Bronx, deliberately avoiding all of Morgan's hangouts. There were plenty of dives where a man could get quietly shitfaced; plenty of bars where people only knew you well enough to say hello. Or didn't know you at all.

He had begun in the West Bronx, a saloon across the street from the Forty-sixth precinct. Then, suddenly, there were too many familiar faces, and he went over to the Church Key, which was around the corner from the Four-Four. He had started out with beer, but switched to vodka and grapefruit juice, and then vodka on the rocks when the grapefruit juice began giving him gas. After a few drinks at the Church Key, Murphy called the bartender over.

"You know what's wrong with this saloon? Too many fuckin' cops. You just can't relax with so many cops around."

"And what are you?" the bartender asked.

"A proctologist. I see assholes all day long, I don't wanna have 'em in my face at night, too."

Murphy drove north, and began a tour of the Irish gin mills along Fordham Road. In some locations they came thick and fast, two or three to a block on both sides of the street. Murphy visited them all. He saw no cops in these bars. There were mostly Irish working people from the neighborhood with a sprinkling of Puerto Ricans. No jukeboxes, just the TV running the same old late movie in every joint he entered. They pinned him as a cop right away, and gave him a couple of stools on either side. These were the bars where numbers and sports actions was taken, where an occasional truck backed up and left a load of TVs or sports jackets, where you could find somebody who'd collect a debt for you, somebody who might even kill for you if the price was right. Murphy spotted a few familiar faces, guys he had collared at one time or another—you never forgot them. Thieves, gorillas, small-time Shylocks, guys trying to supplement their income with an occasional felony. Well, fuck them, too. If they didn't booze so much and play the horses and chase broads, they wouldn't need the extra money. He wasn't going to worry about them.

Next, he hit the Italian restaurants along Arthur Avenue where all the wise guys drank. Sevilles and Mercedes 450s were double parked outside. Inside, the jukebox was playing Jimmy Roselli, there were murals of gondoliers and palaces and a scowling bartender with an eighteen-hundred-dollar watch. The pinky-ring crowd—stout, saturnine men bulging out of four-hundred-dollar suits, overdressed, over-coiffed women angrily stubbing out lipstick-smudged cigarettes.

Murphy got the big greeting here. The boss with the gravelly voice came over, put his arm around him, bought him a drink. The detectives all ran off to hide in the darkened dining room. Murphy saw them—guys from the various squads, who loved to drink with the rackets people, who dressed like them, thought like them, and dreamt of leaving the job to cross over to the more lucrative side. They ran like thieves because they thought he might be spying for I.A.D. As tough as they thought they were, they hid in the dark to protect their pensions.

White Plains Road, Westchester Avenue, more rackets bars, more cars, more Jimmy Roselli, big greetings. "Put your money away, your money's no good in this joint." "Buy my friend Johnny Murphy a drink." More discontented chippies—one thing you had to say for these guys: they had their wives trained—more nervous cops, who faded into the woodwork when he came in. There were more familiar faces, mostly numbers guys who bled the South Bronx white, and spent the money on cars, jewelry, and bitchy mistresses. Murphy felt their contempt behind those elaborate, patronizing greetings. They thought cops were boobs who risked their lives for starvation wages, humble, ass-kissing peasants who could be bought for a drink and a pat on the back. They had it all figured, alright. So how come so many of them ended up doing twenty, thirty years hard time in some state prison, while others figured themselves right into the trunk of a car with two holes in their heads? Murphy laughed and shook their hands and took their drinks and ogled their women and watched the detectives scamper for cover. They were real smart boys, alright. Everywhere he went, all he saw was real smart boys.

By three-thirty he was drunker than he had been in seven years. Amazing what the whiskey did, flowing right up to the brain, washing all the cobwebs away, making things seem so clear and obvious. It made drinking worthwhile, because you couldn't get this clarity any other way. You had to drink a quart of booze, that was it. That was probably what she got out of that fucking smack: some kind of experience or state of mind that she couldn't get any other way. It made shooting dope worthwhile.

Isabella. She was never far from his thoughts, even when he was drunk, even when he tried to squeeze her face out of his mind. But that did make shooting dope worthwhile; he would tell her the next time they got together.

Only he was never going to see her again . . . never. It was just asking for trouble hanging out with a broad like that. And if he didn't see her in the flesh, then it wouldn't take long for her face to stop popping up in his head at odd moments, and he would soon forget that sad smile that made him go weak and tender even when he saw it in his mind's eye.

His mind reeling with thoughts of Isabella, Mary, the kids, Murphy headed south. And then he began to see that kid falling. It started with quick flashes, a glimmer of light from between the elevated tracks, a movement he picked up out of the corner of his eye. Then, the details began to come back to him. The kid had fallen with his arms outstretched, and his legs kicking as if he were trying to fly. Sure, you would do that. If you knew you were falling to your death you'd flap your arms and try to fly, praying for a miracle. In the split second it would take, you would know that only a miracle could save you.

Murphy had to pull over. For a moment back there he had been falling, himself. He had felt the terror that boy had felt. It wasn't fear of death, because the boy had known he was dying. It was an overwhelming flood of sorrow and regret, the corpse mourning itself.

Murphy opened the window, and let the cold air hit him. He smoked a cigarette, and struggled with that fear. He heard the screams now. With all the noise at the fire he hadn't heard anything. But now, in the silence of the car, the boy screamed all the way down to the ground. It was a sound Murphy had to supply, but he knew it was right. He had heard people scream in pain, in rage, in sorrow—he knew what it had sounded like.

Murphy put his hands to his ears. He started the car and revved the motor; he blasted the radio. He peeled out and sped down Westchester Avenue, skidding slightly in the slush. On either side of him loomed the pillars of the elevated subway. He might be able to stop the sound of that boy's screams by smashing into one of them. But that wasn't good enough. There was one sure way of restoring that blessed, drunken silence he was seeking.

Murphy screeched to a stop in front of the Emerald Bar, the place he had been avoiding all night.

42

Charlotte had been gone for three days. When she finally showed up at Gloria's door, she was all matted and dirty and wild-eyed.

"The little pussycat always finds its way home," Gloria said bitterly. "Go out sellin' ass all over. How many funky dicks did you deal with this time, huh? Bringin' all that shit home for Mama to clean up." But she stepped away, and let Charlotte stagger in. "You're just a worthless slut after all, ain't you, Charlotte?"

Charlotte teetered in the middle of the room. "Shut your mouth, bitch," she said, raising her hand threateningly.

"Sure," Gloria said, "sure, I'll shut up. I oughta throw you out on your ass." She didn't mean it, of course. She'd been worried sick the past three days.

Charlotte's hands were ice cold. Gloria blew on them and rubbed them between her breasts. "I'll warm you up, baby," she said. "I'm sorry I was mean." The straps on Charlotte's shoes had broken. Gloria washed her feet with a wet towel, kissing her between the toes. She ran a nice, warm bubble bath, and eased Charlotte into the tub. "Now, that's better, isn't it?"

Charlotte closed her eyes and sank dreamily into the fragrant suds. "You see how well I take care of you, pussy, you see?" Gloria whispered.

"I'm the last woman in the world," Charlotte said. "That's why they all cryin' for me out there." She pushed Gloria's hand off her breast. "Back up, girl. Don't go touchin' me like that."

"I'm sorry, baby," Gloria said, wiping her soapy hands. "I won't do nothin' until you say it's okay."

Gloria went out into the kitchen and made coffee. She came back to wash Charlotte's back with a special Japanese sponge she had bought on 149th Street the day before.

Charlotte arched her back, and purred like a cat. "You see, baby," Gloria murmured, letting the sponge drift gently over Charlotte's breasts, moving slowly, cautiously toward the nipples. "I can do real nice things. Nobody will ever treat you as good as me . . ."

She got on her knees and made Charlotte stand in front of the medicine chest while she dried her, starting with her feet and working her way up until she could see her hands in the mirror. She pressed her lips to the inside of Charlotte's thigh. "Oh baby, you smell so good now. You smell like heaven."

"Heaven," Charlotte echoed. "Heaven."

Even with the stereo on and the bathroom door closed Gloria heard the soft knocking at the door. It had to be some strung-out junkie. Who else would come out at four o'clock on a freezing night like this? Well, she wasn't letting anybody in; she had better things to do.

But the knocking was insistent. She heard someone calling her through the door. She went into the bedroom for the sawed-off. "Who is it?" she demanded loudly.

"Open up. Police." The voice was muffled, but she recognized it as Hernando's. He and that weird faggot Jose were giggling out in the hall. They were stoned. Hernando's eyes were turning like little pinwheels. "What's this, World War Three?" he said, pointing at the sawed-off.

"I didn't know who it was," Gloria said.

"This how you say hello to your friends?" Hernando asked.

"Bitch don't know how to use the fuckin' piece anyhow," Jose mumbled, glaring sidelong at Gloria as though he were ready to spring at her throat.

"I can use it," Gloria said, hefting the shotgun. "And I will, too."

"Whoa," Hernando said. "Don't go fightin' in the middle of the hall. We're all friends, right?"

Gloria was reluctant to let them in. She had the gun. Two barrels would blow both these scumbags right through the wall. But then she would have to go out on the lam; leave her nice little pad, cut Charlotte loose. Hernando was her connection; she couldn't do business without him. Anyway, as soon as she cocked the shotgun they would be on her. The truth was that as soon as she had opened the door Gloria had become a loser. There was nothing she could do about it. She stepped away from the door, and let them in.

"Thanks, baby," Hernando said. "You almost hurt my feelings pointing that fuckin' piece at me like that." He sniffed suspiciously around the apartment. "You got a party goin' or something that we ain't invited to?"

"I got nothin'," Gloria said anxiously. "But it's four o'clock in the morning. I didn't know who was out there."

Hernando peeked in the bedroom. "That's right. Can't be too careful these days."

Charlotte was obviously still in the bathroom. Gloria hoped she stayed there until Hernando left. Hernando didn't like women.

"What are you doin' out here so late?" she asked.

Hernando caught the fear in her voice, and smiled. "You like holdin' that piece, Gloria?" he asked. "You ain't got no reason to be havin' it out here like this. You don't need no protection from me, baby. I'm your friend."

"I know that," Gloria said. She went into the bedroom, and put the shotgun behind the door where she could get to it in a hurry.

"We were just sittin' up in the pad with nothin' to do," Hernando said. "There was nothin' on the tube but a Western, and I hate fuckin' Westerns. Been playin' them same tapes all night long. You know, sometimes havin' nothin' to do is cool. I mean you just don't do nothin', so what? But sometimes, man, it makes you crazy. Didn't have nothin' to drink in the house, and all the bars are closed."

"You could go to an after-hours," Gloria suggested.

"That's what my boy wanted to do," Hernando said. "Hey Jose, you and Gloria ought to get together."

Jose's hands trembled as he lit a cigarette. He threw the

match down on the rug, and looked up at Gloria, daring her to say something about it.

"I hate them after-hours joints," Hernando said. "All these dudes snortin' coke. Bitches runnin' around half naked. With everybody holdin', you know something's gonna go down. Every time I'm in one of those fuckin' bars somebody gets offed."

"That's because you off them," Jose said, with a malicious look at Gloria.

Hernando stepped back and cuffed him lightly on the side of the head. "Shut up and be nice, man. You got something to drink here, baby?" he asked Gloria.

"Sure, sure, I got a bottle of rum," she said, going out into the kitchen. "You want it with ice."

"I'd like a rum and Coke," Hernando called from the living room.

"Okay, I can do that."

"And bring the bottle out with you," Jose said.

Gloria brought the Don Pepe rum and a bottle of Jamaica Cola—the cheap soda that she bought on sale at the A & P—out into the living room. "I'll get the ice," she said.

"Don't need no ice as long as the soda's cold," Hernando said. "But I'll tell you what you can do," he said, taking a quick shot out of the bottle. "You can get the fifteen hundred you owe me as long as I'm here."

Gloria looked out into the kitchen at the coffee can where she kept all the money. "You said you'd come by for it on Saturday."

"This way I save myself a trip."

Gloria sneaked a look at the bathroom. The door was closed. It was quiet.

"Well, what do you say, baby, you got the bread?"

Hernando had tilted his head expectantly. He knew she didn't have it. He was just playing with her.

"I don't have all of it," Gloria said.

"Shit, you mean you didn't move them twenty bags I gave you in a week? With all them junkies I see hangin' around your pad?"

Twenty bags, twenty quarter grams at seventy-five dollars each. Gloria had moved ten right away. The rest had gone to Charlotte. Every time she got too restless and crazy Gloria would cook up another bag for her. It was suicide, and

Gloria knew it. She had tried to step on the ten bags, put another cut on them so she could have twenty, and cover her losses. But these South Bronx junkies were like connoisseurs. Once they'd tasted the real, you couldn't fool them with the diluted. Dumb, useless motherfuckers in every department, but they knew what they were putting in their arms. Gloria cursed herself. Going out on a limb for some strung-out, beat-up hooker who'd probably take off for good with the first pimp who came along. Putting herself in a jackpot just for a little pussy. Gloria felt the hot tears welling in her eyes. She couldn't stop them, couldn't throttle the fearful sob in her voice.

"I had a little trouble with this load," Gloria said.

Hernando leaned back and put his hand in his pocket. Jose stopped fidgeting, and became very attentive. "What kinda trouble?"

"I gave five out on credit, you know," Gloria said, talking real fast. It was hopeless—they weren't going to believe her, but she had to see this story through, at least make it sound right. "It's people I know. They're good for the bread. I make them pay what they owe before I give them anything else."

"You'll get burned doin' that one day," Hernando said. "How about the other five?"

Gloria tried a nervous laugh. "You're not gonna believe this, but they got wet. It was so stupid. I had the dope out on the table, and there must have been a puddle of water or soda or something. You know how fast that shit soaks up moisture."

"You were trying to stretch the dope, weren't you, Gloria?" Hernando asked.

"No, I . . ."

"Don't bullshit me, bitch," he snarled. "I know it all. I know every move you hustlers make. You're makin' money with me, but you want to make more. You want to rip me off and rip off the junkies because you're a fuckin' low-life, and you just ain't happy unless you're rippin' somebody off." He leaned forward, and pointed menacingly. "Well, let me tell you something right now . . ." He stopped and looked over Gloria's shoulder. Jose's eyes widened in astonishment. Gloria didn't have to turn around; she knew Charlotte was standing there.

"Dig this," Jose said with a shrill laugh.

Charlotte had come out of the bathroom. She was nude. Drops of bath water glistened on her light brown skin. Her wig was combed, her cheekbones rouged, and she had put on a thick coat of vermilion lipstick. Crazy bitch. All the time Gloria thought she was hiding she had been in there making up. Crazy bitch.

"Well, at least we know where all that dope's been going," Hernando said.

"You got it, bro," Jose said. He held out his palm. Hernando slapped it absently.

"You got yourself a new old lady?" he asked.

"Jailhouse boyfriend," Jose said. He raised his hand. Hernando held out his palm, and Jose slapped it.

"It's nothing like that," Gloria said. "I just let the chick stay here for a few days."

Jose got up and sauntered across the room to Charlotte. "Hey, baby, what's happening?"

"Don't worry about her," Gloria said. "She's okay . . ."

"I ain't worried," Jose said, smiling seductively at Charlotte. "I'm interested."

"Okay," Hernando said sourly. "Everybody knows you got a joint now. Let's take care of business."

Charlotte stared unblinkingly into Jose's eyes. He stepped back, and waved his hand in front of her face. "You got this chick hypnotized?"

"She's alright," Gloria said.

"Why don't you stop messin' with the bitch?" Hernando said. "*Esta tostada*, can't you see that? She's nuts."

Jose turned to Hernando in mock protest. "Hey, man, don't talk that way about my old lady." He touched Charlotte's shoulder. "Hey, baby, talk to me, baby."

"I can see where all those wet bags of dope went," Hernando said.

"No," Gloria said.

"You've been pimping for yourself with my fuckin' dope."

"No, man, I'm just lettin' the chick crash here for a couple of days. She's real fucked up, you know, and . . ."

"She is not," Jose said. He wheeled on Gloria and shouted. "You give my old lady some respect, you understand?"

Charlotte seemed to come out of her trance. She smiled

260

at Jose when he turned back to her. "Pretty little boy," she whispered.

"That's me, baby," Jose said, stepping back to give her a better look.

Charlotte stretched her arms up over her head. "Did you ever see a snake, little boy?"

Jose laughed; his whole body shook with hilarity. "Check this number out," he said.

"The bitch is burnt out," Hernando said. "Leave her."

Charlotte began to sway. "A snake has a dance, pretty boy," she whispered caressingly. "A snake has style." She ran her hands over her breasts, down between her legs:

Jose whooped and clutched his genitals. "You got style, baby. You got it."

Charlotte swayed across the room toward him. "A snake'll sneak up on you every time, baby. Give you that smile." She darted her tongue snakelike out of her mouth. "Little tongue shootin' out . . ."

"Oh yeah," Jose said. "Do it, baby. Do it to it."

Charlotte smiled languidly, and slid her hands slowly up her body. She kissed her fingers, sucking every one coyly.

"Do it, baby," Jose said. "You turnin' me on now, mama."

"A snake's a cold killer, baby," Charlotte said, undulating right up to Jose. "But you don't care. You too busy lookin'."

She smiled and stretched, and slid her hands up into her wig. Then she hissed, and slapped Jose in the face.

Jose shrieked and staggered back, his hand to his cheek. Blood spurted out from between his fingers.

"She cut me," he screamed. "She cut my face. She's got a razor."

Hernando got up and smashed Charlotte on the side of the head with the bottle of rum. She snarled like an animal, and her eyes bulged.

"My fuckin' face," Jose shrieked.

Charlotte came at Hernando, the razor held high. He sidestepped, and hit her flush in the face, breaking the bottle against her forehead. She fell back into Gloria's arms. "Alright, alright," Gloria said. "Alright, Hernando, I'll take care of her."

"You fuckin' cunt," Jose shrieked. He lunged forward,

and grabbed the broken bottle out of Hernando's hand. Gloria tried to pull Charlotte out of the way, but Jose was on her in a second, slashing at her body with the jagged glass. It sounded as though he was ripping fabric off a couch. Covered with blood, Gloria dropped Charlotte, and ran for the bedroom, but Hernando kicked her legs out from under her.

"You killed her, you killed her," Gloria screamed.

Hernando found the shotgun behind the bedroom door. "It's your fault for having her around. So shut your mouth."

Jose sank to his knees in a corner, whimpering and holding his face.

"Blood," Gloria screamed, looking wildly around the room. "Blood."

Hernando stuck the shotgun in her face. "Shut up. Shut up." He shoved the barrel into her mouth. "Bite it," he said. "Open your fuckin' mouth and bite it."

Gloria opened her mouth to protest, and Hernando jammed the barrel against her teeth, and down her throat until she was gagging and pleading mutely for mercy.

"Suck on this for a while, bitch, and when it comes you'll really feel it."

"Kill her," Jose shrieked hoarsely. "Blow her fuckin' brains out."

Gloria shook her head, and tried to speak. Hernando cocked the shotgun slowly. Gloria's struggles became more frantic. He looked over at Charlotte. She was on her back staring at the ceiling. Something was gurgling in her throat. Her body was crisscrossed with crimson slashes. "Your old lady's dyin', Gloria," he said. "And you're gonna get popped for it. That's right—you. You already did time for murder, so they're gonna come right back to you again. You got the bitch's blood all over you, all over your pad."

"Kill her," Jose screamed hysterically. "She's gonna give us up if you don't."

Hernando smiled, and eased the barrel of the shotgun farther down Gloria's throat. "She ain't gonna give nothin' up 'cause it's her ass just as much as ours." He stepped away, and pulled the shotgun out of Gloria's mouth. "You better get yourself a mattress or somethin' to soak up the blood." He put Gloria's shotgun under his coat. "Get one of them junkies to help you, and get this body outta here before it starts to stink. Then you'd better clean the pad up too." Hernando opened the door, and called to Jose. "C'mon, man, let's go."

Jose stamped his foot, and screeched. "Kill her man, you're crazy. She's gonna give us up."

"Gloria's gonna do the right thing, ain't you, Gloria?" Hernando said. " 'Cause Gloria don't wanna go back to the joint, and she knows she will if her girlfriend don't get buried in a hurry."

"My face," Jose cried. "My face." He sounded like a mourning woman.

"You got a scar now, honey," Hernando said. "You're real macho now. *Vaya, chamaco, vaya.*"

He closed the door, leaving Gloria in the middle of her bloody living room.

First, the drinking had been good. It had been necessary. The booze had lit up his brain, shown him pictures, made him think. But then the pictures had become too vivid, the thoughts had gone out of control. Now he was drinking to put out the lights. No more revelation—he wanted oblivion.

But he couldn't get it. Not while that bastard Morgan was down at the other end of the bar telling war stories, and acting as if nothing had happened. Murphy wasn't even drunk, just sodden with alcohol. And the pictures weren't going away.

"Fourteen years old, and you should have seen the knockers on her," Morgan said. He was in the midst of an admiring circle of younger cops who respected his legend and believed everything he said. And it was all true enough. Morgan wasn't a bullshitter. It was what he left out that marked him, not what he admitted to.

"I told her she could make three hundred an hour on Lexington Avenue," Morgan said.

"Was this before or after?" a young cop challenged.

"During, I don't know. A little piece of ass like that is just wasting her time up here pipin' truck drivers for twenty bucks . . ."

"Why don't you put her on the street?" somebody asked. They were needling him, putting him through his paces. And he loved it.

"Maybe I will," he said. "Maybe I'll take every teeny-bopper off the streets, and put them down on the East Side."

"Morgan, the pimp," a detective named Freed said. "Somehow I just can't see you with one of them big Stetsons that they all wear."

"Morgan, a pimp?" a black cop named Robinson said, shaking his head. Everybody laughed at the thought.

"Why not?" Morgan said. "Did you ever know a pimp who was in hock? Did you ever know a cop who wasn't?" He leaned over the bar, and called to Murphy. "Hey, I'm gonna open up a cathouse, Murf . . ."

Murphy ignored him. Morgan slammed his glass down on the bar. "Hey, Murf," he hollered, "come down here, and have a drink. I'm tired of talkin' to these donkeys."

Lureen waddled up, shaking her head, and grabbed Murphy's glass.

"Hey, where you goin' with that?" he said.

"Well, I'm takin' it down to the other end of the bar," she said.

"Who the fuck elected you social director?" he said through clenched teeth. "Leave it here."

Frightened by something in his voice, Lureen stifled her automatic riposte. She put Murphy's glass back in front of him, and slid out from under the bar, going to a table in the far corner.

Murphy caught Morgan's watchful, curious glance in the mirror. He got up and went to the jukebox. Morgan lumbered up behind him. Murphy could feel Morgan's boozy breath on the back of his neck.

"Hey Murf," he said, quietly conspiratorial. "How do you like that sonofabitch?"

"Which sonofabitch?" Murphy played *Danny Boy* and the Clancy Brothers, and headed back to his stool. Morgan followed, still affable, still watching.

"Connolly, our fearless leader," he said with casual sarcasm. "That fuckin' banana. Who does he think he's playin' with, a bunch of chickenshit rookies? I mean we've been on this job too long, you know what I mean? They might get us for coopin' or scorin a little nooky on the side, or maybe even for shakin' down a *bodega*. None of us are mental giants, let's face the facts." Morgan lowered his voice. "But when he comes in with this phony witness shit . . ."

Murphy turned to face him. He wanted to look right into Morgan's eyes when he told him. "They got witnesses, Einstein," he said.

Morgan winced. He steadied himself. "Deaf and dumb ones, right?"

"Real live ones, Godzilla," Murphy sneered. "The kind that put you away."

"Hold it, Murphy." Morgan leaned in, putting both hands on the bar, boxing Murphy in. "What are you tryin' to say?"

Murphy shoved his arm away. "Get outta my face, Morgan. You make me wanna puke." He scooped his money off the bar, and headed out the door.

"Hey, Murphy," Morgan called after him. "Wait a second, I wanna talk to you."

Murphy gave him the finger, and stormed out the door.

"Hey scumbag, wait a second, I said." Morgan ran out after Murphy, and caught up to him on the street. "Hey, prick, you stop when I talk to you."

Murphy kept walking. Morgan grabbed him by the shoulder, and spun him around. "What the fuck are you talkin' about, witnesses?"

"They got that little chick who was hidin' up on the roof," Murphy said.

Morgan sobered up fast. "What little chick?"

"And they got me and Corelli, too." Murphy patted Morgan on the shoulder. "A-1 motherfuckin' police work, Officer Morgan. Some kid's on a roof not botherin' anybody, and you throw him off . . ."

Morgan looked nervously at the bar. His buddies had come out and were standing by the door, watching. "Shut up, will ya," he said. "You'll blow the whole thing."

"You fuckin' creep," Murphy screamed. "I wish I could. I wish I was man enough to turn your ass in."

"Shut up," Morgan yelled. He reared back and punched Murphy in the face, knocking him to his knees.

With a roar of relief Murphy rushed him. This was what he had been building up to all night long. He butted Morgan, and took a vicious blow on the back of the neck, but he managed to dig his fingers into Morgan's scrotum. He jerked up, and Morgan yelped, tearing at his hair, and slipped backward on the ice. With grim satisfaction Murphy heard Morgan's head crack on the sidewalk. He tried to scamper over the body. He was going to grab Morgan's ears and smash his head against the sidewalk until there was nothing but bloody pulp, but he rolled over and got to his feet.

"Fuckin' stool pigeon," Morgan growled. He kicked Murphy in the ribs. Murphy fell back, and Morgan raised his foot again to stomp his face but Murphy got hold of his ankle and twisted. Morgan came down with his foot on Murphy's neck.

Suddenly, there were a thousand hands around them, a chorus of anxious voices urging them to "Break it up," "Stop killin' each other." Murphy jammed his thumbs in Morgan's eyes. He rolled Morgan over and tried to shove his fingers in his nostrils. Somebody had him by the neck. Hands were pulling at his wrists. "Guy's like a bulldog," he heard somebody say. Then the low moan of sirens, and something crashed on his shoulder bone, making his whole arm go numb. Finley, Murphy thought. He rolled off Morgan, and jumped to his feet. Sergeant Clendennon was standing there, a blackjack dangling from his wrist.

"You sapped me, Clendennon," Murphy yelled.

"I didn't think a tickle would work," Clendennon said.

"You gonna write me up for this?"

"Write you up? You piece of shit, you bring me out of my nice warm station on a bullshit beef like this. I gotta stop two cops from killing each other? You're lucky I don't shoot you, asshole. Now get out of here. Go run your car into a tree." He turned to Morgan, who had shrugged off the aid of two patrolmen, and was glaring insanely at Murphy. "Go home, tough guy, it's a draw. Both of yiz call in sick tomorrow."

"That cocksucker," Morgan began. He made a move toward Murphy, but Clendennon raised his blackjack. "Go home, I said. Die in bed, or in some gutter in a different precinct but don't make me do any more paperwork than I have to." He walked over to the entrance of the Emerald, where Lureen stood, arms folded shaking her head.

"Give last call, and close this dump up," he said.

"That's right," Lureen said indignantly. "Blame me for this. That's typical."

"You keep runnin' your mouth, and I'm gonna blame you right outta the neighborhood," Clendennon said.

As he walked away, Lureen muttered under her breath. "Damm cops. When they ain't got nobody else to beat up, they beat up on each other."

It took Charlotte most of the morning to die. Gloria sat on the couch, her legs drawn up under her, whimpering like a little girl and watching. Charlotte didn't move very much. She just stared up at the ceiling, making funny noises in her throat. The room was gray with dawn before the noises finally stopped. Then Charlotte's head slowly flopped over, her sightless eyes staring straight at Gloria.

"Honey?" Gloria called tentatively. "You alright?" She got up and tiptoed over to Charlotte's body (be quiet, don't wake the dead). There was blood all over the place. It was spattered on the walls and the ceiling, in the corner where Jose had fallen, on the couch where he had thrown the bloody bottle, and on the rug under Charlotte. Gloria knew she could scrub the blood off the walls and the floor, but the rug was ruined. She would have to cut the bloody piece out of it. But then everybody who came in would know that something had happened. The whole rug would have to go.

Gloria was thinking clearly now. She went out into the kitchen and emptied the coffee can. There was eight hundred and seventeen dollars in it, enough to get her out of this neighborhood and into a fleabag hotel on the Upper West Side. She would leave the dishes and silverware, and travel light. Stepping gingerly around Charlotte's body, she went into the bedroom and packed all the clothes and souvenirs she could fit into one suitcase. The stereo and the TV she would sell to someone in the neighborhood; they'd only get ripped off, anyway, in the single occupancy dumps she was heading for.

Gloria saved the worst job until last. Charlotte lay quietly in the living room, waiting. Gloria got a few towels out of the bathroom. She didn't want any blood on her hands, didn't want to have to look at it. She moved the furniture away, and began rolling the rug toward Charlotte, starting with the dry part. Gloria closed her eyes but that was worse because she suddenly touched Charlotte's outstretched arm. It was still warm, just as it had been in the bathtub. Gloria brought Charlotte's hand to her lips. "I'm sorry, baby," she sobbed. "Poor baby, I'm sorry." Was there nobody who

267

could offer a prayer? Everybody had to have a few words said over them. Gloria stopped. God would punish her if she let Charlotte die like this. She went cold with foreboding. God was in this room, watching. She had never felt his presence as strongly as she did now. "God," she prayed, "please accept the soul of this poor girl Charlotte—I don't know her last name. She was a good person, and she was killed for no reason . . . and me, too." She wailed and dropped to her knees by Charlotte's body. "Forgive me for not protecting her. Forgive me, baby. Forgive me for living in sin and committing crimes. God, oh God . . . And for not being the woman my mother wanted me to be . . . forgive me."

She stayed on her knees crying until her chest ached, and there was a jagged lump in her throat. Then she pushed Charlotte's arms up against her sides, and put her legs together She rolled Charlotte's body up in the rug, ripped strips from her bedsheet, and tied it at both ends. She would have to wait until it got dark again before she could take the rug downstairs, and dump it in the vacant lot across the street. The garbage trucks never came there, and it was too cold for the kids to play. If she was lucky, they might not find Charlotte's body until spring

Gloria was calm now. She had done her planning and her praying. She had even thought briefly of vengeance, but that would have to wait. In spite of her thick, strong body, in spite of her thoughts and desires, she was a woman. And she was alone.

"I'm sorry, baby," Gloria said to the rolled-up rug on the floor in front of her. "I could have saved you. But I was a loser as soon as I opened the door."

43

Corelli had spent most of the night looking for Murphy. He covered all the cop hangouts in the area, even drove by the hospital to see if that skinny nurse had seen him. But she wasn't there. "Night off," they told him. He thought for a moment about flashing the shield and getting her address, but decided against it. If Murphy was shacked up, he was safe. It was only if he was roaming around, drinking and brooding, that Corelli had to worry.

At about three in the morning he took a shot in the dark and called Murphy's house. The phone rang for a long time, and then a querulous female voice answered. Corelli hung up without even asking for Murphy. You didn't come home to a woman who sounded like that.

He ended up in the New Era, a disco on Evergreen Avenue where some of the younger cops hung out. It was dark and noisy and packed to the rafters. Corelli elbowed his way to the bar. A couple of drinks, a look at the chicks, and then he would go home. He had to be up at ten to go shopping with Teresa. She had found a jeweler in Long Island City who sold antique gold rings. That's what she wanted all of a sudden, an antique ring. Then, after that, they had to go over to the printers to pick up the invitations. Three hundred people were coming to this wedding. They were going to have prime ribs, two bands, and a violin duo that went around playing requests. All the ushers and maids of honor had to wear matching outfits. Nobody could wear white but Teresa and him. It was a big production, and they kept making it bigger, adding things all the time. They thought they could bury him under an avalanche of responsibilities, making it impossible for him to wriggle out. But it wouldn't work. He would take off on his wedding day. He'd leave Teresa, her antique ring, and her tits standing at the altar. He'd stick the old man for a thirty-thousand-dollar affair that nobody would come to. Because there is no wedding without the groom, assholes—that is a little detail they might have forgotten. He was only going through all this for Teresa. She pouted and pleaded and gave him little hummingbird kisses and he gave in to everything. "You're spoiling that girl," his mother said. "You're gonna be sorry." But he didn't care. He liked spoiling her. He liked making her happy. "Never let a woman make you forget who you are," his mother said. Well, who was he? A bust-out cop with nothing to look forward to. Maybe this wedding would change things. Maybe Teresa would bring him luck.

"Hey, space cadet . . ."

It was a familiar voice. Corelli squinted through the darkness.

"Down here."

Ida was on her knees by his stool. "Remember what you said the last time I saw you?" she said. "That I would have to come back on my knees and apologize. Well . . ." She reached around and grabbed his knees. "I'm sorry, I'm sorry."

"Hey, nutjob." He lifted her under the arms. How could a girl with such big tits be so light? "What are you doing here?"

She tossed back her long dark hair. "Looking for you."

He slapped her lightly on the cheek. "Don't lie to a cop. I never come here."

"So who am I talking to, your twin brother?" She leaned toward him and kissed him on the lips. "Hmm, *sabroso*," she said. Her eyes were shining. She was stoned and horny. She was inspired. "C'mon, let's dance," she said, pulling him out onto the floor.

"You know I can't dance *salsa*," he said.

"So watch me, maybe you'll learn something."

She was wearing a silver bodystocking that glowed under the lights. She danced for him, her hips swaying, her hair whipping around as she turned. Other people on the floor stopped to watch admiringly. That turned her on even more. She whirled and dipped, a little flamenco here, a bump and grind there; she was gasping for breath by the time the record ended.

"You could be a professional," he said.

She brandished her tiny fist. "Professional what?"

"Professional anything you want." He slid his fingers down her shoulders, just grazing the sides of her breasts. She shuddered, and hugged him, pressing her lips against his neck.

"How do you get this thing off, with a blow torch?" he said, running his hands up and down her back, looking for a zipper.

"It's a secret," she said. "Wanna learn it?"

They smoked a joint in the car on the way to Ida's house. Corelli got dizzy, and had to open the window to stick his head out into the cold air. "This shit is strong," he said.

"Sensamila," said Ida. "Pure female grass. No seeds. No contamination by the male . . ."

Corelli grabbed for her. "I'll contaminate you."

By the time they got to Ida's, the dizziness had passed and he was philosophical. He returned her embraces in the elevator, but it was as if he were a million miles away, and watching himself through a telescope.

"I gotta go shopping tomorrow," he said as they came into the apartment.

"So, we'll have to hurry," said Ida. She unzipped the bodystocking down the front and stepped daintily out of it. Still wearing her high heels, she stood over Corelli and helped him undress.

"Did your boobs get bigger?" he asked.

"I don't think so. I did lose twelve pounds, so maybe they just seem bigger."

"Twelve pounds? What for? You don't have to go on a diet."

She bent down to unlace his shoes. "I didn't. Just haven't had an appetite the last few weeks."

"All that cocaine," he said.

"No, that's not it." She slid his pants down around his ankles. "If you wanna know the truth, I think it was because I was missing you."

"Who said I wanted to know the truth?" he said, lying back.

It was different with her now. Corelli kept thinking it was the grass. She was calmer somehow, not as frantic. Everything took longer. She lingered over him, savored him. There

271

were no shouts, no sharp bites or digging of nails. It was as if she had been with another guy, who had taught her a whole new way of lovemaking.

"Who you been hangin' around with lately?" he asked.

"Nobody," she said. "I haven't been with anybody since the last time with you."

"Yeah, sure, tell me another one."

"It's true. Whether you believe it or not, it's still true."

Then something struck him, something he had never noticed before. From the back with her hair falling over her shoulders Ida looked just like Teresa. They were about the same size, had the same black hair, skinny arms, narrow shoulders, huge knockers, tight little asses. Even in profile, looking at Ida, Corelli would get flashes of Teresa. There was that look of intense concentration in the eyes, a kind of power they both seemed to have. Corelli closed his eyes. It was the grass. From the time he had first smoked it in the service it always made him feel weird. Still, it suddenly seemed as if Ida and Teresa were really the same girl. Teresa, the way she flirted and teased, really wanted to be like Ida. She wanted to wear a silver bodystocking, take a couple of quaaludes and dance her ass off in a disco with everybody looking at her tits and ass, all the guys getting hard-ons. She wanted to hump in the back seat of a car, or on the cold tile floor under a stairway or against a tree in the park, screaming and biting and taking it up the ass. But she never would because she was a nice, respectable girl from a nice family. And she had to behave in a certain way. Corelli remembered his brother's wedding. When it came time to kiss the bride, his new sister-in-law, he had bent down to plant the usual sexless smack, and she had stuck her tongue down his throat so far he had almost gagged. Then, she pulled away with that innocent, beatific expression with only the tiniest glint in her eye to show what she had done. Would Teresa do that? Would she walk down the aisle checking out the ushers, looking at the bulges in their pants? That was another thing about chicks like Teresa and Ida—you could never really, completely know what they were thinking.

And Ida. She dreamt of having all the things Teresa had. She wanted to be respectable. To hide her hair under a hat, wear long, black dresses and a veil to church. To be a mother and a wife with a hard-working husband and a nice split level out in the suburbs. Three kids, a big kitchen with the TV going all the time, a mother and sisters to gossip with, the loose flesh on the arms and under the ass that comes with respectability. She wanted stability as much as Teresa wanted insanity. But Ida would never get it. No man would ever come to her for security, just as no man would come to Teresa for excitement. They were stuck. It would be nice if the two of them could change places for a couple of weeks, each living the other's life with nobody knowing, so they could slip right back into their own lives when it was over. But that couldn't be.

And that was why they had him! Holy shit, what a revelation. He was their bridge between reality and fantasy. Corelli looked down at this stoned-out barmaid dozing peacefully under his arm. He was her legitimate lover. When she straddled him with her eyes closed, biting her lips, she was dreaming of station wagons and christenings. And Teresa? Well, she knew about his life as a cop, the partying, the other women. She questioned him all the time, avid for details. She wanted to hear about every bimbo he'd ever had, every freak scene he'd ever been in, so she could be all those women when they made love. Yeah, that was it. He was nothing but a tool. Well, that was good, it made them even.

"I'm getting married," he told Ida as he was getting dressed.

"How come I didn't get my invitation?" she asked.

He stood by the door, uncertain what to say. "So I guess I'll say good-bye, and nice knowin' you, and all that . . ."

She shrugged. "That's up to you."

"What do you mean?"

"You can come see me any time you want, baby." She kissed him lightly on the cheek. "Just call first."

"You mean you're not gonna stab me . . ."

"Not me, baby. It's your wife you'll have to watch out for now."

44

Corelli's father was waiting for him in the kitchen when he got home.

"Better phone the station house," he said. "Three times they called already for you."

"Oh shit, what happened now?" Corelli said, reaching for the phone. He got Clendennon on the desk.

"You seen your partner tonight?"

"No, I was looking for him. Where is he?"

"Last time I saw him he was trying to pull Morgan's nostrils apart in front of the Emerald."

"Morgan . . ." Corelli's palms got clammy. "What was it all about? How did it start?"

"They were both drinkin' pretty good," Clendennon said. His tone was guarded. He knew what it was about. "I don't know what started it, but Murphy was in pretty bad shape."

"Beaten up?"

"Beaten up, drunk, fucked-up, you name it. I called his house, but he never made it out there. So that means he's wandering around here. It would be nice if somebody found him before he did something stupid."

"I'll find him," Corelli said.

He jumped back in his car, and sped down to the South Bronx. The Emerald was closed, and Murphy never went to any of the other after-hours joints in the neighborhood. Corelli checked out the White Castle by the highway, the Dunkin' Donuts on Fordham Road, the Greek joint on Westchester Avenue. No Murphy. Now he was starting to worry. It was a big city. Murphy could be anywhere by now.

And then he saw him, sitting with his head in his hands on a bench in Crotona Park, not far from where they had chased the track star. He drove to a candy store on the corner, and got two coffees to go. Then, he pulled off the street into the park. Murphy didn't even look up as he drove by.

"It's a little cold to be sunbathing," Corelli said.

"If I start now I'll have a great tan by July Fourth," Murphy said. He took his hands slowly away from his face. There were traces of dried blood around his nose and mouth, and he had a big purple swelling over his eye. "But you should see the other guy," he said before Corelli could ask how it had happened.

"The other guy's probably got a little lipstick on his collar, if I know you," Corelli said. "You want coffee?"

Murphy nodded.

"Do I have to come out there to deliver it?"

Murphy nodded again. "The fresh air'll do you good."

Corelli got out of the car. "I don't see where it's done any wonders for you." He sat down on the bench, and passed Murphy a container.

"You didn't happen to bring any cigarettes?" Murphy asked.

"As a matter of fact . . . ." Corelli remembered that Ida had left her cigarettes in the car. He brought them out to Murphy, who made a face.

"Virginia Slims?"

"They belong to a young lady of my acquaintance," Corelli said.

Murphy's fingers were too cold to hold the match. Corelli had to light the cigarette for him.

"Just passing through?" Murphy asked.

"Clendennon called me."

"Uh huh." Murphy took a careful sip of the steaming coffee. "You like being my den mother?"

"I'm your friend, ain't I?" Corelli said. "I'm glad they called me. If somebody's gotta look out for you, I don't want nobody to do it but me."

"Nobody's gotta look out for me," Murphy said. "I'm alright. I'm doin' fine."

"Oh yeah. If you were doin' any better you'd be dead. As it is, you'll probably end up with pneumonia. What the hell are you doin' out here, anyway?"

"Thinking," Murphy said.

"There you go, braggin' again," Corelli said, trying to

275

keep it light, to avoid the subject that was screaming all around them.

"I'm thinking of giving Morgan and Finley up, Andy," Murphy said.

There, it was out in the open. But that would only make things worse.

"Would you back me up if I did?" Murphy asked.

Corelli took a deep breath and closed his eyes.

"Thinkin' it over?" Murphy asked.

"Nope."

"They killed that kid for no reason, Andy."

"I know that," Corelli said.

"They're no goddamn good, the two of them. And you know it."

"I ain't a stool pigeon, Murf," Corelli said.

"No," Murphy said pointedly, "you're a cop."

"A cop? Am I supposed to hear the violins playin' when you say that?"

"You're supposed to report a crime."

"Aw, c'mon, Murf, lighten up. Since when are you livin' by the book? Face the facts, face reality. The kid's dead. There's nothing we can do for him. We'll only end up making trouble for ourselves."

"So we let these two scumbags get away with murder," Murphy said angrily. "So another P.R. is dead. Why worry about it?"

"I didn't say that," Corelli said defensively.

But Murphy was off and running, repeating thoughts he had obviously been mulling over all night. "We've got plenty of people to blame. It's the neighborhood, it's the world, conditions in general." His voice was hoarse with scorn. "These people are gettin' shit on every day. A little more or less won't make any difference."

And Corelli was getting edgy, losing his temper with this man for the first time in six years. "Don't put words in my mouth, Murf."

Murphy shoved Corelli so hard a little coffee sloshed onto his Jordache corduroys. "We're cops, so automatically we gotta stick together, cover each other. But meanwhile, if that kid had been Irish or Italian . . ."

"He wouldn't have been living up here in the first place," Corelli said. "He'd be in Ireland gettin' blown away by some bomb in a fuckin' saloon. Or in Italy gettin' murdered by one of his own. You been readin' the papers lately? People are droppin' like flies all over the place. We ain't gonna change the world by giving two cops away."

Murphy shook his head sorrowfully. "That's all talk, Andy, and you know it. Both of us know what's right, but we ain't got the guts to do it."

"Guts!" Corelli threw his coffee container against the side of his car; it was either that or throw it in his partner's face. "You mean brains, don't you? Guts is something we all got too much of. I mean, shit, I'll go through fire with you, Murf, and you know it. Both of us have done things on this job that no smart guy would ever do. Not for twenty-four grand, and you gotta pay for your own uniform. Not for fifty grand, and a fuckin' limo picks you up every morning. But even I ain't brave enough to turn in two cops. Or is that stupid enough? I get guts and stupidity confused sometimes these days. I mean it takes a lotta guts and no fuckin' brains at all to make trouble for yourself when you ain't gonna do anybody any good."

"You're not makin' sense, Andy," Murphy said quietly.

"Okay, see if you can follow this." Corelli spoke with irritating slowness and clarity. "I am not a stool pigeon. Period."

Murphy turned slowly to him. "Is that what I would be, Andy?"

"Check out the uniforms, Murf. Those guys are on our team whether we like it or not."

Murphy persisted. "Would I be a stool pigeon to you, Andy? Would I?"

Corelli exploded. "You want me to say it? All right. If you turn two cops in you're a fuckin' stool pigeon rat bastard, that's what you are."

Murphy winced, and touched the bruise over his eye. "That's all I wanted to know." He got up and limped away without another word.

Corelli watched Murphy walk down the hill and disappear behind the handball courts. All the anger seeped out of him, replaced by a sadness so sharp he could feel it in his chest. He had felt Murphy's loneliness—in his pained, limping gait, in the desperate look in his eyes. He had felt it all the while they were talking, and had done nothing. And as Murphy had walked away he wanted to call him back, to go to him and put his arm around him, and tell him the truth. That he loved him and owed him everything. That in the six years they had been together Murphy had made a cop out of him; a man as well. That he looked up to Murphy, quoted him in his absence, bored people, especially Teresa, with Murphy stories, Murphy sayings, the wisdom of John Murphy. That Murphy had more heart than any man he had ever met, or ever would meet. And that he didn't want their friendship to end because two shitbums had thrown a kid off a roof. But all of this would have been useless. Murphy would simply have asked him: "Are you going to back me up?" And he would have said no.

It was too bad. Corelli remembered when he'd had that revelation in Ida's apartment the first thing he'd thought was how he would tell Murphy all about it. How they would drive through the sector, Murphy smirking at the wheel while Corelli expounded. How Murphy would deflate him with a few expert little harpoons, but at the same time, without really saying anything, would let him know if he was on the right track or not. There was no one else he could talk to like Murphy, and he realized now he'd never really even talked to him. Now he would have to keep all these great thoughts and revelations to himself. It would probably be easier just to stop thinking.

Corelli drove home, imagining the conversation about Ida and Teresa, the two women in his life, his romantic theories, Murphy's dour responses, a conversation they would never have.

45

After a Saturday of gloom and silence, Mary Murphy awoke early and took the kids to eight o'clock mass. She left a note on the kitchen table. "Have gone to my sister Florence's. Don't worry about us."

Murphy saw the car was outside, which meant her sister must have come to pick her up. She had made coffee and left pancake batter in the refrigerator. He had a beer and a half a pack of cigarettes for breakfast.

It was Super Bowl Sunday, the coldest January thirteenth since 1886. Murphy calculated the time it would take for Mary to get to her sister's, have Sunday dinner, cry on a couple of shoulders about her tragic marriage, and drive back. He figured he had until six o'clock to get out of the house.

A little before noon his brother Paul called. "The old man wants to visit Mom's grave," he said.

"Today? What's the occasion?"

"It's the Super Bowl and it's fuckin' freezin', that's the occasion," his brother said impatiently.

"Just tell him I wasn't home," Murphy said.

"Fuck you. You avoid too many of these little functions, but you're comin' to this one or I'm going to tell the old man the truth."

"That's nice."

"If I have to freeze my nuts off, you can bet your ass I'm gonna have company," Paulie said.

Murphy's mother was buried in the family plot in St. Raymond's cemetery just outside the Bronx. It was easy to spot his father and three brothers. They were the only people present in this huge Catholic burial ground. Everyone else had forsworn piety for a warm house and a football game. All four of them were holding bouquets. Murphy cursed himself—he had forgotten to buy one. But his father didn't seem to notice.

"Better late than never, John," he said.

"I had to came all the way in from Mineola," Murphy said. His brothers glared at him, but his father had already turned back to the grave. "Kathleen," he said to his long-dead wife, "I feel the moment of our reunion approaching."

Murphy's brother Eddie shifted slightly and coughed. The old man turned with a fierce look. "Stop fidgeting, Ed."

Eddie's red face got a touch redder, but he kept silent. No one ever talked back to the old man.

"I woke up this morning in severe pain, Kathleen," the old man continued. "It felt like I had a five-hundred-pound weight on my chest. I know my days are numbered. I wanted to bring the family together one more time." He turned and looked balefully at his shivering sons. "Because God knows what will happen after I'm gone."

They laid their bouquets at their mother's grave. The ground was frozen solid, the wind howled in their ears. Each of them sank into their coats. Except the old man; he stood erect and hatless by the grave.

Murphy tried to remember what his mother had looked like. He squinted back into his memory, but could only come up with the image of a white-haired woman, wasted by cancer, beckoning on her death bed. That musty old bedroom she had shared with the old man, the crucifix over the bed. They had all gone in and stood by the bed. She had moved her parched lips, trying to speak. But nothing had come out.

"Your children have done well by you, Kathleen," the old man said. "You said you always wanted one of your sons to be a priest so you would always have someone to say prayers over you. And you have Vincent, just as we planned."

Murphy looked over at his brother Vincent, standing impassively with his missal. *You see, asshole, that's why they cut your nuts off and gave you that choker to wear, so you could say a few words for your mother once a year.*

"You can still be proud of your other boys, Kathleen," the old man said. "They're making their ways in the Department, raising their children. Paulie took a business course, and has gotten very sharp about investment. He's put some of our savings in an oil-gas lease down in Oklahoma, and our prayers go out for its success."

280

The old hypocrite. For a guy with a five-hundred-pound weight on his chest, he's awful concerned about striking oil.

Afterwards, they all drove back to the family house in Mott Haven, the three-story shingled job where Murphy had grown up. The old man had gotten a taste for Drambuie, so everybody had to have a few snorts. Then they all sat around the parlor, and the old man berated them, one at a time. Vincent, of course, was exempt. But the rest of them got it—who didn't call enough, who had promised to get the old man a new TV and had never come through, who was supposed to drive the old man to Poughkeepsie to see his old partner from the Seven-Four. Chickenshit complaints, directed mostly at Paul and Eddie. The old man was saving the heavy artillery for his youngest.

"I ran into Pat Ward at the Holy Name Society dinner last week, John. He said he was still looking for your name on the sergeant's list."

Murphy thought of Isabella. She had asked him why he wasn't a sergeant. Maybe she and the old man would get along. *Pop, this is my new girl. She's a Puerto Rican and a heroin user.* "I haven't taken the test," Murphy said.

"Ward says it's a piece of cake," the old man said. "Since they've been upgrading all the niggers, they've lowered the passing grade to seventy-five. What was it when you took the test, Paul?"

"Ninety-one, Pop," Paulie said smugly.

"There, you see?" the old man said. "Ward said he could see to it that you got the stripes if your name ever popped up."

"Maybe I'll take the test next year," Murphy said, just to mollify the old man.

"That extra money would come in handy, you know," the old man said. "Might smooth things over at home a little."

Vincent looked discreetly into his glass. Mary had been talking to him again, and he had gone blabbing to the old man. It was okay to run crying to a priest, but not to his own brother. Murphy wondered what they would all do if he walked over and decked the bastard right now.

"It would get you out of the Four-One, anyway," Eddie said.

"I could slide you into a warrant detail," Paulie said, eager to impress the old man.

"Sure you could, Paulie," Murphy said. "Just like you

slid me into the Bank Squad and into Traffic and Borough Planning and all the other favors you were gonna do me."

"Paul's been tryin', John, and you know it," the old man said sternly. "Everybody's been tryin', pullin' strings, collectin' favors ... Everybody but you."

There was a moment of silence as the old man worked up a head of steam. "You haven't used the job properly, and it wasn't for lack of advice or help from your brothers and me. You have nobody to blame but yourself."

"I'm not blaming anybody for anything," Murphy said.

Sensing a quarrel, Vincent stepped in. "I think the important thing is to get John out of Fort Apache. With what's been going on up there lately it's not a fit place for man or beast."

"A hundred thousand people live up there, Vincent," Murphy said. Only his family could make him talk like a liberal.

"Call that living?" Paulie said.

"Is that where you got the shiner, John?" the old man asked. It was the first mention anyone had made of Murphy's battered face. "I've never seen you with a mark on you since you were a kid."

And the only time I ever got marked up as a kid was when my older brothers ganged up on me, Murphy wanted to say. "I got it during that riot the other day," he said.

"Which one?" Paulie said. "I hear they're a daily occurrence."

"Who's the new man up there?" the old man asked. "Do we have any clout with him, Eddie?"

"Not with Dennis Connolly, Pop. He's a loner. No family on the job."

"He's no politician," Paulie said. "He was with I.A.D. for a long time."

"Wasn't he the lieutenant who bad-mouthed you when your partner was shot, John?"

"Yeah." You had to hand the old man, he had a memory like a cop.

"Well, then, we'd better get you out of his clutches."

"It's not as bad as all that."

"Didn't a kid get killed the other day up there?" Eddie asked.

"Yeah," Murphy said, "during that fire. They think he got thrown off a roof."

"With the rest of the garbage," the old man said.

Vincent looked pained. "Now, Pop, you know it hurts me when you talk like that."

The old man got truculent. Not even God's middleman was allowed to reprove him. "Vincent, there are some things you don't understand, never having walked the streets like your brothers and I. These people are animals. They're worse, because even animals don't foul their own nests . . ."

"They think two cops did it," Murphy said. It was nice dropping that little bombshell. And the next one would be even better. *I know who did it, Pop, and I'm gonna turn 'em in.*

"Oh Jesus Christ, not this again," Paulie said.

"And you know with Connolly in command, it won't die," Eddie said. "The only thing he's good for is nailin' cops."

"Well, I think they oughta get a medal," the old man said obstinately, daring Vincent to rebuke him again. "There's not enough of that bein' done, which is why this city's goin' to the dogs. Why I remember when we used to catch a nigger on Parkside Avenue. Down in the basement he went, and he caught a beating he never forgot if he had enough brains left to remember anything when he got out of there."

"Those days are gone, Pop," Paulie said.

"That's what we did, and I'm not ashamed of it," the old man said. "You could walk the streets of that neighborhood at any hour until the day I retired. We kept it safe. That's what cops are for, isn't it? You bet your ass it is. Why, a woman isn't safe in broad daylight right in the middle of Manhattan, and it's because they don't let the cops do their jobs." He looked scornfully at his sons. "That is, if there are any cops left who are men enough to do a proper job." He poured himself another shot of Drambuie. His hand was steady, his tone righteous. He was without doubt.

"Johnny," he said, raising his glass, "if you know these men, tell them your father, who put thirty-five years in on this job, thinks they're heroes. Tell them he drank a toast to them. You tell them that for me."

46

Murphy left his father's house early, saying he wanted to get home before dark. He drove straight to the nurse's building, stopping only to get a six-pack to wash the syrupy Drambuie out of his mouth. But when he stood in the lobby looking at her name in the directory, he couldn't ring the bell. Maybe she lived with her family, in which case a red-faced, stammering cop with booze on his breath would be an embarrassment. Maybe she was shacked up with somebody: that black orderly from the hospital or the little intern who seemed to watch every move she made. Maybe she was lying there in the darkness with a needle in her arm, and didn't want to be bothered. He finally went out and sat in his car, determined to wait all night, if necessary, to see her.

It didn't take that long. After about an hour he saw her get out of a bus on the corner. She walked slowly, head down, hands in pockets, cringing from the cold. She walked right by the car without seeing him. He kicked the passenger door open.

"Freeze!"

She didn't even flinch, too tired or jaded to let anything get to her. "I am freezing," she said.

"You're under arrest for not soliciting an officer of the law."

She peered into the car. "I thought I was never going to see you again."

"I'll make any sacrifice for my country, even seeing you," he said. "Now get in the car, and take your clothes off."

She smiled, but shook her head. "Another time, okay? I worked a double last night, and I'm really wiped out."

"Vee haf facilities in ze Zunzet Motel to revive you, Fraulein. Do not fuck mit ze Geshtapo if you don't know vat's good for you."

"I'm just going to take a hot bath and go to sleep."

"Ve haf in room 302 a bass zat vill make out of you a new voman . . ."

She laughed. "A bass?" She pushed his leg aside, and got into the car. "This bass better be good. Hey . . ." She touched his swollen eye. "What happened to you?"

"I got mugged by the sidewalk. Keep your hand there. It's starting to feel better already."

"I've got the magic touch," she said.

"Good, I've something else for you to work on."

"I don't know if it's that magic."

They drove to the Sunset Motel. Room 302 was taken. "The joint's half empty, how could you give that room away?" Murphy complained to the clerk.

"Nobody told me you were coming, your lordship," the clerk said. "But the bridal suite is available. That's room 304. I promise you won't know the difference."

The nurse made light of it. "If you like that room so much, why don't you buy it?" she said as they walked down the corridor. "A condominium in the Sunset Motel. You'd have a place to retire to."

But Murphy was troubled. "I wanted that room again. I don't know why, I just did."

"Don't be sentimental," the nurse said. "That's the worst thing you can be."

She ran into the bathroom and slammed the door as soon as they got into the room. "It's hot," she called over the sound of the rushing water. "It never gets this hot in my apartment."

Steam seeped through the door. "Want me to wash your back?" Murphy asked.

"No, just let me soak for a while."

She'd taken her bag into the bathroom with her. She could be shooting up, sitting on the toilet seat while the bath ran, tying off with her stockings, cooking the shit up over the sink while he lay out in the next room waiting. How many times had she done that? How many poor slobs had been kept waiting in the next room?

"You on your lunch hour?" she asked.

"No, I'm off today," Murphy said, wondering if he should break in on her.

"Sunday, and you're down here? How'd you manage to sneak away from your wife?"

Murphy was insulted. "I didn't sneak away, I left."

Even through the closed door with the water running she sensed his annoyance.

"Don't get your feelings all hurt. But you know Sunday is family day."

"Well, not for me," Murphy said. And then he added tentatively: "I'm cuttin' out for good, anyway. My wife knows that."

There was no response from the bathroom. The water had stopped, and he heard only the faint splashing as she relaxed in the tub.

"I'm thinking of getting a place for myself," he said. "Somewhere in the Bronx, you know, so I can be near the Four-One. This drive's been killing me lately."

There was still no response from the bathroom. "Maybe I can get something in Co-op City," Murphy said. "Or maybe up in Pelham. There's still some nice sections around there."

"You mean with no Puerto Ricans?" she asked.

"I'd like to bring one with me," Murphy said. "If I were to get a place would you wanna move in?"

It got very quiet, as if she had suddenly disappeared. Murphy lit a cigarette. He wasn't going to fill the silence the way he always did. She would have to speak up this time.

"You're just getting out of one marriage," she said. "Don't you think you'll want a little time to yourself?"

"I've had about ten years to myself," Murphy said. "It's made me real lonely, you know. And since I've met you, I've gotten lonelier."

"I'm sorry."

"It's not your fault, it just happened. It's no big deal, you know. It's just, I'll be goin' along okay, and then I start thinkin' about you and I get lonely."

More silence. This time he had to break it. "Maybe I'm taking this whole thing too seriously," he said.

And still more silence until she called raucously: "Hey, Murphy, get your ass in here and wash my back."

The creaking of the bed springs awakened him. She had gotten up, and was tiptoeing around the room gathering her clothes. He watched her dress stealthily, and when he was

286

sure she wasn't going to wake him, but slip out of the room and out of his life, he stretched and yawned and rubbed his eyes, waking up as conspicuously as he could.

She stood at the foot of the bed watching him. It was too dark to read her expression.

"Didn't your mother tell you not to rub your eyes like that?" she said.

"If I listened to my mother, I wouldn't be here."

"Maybe you'd be better off."

He turned on the lamp. "Where you going?"

She squinted into the light at him. "Home, lover. Can't stay here forever."

"Sure you can."

"Then it wouldn't be as much fun."

"Speak for yourself," he said.

She sat down on the bed and kissed him lightly on the forehead. "You're sweet."

Murphy offered the pack of cigarettes. She shook her head, and played absently with his hair.

"How you gonna get back without a car?" he asked.

"I'll call a cab."

She started to get up, but Murphy pushed down on her wrist. "What's the matter with you, anyway?"

She smiled, all wide-eyed and innocent, like a crook trying to get away with something. "Nothing, really. I just have to go, that's all."

It's great to be a cop, he thought. You learn every style of lying there is, and eventually one of them pops up on the face of someone you love. "I know you like me, Isabella," he said. "I know you do."

"I do, baby, but I gotta get back," she said with gentle firmness, trying to ease out of his grasp.

He released her. "If you wanna get high . . ."

"Oh yeah," she said with sudden bitterness. Her lower lip drooped, her eyes closed, and she scratched her face like a street junkie. "Yeah, Jim, I gotta get down, baby, gotsta get my medicine, you dig." Then, she was out of it, up and striding angrily around the room. "You cops are weird. It's like you see everything, but you don't really know anything."

"All I was gonna say was . . ."

"You think I'm a junkie? You think I'm strung out? You see, that's what I mean. You could stay in this neighborhood

287

for the rest of your life and you'd never understand. Look . . ." She came back to the bed, and took his hand, staring earnestly into his eyes. Either this was a new style of lying, or she was telling the truth. "What it is . . . is . . . I get high once in a while. No big thing. Just like everyone else in the hospital, even the doctors."

"Like everyone else in the country," Murphy said.

"That's right."

"Only everyone else in the country doesn't stick needles in their arms."

She dropped his hand. "Hang around with a cop long enough, and you end up getting the third degree."

"Look," Murphy said, "I don't care what you do."

She didn't hear him. "Smack's a cheap vacation for me," she said, eager now to justify herself. "It's like a few hours floating on a raft in the Caribbean. It's like lying down on the bed and pulling the nice, cool covers over you. Everything gets nice and quiet. I don't have to hear nothin' or see nothin' . . ."

"If you want it so bad, let me get it for you," Murphy interrupted.

She stared in astonishment. "You?"

"Yeah, me. They keep it around the precinct to give to stoolies. There's plenty of it, just as good as whatever you get. Probably comes from the same place."

She came back and sat on the bed. "No lectures? No slide shows? No ultimatums to clean up my act?"

He stroked her cheek. "You see? You could be around cops for the rest of your life, and you'd never understand them."

She waited until he got dressed, and he drove her back across the bridge into the Bronx. She seemed cheerful enough, but as soon as they hit the dismal streets she quieted down, and looked out of the window. It was gray and rainy. The wipers ticked back and forth. Everything seemed dismal and hopeless.

"How about we get out of the Bronx one night?" Murphy said.

"Sounds good."

"Go to a show downtown."

"Sure, why not?"

"A little change of scene . . ."

Somewhere, sirens were wailing. She looked out of the window, trying to locate them. "It stays in your head no matter where you go, though. Especially when you know you're coming back to it. Sometimes, I'll be someplace, and I'll turn real fast, and I think I see blood on the walls like in Emergency. Or I'll see an old man sitting in the park, and his mouth kinda drops open, and it's like he's dead. People pass you, and they're laughing, only you think they're screaming."

"Some things you can never get out of your mind," Murphy said. "Some things are real tough to live with."

She didn't respond. She was a million miles away.

"You know that kid who got killed the other day?" Murphy said. "Thrown off the roof?"

"You're not going to tell me you did it, are you?" she asked.

"No."

"Well, that's a relief. I mean because we figured it was cops."

"You did, huh? Just like that, huh?"

"Well, don't take it personally," she said. "People were throwin' garbage down on 'em . . ."

"This kid wasn't," Murphy said.

"So he was in the wrong place at the wrong time."

"This kid wasn't doing anything," Murphy said, his voice breaking.

The nurse became quiet and attentive.

"The kid was just up there watchin' the fun," Murphy said. "My partner and I were across the street on another roof. Two guys from our precinct came up and threw him off."

The nurse looked out of the window.

"We saw them do it," Murphy said.

"Uh huh."

Murphy couldn't understand her indifference. "You understand what I'm saying? I know who killed that kid."

Why didn't she say something, or at least look at him?

"I could turn 'em in right now," he said. "I should, shouldn't I? Oh, it would end me up here. None of the men would have anything to do with me. I'd probably have to put in my papers."

"Are you asking me what to do?" she said impatiently.

"I don't know. I'm just talkin'."

"Just make it easy on yourself," she said, surprisingly cool and dispassionate. "It doesn't make much difference now, does it? I mean you'll never bring that kid back, no matter what you do. And like you said, if you rat out those two cops . . ."

"Rat out?"

She turned to him with feigned innocence. "Well, that's what you're talking about, isn't it? I mean, if you had seen my brother throw this kid off the roof, there'd be no problem at all, would there?" Now he could feel the sarcasm in her voice, slicing surgically through him. "You'd arrest my brother in a second, wouldn't you?"

"Yeah . . ."

"It's only because they're cops that you've got all this conscience about it."

Murphy was stricken by her logic. "That's wrong, I know, but . . ."

"Hey baby, nothing's wrong," she said harshly. "You do what you have to do. Which means you take care of yourself. Everybody knows that."

"That's not why . . . You see, there's a loyalty that cops feel for one another. Like, they feel it's them against the world, and most of the time it is."

"You can let me off here," the nurse said.

"I'm not trying to cop out," Murphy said.

She gave him that wide-eyed phony smile again. "I didn't say you were, baby, did I? I just said to let me out here."

"This ain't your block."

"I know. I gotta go to the store first."

"Yeah, but it's rainin'," he said.

"I won't melt," she said. "Just let me off here, man." There was an edge in her voice as if she would start screaming if he didn't stop the car. Murphy pulled over to the curb.

The nurse opened the door and put her foot out. Then she looked back quickly at Murphy. He could see why she had been facing out of the window all this time. She had tears in her eyes. She leaned over and kissed him on the cheek.

" 'Bye, baby."

Murphy reached for her, but he was too slow; she was out of the car. "Will I see you again?" he asked.

She managed a weak smile. "Sure . . . sure you will." And she was gone, vanishing in the darkness under the broken streetlights. Murphy looked around. There wasn't a store open for blocks.

Jose had been drinking all day, but nothing killed the pain. His cheek throbbed so badly it seemed as though his whole head was going to explode. He had bloodied every towel in the house, had held ice to the wound, had even let Hernando drop a little iodine into its jagged crevice. Nothing had stopped the bleeding. So Hernando had to use the old jailhouse remedy—fire. He had passed a kitchen match over Jose's face several times until the charred flesh closed sufficiently over the wound to stop the bleeding. It had hurt so bad. Jose had tried not to cry out. He knew Hernando would mock him. It had been okay until he looked in the mirror and saw that blackened gash going from his cheekbone to his chin. Then, he had begun to weep. "Oh, shit, man, I'm gonna be so ugly now . . ."

"What do you mean, now?" Hernando said, chuckling over his work.

Jose had wanted to run to the Emergency Room to get it stitched up, but Hernando said he couldn't for at least three days. Anywhere he went—a private doctor, a hospital—they'd take a blood test, and they'd find traces of heroin. If the people were cool they would let it slide. If not, they'd call the cops, the social workers, the detox people. They'd be asking Jose how he got cut up in the first place. They'd put him in a prison ward until Legal Aid came over to get him out, asking his address and all those personal questions. As soon as they found out he had a record, the cops would be around all the time looking to pin something on him. They might even slip him some kind of down or tranquilizer that would make him talk in his sleep. You never knew what these mother-fuckers would do. So, Hernando said, it was better for Jose to wait a few days until all the dope pissed out of his system. Then he could go anywhere, and everything would be cool. Of course he couldn't get high at all now, not until his face was taken care of; he couldn't even use strong painkillers like Percodan, because you had to show a scrip for them or they put you through the same hassle. The only thing Jose could do was drink, and try to pass out. He got a couple of quarts of 151 proof Puerto Rican rum, but it didn't work. He drank until he puked. Then he drank until he couldn't stand up. He lay on the bathroom floor gagging on his own noxious spittle. He could feel the darkness settling over him, but his cheek still glowed fiery red, no matter what he did.

And now the rum and the burning pain had made him crazy. He prowled the room, obsessed by fantasies of blood and vengeance, rehashing old grudges, remembering every slight that he had ever suffered, vowing to punish the transgressors.

Hernando sat hunched over the glass table cutting dope. He dropped an eighth of an ounce of pure on the table, and then seven-eighths of mannite. Frank, the orderly, had copped him two five-pound jars of the shit, so he was set for a long time. He strained the mixture twenty or thirty times, over and over again, moving in a trancelike fashion. He loved to cut dope, loved to package it, too, getting out the triple-beam scale, weighing a quarter gram of the mixture and spooning it into a glasseine envelope, then folding it and snapping a rubber band around it. A seventy-five-dollar package out of one-thirty-second of a gram of dope—that's what it amounted to. You could make between thirty-five and forty thousand bucks on one ounce of this dope. That's why that pretty little Chino was coming all the way up to the Bronx to cop. That was why he had paid twelve thousand for that ounce, and he'd pay Garcia's price for the pound. Because he was making money. Everybody made money off this shit. Even the junkies got off, so you couldn't say they were losing.

Jose's shrill curse cut through Hernando's reverie. "That fuckin' bitch . . ."

"Hey, man, slow down, you gonna make me lose count," Hernando said.

Jose pointed out the window. "It's that bitch from the hospital. She's with that cop again."

"She's really gettin' it on with him, ain't she?" Hernando said.

Jose kicked at the sofa. "That fuckin' slut."

"C'mon, baby, you're just jealous," Hernando said with a sly smile.

"Jealous? What would I want with a slut like that?"

"I'm not talkin' about the nurse," Hernando said. "The cop's more your speed, ain't he, Joselito?"

"Hey, man, that cunt is gonna give us up, man, I can tell," Jose said urgently.

"She ain't givin' nothin' up," Hernando said quietly.

Jose whipped out that Police Special for the hundredth time that day. "That's right, she ain't 'cause I'm gonna off her, man. I'm gonna lay *El Tremendo* right upside her fuckin' head. I'll take that bitch out just like I did to that fuckin' *puta*."

"*Cuidado*, bro," Hernando said. "Cool your act, my man. You just get too excited behind this shit. You go around gettin' yourself all messed up and everybody else, too."

"Why won't you listen to me?" Jose screamed in agony.

"I hear you, baby," Hernando said. "And I'm tellin' you not to worry about it. You got the man on the case. Number One . . ."

"What are you gonna do?" Jose asked excitedly.

"I ain't gonna do nothin'."

Jose came to the table, his expression worshipful. "You're gonna burn her, ain't you, man?"

"No, man." Hernando looked pityingly up at Jose. "I'm gonna let her burn herself."

He took a spoonful of pure heroin and dropped it in an envelope. "Straight with no chaser," he said. "This bitch is gonna get high."

There was a timid knock on the door. Hernando bopped slowly over, and looked through the peephole. "Hey, baby," he said expansively. He stepped back and opened the door. The nurse stood in the hall shaking the rain out of her hair.

"Hey, baby, nice to see you," Hernando said. "C'mon in outta the cold."

47

Chino's phone had begun ringing at seven o'clock in the morning. He tried to outlast it, but whoever was on the other end knew he was home. After what seemed like a thousand rings he picked it up.

It was Nolan. "This is your big day, birthday boy."

"What's so big about it?" Chino mumbled sleepily.

"You're gonna have a meet with Garcia, the drug king-pin of Upper Manhattan."

"That's not until two o'clock in the afternoon," Chino said. "Why the fuck are you callin' me now?"

"Our superiors at D.E.A. want to make sure we don't get our signals crossed. We've been cordially invited to a briefing at nine-thirty downtown."

"Oh shit . . ."

"We'll pick you up in a half hour," Nolan said. "Make sure you've got your briefs on for the briefing."

Chino fumbled around for the vial of coke on the night table to see if he had enough for one and one to get his head straight. "Make it an hour," he said.

"Hey, you wanna knock off a little morning piece with that little underage runaway you picked up last night, I understand. Make it an hour."

There was nobody in bed with Chino. When he was working on a case as complicated as this he didn't chase around. He preferred coming home alone, smoking a joint and thinking it over. There was always plenty of time, and plenty of chicks when there was nothing else happening. There would be that barmaid, and little Toni the junkie. He would backtrack on all of them just as soon as he got himself out of this jackpot.

At nine-thirty he was ushered into a paneled conference room at D.E.A. Headquarters on 57th Street. There was a silver-haired man in a gray suit at the head of the table. He had a pair of half-moon spectacles, which he put on and took off at such odd moments that Chino thought he was signalling somebody. Two bulky guys in short-sleeved white shirts sat on either side of him. They had short military-type haircuts and thick cop forearms. The pale, skinny guy who had given Chino the money to cop was there, and there was a black guy in a blue suit who puffed calmly on a pipe. They didn't get up, didn't introduce themselves, didn't smile. They were taking this whole thing very seriously.

"First, I'd like to congratulate you gentlemen," the silver-haired guy said. "You've done a fine job on this."

Nolan took the compliment in his stride. "It's nothing we don't do every day."

"And do very well."

Fabrizio wrote "So where's the money?????" on the legal pad in front of him.

"Now we're getting into a more intensive phase of this operation," Silver-hair said. He slid an envelope down the table to them. It was full of grainy black and white photos of a stocky, dark-haired man in an overcoat with a fur collar. Some looked like telephoto shots, others had been taken at night, probably with an infrared outfit. It was all spy stuff.

"This is our target, Anton Grigorihou," Silver-hair said. "He's in the country now. Came in last night with a few valises, one of which we're pretty sure is full of pure heroin processed at a lab in Afghanistan. Now, we'd love to catch him with that valise, but obviously we have to move carefully. He has diplomatic immunity, of course, and we really need an absolutely air-tight case before we can make any moves. Which is why we started this operation in the first place." He looked over at the bulky guy on his right. "Do you have that device?"

The bulky guy opened his attache case and took out a tiny microphone. He turned to face Chino, and spoke in a raspy voice that was accustomed to command. "Now we're gonna put this wire on you, Mr. Mendoza," he said. "This has an extremely sensitive transmitter, which can . . ."

"I can't use the wire," Chino said.

The bulky man raised his eyebrows. Nolan interjected hurriedly.

"You see, sir, a guy as smart as Garcia will almost certainly make Mr. Mendoza undergo a body search before he speaks to him. Drug dealers are very knowledgeable about listening devices these days, sir."

"That's why he picked the hospital for a meet," Chino said. "He'll walk me back and forth and in and out of the cafeteria, all the noisiest places in the building, just to be sure he's not bugged."

Silver-hair sniffed. "I didn't realize these people were so sophisticated."

"They run large organizations, and they make millions of dollars a year," Nolan said respectfully. "They're pretty slick."

"Fine," Silver-hair said, "we'll dispense with the transmitter. Mr. Mendoza, during the course of your conversation with Garcia do you think you could steer the subject over to who is supplying him?"

"That's not a good idea," Chino said.

This time Silver-hair raised his eyebrows. "Oh, and why not?"

Nolan cleared his throat and squeezed Chino's knee under the table. "You see, sir, if Mr. Mendoza asks about Garcia's supplier, he might create suspicion that he wants to go around Garcia and deal with the source. A man with as much money as Mr. Mendoza is supposed to have could easily do business without the middleman. Garcia keeps his supplier out of it. It's not considered good manners to ask about it."

"By all means let's not commit a breach of manners," Silver-hair said with obvious irony. He looked over at the pale, skinny guy. "Now as to the transaction you will effect, we have a hundred and fifty thousand in hundred-dollar bills . . ."

"I'm not making a buy today," Chino said. "I won't need the money."

Silver-hair put his glasses on. "Three strikes, Mr. Mendoza, and you're out."

"Sure, boss, anything you say," Chino said. "Send somebody else up there to meet Garcia today. Why don't you go?"

"The point is," Nolan said, with an angry look at Chino, "that such a large buy is usually discussed a few times. You know, negotiated. Garcia won't be carrying the drugs, so there's no reason for Mr. Mendoza to bring the money."

"If I show up at the hospital with a hundred and fifty thousand in nice new bills I might as well glue my shield to my forehead for all the good I'm going to do," Chino said. "I can't show that I'm eager or in a hurry to make the buy. I have to negotiate, try to get the price down, even threaten to kill the deal. That means I have to have a couple of meetings with this guy before we set the buy." Chino got up and pointed across the table at Silver-hair. "You let me do my thing, and when the time comes you'll collar Garcia with the money, the drugs, and an intense desire to tell you about his supplier, I promise you that."

There was a little irritable shuffling from the two bulky guys, but Silver-hair sat, still and composed, looking over his glasses at Chino.

"Alright, Mr. Mendoza," Silver-hair said. "We'll accept that."

In the corridor Chino grabbed Nolan angrily. "Hey, man, I can speak for myself. You don't have to translate to the white folks for me."

"These are important people, asshole," Nolan said. "You stay on their good side and they can help you out. You're not gonna be on this job forever, you know."

"Yeah, well, I don't like you treating me like your poor, dumb nigger," Chino said.

"We're all niggers to those guys," Nolan said.

"Yeah," Fabrizio said. "We're even niggers to that nigger with the pipe."

Isabella started to nod while the needle was still in her arm. Her consciousness was split into warring halves. One watched and warned and tried to rouse her; the other sank gratefully into the deep, black oblivion that was falling around her. It was hard to resist the rush. If you closed your eyes you would begin to fall through the polished metal corridors, faster and faster, spinning now, out of control, the wind roaring in your ears. Everything was soft, thick blackness. It was all around you. You could lie back in the blackness, become part of it.

"O.D., O.D.," Isabella moaned. She tore the needle out of her arm and flung herself off the bed onto the floor. As beautiful as it was to yield, it was torment to fight the rush. Your breath snagged painfully in your chest. Every time you tried to stand, the blackness wound itself tightly around you like a scarf, blinding, choking, driving you back to your knees. Isabella held her hands up to her eyes. Her fingertips were blue, the way they had looked when she smeared ink on them in public school. "No oxygen," she said. Through the pain and the panic the explanation was very clear. Oxygen was being cut off to the small blood vessels, the capillaries, in her extremities. But soon this deprivation would spread. Her lips were probably blue already. Isabella crawled frantically around the room. Do anything, just keep moving, keep the blood circulating.

A cold bath. She managed to stay on her feet long enough to stagger into the bathroom. The blue was spreading through her hands like ink through a blotter. She was too weak to turn the cold water on. She fell over onto the cool tile of the bathroom floor. Oh shit, why not just enjoy it? If this was death, it wasn't so bad. It was so nice when you gave in.

"No, no, no. . ." Isabella repeated the word over and over again. Just keep moving toward the door. Once she got outside, someone would help her. Just keep moving.

The door was locked, bolted. A police lock, a chain, everything that kept people out was keeping her in. She grasped the doorknob and pulled herself up. Be calm . . . Flip the locks, take the rod away. Calm . . . Calm.

The chain wouldn't come loose. It clung to its runner. It wants me to die. And I could. I could sit here against the door. It's so comfortable like this. I could just sit here, and . . .

"NO!"

She dug her nails into her wrists, bit her knuckles, praying for pain, because pain meant her body was still functioning. I want to live . . . I want to live . . .

She wrenched the chain. She couldn't get up off her knees, but it was alright. The chain came loose. She got both hands on the doorknob.

"I want to live," she said, trying to scream. "I want to . . ."

The darkness overtook her, surrounded her, devoured her. She fell back.

And the door swung slowly open.

Chino dressed for the meet. Nothing fancy. The purple velour pullover with the mandatory gold chain. Sasson jeans, Bally loafers, that leather aviator jacket. A touch of New Wave—Garcia would appreciate it.

A gun was permissible for this get-together. It was in a

public place, so the weapons were only decoration. Garcia and his people would certainly be heeled; he could also allow himself the luxury. Chino slid a 9-mm automatic in his ankle holster. It was the weapon of choice among drug dealers, favored for its accuracy and power. He snapped in a clip, and put a shell in the chamber just to show off. Everybody always made a big deal of flashing, then stashing, their pieces at these meets, so he might as well have something nice to flash.

Chino wasn't scared. His cover was solid. He was the man from Queens who lost his connection in the Eldridge Street busts. He had already tightened up some stoolies in Jamaica to vouch for him if anybody checked. He knew what he was talking about, he had the bread. He'd have no trouble with Garcia. The big guys were actually easier to deal with than street dudes like Hernando and Jose. They were smarter, which meant they could be fooled by a smart story. With a cat like Jose, you had to hope he understood you because he might blow you away if he didn't.

Chino was confident as he walked through the Emergency Room parking lot of Jefferson Hospital. He didn't see Nolan and Fabrizio, but he knew they were around somewhere, dressed as janitors or visitors, blending in with the scenery. They would be right there if he needed them, but he wouldn't. Everything would go real smooth with Mr. Garcia.

They were sitting in the waiting room. Chino spotted Garcia even before he saw Hernando. He was into the Continental look—dark, conservative suit, Cardin raincoat thrown over his shoulders. A real charmer, too, *un guapo*, the chicks must really flip for this dude. He had two guys with him, two Spanish cats who were dressed like the boss but didn't have his flair. They were sitting around looking tough while Garcia paced nervously.

"Hey, Chino."

Hernando was standing by the candy machines. "Right on time, man. C'mon, let's meet the man."

Garcia took him in from head to toe. His two boys got up and stood protectively around him. Garcia kept his hands in his pockets, and didn't shake hands. But his manner was friendly.

"Chino, they call you? Let's take a walk Chino, okay?"

"Sure."

They took him through the corridor toward the cafeteria.

Garcia looked over his shoulder several times, then turned quickly and took Chino by the arm. "I'm sorry, but I'm gonna have to look you over." He sounded sincerely regretful.

Chino raised his arms and backed against the wall. "I understand."

Garcia patted his chest and back and slid down both sides of his legs looking for wires. He didn't get low enough to feel the automatic, but stepped away with an apologetic smile. "Okay, I guess we can talk."

"Too bad," Chino said. "I was starting to like that."

Garcia's expression softened. Maybe this man-about-town had a little *pato* in him. In that case, there were all kinds of ways to play him. This cat was going to be a piece of cake.

But when they turned the corner Chino saw something that turned his stomach. Two guys in blue suits were leaning against the wall. Two young white guys, one blonde, the other pinkly bald. They were leaning against a blank wall doing absolutely nothing, holding their topcoats and trying to look innocent. Across the lobby, two more were standing at the newsstand. White guys with baggy suits looking around, chatting, their eyes roving everywhere but in the direction of Garcia and his little group. White guys trying to be inconspicuous in the South Bronx.

They read "Fed" all the way. It was bad enough that they stuck out like sore thumbs in this hospital, but they hadn't even tried to disguise themselves. And what the hell were they doing here anyway? Had old Silver-hair decided he wanted some of his own ace operatives on the job?

If he had, he had ruined his own operation. There was an old undercover maxim: If you can see your back up, so can the target. Garcia was smart. He spent most of his day looking out for guys like this. He had to have spotted them. Assholes. Fucking stupid assholes. Not only had they blown their own operation, but they had ruined Chino as well. Now he couldn't work Garcia or any of his network. They would spread his name all over Washington Heights. Undercovers learned that guys you put away couldn't hurt you. It was the ones who walked, like Garcia. The ones on the outside.

"I understand you want to buy something from me?" Garcia said.

"Yeah," Chino said cautiously. Maybe Garcia hadn't

spotted them after all. It was possible that he was preoccupied with the deal, that he was nearsighted and too vain to wear glasses, that he was checking out Chino's ass when his eyes should have been elsewhere.

"I'll put the price on a piece of paper," Garcia said. "Just a number. And that's it, take it or leave it."

"Okay, okay," Chino said, "don't keep me in suspense." His high spirits were returning. It looked as though he had lucked out. "I'll need a sample, too."

"Yeah, yeah, I know. I brought you a taste."

They walked through the cafeteria. A big, black orderly got up and waved to Hernando.

"Hey Frank," Hernando said casually. "I'll speak to you later, man."

The orderly sat down with a hurt look.

"That's my cut connection," Hernando said. "He works in the pharmacy, and rips off all kinds of shit for me."

"Let's step in the bathroom for a second," Garcia said. He smiled and held the door for Chino.

"I do my best work in bathrooms," Chino said.

"I'm sure you do," Garcia said.

Chino turned to face Garcia, and caught a knee right in the groin. He saw them after all, Chino thought. He retreated to a corner, doubled over, pretending to be more hurt than he was.

"What's the matter . . ."

"You fuckin' stoolie." Garcia kicked him in the side of the head. Chino was thinking fast. He doesn't know I'm a cop. Okay, that's better. So I take a beating. As long as they don't know I'm a cop I can always come back. I can always come back.

Chino got up, and walked right into a right hand from one of Garcia's gorillas. He fell back against a urinal.

Garcia grabbed Hernando by the collar and threw him against the wall. "You set me up with a stoolie, you stupid motherfucker. The whole fuckin' place is crawlin' with fuckin' cops."

Hernando clasped his hands. "I swear, I didn't know nothin' about this. I swear on my mother . . ."

"You're finished, asshole," Garcia shouted. "You don't work for me no more, understand? You're lucky I don't blow your fuckin' stupid brains out."

"But it wasn't me, Mr. Garcia," Hernando said. "It was him." He pointed to Jose, who was staring down at Chino in disbelief. Through the blur of pain Chino caught Jose's look. The kid was starting to freak. Nobody had noticed it yet because nobody was looking at him. Chino crawled closer to the stall.

Hernando slapped Jose on the side of the head. "You stupid junkie motherfucker," he said, punctuating each word with a slap. "It was him, Mr. Garcia." He grabbed Jose by the hair and slammed his head against the wall. "I told you I didn't trust the dude, didn't I? Didn't I tell you that?"

Jose sobbed. "I'm sorry." He extended his hands piteously. "I didn't know, man."

Chino moaned and doubled over, managing to get his hand near his gun.

Tears were pouring down Jose's face, and he was trembling violently. "I'll kill him," he said grinding his teeth. "I'll kill the fuckin' stoolie."

Garcia looked thoughtful. "That's an idea." He spoke to Hernando, the sane one. "You take care of this, and maybe I'll let you back."

"I'll kill him Hernando," Jose said. Somehow his wound had opened, and blood was filling the makeshift bandage he had plastered on his face.

"Calm down," Garcia said. "You just give us a few minutes to get out of here, and . . ."

"I'll kill him." Jose ripped the bloody bandage off his face with a shriek. He reached into his pocket, screaming incoherently.

Chino dove into the stall. The last thing he heard before Jose started shooting was Garcia yelling: "Not now, you crazy bastard." He couldn't get the door closed. "Oh God, save me," he cried, trying to wedge himself in behind the toilet bowl. It sounded as though a cannon was going off in this little room. One-two-three-four—the bullets ricocheted like maddened insects off the walls. He got his own gun out, and waited. It was quiet, except for a peculiar sound that took him a while to identify—the sound of his own whimpering breath.

He slid slowly out along the bathroom floor. There was blood all over the walls. Garcia was kneeling on the floor holding his stomach. He seemed about to burst into tears.

"What happened?" he asked.

Chino ran outside. A hospital security guard was lying by the elevator. A woman stood over him screaming hysterically.

"They took them," a nurse said, pressing her palms against her cheeks and staring up at the floor indicator on the elevator. "They took all the people out of Admission. And when Mr. Cleveland tried to stop them they shot him, and took his gun." She pointed at six, the floor where the elevator had stopped. "That's where the Administrator's office is. Oh God, oh God, oh God . . ."

Nolan and Fabrizio came running up. They were wearing maintenance uniforms. "What the hell happened?" Nolan asked.

Chino leaned against the wall. "A mess," he said. "A mess."

And the woman's screaming continued, each shriek coming out at precise intervals like the tolling of chimes.

48

The Four-One got seven 911 emergency calls from Jefferson Hospital, each one describing a different incident that had occurred as a result of Chino's aborted meeting with Garcia. One man on an upper floor of the hospital merely reported shots fired somewhere in the building. Another saw Chino ranting on the ground floor about how he wanted to kill all those "CIA assholes," and called in a psycho complaint. No one reported the shooting of the security guard; everyone just automatically assumed it had been done. And when an intern found Garcia bleeding on the bathroom floor, he got two orderlies with a stretcher, and transferred Garcia to Emergency without notifying anybody. When Applebaum arrived he expected to find the usual insanity and exaggeration in the complaints. Only one car had responded to the hospital, and the two cops came running over to Applebaum as he waddled into the lobby.

"Hey, Sarge, we've got a massacre here."

"What do you mean?"

"We've got two guys shot, and two drug dealers holding hostages in the Administrator's office."

"Hostages!" He shoved one of the cops toward the exit. "Go out and call the house. Get the Lieutenant over here, call in a 10–13, and tell the Dispatcher to get the Hostage Squad over here right away. You . . ." He grabbed the other cop by the arm, and dragged him toward the elevator. "Take me to the room where the hostages are."

Chino was squatting in front of the Administrator's office, keeping guard while Nolan called the office, and Fabrizio went to the car for the shotguns. He jumped up and saluted Applebaum. "Hey Sarge . . . Julio Mendoza, Narcotics undercover, on temporary assignment to the D.E.A."

"You got something to show me?" Applebaum asked. "A shield, maybe, or an I.D. card?"

"Nothing, Sarge. I was on assignment today in the hospital. Which is why this all happened."

Applebaum nodded patiently. That was all he needed, a psycho. "Well, Mr. Mendoza, if you just sit down against the wall over there we'll hear your report as soon as we're ready."

"What the fuck are you talkin' about, man, I'm a cop," Chino snarled. "I've dealt with enough assholes today, so don't get on my case . . ."

Applebaum was the soul of patience. "If you'll excuse me, Mr. Mendoza . . ."

Nolan came running out of the office. "How are you, Sarge?" he said, saluting.

"I suppose you're a cop masquerading as a janitor," Applebaum said.

Nolan flashed his shield. "Narcotics Task Force on loan to the D.E.A. This is Mr. Mendoza, my associate."

Applebaum didn't bother to apologize. "Well, tell me what happened here."

"I had a meet with a dealer, but he spotted the surveillance," Chino said. "These two crazy bastards in there deal for him. They got nuts when they found out I was a cop, and started shooting. The dealer got hit. They ran out in the lobby. I don't exactly know what happened then, but they shot a security guy, took his gun, and emptied out the Admissions office, and brought 'em all up here where they got the Administrator and his secretary."

"Well, how many people do they have in there?" Applebaum asked.

"Nobody knows. This one nurse says they filled the elevator, which would mean twenty people, maybe more."

Applebaum wiped his forehead. "Twenty people, *oy gottenu.*" He looked into the crowd of nurses and hospital employees who had gathered around the desk. "Is there an assistant Administrator here?"

"He's gone for the day."

"Well, is anybody in charge?" Applebaum said in exasperation.

A wiry black man in the gray hospital security uniform inched forward shyly. "I guess me," he said. "I'm in charge of security on this shift."

Applebaum checked out his bars and his nameplate. "Okay, Captain Benton, you're the boss. You get somebody to get a list of all the employees of the Admissions office who were at work today, and then start checking out who's sick or on vacation or went home early. Maybe we can start finding out who's in that room. And before you go, tell me the extension number in the Administrator's office."

"Three fifty-six," Benton said, and bolted for the elevator.

"Did any of you guys make contact?" Applebaum asked Chino.

"I don't think either of those two dudes wants to talk to me."

"Right." He faced the bystanders. "I need an office with a phone."

They took him into the Head Resident's office. He sat down, pushed back his hat and took a deep breath. Chino had come in after him, and stood in the doorway. "In these hostage situations you gotta make contact right away."

"These guys are freaked out, Sarge," Chino said. "I know them."

"Yeah, well, you gotta open up the lines of communication," Applebaum said, dialing three fifty-six. The phone was snatched up on the first ring. Applebaum could hear the sound of sobs and low voices at the other end. He put on his friendliest voice. "This is Sergeant Applebaum of the Forty-first precinct. Who am I speaking to, please?"

"I ain't talkin' to no fuckin' sergeants, man," a voice said. "I want the Commissioner, I want the Mayor. Or else I'm gonna start executing some people around here." And he hung up.

Applebaum drummed on the desk for a moment, then jumped up and ran out into the hall. "I need a floor plan of the building. Anyone know where that is?" About a half dozen people scurried off in different directions. "Thank you," Applebaum called after them.

Murphy and Corelli had driven in silence for the first hour of their tour, each absorbed in his own thoughts. The radio was quiet, the streets were dead. On a day when they would have welcomed the work, there was none, so they were stuck together in the car, stuck with the ashes of their friendship. The radio call came as a relief.

"All units proceed to Jefferson Hospital forthwith."

"That's probably your girlfriend," Corelli said. "She just can't get enough, can she?"

Murphy kicked down on the accelerator. "Let's at least see if we can get there first."

"Yeah, it would be pretty embarrassing to have sloppy seconds on your own old lady," Corelli said.

Murphy forced a smile. The jokes were the same, but the two of them were different. It just wasn't going to be as much fun anymore.

Workmen were putting up police barricades as they arrived at the hospital. Heffernan was in the lobby writing feverishly in his memo book as Perez, the intern, read from a patient's chart. "Garcia was shot once in the stomach."

"Alright, we got the casualty list squared away," Heffernan said, shutting his book.

"You may not, Lieutenant," a lithe, dark Spanish guy said. "Garcia had two guys with him. Four shots fired at close quarters. One of them might have gotten hit."

"Jesus, this is a nightmare," Heffernan said. "What happened to these hooples?"

"I guess they just split," the Spanish guy said.

"They couldn't have done that." A hospital cop came forward. "As soon as I heard the shots I put a man on

306

every door, and locked all the unattended exits. There's no way anybody could have gotten out of here."

A nerve under Heffernan's eye began to twitch. He slapped at it in irritation. "So these guys are roaming around here, too."

"And they're armed," the Spanish guy said.

The nerve didn't stop. Heffernan rubbed his face angrily. "We're gonna have to flush these bastards out. We'd better evacuate the hospital."

"But, Lieutenant, that's impossible," Dr. Perez said. "We have many patients who aren't ambulatory."

"So we'll carry them out," Heffernan said. He turned to give instructions to the men around him, but Perez pursued him.

"Please, Lieutenant, if these men are wounded and desperate, there's no telling what they'll do. With all these sick, helpless people . . ."

"You got a better idea, Doc?" Heffernan asked angrily. "Or do you just want us to let these guys go?"

Perez took the suggestion seriously. "Why not? If you know who they are, you can always pick them up some other time . . ."

"Listen, Doc, there must be somebody who needs an enema in this hospital," Heffernan said.

"But, Lieutenant . . ."

Heffernan's voice cracked in irritation. "Will somebody get this idiot away from me?"

The Spanish guy drew Perez aside, speaking in Spanish.

"What the hell's goin' on here, anyway?" Murphy asked Patterson.

Patterson pointed to the Spanish guy who was trying to pacify the intern. "That dude's an undercover. He and his boys blew a collar. The perps shot two guys and took about twenty doctors and nurses hostage."

"Nurses?" Murphy looked around in alarm. "Where are they? Do they have any of the names?" He didn't wait for an answer, but rushed over and grabbed Perez. "Hey, Doc, where's Isabella, do you know?"

Perez looked at him strangely. "Isabella?"

"Isabella Ortiz. She's a nurse in Emergency."

"I know who she is."

"Where is she, Doc? I know she's supposed to work today."

Perez started to speak, then changed his mind, and gestured helplessly.

"Is she one of the hostages?" Murphy asked. He shook Perez by the shoulders. "C'mon, tell me."

Perez jerked out of Murphy's grasp. "Leave me alone," he said. "Just leave me alone, all of you." He ran through the lobby.

Murphy started after him. "Hey, wait a minute."

"Will ya let that asshole go, Murphy?" Heffernan said. "Get your ass over here, we got work to do." Heffernan checked his men. "How many horses do I have here? Six? Shit! That's not enough." He snatched Donahue's walkie-talkie. "Applebaum . . . Applebaum, where the fuck are you?" Applebaum's voice croaked back at him. "Up in front of the Administrator's office, Loot. Over."

"Did you call in for more troops?" Heffernan asked. He hated to say "over," but he knew the literal-minded Applebaum wouldn't answer until he did. "Over."

"I did it first thing . . . over."

"So how come there aren't swarms of bluecoats comin' from all directions?" Heffernan asked with despairing sarcasm. "Call Borough, call Emergency Service. Get some fuckin' manpower over here." He gave the walkie-talkie to Donahue, then grabbed it back and shouted "Over and out."

"We'll have to do a search of every floor in the hospital," Heffernan told the cops gathered around him. "Every room, office, broom closet, the landings on both ends of each floor, every square inch." Heffernan's red face got redder. "And be careful, because these two guys must be jumpin' outta their skins by now. Go up in teams, each team taking a floor. I guess we might as well start with the ground floor, and work our way up."

"Aren't there some unused floors in this hospital?" Murphy asked.

"Yeah, from eight up to eleven's not in use anymore."

" 'Cause if nobody's found these guys yet, maybe they're hiding on one of the vacant floors."

"Okay," Heffernan said, "three floors, one to a team. Don't try to take these guys if you don't have to. Call down to the other units. Once we know where they are we can get a whole army to take them out."

"What floor you want?" Patterson asked.

"I'll take eleven," Corelli said. "It's my lucky number."

Murphy went after Heffernan. "Hey, Loot, where they holdin' the hostages?"

"Sixth floor Administrator's office."

"Do they know who's in there? Do they have any names?"

"We'll get their names, when we get 'em out," Heffernan said. "You got a girlfriend in there, huh? I'm sorry to hear about it. Now go to work and don't bother me with your personal problems."

Corelli was waiting for Murphy at the elevator. "You think your girlfriend's one of the hostages?"

"I don't know, I don't know." Murphy scratched his head feverishly, clawing at the skin on the back on his neck. "Did you see the way that intern acted, Andy? He ran away from me."

"The guy's a whacko, Murf."

"No," Murphy said, nodding convulsively, "it's true. The guy knew something. That's why he ran away."

The elevator door opened onto the eleventh floor, affording a perfect view of its vacant, silent corridor. Murphy started out, but Corelli grasped him firmly by the shoulders. "Take five, Murf, cool yourself down. I don't wanna go out there with no basket case."

"I'm alright, Andy, don't worry." He stepped out of the elevator, and walked toward the corridor, taking his gun out. He turned and beckoned to Corelli. "C'mon." Corelli hung back. "Alright, fuck you, then," Murphy hissed, and quickened his pace.

Corelli jumped out after him. "Not so fast," he whispered. "Take it easy."

Murphy turned, his finger to his lips, and touched his ear. Corelli moved forward, straining to hear. There was something that could be the murmuring of voices coming from a room further down the hall. Two guys came out of a room on the left-hand side. One of them had his arm in a makeshift sling. They were followed by a big, black orderly in a white uniform.

"That's one of them," Murphy said. He dropped to one knee and shouted "Freeze."

The two guys stopped dead like statues. You could tell they'd had plenty of practice. The black orderly said something, and came toward them, waving something.

"It's a fuckin' gun," Corelli shouted. He and Murphy fired almost simultaneously. The shots echoed through the hollow corridor, mixing with the piercing scream of the black orderly, who went down clutching his knee.

Murphy and Corelli ran down the corridor. The black guy was writhing, and yelling with pain and rage. The two other guys stood perfectly still watching.

"You dumb motherfuckers," the orderly cried.

"Stay away from that gun, or I'll blow your fuckin' brains out," Murphy said.

"I'm a cop, you stupid, honky motherfucker."

"Yeah, you're the Commissioner, right?" Corelli said.

The black guy sat up and examined his bloody kneecap. "Oh Jesus, you made a fuckin' cripple out of me, you stupid . . ." He turned over slightly. "Here, hurry up, my wallet's in my back pocket. Get it. C'mon, you bastard, I'm dyin' here."

Murphy slipped the wallet out of the orderly's pocket, and let it fall open. There was a gold detective shield hooked to one of the compartments. Murphy let the wallet drop.

"But you were hangin' out with that dealer . . ."

"Undercover, you ever hear of undercover? Sure you did. But all you saw was the nigger you thought was fuckin' your old lady. Right, you Irish pig." Sweat was pouring off him. He rolled over in agony. "Well, get me a fuckin' doctor," he yelled. "Oh, let me just get my fuckin' gun, and I'll get you, man. I'll get you for this."

"He's delirious," Corelli said quietly.

"Yeah." Murphy retrieved the orderly's gun. He walked back and handed it to him. "Here. We'll get your two prisoners downstairs, and send a stretcher up for you."

"You fucked up everything, you know that," the orderly yelled at Murphy. "And I'm gonna get you for it." He was still yelling as the elevator door closed. They heard his curses all the way down to the first floor.

"It was my shot," Murphy said.

Corelli laughed. "I know it was. I was aimin' for his head."

They cuffed the two prisoners together, and marched them out of the elevator and into the lobby. Heffernan had met Connolly at the door, and was briefing him. "Are those the guys with Garcia?" he called.

"Yeah."

Heffernan came over. "Jesus, am I relieved."

Connolly was a few steps behind him. "Well, that removes one problem from this situation." He nodded coldly at Murphy. "You men have any trouble up there?"

"We had a little trouble, yeah, Captain," Murphy said. "I shot a cop."

49

Hernando had lined up all the hostages against the door. "When the cops break in, people, you're gonna be the first to get it. And lemme tell you . . ." He pointed his .38 Police Special at them. "Them cops are gonna come in smokin'." He bopped over to Jose with his palm out. "Right, bro?"

Jose slapped him five. "Right, man."

Hernando had never been so happy. He strutted around the office chanting "Take it to the street now, Take it to the street." The hostages watched him nervously, following his movements like spectators at a tennns game. Back and forth he walked, smiling broadly, singing to himself.

"You did it, bro," he said to Jose. "You put one right in that motherfucker."

"Yeah, I did it." Jose tried to pick up on some of Hernando's spirit. He tried to laugh, but the left side of his face felt as though it was on fire. The pain had spread up into his head, and even down through his shoulders.

"He had it coming, too, man."

"He did, he did," Jose agreed frantically. "Talkin' to us like that. I'd never let any man treat me like that . . ." Suddenly, he couldn't stand it any longer. "Get me something," he screamed insanely. "Please get me something, Hernando . . ."

Hernando's good cheer rode over his hysteria. "You proved yourself today, man. You really are a stone killer."

"I proved myself," Jose sobbed. "I know I did. But can you get me something, man?"

The hostages now turned their horrified attention to this skinny, seemingly spastic kid with the discolored, purulent wound on his cheek. He was the crazy one. He'd pull the trigger first.

"You're gonna get something," Hernando said soothingly. "You'll get anything you want. You just keep your heart, Jose, man, because we're gonna win this one, and when we do we're gonna have every fuckin' thing we want."

"Motherfucker can't talk that way to you," Jose said. "I killed him right there."

"You bellyshot him, baby," Hernando said. "He won't forget you."

"No," Jose said. "He won't." He waved his left hand in front of his face. If he could just get his fingers in there, and tear that scratch out. He could feel the heat of his face on his hand. And he screamed, a tormented scream from the depths of his chest. He screamed and tore at his hair. "Get me something, man."

And the phone rang.

Detective Frank Russo had been on the Hostage Negotiating Squad for six years. In that time he'd had shingles, a hiatus hernia, and incipient psoriasis, which he controlled with heavy cortisone shots that usually ruined his weekend as well as chronic hemorrhoids. He'd put on about twenty pounds, and become a chain smoker. And he had volunteered for this detail because it promised relief from the stresses of ordinary police work.

Now he was sitting at a phone talking to a guy he knew was big trouble. The corridor was jammed with cops, hospital personnel, technicians. Emergency Service had shown up with their special explosive battering ram that detonated a charge of TNT on contact. They were ready to go in, but Russo didn't think that was a good idea for the moment. He didn't know where the hostages had been positioned—how close to the door, how vulnerable to quick attack if the door was broken down. He didn't know what kind of people he was dealing with.

Mendoza, the undercover, had told Russo their names. He had also told Russo how crazy they both were. Mendoza had taken him aside and said: "If you get these guys with your mouth, you're a genius."

"Hernando," he said cheerfully into the phone. "I'm Detective Frank Russo."

"I'll only talk to the Commissioner," Hernando said. "I already told you pigs that. You wanna mess with my head, I'll just start chalkin' them off in here."

"We're not messing with your head at all, Hernando. We're very serious. I work for the Commissioner, you see, and he sent me down to get an idea about what your demands are."

"I'll tell you right now, loud and clear. My unconditional, did you catch that unconditional, demands are as follows. I will exchange my hostages for the Mayor and the Commissioner. They will arrive here with five million dollars in small denominations. As soon as they walk in, I let these people go. Then, a plane shall take us to Tripoli in Libya where my man and I will request asylum. The Mayor and the Commissioner can go home as soon as we land."

"Well, that's a clear presentation alright, and thanks for giving it to me like this," Russo said. "I'll be back to you."

"Hey, man, don't try to con me. You get punished for that, now." Russo heard the sudden report of a pistol, and a chorus of terrified screams. "There's one doctor, who needs a doctor. Next one's gonna need an undertaker."

Russo flinched and put his hand over the phone. "He just shot someone in there," he told Inspector Krieger. "Hey, Hernando, if you shoot everybody we won't be able to make a deal," Russo said jokingly.

"So what? You know the kind of man you're dealing with here? The kind of mind you're up against, motherfucker? I got a box with a hundred shells in my pocket. If I don't get what I want in thirty minutes I'm gonna burn everybody in here, that's a promise. And then, just before you cops come in to burn me, I'll open up the door, and give myself up. Right

313

there in front of the press and all the political big shots. You won't dare do anything to me. They'll give me life for killin' those twenty-seven people. And I'll be out in fifteen years. So why don't you start the ball rollin' on my money, okay? Because you ain't gonna bullshit me. I'm right on top of this case."

And he hung up.

Russo looked down at the telephone reproachfully, as if it had failed him. He lit a cigarette and jotted some notes, doing his best to avoid the inquiring eyes of the policemen wedged into the office with him.

"Well, what do you think, Russo?" Inspector Krieger demanded. "Can we do business with this guy or not?"

"I handled it wrong," Russo said. "That thing about shooting the hostages . . ." Russo winced. "That was probably the stupidest thing I could have said to a guy like that."

"That's done. You can't take it back. Now, what about this guy?"

"There are two kinds of hostage takers, Inspector," Russo said. "The ones who want to walk out and the ones who want to be carried out in a body bag. Hernando is definitely a bag man."

"Alright." Krieger turned to Connolly. "We're going in. Get the Emergency Service personnel in here."

Russo walked out of the room muttering, "It's my fault. I handled it all wrong."

Mendoza sat in on the planning session. They spread the floor plan out on the desk. "The Administrator's office is divided into two sections," Inspector Krieger said. "The anteroom and the office. Now, we don't really know where the hostages are located . . ."

Benson, the security man, coughed shyly. "I'm almost positive that they would have to be in the anteroom, sir."

"Why is that?"

"We installed a self-lock device on the office door a few years ago when we were having all these demonstrations up here," Benson said. "As soon as the door closes it is locked and can only be opened from the inside."

Connolly looked at Krieger. "We could send two men in through the office, and coordinate this with a rush on the front door. Hitting them from two sides might minimize hostage casualties."

"Yeah." Krieger was annoyed that Connolly had come up with such a good idea. "That's what we'll do."

"In which direction does the office door open, Mr. Benson?" Connolly asked.

Benson pantomimed the movements. "You push to get in, pull to get out."

"We'll have to tell that to the men who go through the office," Connolly said.

"How are we going to get them in there?" Krieger asked.

"No problem," the Emergency Services lieutenant said. "We rig them up with harnesses, and dangle them off the roof. When they reach the sixth floor, they cut into the window with a circular glass cutter, and drop the harness as they're entering the window."

"Inspector Krieger, I'd like to have that detail," Mendoza said. "I know Emergency Services handles this kind of thing usually, but I think the guys have to know who they're looking for. You've got almost thirty people in a small space. Hernando's smart enough to wear one of their white coats, so he could pass for a hostage. This was my squeal. I worked on these guys. Anyway, I know them."

"Okay, Detective, you got the detail," Krieger said. "Now we need one more man who knows these two mutts."

Krieger went out into the hall where all the cops were milling around, waiting for instructions. "We need a volunteer," he announced. "One of the guys in there works in the hospital Detox Center. He's a known heroin dealer named Hernando."

Murphy raised his hand. "Is he a little guy, big bushy Afro and a scraggly beard?"

Krieger looked back at Mendoza, who nodded. "That's him."

"I know that guy," Murphy said. "I'll go in and get him."

It was cold on the roof. The Emergency Service guys gave Murphy and Chino thick pairs of gloves, and stuck the glass cutters in their belts. Then, the sergeant offered a quick lesson in rappeling. "You just push off with your feet against the building, and let your weight carry you down. Don't worry, you won't fall. You're safer in this rig than you are at home in bed."

Inspector Krieger checked his watch. "We'll give you two minutes from the time you go down. You'll have to work fast. Get into the room as quick as you can so you'll have plenty of time to prepare for the attack. Have you checked your guns?"

Both men obediently took out their pistols, flicked them open, and checked the loads.

"Alright." Krieger shook hands with both of them. "Shoot straight and don't miss," he said. He stood on the edge of the roof as the two men were lowered. Then, he called down to Connolly on the walkie-talkie. "Start the count-down."

Connolly signalled Russo, who picked up the phone. The Emergency Service guys were using the regular iron battering ram for this door. Nolan and Fabrizio were on one side of the door with their shotguns. They had insisted on being in on the attack. "That's our partner," Nolan had said. "You can't expect us to sit around playin' with ourselves while he's risking his life. No way."

Corelli was on the other side of the door for the same reason. Other cops were lined up in a wedge behind the battering ram. It was dead quiet in the hall as the men checked their watches. The only sound was Russo's mild, friendly voice. He gave Connolly the thumbs-up signal. He was trying a new tack with Hernando, and it seemed to be working. He was using the "detail" approach.

"Just exactly what denominations do you want the five million to be in?" he asked.

"Fives, tens, and twenties," Hernando said.

"Right." Russo made believe he was writing. "Just let me get that down. And now how many of each denomination?"

"How many of each, I'll have to think about that."

It took a little longer to get into the office than they had planned. The glass cutter was harder to use than it seemed. You had to press down, and keep it at the right angle, or it wouldn't cut cleanly. The harnesses had a million hooks and buckles. If you weren't used to them, it took a while.

316

By the time they got in, they had less than thirty seconds to go.

They moved to the door. They could hear Hernando talking on the phone. "A hundred thousand fives, a hundred thousand tens, and a hundred thousand twenties."

Chino grabbed the doorknob. "Push to get in, pull to get out," he whispered.

Murphy nodded. "Shoot straight ahead," he whispered. "No crossfire."

"Okay." He took a crumpled piece of paper out of his pocket, a rough layout of the anteroom that one of the maintenance men had sketched out for him. "Here's the phone," he said pointing to the right corner of the room where the receptionist's desk was located.

"That's Hernando," Murphy whispered. "I get him." He pointed to the left side of the room. "Jose. That's you."

Chino nodded. "I open the door. You go in low. I'll come over you."

Murphy nodded, and checked out his watch. "Now!"

Hernando had gotten into a very complicated conversation with the cop on the outside. He was sitting on the desk, the pistol held loosely in his lap. "I don't care how heavy it will be, I still want the bread in small bills."

One of the hostages, a dermatology resident, had offered to look at Jose's face. Jose put the gun in his belt, and let the doctor approach. He could hardly see out of his left eye, and had to turn to the right to get a look at the man. "Don't touch it," he warned.

He heard a scream. "Freeze, you bastards!"

Hernando had dropped the phone and was twisting around, firing his gun.

The doctor suddenly disappeared from view. Jose felt someone shove him real hard. He tried to get the pistol out of his belt, but they shoved him again . . . and again . . .

Murphy emptied his gun into the little drug dealer. The guy was an easy target, sitting up on the desk, away from the hostages. Murphy hit him in the shoulder first. He turned, yelling savagely, and firing his own gun. His bullets went into the ceiling. Murphy just kept shooting until it was

317

over. He didn't look once at the other target. He had to trust this undercover guy to do his job.

Jose had his back to the door when Chino jumped out. He didn't see Chino, but a hostage who was standing in front of him did. The hostage dove for cover just as Chino raised his pistol. Murphy had come out a split second after him, but had already started shooting. Chino didn't look anywhere but at Jose. He aimed at his upper back, and started squeezing shots off. Jose jumped with the impact of every bullet. The third shot turned him around. He was trying to get a gun out of his belt. Chino hit him in the chest, and he flew back as if somebody had jerked him with a rope.

The hostages were crawling over each other to get out of the line of fire. The room was suddenly full of cops. Chino hadn't seen them break in. He hadn't seen anything but the space between Jose's shoulder blades. Nolan and Fabrizio were pushing through, trying to get to him. He dropped to one knee just to clear his head a little. From there he got a better view of the man he had just killed. Chino shut his eyes tightly, and tried to think of something pleasant like getting his name in the paper. They would have to do it this time. Those bastards would have to give him credit.

It had taken two shots with the battering ram to get the door down, and by that time the shooting was over. The hostages were all piled up against the door, and they ran out of the room as the cops tried to get in.

Corelli put his head down and bulled through the crowd. Murphy was standing over the body of the guy he had just shot. The man lay on the desk, one leg bent under him, his eyes bulging, his lips drawn back against his teeth as if he had been screaming curses of hate when he died. It was the same expression Corelli had seen on animals that had been run over on the road.

"Murf, you okay?" he asked.

Murphy nodded. "It was easy, Andy. He had his back to me."

"They were talking to him on the phone," Corelli said.

"He threw two shots into the ceiling, Andy. Dumb bastard probably never shot a .38 in his life."

Corelli tried to lead Murphy away. "C'mon, Murf, let's go sit down somewhere."

"She wasn't in here," Murphy said. "There was a nurse with long black hair, but it wasn't her."

"That's great, man. That means she's okay after all."

Connolly was standing by the door. "Take him home," he said to Corelli. "We can take care of all his paperwork tomorrow."

Murphy walked down the corridor, shuffling his feet like an old man, his arms hanging at his sides, the pistol still in his hand. "I gotta talk to her, Andy," he said. "I'm just goin' down to Emergency. Maybe she's there."

They had taken the hostages down to the Emergency Room. The doctor that Hernando had shot had fainted from loss of blood, but his wound wasn't serious. Two of the nurses had been pistol whipped by Jose, and a few more had suffered minor lacerations when the shooting started, but there were no serious injuries.

Frank Russell, the black undercover cop, was in a treatmen room, hooked to a glucose I.V., waiting for the surgeon to come down and dig Murphy's bullet out of his leg. He had refused sedation until he spoke to a "boss."

"I want that asshole busted," he said. "I want somebody to come down here, and tell me that sonofabitch is off this job."

He raised himself up on his elbows as Murphy and Corelli passed. "Hey, Murphy, you stupid, honky motherfucker, come over here!"

Corelli leaned into the room. "Hey, man, why don't you lay off for a second?"

"Get the fuck outta my face, boy," Frank said. "Hey, Murphy," he called. "Take a look in that treatment room across from me. Go ahead, you stupid bastard. Go ahead."

Murphy turned slowly and walked back. A group of nurses were standing in front of the room, some of them weeping. Inside, Isabella was under a sheet on a table. A nurse's aid was taking the intravenous tubes out of her arm.

Murphy shoved his way through, and stood at the foot of the table.

"You see what you did?" Frank called. "I warned you to stay away, but you had to keep comin' around stickin' your Irish puss where it didn't belong. They hot-shotted her because she was your old lady. You happy now?"

319

"What are you doing?" Murphy said sharply.

The nurse's aid backed away, frightened by the look on his face. "I'm just taking the I.V. out."

"That's no way to treat an overdose," Murphy said. He picked Isabella up, and wrapped the sheet around her. "She's still warm. She's still alive."

"No," the nurse's aid said. "No, the doctor . . ."

"You've gotta keep her moving. Gotta keep the blood going." He lifted Isabella off the table. "C'mon, baby, you'll be all right. We just have to keep you moving, that's all."

The nurse's aid ran out of the room. "Somebody help," she cried. "He's taking her . . ."

Murphy grasped Isabella by the waist. Her head fell back, and he pushed it against his shoulder. "C'mon, baby, let's go for a little walk," he whispered in her ear. He carried her out into the corridor. "Just get those feet going, Isabella, and you'll be fine," he whispered. "They don't know. They're all assholes, every single one of them. But we'll show 'em."

Corelli came up alongside of him. "Murf, wait a second."

"Gotta keep her movin' Andy, you know that. C'mon, baby . . ." He shook Isabella, and her head lolled back again. "Come on, don't give up on me now."

Nurses and paramedics closed in on Murphy.

"He's in shock."

"Somebody just grab him, and take her away."

"This is awful."

Applebaum blocked Murphy's path, beckoning to the other cops. "There's nothing you can do for her, Murphy."

"Try to take it easy, Murf," Donahue said.

"Leave us alone, you sonsabitches. What the fuck do you know about it?" Isabella's body started to slide from his grasp. "That's it," he said excitedly. "She's moving, you see?"

"No, Murf, she's not," Corelli said.

The cops formed a protective circle around him, and began to close in. Murphy stopped walking. He picked Isabella up, and hugged her to his chest. "You guys tryin' to tell me how to treat an overdose? You know how many people I've walked around up here? Picked 'em up half dead and walked 'em around, and stuck their heads under a johnny pump. You know how many people I've done that for?"

320

Patterson lifted Isabella's body out of Murphy's arms. Murphy looked at the cops standing around him. "Do you know how many lives I've saved, you cocksuckers?" he shouted. "Do you?"

50

Connolly was jubilant. He kept Kathleen up half the night talking about the action in the hospital that day. He was amazed at the courage and the camaraderie the men had displayed. The way they had performed under pressure. Heffernan and Applebaum taking complete control of the situation, Mendoza, that young undercover, staying around to help out, and then going in after those men themselves because it was his case and he felt responsible. Murphy, volunteering with such alacrity that the other men didn't have time to raise their hands. Now that was a real surprise. He never would have thought Murphy capable of such heroism. He was too much the shrewd street cop, playing the angles, getting through the day. But he had volunteered to do the one thing a cop dreads the most—go through a closed door. He and Mendoza had risked their lives to save others. Corny as it sounded, there was no other way to put it.

"I never thought cops could behave like that, and I've been one for almost eighteen years," Connolly said.

"Well, you've always dealt with the bad pennies, Dennis," Kathleen said with a frayed, patient smile.

But that was just it: these were the bad pennies. The ones that Dugan had warned him about. The ones who had to be prodded, bribed, and threatened into doing their work. Was that over now? Had the precinct really turned around?

Kathleen did everything but go into a coma to show she was sleepy. Of course she didn't want to talk about any of this. It wasn't her life, it didn't mean anything to her. Connolly

321

went up to bed with her, but lying in the darkness was agony to him.

"Think maybe I'll go in early this morning," he said. "Just to make sure everything's under control."

She reached around and patted his hand. "That's a good idea, dear." She was snoring lightly by the time he got his pants on.

Connolly got to the Four-One a little before seven. If the place had turned around if the men had experienced a great conversion, you couldn't tell by the look of the precinct. The cops on duty wandered listlessly about. Only Clendennon acknowledged his arrival.

"You're here kind of early, boss."

"Have to finish some work," Connolly said brusquely. "Had a little interruption yesterday."

Clendennon handed him a copy of the *Daily News.* "Wanna read about the heroes of Fort Apache? If this keeps up we'll have to change the name to the fightin' Forty-One."

Suppressing his excitement, Connolly took the paper into his office. There it was on the front page again. His precinct, his men. Just let those Headquarters back-stabbers try to move him out of this job now. The official story was that Mendoza had come to the hospital to arrest the two dead men, who were considered the biggest drug dealers in the South Bronx. They had caught on somehow, and the rest was history. Murphy and Mendoza were both mentioned several times, as were Connolly and Inspector Krieger, who were credited with planning the two-pronged attack that saved the lives of the hostages. All that stuff about Garcia had been omitted. The D.E.A. didn't want to expose its undercover operations. And the detective, who had been accidentally shot by Murphy, had agreed to let the matter drop. He was D.E.A., too, and would only compromise himself by making an issue of the shooting. The public would read a simple, inspirational story about police heroism. What went on behind the scenes would stay there—where it belonged.

A little before eight, Headquarters called. A certain Senator Bennett from North Carolina was going to pay a surprise visit to the area to check on the progress of a housing project the federal government was supposed to be building on Charlotte Street. He would need an escort. Connolly rang Clendennon at the desk.

"There are no projects in construction on Charlotte Street, are there?"

"No, sir."

"Send two cars to cover the area. A senator from North Carolina is coming to inspect a vacant lot."

At nine o'clock two rookies on the eight-to-four discovered Arthur Mitchell's body. His wife had reported him missing when he didn't return home from work. She had given a detailed description of her husband and his car. But Mitchell's Seville had been stripped to the bone within hours, and passing radio cars saw only another anonymous hulk. The rookies had noticed a license plate in the gutter. It checked out as Mitchell's. Then just out of curiosity, they had wandered into the gutted tenement building where Arthur Mitchell's corpse had been sitting in a chair facing the window for eight days.

Clendennon had been going off when he got his instructions from Connolly. He left a note for the day desk sergeant. During the eight-to-four turnout, the sergeant had instructed two cars to cover the area, chase the bums and winos before the senator got there, and make sure nobody threw rocks at him. They were parked by the curb when Senator Bennett arrived, followed by two TV mobile units, and an "Eyewitness News" car. He got out and made some ironic remarks about the wonderful project that was going up on this location, and how pleased he was sure the people were going to be. One of his aides had spotted a big pile of garbage on the other side of the lot, and decided that it would make an ideal backdrop for the Senator's press conference. So, the whole convoy moved to another location. In the midst of a tirade on urban blight and government spending, Senator Bennett noticed an arm protruding from a piece of rolled-up carpet. Indignantly, he directed the attention of the police to this appendage, and with cameras rolling and flashbulbs popping, Charlotte made her TV debut.

The senator from North Carolina favored his aide with a tight little smile. The headline was obvious: SENATOR DISCOVERS BODY IN THE SOUTH BRONX. Reelection was almost assured.

At ten-thirty Dacey called. "I just thought you ought to know, Dennis. It looks like we've solved the cop killings."

The two guns found on the drug dealers had belonged to the dead rookies. In addition, Dacey said, the wife of one of the men had told detectives that her husband had bragged about killing the two cops on the morning it happened, before it had hit the wires.

"We'll wait a couple of weeks, and if we don't get anything better I'll see if we can close the books on this one," Dacey said. "I've already told the papers about it."

Connolly thanked him for calling.

"I always do the right thing, Dennis, you know that. How are things over there?"

"Busy," Connolly said. "Very busy."

He hung up the phone, and looked into John Murphy's bloodshot eyes. Connolly started. The man had slipped into his office without a sound. He was pale and unshaven, and didn't look much like a hero. Probably in shock, Connolly decided.

"Murphy," he said, "I didn't hear you come in. What can I do for you?"

Murphy squinted slightly. He had the perplexed look of a man who was trying to remember something. Then he nodded. "You've got your rat, Captain."

"What's that supposed to mean?"

"I'm giving Morgan and Finley up," Murphy said. "They pushed that kid off the roof."

Easy, Connolly cautioned himself. Get it right. The man's in shock. The whole thing might be a fantasy.

"How do you know?"

"I saw them do it," Murphy said. "I am what is known as a star witness."

"And your partner, did he see them, too?"

Murphy shook his head. "You'll have to ask him."

"Wasn't he on the roof with you?"

"You'll have to ask him, I said." He was rattled enough; it would be foolish to push him further.

"I will ask him," Connolly said, reaching for the phone. He called the Bronx D.A.'s office, and told them to send an Assistant District Attorney and a stenographer to his office right away. "One of my men wants to make a statement about the Quinones murder."

"You sure took your time coming in with this," he said.

"I had to think it over. It's a big move becoming a rat."

"You're not a rat, or a stoolie," Connolly said. "You're a police officer doing your job."

"It would seem more natural to you," Murphy said with quiet contempt. "You . . ."

"These men are murderers," Connolly said quickly, interrupting before Murphy said something that might lead to open conflict. He didn't want to antagonize the man, didn't want him walking out before the stenographer got here. "You're doing the right thing."

"Don't say that," Murphy said, with sudden heat. He walked to the window. "Ten years ago, right outside this house, I saw Morgan slam his car on some kid's head. He did it three times, while we all stood around watching, cheerin' him on. I should have turned him in then, Captain. If I did, that Quinones boy would be alive today. Instead, I went around tellin' everybody what a time bomb Morgan was, and how he was gonna explode one day. And guess what, he did." Murphy tapped his forehead. "So I guess that makes me real smart. Because I'm gonna give him up now when I can't do the kid or Morgan any good, and all I can do is soothe my own conscience."

"I still say you're doing the right thing," Connolly said.

"So I lose twenty-eight thousand friends, and make one. You. Horseshit's still horseshit even when you put sugar on it. I'm a stool pigeon, plain and simple. So let me tell my little story and get out of here."

51

The Assistant D.A. took a detailed statement from Murphy. Cases against cops were the most difficult to win, so he knew he had to have a good one. He questioned Murphy about the weather, the visibility, Murphy's personal relationship with Morgan and Finley, everything that a good defense lawyer would ask. When he left he was satisfied.

"You're a really good witness," he told Murphy.

"Whoopee," Murphy said. "You made my day."

"You know they'll probably call you into the grand jury on this," Connolly said.

"Yeah, I know."

"The men will know about it by then."

"They know about it now." Murphy looked through the smoked glass. "They saw the stenographer. They know I ain't in here dictatin' my memoirs." Murphy rose stiffly. "Anyway, there was something else I came in here to do." He took his shield out of his back pocket and dropped it on Connolly's desk.

"What's that supposed to mean?" Connolly asked.

"What does it look like? I'm through, as of today. My last official act as a police officer was turning in two of my fellow officers. The end of a distinguished career."

"You're a good cop, Murphy, but I don't think you'd be much good at anything else," Connolly said.

"So I'll run for President, what do you care?"

"I care because I'll need good cops if I'm going to run this precinct the right way."

"There is no right way. There's your way and Dugan's way and my way, and all of them are useless. Because in the end you don't run this precinct, it runs you . . . right into the ground."

"You're under a lot of stress, Murphy." Connolly picked

up the shield and held it out to him. "Why don't you take a couple of days and think it over?"

"That's all I've been doin' all night long. Thinkin'. And you know what I came up with? I'm a very rare individual, Captain. Everything I touch turns to shit. My life's in a shambles. My marriage is wrecked and my kids will end up hating me, if they don't already. This fuckin' job has twisted me so bad I hate everybody. Everything I do is wrong. I'm poison, Captain. Just ask my partner. Or ask that nurse over at Jefferson Hospital, the one in the morgue. Or ask Morgan and Finley."

Connolly pushed the shield at Murphy. "Just give yourself a few days. You can always come back and throw it in my face."

Murphy grabbed the shield away from Connolly. "You are a simple bastard, aren't you? Okay. You don't want this?" He flipped his shield into the trash can. "Leave it for the sweeper."

52

Murphy walked the gamut from Connolly's office to the door of the precinct. He could hear some of the men muttering behind him. The word was out. And this was only the beginning. He would walk many gamuts before this nightmare ended. In and out of hearing rooms, courtrooms, office buildings, past rows of hostile, questioning eyes. Lowlifes who beat their wives and shook down dope dealers would feel righteous at his expense. Men he had worked and drank with for years would turn away without giving him a chance. He had seen it happen many times. They forgot everything that had gone before. Friendship, favors, everything went by the board. It was almost as if they had been waiting all this time for a reason to hate you, and they finally had it.

Murphy got into his car and watched the precinct recede into the distance through his rear view mirror. Wait until the old man found out what he had done. Jesus, he'd never be able to hold his head up at the Holy Name Society again. His brothers would be ecstatic. Here would be conclusive proof that he was the worst kid in the family. They'd all be safe from the old man's mouth as long as this cloud hung over the family. Well, fuck them, too.

"Freeze!"

Corelli popped up from the back seat, and stuck his finger in Murphy's face.

"Christ, I thought it was a hit," Murphy said.

Corelli swung over into the front seat. "You ain't worth killin'."

"Don't be so sure. I just gave Morgan and Finley up."

"So what else is new? I knew you were gonna do it all along."

"They'll subpoena you, you know."

Corelli seemed unconcerned. "That is what they do, the little devils."

"I didn't say nothin' about you, Andy. You can come in with any kind of story you want to."

"Let's not get carried away here," Corelli said. "I ain't gonna commit perjury to protect those two humps. No way."

"You can always say you didn't see nothin'."

"And leave you hangin'? What kind of friend would I be if I did a thing like that? I mean, I'll go up against the department, I'll go up against the goddamn world for you, my man." Corelli stretched contentedly. "And besides, I won't catch any flak. You're the stoolie. I'm just the hostile witness being forced to testify. Just goin' along with the program."

Murphy laughed for the first time in days. "Smart boy. You've got it all figured out."

"Somebody's gotta do the thinkin' in this little partnership."

"Not any more," Murphy said. "I just dissolved the partnership. I put in my papers, Andy."

Corelli sat up in alarm. "You kiddin' or what? You

gonna leave me up here in the garden spot of the western world?"

"I'm gettin' out. You're the one who's always schemin' to quit, and I end up doin' it."

Corelli put his arm around Murphy's shoulders. "I hate to tell you this, kid, but you're not suited to the outside world."

"This job's been killin' me, Andy," Murphy said.

"So would any job. You think you'd be better off pumpin' gas, or deliverin' the mail? You think you're gonna find some meaningful experience out there? I mean, like who's breakin' down your door?"

"I'll have my pension," Murphy said. "I'll get something."

"Sure you will. Wearin' a square badge and guardin' somebody's supermarket, that's what you'll find. Face it, Murf, you're a cop."

"Not anymore, I'm not."

They passed the Senior Citizens' Center on Jerome Avenue. The track star was lurking in a doorway down the block as two old ladies crossed the street.

"Look at that guy," Corelli said.

Murphy kept his eyes on the road. "I don't see anybody."

"He's gonna do it again." Corelli watched Murphy's eyes go to the mirror to check the kid out. "You know, if you staked out all the old-age places around here, you could catch that kid."

"Brilliant plan, Officer Corelli," Murphy said. "Now if you will submit it in triplicate to the . . . holy shit." Murphy braked involuntarily. Corelli turned in time to see the kid race across the street holding two pocketbooks. One of the old ladies was crawling on the sidewalk to retrieve her glasses. The other was lying flat on her back.

"You gonna let him get away with this, Murf?"

"What do you want me to do, make a citizen's arrest?"

"He's gonna kill one of these old ladies one of these days. He's gettin' rougher with them all the time."

Murphy turned the wheel furiously, and skidded into a U-turn. "This time I'm gonna run the bastard over," he said.

The track star saw them coming. He ran down a side street toward the Cross-Bronx Expressway. "Better get him before he hits those stairs," Corelli said. "Otherwise we'll have to run."

Murphy floored the gas pedal, but it was too late. The track star had run up the narrow foot ramp that led to the overpass. Murphy lurched to a stop in front of the ramp and opened the door. "I'm gonna get this guy," he shouted.

The track star was halfway up the ramp, running with defiant ease. Murphy ran right into a gust of wind. He put his head down and kept going. There was no need to look up, not as long as he was on the ramp or the overpass. When he got to the steps leading down to the street on the other side of the highway, Murphy checked his progress. The kid was skipping along, taking two steps at a time. Murphy hadn't lost any ground, and now he had a chance to gain some. He jumped down a section of steps, about fifteen of them, and came down on his knees on the landing. The track star figured he was way ahead. He hadn't looked back. So if he could do it again . . .

Murphy jumped down the second section, landing on his heels and slipping backward on the wet pavement. He managed to break his fall with his elbows, feeling a bolt of pain shoot through his arms. I'll feel this tomorrow, he thought. But for now he was only one landing away from this kid, and it would be worth breaking his neck to catch him.

Murphy limped to the top of the steps. If he just dove, maybe he would land on him, or at least close enough to grab his ankles. Just let me get my hands on any part of you, motherfucker, and you won't get away. He crouched to dive, but the track star turned. He was close enough to see the kid's eyes pop. No cop had ever been this close to the track star before. He jumped the remaining couple of steps and landed, with his legs churning. In a matter of seconds he was a hundred feet away, and gaining. Murphy limped along in despair. He'd never catch this kid. Never. But wait, they were running down a long, wide boulevard now. There were no fences to jump, or side streets to disappear into. The kid had pulled his one evasive move—running down the highway steps—and that hadn't worked. Now it was just a matter of endurance. Murphy didn't have to catch him, not yet, not for a while. All he had to do was keep him in sight. As long as he kept him in sight he had a chance.

THE BEST OF THE BESTSELLERS
FROM WARNER BOOKS

REELING
by Pauline Kael   (83-420, $2.95)
Rich, varied, 720 pages containing 74 brilliant pieces
covering the period between 1972-75, this is the fifth
collection of movie criticism by the film critic *Newsday*
calls "the most accomplished practitioner of film criticism in America today, and possibly the most important
film critic this country has ever produced.

P.S. YOUR CAT IS DEAD
by James Kirkwood   (95-948, $2.75)
It's New Year's Eve. Your best friend died in September.
You've been robbed twice. Your girlfriend is leaving you.
You've just lost your job. And the only one left to talk to
is a gay burglar you've got tied up in the kitchen.

AUDREY ROSE
by Frank De Felitta   (96-947, $3.25)
The Templetons have a near-perfect life and a lovely
daughter, until a stranger enters their lives and claims that
their daughter, Ivy, possesses the soul of his own daughter, Audrey Rose, who had been killed at the exact moment
that Ivy was born. And suddenly their lives are shattered
by event after terrifying event.

A STRANGER IN THE MIRROR
by Sidney Sheldon   (93-814, $2.95)
Toby Temple is a lonely, desperate superstar. Jill Castle
is a disillusioned girl, still dreaming of stardom and
carrying a terrible secret. This is their love story. A brilliant, compulsive tale of emotions, ambitions, and mach-
inations in that vast underworld called Hollywood.

COAL MINER'S DAUGHTER
by Loretta Lynn with George Veesey   (91-477, $2.50)
America's Queen of Country Music tells her own story in
her own words. "How a coal miner's daughter made it
from Butcher Holler to Nashville . . . it's funny, sad, intense, but what makes it is Loretta Lynne herself . . . a
remarkable combination of innocence, strength, and
country shrewdness."   —*Publishers Weekly*

PROVOCATIVE READING
FROM WARNER BOOKS

THE BEST OF THE BESTSELLERS
FROM WARNER BOOKS

DEAD AND BURIED
by Chelsea Quinn Yarbro   (91-268, $2.50)

He thought dead men told no tales. The murders were bad enough but what Sheriff Dan Gillis couldn't understand were the new-comers to Potter's Bluff, and their eerie resemblance to people he had seen DEAD AND BURIED. Was he imagining things? Or was something evil preying on the sleepy town of Potter's Bluff—something as shadowy as the faceless killers who roamed the land.

RAKEHELL DYNASTY
by Michael William Scott   (95-201, $2.75)

This is the bold, sweeping, passionate story of a great New England shipping family caught up in the winds of change—and of the one man who would dare to sail his dream ship to the frightening, beautiful land of China. He was Jonathan Rakehell, and his destiny would change the course of history.

P.S. YOUR CAT IS DEAD!
by James Kirkwood   (95-948, $2.75)

It's New Year's Eve. Your best friend died in September, you've been robbed twice, your girlfriend is leaving you, you've just lost your job . . . and the only one left to talk to is a gay burglar you've got tied up in the kitchen. "Kirkwood is a fine writer, and keeps the suspense taut all the way."
                          —The New York Times Book Review.

ACT OF VENGEANCE
by Trevor Armbrister   (85-707, $2.75)

This is the true story behind one of the most frightening assassination plots of our time: the terrible corruption of a powerful labor union, the twisted lives of the men and women willing to kill for pay, the eventual triumph of justice—and the vision and spirit of a great man.

ALINE
by Carole Klein   (93-526, $2.95)

She was an eminent theatrical designer; he was an unknown. She was a 44-year-old sophisticated New Yorker; he was a 25-year-old hillbilly from North Carolina. From the moment he glimpsed her "flower face," their fiery relationship grew, ripening and exploding into one of the most turbulent and passionate love stories the world has ever known. "A richly detailed portrait of the woman and the many worlds through which she moved . . . a rare and unforgettable personage."
                          —New York Times

OUTSTANDING READING FROM
WARNER BOOKS

THE EXECUTIONER'S SONG
by Norman Mailer   (80-558, $3.95)

The execution is what the public remembers: on January 17, 1977, a firing squad at Utah State Prison put an end to the life of convicted murderer Gary Gilmore. But by then the real story was over—the true tale of violence and fear, jealousy and loss, of a love that was defiant even in death. Winner of the Pulitzer Prize. "The big book no one but Mailer could have dared . . . an absolutely astonishing book."—Joan Didion, *New York Times Book Review*.

ACT OF VENGEANCE
by Trevor Armbrister   (85-707, $2.75)

This is the true story behind one of the most frightening assassination plots of our time: the terrible corruption of a powerful labor union, the twisted lives of the men and women willing to kill for pay, the eventual triumph of justice—and the vision and spirit of a great man.

HANTA YO
by Ruth Beebe Hill   (96-298, $3.50)

You become a member of the Mahto band in their seasonal migrations at the turn of the eighteenth century. You gallop with the warriors triumphantly journeying home with scalps, horses and captive women. You join in ceremonies of grief and joy where women trill, men dance, and the kill-tales are told. "Reading *Hanto Yo* is like entering a trance."—*New York Times*

MS READ-a-thon— a simple way to start youngsters reading

Boys and girls between 6 and 14 can join the MS READ-a-thon and help find a cure for Multiple Sclerosis by reading books. And they get two rewards — the enjoyment of reading, and the great feeling that comes from helping others.

Parents and educators: For complete information call your local MS chapter. Or mail the coupon below.

Kids can help, too!